Shadow of the Phantom

Siara Brandt

I

BOOKS BY SIARA BRANDT

III

*Based on the novel Le Fantome De L'Opera
by
Gaston Leroux*

Thanks to all the artists who brought me to this place. To the beautiful Naruto music that helped me envision the chapters. And, finally, to all those who find beauty in the shadows.

Prologue

A phantom moon rode the sky, a hunger moon whose wan face looked down from afar while the vesper bells of Paris dolorously struck the hour in the distance. The descending orb was an imperfect circle. One edge was uneven and blurred as if a portion of it had been hastily erased by an artist's frantic hand in a moment of fervent dissatisfaction over an inadequate rendering of moonlit nightfall. As the ghostly sphere waned, its light grew paler still. It was as if the dark half of the earth and the vault of the heavens over it had been stripped of color until only the starkest contrasts of black and white remained.

As the moonlight filtered down through the leafless trees of the Bois de Boulogne, it glistened on a snow-mantled landscape, one that was heavily-etched in shadow for the Bois at night was a place of mystery and secrets. Once the vast woodland had been a lair for thieves and the scene of violence for the unwary, but that had been in a time long past. Now, in a more civilized era, with its winding paths and pavilions, its waterfalls and botanical gardens, the park served as *the* milieu for the aristocracy as well as a gathering place for those not quite so privileged.

But the Bois by night remained something very different from the Bois by day. When night flung down her ebon veil, distorted silhouettes of deepest black altered the landscape so that nothing resembled its daytime form. Elongated shadows became otherworldly, illusory phantasms that were more suited to the realm of nightmares than the realm of reality. Even the trees loomed in monstrously exaggerated proportions, their naked, gnarled limbs flung outward and upward into grotesque convolutions that reached heavenward like the writhing torment of the damned that had been suddenly frozen that way.

It was the dead of winter, so every branch and every blade of grass was hoar-frosted, making the woodland sparkle like some enchanted fairyland in the moonlight. But the weather had begun to warm on a sudden so that a faint mist was also rising in eerie slow motion from the snow-laden ground. It lent to the deserted woodland a diaphanous, otherworldly luminescence, a softness, an almost ethereal radiance that spoke of ghosts and hauntings and other restless lingerings of the soul.

But the Bois was not as deserted as it had at first seemed. The heavy pounding of hooves disturbed the wintry stillness as a horse and rider suddenly emerged from the deepest shadows beneath the trees. Like the relentless swooping of some predatory bird, the ominous vision in black took on the aspect of some moon-struck apparition come forth from the grave. The trees blurred on one side of the path that the massive black stallion followed. The edge of one of the small lakes rushed by on the other. A distorted reflection of the lopsided moon floated on the rippling surface of the lake where the perpetually-agitated water was deepest and remained unfrozen, seething into a turbulent and frothy vapor at all times.

In that witching hour of night when everything else seemed to be suspended in a state of melancholy gloom, iron-shod hooves echoed hollowly on the planks of a wooden bridge. Before reaching the end of the bridge, the horse yielded to the strong hand of its rider. The powerful animal continued to toss its head and paw the wooden planks for a few paces, but the sound of hooves finally died and the Bois was silent again. Only the incessant murmur of the Grand Cascade and the heavy breathing of the horse filled the night.

The moon had retreated behind a dense bank of clouds so that everything was thrown into sudden darkness. The still-restive horse and the black-shrouded figure sitting astride its broad back all but disappeared as they blended with the shadows. But in that final moment of illumination, the bold silhouette of the man and the horse had seemed like the vision of one fallen from grace, or a vengeful wraith obeying some ghostly summons and seeking the resolution of some earthly quest that as yet remained unfulfilled.

The rider lifted his face and his black hood fell back to reveal a half-mask. Its ashen hue was a startling contrast to the long, raven-black hair and the heavy black cape that fell in thick folds down his back. Below the mask, the lean, masculine line of the rider's jaw showed strength as it flexed with the tensing of the muscles there. The moon was reflected in the depths of indigo eyes, eyes that seemed, at the moment, nearly as black as the surrounding shadows. Those eyes narrowed slightly as the man silently contemplated the mission that had brought him forth from his deep and solitary underground abode. Distracted from his thoughts for a moment, his dark gaze slid upward, for he had seen a brief flash of light in the star-flung vault of darkness above him. A falling star. A thing to make a wish upon. If life and circumstance had not already gone far in banishing such sentimental musings from his mind.

And yet, despite his habitual cynicism, he was drawn into an unaccustomed state of reverie, for at precisely the same moment that he saw the falling star, a vagrant wind stirred the leafless branches around him. It touched him as lightly as a caress, was soft as a lover's sigh. That same wind lifted a few strands of ebony hair and blew them across the unmasked portion of his face. Lost in his dark and brooding thoughts, he made no move to brush the rogue strands away but sat as unmoving as a statue that had been carved from a slab of black marble.

The mist was heavier here between the two lakes. It hovered over the surface of the water and seeped through the planks of the bridge, so that anyone watching might have thought that the man and the horse had emerged ghostlike from the mist itself. The cascading waterfall, the centerpiece of the Bois, remained a dramatic backdrop behind them and it drew the man's frowning gaze for a moment before he again scanned the shadows with a watchful eye.

But there was little need for vigilance at this hour, especially on this lonely winter's night. The Bois was empty and the winding trail was deserted before and behind him as far as he could see. Only in these deserted hours could he move about so freely. Only in the dead of night could he go forth with ease, secure in his solitude, without the fear that chance eyes might look upon him, first with curiosity, and then with the inevitable apprehension that always followed.

But he had no thought for chance meetings at the moment. He had come seeking a distraction from the restlessness that had been plaguing him all day. That vexing state of unrest had grown steadily with the passage of the long day until he had become too impatient to stay confined. His solitude this night, instead of being a comfort, had become more like a prison.

And yet he was used to the darkness. It was his accustomed environment and he felt more at ease in the shadows than he did in the harsh glare of day. As he dismounted in a single, lithe motion, there was a smooth and fluid grace about him. With an unconscious flourish, he tossed the long black cape back over one broad shoulder. It swirled about his boots a little before it settled, revealing a portion of the lean but heavily-muscled body beneath it. With his tall, powerful physique and his wide shoulders, he was a commanding presence, like the ghost of some dark, ancient prince of bygone days, one that might have easily graced the stage of the Opera House itself.

He stood at the head of the horse, holding the reins in a black-gloved hand. "Easy," he breathed, soothing the horse and stroking the sleek, velvety neck.

He had his choice of mounts from the underground stable of the Opera House. But this horse, this coal-black, half-tamed stallion that was shunned by everyone else as being dangerously unpredictable, was his favorite, for the truth of it was that out of all the rest in the Opera's stables, the sheer wildness of the animal most closely matched his own dark temperament. Even now the horse stamped its hooves in a display of impatience and tossed its long black mane. Yet, for all its wildness, the animal stood obediently for the man.

Still idly soothing the animal, the man waited, prey to his own internal unrest, for the day, and then the night, had dragged out endlessly, keeping him immured in a dark and restless mood even after he had come forth from his dark refuge.

He glanced up at the ponderous oak limbs above him at precisely the same moment that the moon suddenly pierced the bank of black clouds. It immediately bathed him in a flood of light that blazed his mask and his hair into silver fire. The unmasked portion of his face remained devoid of expression, and yet there was an intensity, a dark gleam in the depths of his eyes that bore witness to deeper emotions that, in spite of his efforts at control, continued to war within him.

It had been less than a day. Mere hours had passed since he had made his final decision and then had taken the steps to see it through. Yet those hours had seemed like an eternity and he had found his patience sorely tested. He had not expected the Persian to bring him word this night and yet he could think of nothing else but the long-awaited reply to his missive. He knew full well that his impatience could only be relieved when he had her answer though he also realized that the passing of this night would most likely offer no relief for his inner turmoil. The night was almost over. The morning would drag out just as interminably. Thus, having no choice, he strove for patience with a will of iron. He had decided on his course and there was no turning back now, no matter what the outcome. And yet, amazingly, he was still plagued by uncertainty. Why this one woman had become such a disruption in his life, he did not know. He marveled at the very fact that he had allowed it to be so, and that she had changed him so much.

He trusted the Persian implicitly with the task he had given him. He would accomplish it with his usual discretion and tact. The man had shown not only his competence, but his steadfast loyalty many times over the years. There was a deep and abiding bond between them, something that had come about during those dangerous days at Mezzanderan, that world of assassins and corruption and ruthlessness and more brutality than he would have thought men could be capable of. He had been drawn deeply into the court intrigue there, until the time had come when it was decided he knew too much. An assassination attempt had already been made on the Persian's life, one that had very nearly succeeded. Fleeing Persia, the two men had barely escaped with their lives. Desperate, pursued, with the Persian barely clinging to life, they had made the journey back to France together.

His perusal of the past did not distract him for long. Distant hoof beats echoed in the stillness. He turned, fixed on that steadily-increasing sound, and watched the path he had just travelled, until out of the wavering mist he saw a horse and rider approaching. It was the Persian.

He tried to tell himself that whatever her answer might be, he would quietly accept her decision. Yet deep down he knew that was far from true. All along he had tried not to let himself have hope, but, despite his best efforts, hope insisted on residing like a living, breathing entity inside him. His own bleak, often brutal past should have warned him against the folly of leaving his heart so open and vulnerable. But there was no changing what he had done and reality, no matter how painful it might prove to be in the end, must eventually be faced. He reminded himself that he had faced far worse in his lifetime and that this small thing was of little consequence. And yet, at the same time, he scorned himself for waiting there with such breathless anticipation.

His broad shoulders lifted and fell as he waited. His deep sigh was merely another indication of how far things had gone with him. If anything he grew more anticipatory as the Persian drew nearer.

He waited until after the Persian had dismounted, and then he put the question quietly. "You have spoken to her?" His voice was deep and masculine, with a strength that carried through the mist-laden darkness, even over the murmur of the Grand Cascade.

"Yes," came the reply.

The Persian, who knew him better than anyone else, felt the intensity of the dark gaze behind the mask. He had first met him when he had been a young man newly arrived in Persia, a fledgling experiencing his first taste of freedom. With the restraints of the past gone, he had embraced life with a boldness, a recklessness even, that few men experience even over the course of an entire lifetime. Grasping the fullness of all that the world presented him for the first time, he had been as wild and intractable as any untamed horse that had never known the guiding hand of man. His hunger for adventure and his thirst for knowledge had been boundless and he had pursued both avidly and fearlessly.

The horse snorted suddenly and impatiently stamped one iron-shod hoof, making the Persian think how alike the two were, the man and the horse. Only yesterday the stallion had been declared a monster, a devil who had bitten and then nearly trampled the handler until the man had finally declared he would no longer work with the horse. The Persian himself, although he had been born to the saddle, would never have attempted to ride such an animal. And yet the beast was docile enough with this man who knew how to handle him, but wasn't that because the man was a little untamed himself?

"Has she answered so quickly?" The masked man asked.

"Earlier this evening, yes," came the Persian's answer. "I have been searching for you, not realizing that you were still here."

6

And then, sensing the almost palpable undercurrent of impatience in the other man, the Persian said straight out, "I told her that she has a patron if she wishes one."

There was a searching look in the other man's eyes for the briefest of moments, but that was quickly veiled. "And is she-agreeable?"

The Persian nodded. "She was surprised by the offer at first. But she did seem most eager after she had some time to think the thing through. She was curious, of course, about your identity, which, as I explained to her, must remain a mystery. Yet she seemed, dare I say, intrigued, if not flattered, by the idea. Here is her note."

Saying no word, the man in the mask took the note in one black-gloved hand hesitantly, as if it were some fragile artifact that needed to be handled carefully. "Then it is done," he said with his head still bowed. He looked up and said more firmly, "I can hardly back out now. It seems that fate will play itself out, regardless of our intentions."

Those words showed how much he still battled inside himself with his decision. It had never been his intention to approach her. Nor to speak to her. But astonishingly he had done those very things, even if it had only been through the Persian. Now he must see it through and find a way to deal with the consequences.

He looked up as the Persian said, "She said she is agreeable if Madame Giry gives her consent."

"Yes, of course."

"She also asked to have more details about the lessons. Where and when they should be given."

"I must give more thought to that," the masked man said. "I have not worked out all the details yet. There is much for me to consider here."

"She is in need of a patron *now*," the Persian said and the other man glanced up sharply at the tone he heard in his voice. The emphasis on the final word was not lost on him. "If you don't step in quickly, then- " the Persian's voice trailed off as he left the rest unsaid.

"Then there will no doubt be others rushing in to offer their patronage," the masked man finished for him, a muscle on the unmasked side of his jaw tensing.

Yes, other men would undoubtedly offer their patronage. He had been aware of that possibility all along. Men with less honorable motives than his. Men who would prey upon her innocence. That they had not come forth already was surprising. Christine was an uncommonly beautiful woman.

"She is in a difficult situation," he said as if still half talking to himself. "I would not take advantage of her circumstances, but if I can offer her *this-* "

"The Viscount Raoul de Chagny has offered to become her patron as well."

The masked face lifted slowly. A flicker of something unreadable darkened the indigo eyes as they contemplated all that the revelation portended.

He turned his face aside for a moment as if he searched the shadows for some unforeseen menace. One corner of his mouth tightened briefly, allowing some of his deeply-rooted cynicism to come to the surface, and he said, with the faintest trace of bitterness in his voice, "The Viscount will try to buy her with money *and* his handsome face. I will teach her to sing."

"Raoul de Chagny knows nothing about her singing," the Persian informed him. "He wishes merely to sponsor her as a dancer."

That surprised the man in the mask. "But she is so much more than that," he said very quietly. His voice lowered and was suddenly laced with sarcasm. "I am sure we can both agree that selfless generosity is not a part of the Viscount's nature. He will undoubtedly expect something in return."

And then he drew himself up and said more forcefully, "You must tell her to choose between us. I will have no interference with my teaching."

"She has already decided," the Persian told him. "She has chosen you."

There was a heavy pause. In that darkest hour before the light, the silence grew deep around them. Save for the murmur of the Grand Cascade, there was no other sound.

"Then all that is left is for her to agree to my conditions," the masked man said. He put the note in his pocket without reading it. "It is done then," he repeated. "The hour is late and the sun is almost up. It is time for me to return."

Sensing that he wanted to be alone, the Persian mounted his horse, bid his farewell and left the other man to his solitary thoughts. The masked man stood unmoving as he contemplated the madness that had spurred him to start this in the first place. It had been an impulsive, reckless thing to do, even rash, and against his better judgment. He still wondered that he would even consider starting something that was so perilous, so dangerous to his peace of mind. To his very existence.

But deep down, he did know why. Because there was too much inside him to stay silent. And because she was like a flame, a light in his darkness, and he was like some helpless moth that didn't have sense enough to stay away from that light, no matter the danger. He was fully aware of all of the reasons why giving her voice lessons would be such a risk. As he stood there in the full blaze of moonlight, he closed his eyes and envisioned her face as she must have looked when she was told about his offer. And then, releasing a sudden breath, he almost winced at the thought of his own marred appearance which was in sharp and painful contrast to the perfect visage of the Viscount. His imperfection was ever in his mind, and he knew above all that he must keep his curse hidden from her at all costs. A bitter smile again tightened one corner of his mouth. He couldn't help but wonder what she would say if she knew that one of his conditions would be that he would never allow her to look upon his face. Or that the Phantom of the Opera himself had summoned her. Such a revelation, he knew, would end the lessons before they even began.

The bitter smile faded and the muscles in his jaw flexed with irony as he wondered how he had let things go so far and what a foolish, irreversible thing had been done. He had come back to France seeking one thing only, and that was solitude. Instead he had found something he had never expected to find. He had found Christine.

Unconsciously, his hand gripped the reins more tightly. Would that he could have been content with his solitude and that his heart had stayed unburdened by what he could only see as an ill-fated arrangement. Far better if he had never laid eyes upon her at all. But her voice had haunted him from the first time he had heard her sing and he had allowed himself to be bewitched by her beauty. Knowing better. His restlessness could have no resolution, no matter what her decision. He knew that. He also knew that the lessons were going to make things so much worse for him, even if they could be given from behind a curtain. *If* she agreed to those terms. And yet, all of that warred with something else that disturbed him just as deeply. He had given her an ultimatum. What if she should turn him down because of that? What if, in thinking the whole thing over more carefully, the Viscount's offer appealed to her more?

He closed his eyes for the space of several heartbeats. Little did she know that she had already become the focus of his music. That should have been enough for him. He had learned to turn his feelings for her into words and music and pour them like hot wax onto a sheet of paper. Even before he had finished the first song, he had started another. He could not bear to see it ended, so deep was his obsession, an obsession that, he fully admitted, if only to himself, had been consuming him more and more lately. And that troubled him. Deeply.

Yet the fact remained that his love for Christine had lifted him to a higher place than he had ever been to before and fettered him there helplessly, like some pinioned moth. On the wings of love he had risen out of his own solitary dark hell. He had been transformed. He could never go back to the way things had been before. Never.

He had learned one thing in life. That one could not change reality, only how one dealt with it. Facing stark reality now, he knew that his weakness for her was certain to bring about some kind of misfortune for him. It seemed inevitable. And yet deep inside him, something belied all his reservations. He wanted this far more than he feared it. Like a siren, she drew him relentlessly onward, even though he knew the danger. She had become a necessary thing for his soul even if she remained a distant dream, one so far from his reach that it might be the moon he was aspiring to touch. And although the lessons of his past were ever in his mind, his eagerness to start the lessons vied with his fears and his misgivings. There were details that needed to be worked out. A schedule. A meeting place. And most importantly, how he would keep a wall between them, for that was uppermost in his mind. She must remain like the stars, beautiful to look at but very, very far away. A barrier must remain between them, a chasm just as deep as the one that separated them now. She would move through his life for a while like a shadow that he could see but never touch. And then one day she would move out of his life again. Like an act on the stage of the Opera House, the curtain would come down and the scene would be over forever. It was a bittersweet realization, but one that he accepted nevertheless. The moment would come when he would lose her and there would be silence and darkness again. And he knew that the loneliness would seem so much deeper than it had been before. Yet his jaw hardened with his resolve. He would accept the loss when it came. He would yield to it and to the things he must live with and without. Because to have her in his life for only a moment was preferable to never having her there at all.

There was no sense thinking about it further. It was done and could not be undone.

With the sound of the Grand Cascade behind him pulling him from his brooding thoughts, he realized he had stayed longer than he should have, for the mantle of night was dissipating and the sky had begun to lighten. Misty dawn was seeping through the Bois. Still he lingered a little longer than was his wont to, entranced by the beauty of the dawn sky. Where the sun struck the frosted grass, a soft, wraith-like mist suffused the air and rose in eerie swirls, just like a restless wraith seeking the light, knowing the light and the warmth, no matter how beautiful, could have only one outcome, and that was to bring about its end.

There was a searching, almost vulnerable look in his eyes as he let himself drink in all the beauty of the surrounding woodland. In that first trembling light of dawn, he uttered a single word in which there was reflected all the helpless yearning of his heart.

"Christine," he whispered and closed his eyes. "You sang and made me want something I never dared to want before."

The frost-clad branches and blades of grass were beginning to thaw and to drip with moisture as they yielded to the warming sunlight that filtered through the Bois. But he who was born to live in the shadows was long gone by then, already headed back to his solitary abode to hide himself from the harsh, unforgiving light of day.

Chapter 1

"You must have a guardian angel, Christine. Look how many opportunities have been presented to you just this past year." Lisette sighed audibly and her lips curved into a pleased smile as she looked over Christine's costume appraisingly. "You look especially beautiful tonight. And, dare I say, *seductive*? That dress is *very* daring."

Christine agreed that the costume was daring. The form-fitting gown of claret-colored velvet boldly showcased the talents of the Opera House's seamstress, Madame Vernay. Her genius and that of her assistant, Remi Botair, were evident in every exquisite detail of the gown. There were deep-red velvet roses fastened at the center of the lace-edged décolletage that plunged deeply, baring both her bosom and her shoulders provocatively. Her loose curls, falling like a shimmering veil all the way to her waist, glistened like burnished copper. Part of her hair had been arranged coquettishly and becomingly on top of her head by Lisette, who had also fixed a scarlet rose just behind one ear. A fringed silk and velvet shawl, which was heavily beaded and embroidered, was draped low around her hips and tied at one side. It sparkled and drew the eye with her every movement.

"Too daring?" Christine questioned as she looked up, her amethyst-hued eyes meeting Lisette's dark gaze in the mirror.

"What is *too* daring?" Lisette asked with a low laugh and a slight, dismissive wave of her hand to emphasize her words. "You're portraying a seductress, Christine, a bewitching gypsy enchantress.

Of course you must look the part. Besides, you have to wear what you are told to wear. When we are on the stage, we must be transformed into something larger than life."

Christine did feel transformed by the gown. In fact, as she looked into the mirror, she hardly recognized herself. "But- "

"But nothing," Lisette interrupted her. "The dress is perfection and Carlotta will be green with envy. Our seamstress is very talented, *non?* And so is Remi. Madame Vernay outdid herself this time. She confided a secret to me earlier today. She said that she enjoys creating costumes for you because you are like a blank canvas on which she can unleash her creative talents to their full extent. I think, Christine," Lisette went on confidentially. "That our Madame Vernay lives vicariously on the stage through you." Lisette laughed quietly under her breath. "On the other hand, she said that fitting Carlotta for a new costume is like stuffing a sausage into a casing."

Lisette picked up a brush and began to fuss with Christine's curls again. "The Viscount will not be able to take his eyes off of you when he sees you tonight. And that is what you want, *n'est-ce pas?*"

When Christine did not answer, Lisette reminded her, "This is the stage, Christine. All eyes *should* be on you. An entire audience of women will have their bosoms half bared and on display for all to see. Why should you be any different?"

But a slight frown continued to mar Christine's face as she stared at her reflection in the huge, gilt-edged mirror in her dressing room. Somehow Raoul *could* find a difference. The truth was that Raoul had recently remarked on the provocative nature of her costumes, even if it was Madame Vernay's doing, and that she must remember that she was displaying herself before an audience that was at least half men. He had also hinted that perhaps their interest might not be only because of her singing or her dancing ability and that as his future wife, he had an interest in the way that she presented herself. So if her dress was daring or provocative in any way, there was every chance that she would hear about it later.

"Trust me, Christine, the Viscount will fall in love with you all over again when he sees you wearing this."

"I am not at all certain that's the reaction he will be having," Christine remarked absently as she stared at her reflection in the mirror. Her lashes suddenly lowered because, for no accountable reason, it was her teacher's reaction she was suddenly envisioning. What, she wondered, would *he* think when he saw her wearing this dress? *If* he was in the audience as he had said he would be.

"I assure you, you will have the man's undivided attention, especially when he sees how other men are looking at you."

Christine blinked for a moment before she realized that Lisette was talking about Raoul. "That is precisely what I am worried about. The last thing I want is another disagreeable, jealous scene with Raoul," she told Lisette.

Lisette made a scoffing sound under her breath. "Every man in love should be a little mad with jealousy."

"Love and jealousy are not the same thing."

"Christine, I did not realize before this what an unromantic girl you have become."

"Isn't what I'm saying only the truth?"

"So jaded, Christine. How did you get to be like this at so young an age?"

The brush that Lisette had been pulling through Christine's glossy curls caught on a tangle. "Sorry. Did I tell you that in spite of the rain that has been falling off and on all day, it is a packed house out there and people are still lined up in the street waiting to enter?"

"Yes, you did mention that earlier."

"Then what is that frown for? You should be enjoying your success, especially since your reviews have been so flattering."

"They are certainly not lining up to see me," Christine told the other woman. "It is a very small part."

"But it *is* a singing part. And a very desirable one. One that has gotten you noticed."

Lisette was right. It was a very coveted part. Christine had been surprised, but thrilled when it had been offered to her. And her reviews had been more than flattering.

"In spite of your very exasperating humility, your audience does want to hear more of you," Lisette went on. "And if the looks that Carlotta has been giving you lately are any indication, *she* fears you are a threat to her. That should tell you a great deal."

"Carlotta thinks of everyone as a threat. That is certainly nothing new. And," Christine added as she frowned into the mirror. "The truth is, I think that my teacher had something to do with my being given the part. Raoul certainly had nothing to do with it. He has discouraged me in every way he can think of, short of coming right out and forbidding me to perform on stage, which I believe he would not hesitate to do if he thought he could get away with it."

"But he *has* agreed to let you continue singing," Lisette reminded her.

"For a time."

After a silence, Lisette asked, "Do you think *he* will be in the audience?"

"He?"

"Your mysterious teacher."

"I don't know."

"Surely it crosses your mind when you step out onto the stage."

"I- Whether he is there or not, I wouldn't know."

"But you would *like* to know, wouldn't you?" Lisette asked and there was something in her voice that made Christine look up with a questioning frown.

"Why do you say it like that?"

"Because your voice changes every time you speak of him. And there is a certain look that comes into your eyes."

Christine's lashes lowered until they were shadowing those eyes. "You are letting your imagination run away with you, Lisette. As you often do. Do you know you have the most exasperating habit of turning everything, absolutely everything, into a romance?"

"What is better than a romance?" Lisette laughed, undaunted. "But are you very certain you have not begun to fall in love with him? Just a little bit?" Lisette asked, only half teasing as she coaxed a rebellious curl into place.

Christine, who was quite used to Lisette's outspoken boldness, said, "How you talk, Lisette. How can I fall in love with a man whose face I have never seen?"

"Yet you are intrigued by him, are you not? Admit it, Christine. Never having seen the man's face only adds to the mystery that surrounds him. You have told me that his voice is very- how did you put it? It was very masculine, very *puissant*. It was not at all the feeble, croaking voice of the doddering old music instructor that we had been expecting. Perhaps you have been imagining fitting a face to the voice?"

Christine's only response was a small, exasperated sigh, but Lisette silently noted that she made no denial.

"Soon you will be marrying a viscount," Lisette went on, changing the subject. "You will have a title. You will be known as Lady de Chagny. Did you ever anticipate something like that happening?"

Christine shook her head silently.

"I should think that would be enough to keep any woman contented. Yet lately you have seemed anything but content. You have seemed more- What is the word? More restless. More distracted."

"I would be contented if I was not envisioning Raoul sitting in his private box fuming over this dress. He will probably feel that I am openly defying him again. We had very strong words about my attire after my last performance."

"Christine, The Viscount Raoul de Chagny has asked you to marry him. As I said before, a little jealousy will do him good and will make him yearn for you all the more. The only thing you need to be thinking about right now is your wedding day and the life of bliss you will lead afterward."

When her words were met with silence, Lisette hesitated with the brush in mid-air and frowned. "You're not having second thoughts, are you?" she asked.

"It would be foolish of me, wouldn't it?"

"*Are* you having second thoughts?"

Second thoughts? Yes, Christine thought to herself. And third and fourth ones. But she didn't say that out loud. She had decided to keep her uncertainties to herself. Still, Lisette was astute enough to notice the lingering shadows in her friend's downcast eyes and the fact that she had not even tried to deny that she might be having doubts about the wedding.

"There's really nothing to think about, is there, Christine? I mean, it's already done. You have accepted his proposal. You surely wouldn't deny yourself this chance to have such a comfortable future, would you? Do you think you will ever get such an offer again?"

"Probably not," Christine said half to herself as Lisette stepped back and declared, finally, that her hair was perfect.

"The Viscount is very handsome," Lisette said, although she did not have to remind Christine of that. "All the women in the Opera House practically swoon over him when he makes an appearance.

And he is one of the wealthiest, most influential men in Paris. What could have you so uncertain?"

After another long, drawn-out sigh, Christine said, "I'm not certain, but I admit that something about this marriage looms over me like a shadow at times. I can't explain why exactly, but I almost fear becoming his wife. When I say "I do", it will be so- so irreversible."

"But that's a good thing. And he loves you, Christine. Anyone could see that. Not many women have the good fortune to marry for love. What could be more important than marrying a man that you can give your heart to?" Lisette looked at her more closely. "You do love him, don't you?"

Again, Christine did not answer.

"Christine?"

"How can I even know what love is supposed to feel like?" Christine suddenly burst out, frustration clearly evident in her voice. "I have never been in love before. How do I even know that he is the kind of man I can give my heart freely to for the rest of my life?"

So far, Raoul de Chagny had proven himself to be a gentleman in every way. But he had also proven himself to be a man who had strong opinions on every subject, opinions that he did not expect her to contradict. That trait certainly would not change once the marriage vows were spoken. Most likely, it would become more pronounced once Raoul had complete control over her. How was it going to be spending a lifetime with a man like that? Just how much adjusting would she be expected to do?

"Every woman has doubts before her wedding," Lisette reassured her as she shrugged one blue-clad shoulder. "Just as any man does."

"And suppose after we say our vows at the altar, we find we don't get along at all? What if it turns out we don't even like each other?" Christine asked. "Then what? How can any woman know how she really feels about a man unless they have spent a great deal of time together? Sometimes I think that he proposed too quickly. Before we had enough time to get to know each other. Sometimes I feel like I barely know him at all. It is like he only presents a side of himself that he wishes me to see, yet I sense that there is so much more under the surface that he keeps hidden from me."

"Marriage is always a gamble," Lisette said thoughtfully. "But we must risk something in order to play the game. And what man does not hide what he does not want the world to see? No one is perfect. You would expect him to make an effort to put his best foot forward. Especially a gentleman like the Viscount. And as for your feelings about him, I suppose no woman can truly say that she loves the man she is marrying before she has a chance to actually live with him. As I said, very few people are fortunate enough to be able to marry for love. But since it is all so uncertain one way or another, you may as well marry a rich man as a penniless one. Poverty certainly does not guarantee happiness. In fact, it is an added strain on any marriage. I have seen that firsthand with my own parents. You, on the other hand, will be starting out your wedded life with a vast fortune already in the bank, not to mention a mansion of your very own. Which, I should think, will be far more preferable than living in a single room here at the Opera House."

"I know I must sound terribly ungrateful," Christine said. "But the thought of leaving all of this behind- " Her words trailed off as she realized she could not possibly express all that she was feeling.

"All *this*?" Lisette echoed. "What would keep you here? What could possibly be more exciting than becoming the wife of the Viscount Raoul de Chagny?"

Christine closed her eyes. "What would you have me say, Lisette? That I will *not* miss the Opera House? The truth is that the thought of leaving all this behind has been in my thoughts a great deal lately."

"Of course you're sad at leaving all of this. It's all that you have known for the past few years. But once you're married you can't expect to go on singing on the stage. That would hardly be proper. You can't expect any man to allow his wife to- Well, no man wants to *share* his wife with the rest of the world. You may have to make a tiny sacrifice and give up your singing, but look what you will get to fill in the void. As the wife of Raoul de Chagny, you will have everything any woman could ask for, not to mention that you will be living in one of the grandest mansions in Paris. If the opportunity presented itself to me, I assure you that I would not think twice about leaving all of this behind. I would be sad to leave you, of course, but I would be happy to never have to work another day in my life and to finally live a life of leisure and luxury. It's like a fairy godmother waved her magic wand and made a happily-ever-after come true for you. And a Christmas wedding? How utterly romantic that will be."

"But you have not had to sit down to one of the de Chagny dinners in that mansion, Lisette. I had hoped I would be welcomed into a loving, caring family, but I'm beginning to wonder if that will be the case."

"They will warm to you Christine. Give them time."

"You don't understand, Lisette. They are- " Christine closed her eyes for a moment. "Behind their polite smiles, they seem very cold blooded and insincere. And when it comes to gossip, they are like ravening wolves on the scent of prey. At times, they are positively bloodthirsty. I don't know if I could ever thrive there."

"They are bound to be different from the people you are used to associating with," Lisette reasoned. "You just have to give them a chance. Most people are standoffish at first."

Standoffish? The word seemed woefully inadequate to Christine.

"It seems I have no choice," she murmured as she stared at her reflection in the mirror. "But what disturbs me the most is that Raoul grew up in that environment. It is very different from my childhood where everything was open and honest and I felt loved. For years, the Opera House has felt like my home."

"You can still come back to the Opera House," Lisette said. "Only instead of being on the stage, you will be watching the performance from the comfort of the de Chagny's private box. Don't you think that will be a novel experience?"

Christine looked a little lost as she thought of how different that would really be. It would not be the same. Not at all.

"With your upcoming wedding, your singing lessons, and your final performances, you will scarcely have a moment to breath, let alone worry yourself over such details, especially ones you have no control over. So just close your eyes and stop thinking about the Opera House. Fate has a greater future in store for you. Don't forget, you were reluctant to agree to the voice lessons in the beginning. Remember I had to talk you into that as well," Lisette went on. "This is no different."

But it was very different, Christine thought. She could quit the lessons whenever she wished to. A marriage could not be so easily ended, no matter how badly it might turn out.

"The lessons were a *choice* for me, Lisette. I could choose whether I wanted to continue them or not. As a married woman . . . "

"As a married woman, of course your life will change and you won't have the same freedoms that you have now. But- well, you will trade your freedom for security and that's what every woman wants. If you recall, you were worried that your voice teacher might turn out to be some ancient, demanding dragon that would make your life a living hell. And that was not the case at all."

"I seem to recall *you* using those words, Lisette."

"Yes, you're right, maybe I did. But the point is that the lessons turned out to be one of the best things you ever did for yourself. You said so yourself."

"But- "

"But what, Christine?"

"But all the hours that I have put into my singing lessons will have been in vain."

How could she even begin to explain to Lisette what those lessons had come to mean to her? How she looked forward to them. How they gave focus to her days.

"And what about your mysterious teacher?" Lisette asked. "Have you already spoken to him to tell him you will no longer be needing the lessons?"

"Yes," Christine said as she looked aside, and for the space of several heartbeats there was a genuinely distressed look on her face.

"And?" Lisette prompted.

"What could he say? He had to accept my decision to end the lessons. But I think that he- "

"He what?"

"He didn't say it, but he seemed as if he was quite- disappointed by my decision. I mean, I could sense that even in the silence that fell between us. It seemed, in that moment, that a vast chasm had begun to separate us."

"Well, he did devote months of his time to the lessons. One would expect him to feel some disappointment. And since he knew the lessons were coming to an end, he would naturally begin to withdraw himself emotionally. I mean, the lessons must have meant a great deal to him or he wouldn't have offered them to you in the first place. He will have some adjusting to do, the same as you."

"Yes," Christine said as she bit her lower lip. "He was very generous with his time. And his talent. I told you that I have never heard such a- a passionate musician."

She could not put into words how the regret in his voice, a regret she was sure he had tried to hide, had affected *her*. So deeply that she had burst into tears after he had said his good-bye after the last lesson had ended and he had left her alone. Had the lessons come to mean so much to *him* as well?

"Even though he will be giving me a few more lessons, telling him was very difficult for me," Christine admitted. "Not only because I felt like I was letting *him* down, but because *I* would be giving up so much."

"That makes sense," Lisette reasoned. "Not everyone is offered free voice lessons."

But it was more than that, Christine thought. It was so much more than that.

"He did choose me over anyone else here in the Opera House," Christine reminded the other woman. "And in the end, I feel that I must have sounded unappreciative and ungrateful."

"He chose you because he heard you sing, Christine, and he was impressed enough to pursue the lessons. If he didn't know what he was doing, he wouldn't have offered the lessons in the first place. And, as it turned out," she pointed out. "It all led to you singing on the stage, which is something you scarcely dared to dream about. Apparently he had faith in you. He recognized talent when he heard it. But life changes. It's as simple as that."

"It is still difficult to think of giving it all up."

"But you will be getting so much more in return. You will be exchanging an uncertain career, some would say a questionable career, for a life of luxury that most women can only dream about. The decision seems very easy to me."

"Maybe it seems easy to you because you have not heard him play," Christine said very quietly. There was a faraway look in her eyes as she stared into the mirror.

"You do not know how deeply his music can reach inside a person." Christine closed her eyes so she did not see Lisette raise her eyebrows. "Sometimes during our lessons I would ask him to play for me. After these last few lessons, I will never be able to do that again."

After a silence, Lisette asked, "Christine, why would you do that? Ask him to play for you? The lessons were all about teaching you to sing. Having him play for you seems almost- " Lisette searched for the right word. "Too intimate."

"It was not like that at all," Christine hastened to explain. "He has always been respectful and courteous in his manner towards me. I asked because when he plays, he touches my heart in a way that it has never been touched before. To close a door between us forever," she went on. "Sometimes I feel as if he is the only one who knows me for who I really am deep inside and I- I don't even know his name or what he looks like. To always wonder- "

"Always wonder what, Christine?"

Christine was staring down at her clasped hands, so she did not see the worried frown on Lisette's face in the mirror.

"Christine, have you let things go so far? A harmless flirtation is one thing, but- "

"Please do not be so melodramatic, Lisette. There has never been anything improper between us. Not even a flirtation."

"Then what does his name matter? Or what he looks like?"

"You're right. They don't. Perhaps I should have given the lessons further thought before I had agreed to them so recklessly. Then I would not find myself so conflicted now."

"What was so reckless about it? Madame Giry herself said this was a rare opportunity for you."

"When I first went to her, I thought she would definitely say no to the lessons," Christine said, thinking back. "But my teacher had already spoken to her so she already knew about them. She said that he would be an excellent instructor and that he was a genius when it comes to music. And he has proven that to be true."

"Have you ever figured out how Madame Giry knows him so well?"

"No, and she still won't tell me his name. She is mysterious, too, as if she does not want to divulge too much information about his identity."

"There might be a very simple reason he has been hiding from you," Lisette told her. "For all we know, he may be shorter than you and is as wide as he is tall. He could be some hunchbacked, black-toothed beast of a man who is covered from head to toe with warts."

Christine stared at her friend in the mirror.

"Obviously, his identity is going to remain a mystery, Christine, as are his looks. Certainly he cannot be as handsome as the Viscount. But as frustrating as it can be, we can't have the answers to everything in life. And second guessing yourself and having self-doubts, especially those you can't do anything about, will get you nowhere in this world. I have to say that I cannot understand this new uncertainty of yours. It is not like you to let doubt and fear drive your decisions."

Christine stared silently into the mirror. Maybe Lisette was right. She knew very well that nothing in life was certain. Maybe she *was* letting her doubts and her fears cloud her judgement.

"You don't want to always wonder what might have been, do you, Christine? Don't let this new doubt stand in the way of your happiness now. If I were offered such an opportunity, I will tell you now that I would not hesitate to accept it. I would be thrilled to have the chance to marry such a sought-after man. If you do not take this opportunity that has been presented to you, you may well regret it for the rest of your life. In any case, it is out of your hands now. You have agreed to the marriage. There is nothing left for you to do now but to see it through."

Lisette frowned thoughtfully as she continued to look at Christine's reflection in the mirror. "Is there something that you're not telling me?"

"No. No secrets," Christine answered, forcing a smile.

"I know this all must seem like such a big adjustment for you," Lisette said sympathetically.

"You're right. I am probably just having a hard time adjusting to the idea of- everything."

"Don't worry about your teacher. I'm sure he will find some other young lady to sponsor and to teach."

Why, Christine wondered, did that thought suddenly cause such an unsettled feeling inside of her?

"Don't think about all these things right now. Just concentrate on your performance tonight. That is enough for anyone to think about. After you sleep on it tonight, you will probably feel very different tomorrow. At least you are not as nervous as Henri Millard must be," Lisette went on, changing the subject. "He said the ghost made him forget his lines the last time he was on stage."

"Henri is always forgetting his lines," Christine reminded her.

"Yes, but he said he saw the ghost right before his last performance," Lisette said significantly. "He appeared in a backstage hallway and then vanished right before his eyes as if he had never existed at all. Monique said she saw him as well a few nights ago. Although Monique says she is not afraid of the ghost and that she is rather intrigued by the idea of the Opera House being haunted. But then Monique is intrigued by any man, dead or alive. She said the same thing everyone else says, that he was wearing a black cape and that he was masked. Since most people who have seen him describe him as wearing a mask, don't you think it is possible that he may have performed on the stage at one time, maybe many years ago? How else would you explain such a costume? Unless he is trying to hide something. Whatever he is, *was*, evidently something keeps him here. But it does seem to me that he is involving himself in earthly affairs quite frequently of late. His last note to Carlotta was very explicit *and* it was signed: O.G. I call that a very bold ghost."

"Another note?"

"Yes, I saw it myself. Gaspar somehow got his hands on it and he let everyone read it. The ghost warned Carlotta about changing the script when she was on stage and that if she was not more considerate of the other performers, she would have to be taught a more lasting lesson."

"Isn't it possible that someone was playing a trick on Carlotta?" Christine asked.

"That's certainly possible. Who wouldn't like to play a trick on Carlotta? Whoever, or *what*ever, the ghost is, he is obviously not only some tormented soul who cannot leave this place for some reason. He is also concerned about what happens on stage. There must be some tragic event behind such a haunting. Something connected to the Opera House itself. A suicide or a murder, perhaps. Or some story of unrequited passion or forbidden love. *Qui sait?* Usually there is no end to the gossip that goes on around here, so you would think that someone would know of such a story if it existed. But no one can recall even a rumor of anything like that happening. Then again, perhaps there was a secret love affair that no one knew about. And a suicide or murder may well have been hushed up, especially if someone important was involved. Or maybe the ghost was a victim of the Commun and he was tortured and left to die in one of the dungeons below us. We will probably never know the real story," Lisette said with a sigh. "Monique thinks that a séance should be held here at the Opera House to try and contact the ghost. But some people are afraid of what that might stir up.

"Obviously the ghost watches the performances since he insists on having his own private box, which Messieurs Peverell and Vaussard have not dared to refuse him. Not yet at least. Not after the last incident. It seems likely that in some way the music keeps him here," Lisette chatted on. "Remi Botair is not the only one who said he heard ghostly music playing in the theater after hours. Remi said the music was so beautiful and so heart-stirring that it brought tears to his eyes and that no mere man could have played like that. But then Remi is always emotional and it does not take much to bring him to tears. *Tu sait ce que je veux dire?*

"What do you think, Christine? Do you think that the Phantom of the Opera will be there in box five listening to you sing tonight?"

"I think, Lisette, that your imagination is running away with you again." But Christine could not help asking, "Has anyone seen any signs of a ghost tonight?"

"Not that I have heard. But the night is not over yet."

After a pause, Lisette asked, "The Viscount will be there tonight in *his* box?"

Christine nodded.

"He will no doubt want to show you off afterwards." Lisette said. "It is very romantic, *non*?"

"What is?"

"I imagine the handsome Viscount will be envisioning that you are secretly singing to him."

Whether that was true or not, Christine didn't know. Raoul had never even asked to hear her sing outside of watching her on stage. He had only complained about the time she devoted to it, hinting that it was a waste of time since she would be marrying him soon and she would be giving that life up.

"Of course you will be singing to him," Lisette said. She looked over Christine's dress again and there was a mischievous glint in her eyes. "But I'll warrant that even ghostly eyes will find you ravishing tonight."

"Ghostly eyes?"

"Yes. The Phantom of the Opera. If he really is there in box five watching you, perhaps you will win his heart tonight as well. If you have not done so already," Lisette teased before she said, "Ah, I've forgotten that I was supposed to bring Carlotta that fur cloak. She will be *furieux* with me for having forgotten it. But what is new about that?"

When the door closed softly behind Lisette, Christine stood up from her chair and paced restlessly across her dressing room in an attempt to settle her thoughts. With only the whisper of her skirts disturbing the silence, there was one thing dominating her mind. And that was that she would be leaving *him*, her unseen teacher when she left the Opera House for the last time. While she tried not to think about it, Lisette had reminded her once again of how much her life would change. I should be thinking about Raoul and my future with him, she told herself sternly. She would be marrying Raoul de Chagny soon and she would have every indulgence she could imagine. But a small part of her couldn't help wondering what the price for such a life of luxury would be.

"How I will leave all this behind," she whispered as she looked around the empty room, yielding for a moment to the tumult inside her now that she was alone, wondering why it ran so deep. Her teacher had said that he would be watching her tonight. She tried to concentrate on that and about giving a good performance. She would not be able to see him in the darkened theater, of course, but he was something for her to focus on.

Fifteen minutes later, as she was climbing the steps to the stage, one of the stage hands handed her a single, perfect, blood-red rose.

"*Voici pour vous.*"

It was not the first time someone had left her a rose. Who had been leaving them Christine didn't know, but she would find them anywhere, even in her dressing room with a brief note attached wishing her luck with her performance. The notes, however, were never signed.

"Who left this?" she asked the stage hand before he turned away from her.

"I don't know," he said. "I found it the same as I found the other ones, with a note addressed to you. You have about ten minutes, Miss Daae. Make sure to be careful of that last step."

The music of the orchestra continued to fill the darkened theater. Christine could also hear the usual muffled voices of workers behind the stage getting ready for the next scene. She lifted the flower and closed her eyes for a long moment as she tested its fragrance. In spite of all that was going on all around her, she felt strangely alone as she stood there waiting for her cue.

Suddenly that changed.

She opened her eyes and looked around but no one was near her. No one was watching her. A piece of scenery was giving the workers trouble and someone swore vehemently under their breath over some crushed fingers. But other than that, there seemed to be nothing out of the ordinary. And yet a strange prickling sensation continued to creep over Christine's flesh, a kind of eerie feeling that she was being watched. Some instinct made her look up.

She tilted her head far back and as she did so, she drew in a startled gasp. In the rigging far above her was a man. He was half concealed by the shadows but she could see that he was dressed entirely in black. He was leaning slightly forward as he looked down and over the railing. Even from this distance she knew that he was looking straight at her.

Half of his body remained obscured in the shadows, but where the light was upon him, she could make out the pale mask that covered half his face and the flowing cape that concealed most of his body. Christine continued to stare as if she were transfixed. She didn't recognize the man - she could barely make out the shadow-etched, unmasked portion of his face - and she wondered what he was doing up there. Had he been watching her all along, or had he happened to look down at her at the very same moment that she had looked up? As she continued to stare upward, he turned away suddenly so that she could only see his profile. He looked intense, intent, even with the covering of the mask. He looked . . .

Just the way the Phantom of the Opera had been described again and again.

Her heart began to beat a little faster. She looked around to see if anyone else had noticed the man. No one had.

The stage hand returned shortly and said, "It's your cue, Miss Daae. Let me help you up the steps."

When she looked back, the masked man had vanished. As if he had never existed at all.

He watched her from the deeply-shadowed recesses of box five. As always, he could see her even though she could not see him. She stood alone on the stage, bathed in the soft glow of the theater lights. Her bare skin was gleaming with a satiny luster. The fringed shawl draped around her hips sparkled as it caught the light. Even more alluring, her unbound hair fell in a profusion of shimmering, copper-tinged ringlets down her back. Her beauty was such that it held him spellbound. He watched her close her eyes as she took a moment to gather herself. He knew her well by now. It was something she did during her lessons, too, before she sang even a note.

There was a beauty and a grace to Christine that had touched him from the very beginning. And now, the way she looked tonight with the exquisite gown emphasizing her womanly curves as she swept onto the stage, she further bewitched and enchanted him. Because she was also a dancer, there was a fluidity and a natural grace to her every movement that caught and held his eye. She was his ideal of beauty, the embodiment of female perfection. She was all that he knew he could never have. It pleased him that she was still holding the rose. In some small way, it made it seem like he was with her on the stage.

The first strains of music filled the darkened theater. She sang the first word and he closed his eyes. Little did she know the power she wielded over him. Hers was a siren's call, a voice that could draw a man to his very death. She was singing a love song and as her haunting voice reached him from the stage, he wondered how such a young woman could possibly know such depths of passion and emotion. He had been aware of it even before her first lesson and he had worked hard to draw it out of her. And now, because of his training, she could, and often did, bring her audience to tears. They were held in thrall by the magic of her voice as she wove a spell around them. With each performance, she was becoming more popular and people wanted to hear even more of her. Of course, that was not likely to happen. Not if the Viscount had his way. But there was tonight.

He stood well back in the darkness, hanging on every perfectly-sung note. Just as she was about to sing the final soul-stirring, heartfelt word of love, she lowered her head and paused for a moment, drawing a deep breath. He held his breath as well. He might have been on the stage singing with her, so attuned was he to her efforts.

The moment did not last long. Carlotta saw to that. She barged onto the stage and began singing her own aria before the end of Christine's song. The man in box five tightened his jaw as he realized that Carlotta was deliberately defying his request. He vowed that it would be the last time Carlotta was allowed to interrupt her. If indeed Christine ever did sing again.

His gaze shifted and hardened even more as he looked at Raoul de Chagny, who in his own private box across the theater directly opposite him, was also intently watching the stage.

Chapter 2

It was a very cold, disagreeable night in Paris. And yet, in spite of that, one might have said that even the weather bowed to the will of the beau monde for the wind that had been raging so tempestuously for the past two days had finally died and the freezing rain that had fallen with such fitful persistence all day had ended, so that now row upon row of black carriages lined the damp, cobblestone streets that radiated outward from the Opera House. There was no performance on stage this night, however. The Viscount Raoul de Chagny was hosting a private party in the Opera House. As the main patron of the Opera House, it was one of the privileges he could, and did, avail himself of whenever he wished. As a member of the aristocracy, his noble lineage went back for at least seven generations and one of the duties of his position was to display his family's wealth and prestige by hosting lavish parties and funding the arts, both of which he did with liberal sufficiency.

Like any rare gem, it was important for fashionable society to be seen in the best setting, and no place was more extravagant than the Paris Opera House. It had been built to be a symbol of opulence for an emperor and so it was resplendent with the very best that the people's money could buy. Tonight the lights were blazing from the windows of the massive, seven-story building to welcome the Viscount's guests, the creme of Paris society who were still arriving in small, animated groups.

The Viscount inclined his head politely as he listened to a comment made by a gentleman at his side. Dressed impeccably in royal blue velvet, the Viscount's manner was, as always, refined and dignified, with a bearing - some might say an arrogance - that came naturally to the affluent, titled aristocracy.

Raoul de Chagny stood out among the throng of men not merely because he was taller than most. It was his poise and his self-assured manner that first drew one's eye. He exuded a rare confidence at all times. His every move was elegance personified, and it was all underscored by the flattering, expensively-tailored clothing that he wore, attire that never failed to set fashion standards. He was a fine figure of a man. The glittering chandeliers overhead emphasized his strong, classically-French features and blazed the red highlights in his chestnut hair to dark fire. His hair was brushed back from his forehead in the smooth, glossy waves that were at that time in style. He was impeccably and stylishly groomed, from his cleanly shaven, slightly-clefted chin that jutted above the snow-white, perfectly knotted cravat at his neck right down to the toes of his highly-polished leather boots. His face was undeniably handsome, his smile charming, his blue eyes perfectly matching, by design of course, the pale blue silk vest that showed beneath his coat.

He laughed his pleasingly-modulated laugh and shrugged one broad, blue-clad shoulder with an air of studied insouciance at some comment made by one of the many fawning guests gathered around him. He turned his smiling attention briefly to a turquoise-gowned woman who was waving her fan indolently before him, then raised his tawny brows as he laughed politely at some remark she had just made. He was more than comfortable in this aristocratic setting. It had been his world since birth. And yet, anyone watching closely might have noticed that his eyes were subtly searching the crowd even as he continued to make small talk with the woman before him. Still, there was no one who would deny that his ability to hide his irritation was admirable.

Christine placed her gloved hand lightly on the railing and leaned carefully forward. She almost sighed with relief when she saw that Raoul wasn't glaring back at her. He hadn't noticed her up here. Not yet at least. At the moment, the only view she had was the back of his head. But if he should turn and see that she was up here on the third floor by herself . . .

The open space below her was a constantly-shifting kaleidoscope of color, a brilliantly-hued rainbow of dazzling silks and satins. In spite of the somewhat scandalous reputation of resembling a Turkish bathhouse, the entire Opera House was the perfect setting for such a blue-blooded gathering. Richly adorned and gilded in gold embellishments everywhere one looked, every exquisitely-designed area of the Opera House was brightly illuminated by the massive, sparkling chandeliers and candelabras that threw a soft luster over everything. In spite of the gaslights, the Viscount had insisted on candles also being lit so that they would throw a flattering luster over everything, especially on the sparkling facets of the many jewels that adorned the throats, earlobes and wrists of the many ladies present, not to mention the jewels that he himself wore on his hands and the large garnet, a de Chagny heirloom, that was nestled in the lace at his throat.

Tonight the Grand Staircase was serving as a multi-level stage for the many people posing down below. On the second floor landing, the staircase separated into two wide flights of steps which led to the Grand Foyer. Flanking the very bottom steps, the pedestals of the staircase were adorned with breath-taking, life-sized bronzed female torcheres from which long glass prisms sparkled. The railings were made from contrasting colors of imported marble and were a work of art themselves. Indeed, everywhere one looked was the splendor and opulence of a king's palace, from the marble columns and the life-size figures of Eurydice, Aurora and Psyche, down to the beautiful mosaics and the gold leaf flourishes that adorned everything. There were seventeen stories altogether, seven of which were below the stage level. The Paris Opera House even boasted its own private stables underneath the forecourt.

Christine continued to look down upon the crowd from one of the curved balconies on the third floor. For a good hour she had maintained her place at Raoul's side to greet his guests until, worn out from the strain of smiling incessantly and having to make never-ending, polite small talk, she had excused herself. While Raoul was perfectly comfortable with it all, she wasn't at all sure what she was supposed to say and what she was not supposed to say. She didn't know the countless names and titles of the guests. Of course Raoul knew them all and he looked perfectly at ease down there. He was obviously in his element as he graciously greeted each and every one of his guests and basked elegantly in his role as host.

But Christine was well aware of the irritation simmering just below the surface of his calm facade. She already knew that he was far better at hiding things than she was, and that, above all else, he considered it absolutely essential to keep up appearances. So only the faintest, briefest hint of annoyance showed on his face as he glanced searchingly around the crowded room without trying to be obvious about it. She knew the cause of that irritation of course. He was looking for her. She had been gone too long and he was wondering where she was. She was supposed to be at his side greeting all those pretentious guests who were peacocking, parading and preening about down below, posing as much as any actor on the stage of the Opera House.

She would have gone down and joined Raoul at that very moment, but Carlotta suddenly made her appearance. No one could fail to notice Carlotta's entrance. Her flamboyance was just as noticeable off stage as it was on. As she swept past the arched entryway that led to the Grand Staircase, all eyes turned to view the dramatic unveiling as Carlotta pushed back the velvet hood of her cloak.

She was holding her dog, Androcles, in her arms. The tiny dog, who was a Great Dane in a Maltese's body, had a high-strung temperament that matched Carlotta's. Even the dog was sparkling with diamonds. Carlotta handed Androcles to one of the men at her side and with a calculated flourish, threw off, first, the cape and then the fox caplet that was draped around her neck to reveal a startling expanse of bare shoulders and bosom. The tightly-cinched burgundy gown she was wearing looked like it could barely contain the overflow of straining, quivering flesh that was on display for all to see. And to ensure that all eyes were drawn to the abundance of Carlotta's feminine charms, a heavy necklace that was dripping with glittering diamonds was nestled right above the deep valley of her impressive cleavage.

An enormous black ostrich feather curved down from Carlotta's elaborately-coiffed hair to tease one shoulder. As she drew Androcles back into her arms and nestled him against her ample bosom, she tossed the dark curls that fell over the other shoulder in a coquettish gesture as she held out her gloved hand and smiled up at Raoul from behind her thick black lashes. From where she stood,

Christine could see an almost predatory gleam in the woman's eyes and in the slight curve of her carmine lips as she watched Raoul lean over her hand. But then any man was fair game where Carlotta was concerned.

Carlotta leaned towards Raoul as he straightened and whispered something in his ear. Then she laid her hand upon his dark blue sleeve and allowed him to lead her up the Grand Staircase toward the Grand Foyer.

Just another minute or two, Christine told herself, and then I'll go down there and join him. She watched Raoul grab a glass of champagne from a passing tray and hand it to Carlotta. Christine seriously considered fortifying herself with a glass of the sparkling beverage, as well, to help her face the rest of the evening.

She knew how important this night was to Raoul. He'd had a dress made especially for her to wear tonight. He had told her repeatedly that he wanted her to look her best and emphasized that this was her first important opportunity to mingle with what he called the right kind of people. The pale pink brocade gown she was wearing was richly adorned with heavy lace and black velvet bows. The dress was tasteful, elegant, and most importantly it was in the very latest style. As a future de Chagny, one of her duties, she knew, was to present herself fashionably at all times. But she was under no delusions. This night was also a rite of passage, a test to see if she was deserving enough of the title Lady de Chagny.

Her dress was certainly fashionable enough, but Christine realized only too well that while she might look like the other women down below her, she was certain she didn't feel like one of them. They all seemed to be mingling and enjoying themselves with very little effort at all, while she, on the other hand, felt very uncomfortable in the midst of it all. In fact, all evening she had felt like she didn't fit in, like she had to speak and behave according to a very restricted script. Nevertheless, she understood that this would be her world soon and she would be expected to play a proper role as Raoul de Chagny's wife. She would be a viscountess. She would be expected to act a certain way, dress a certain way, live a certain way.

Suddenly, that thought almost panicked her. Suddenly, obeying strict rules of conduct at all times seemed not only confining, but suffocating. She didn't know if she would ever be able to fit in. And then she had another, even more troubling thought. Wouldn't it be worse if she *did* fit in? She couldn't help thinking how much more bearable this would all be if Lisette were here. But Lisette had not been invited, of course, because she didn't move in the same social circles.

Raoul was on the Grand Staircase again, sans Carlotta. Another moment of panic assailed her when he suddenly stopped and straightened. She was certain he was about to turn and look up in her direction so she stepped back from the railing. She held her breath, waiting for him to notice her, but a crowd of new guests had just arrived and Raoul immediately went forward to greet them.

She suddenly released the breath she had been holding and sighed with relief as she shrank back even further from the railing until she was concealed by the deep shadow of a column and partially hidden by the generous folds of a heavy velvet curtain. It was the first time that she had felt safe all night. With her back against the column, she glanced towards the window at the end of the long hallway and saw with some surprise that it was snowing. It was late in the year for snow and it surely wouldn't last long, but the softly-drifting snowflakes held her gaze.

As she continued to watch the snow, the sound of the voices below her blended and her thoughts drifted far from Paris. She closed her eyes, drawn back through the years to the snowfalls of her childhood. How long ago it all seemed. It was almost like a different lifetime. Suddenly she was back at the little cottage where the balsam and the roses filled the air with their sweetness and the hollyhocks bloomed along the white picket fence in the summertime. The woods across the road offered her a different view and a different world to explore every season, and down the winding country lane she could reach the seaside after only a short walk. She sank deeper into her daydream until she was once again standing on the soft sand, watching the reflection of the sunrise on the water in the soft glow of an early spring morning.

A more elusive, far more distant memory came to her, that of her mother who had died when Christine was very young. She didn't have many memories of her mother, so she cherished the few that she had been able to hold onto. She knew that her parents had loved each other very much and those days in the cottage by the seashore had seemed idyllic to her. Her fondest memories remained tied to that place.

But then her thoughts shifted and she was remembering that terrible day when everything had changed and her father's unexpected death had brought an end to it all. Years had passed, yet it still seemed like only yesterday since that awful, fateful day when the innocence of childhood had ended abruptly and the life she knew had vanished forever. Even now, the memory was hard to bear. She had been close to her father and her mourning had been so deep that it seemed as if she had died, too. It was as if half her heart had been ripped away and replaced by a huge, gaping hole of grief. It had been worse, so much worse, than any physical pain she had ever endured.

For a long time after she had arrived in Paris, she had felt lost and terribly, terribly alone. And yet, as hard as it was, she had no choice but to go on with her life. In spite of, or maybe because of her grief, she had worked hard to become a dancer because she knew that it had been her father's dream for her. But it had been heartbreaking for her when he hadn't been there to see her the first time she had danced on stage. And he had never heard her sing, nor even known about her voice lessons. Music had been an important part of her father's life. He had been a musician himself. They had travelled together to Paris when she had been seven years old and she had been enraptured by the opera from the very first moment the curtain had risen. She remembered her father laughing down at her and saying that the opera must be her destiny.

What she wouldn't give to see him just one more time, to hear his voice and his laughter. He had always been there for her, guiding her and offering her his wisdom through all the years of her childhood. He would be proud to see how far she had come. And he, of all people, would have understood the uncertainties of these past few years, not only her joys and her accomplishments, but her conflicting emotions and her fears. She couldn't help but wonder what he would say about her upcoming marriage, a marriage that would change everything for her and take her away from the Opera House. The truth was that deep down she, herself, was afraid of so much change in her life. She worried that she was getting too far away from the girl she had once been. Would her father even recognize her if he saw her now? She needed the reassurance that the past would not fade into nothingness, that it would not dissolve into a long ago that she could barely remember. She did not want to lose her memories. They were too much a part of who she was deep inside. But she was afraid that's exactly what would happen once she married Raoul.

She shook her head, forcing herself back into the present. This was not the time to be thinking about such sad things. Especially things she could do nothing about. She still had hours to go to get through the evening. She straightened her shoulders and resolved to let herself enjoy it, even if it was for Raoul's sake.

But as she stood there, it wasn't Raoul that she found herself thinking about. She was wondering if her mysterious teacher was somewhere down there in the crowd. Even if he was there, she wouldn't know it. She could have been introduced to him already without realizing his true identity. But no, that wasn't exactly true. She would recognize his voice immediately, even if he barely spoke. And somehow, wouldn't she also know it the moment she looked into his eyes?

If he was here, she mused, maybe he was feeling as smothered and suffocated by the crowd as she was. It didn't take long for her to lose herself in another daydream. A daydream in which she would not have go back down to that throng of people. She would go up to the rehearsal room instead, a place where she had always felt safe. She closed her eyes as the fantasy grew more detailed. There would be a fire crackling on the hearth as there always was. It would hold the darkness back a bit and add a low, reddish glow to the room. She would be standing before the tall windows looking out at the falling snow when the door would suddenly open behind her. She would turn from the window to see her teacher who would stop immediately when he realized that someone else was in the room. He would pause for a moment on the threshold, but then, realizing it was her, he would enter the room and quietly close the door behind him.

She would hear his familiar low, throaty laugh as he said conspiratorially, "Ah, Christine, I see that your thoughts were the same as mine."

As he stepped forward into the deep glow of the fire, she would see that Lisette had been wrong about him. He would be tall, and he would look, in fact, very much as she had imagined him looking. Intensely, darkly handsome. She would see his smile for the first time as he said to her, "So you have found me out at last. There seems to be no use in me hiding behind a curtain now."

And then he would say to her, as he had said at the beginning of their very first lesson, "You don't have to be afraid of me, Christine."

He would stretch his hands out to the radiating warmth of the fire and, with a brief glance at her over his shoulder, he would say: "It *is* much nicer here away from everyone, isn't it?" And then he would join her at the window and say, "Stay here with me a while and let me tell you why it was necessary for me to keep myself hidden from you."

And then he would begin to tell her a tale of intrigue and daring, a spellbinding tale in which he was the hero who had kept his identity from her for some noble reason, and she would come to know all his secrets. All this he would say while the snow was still falling outside the window and the fire crackled comfortably in the background and no one would pound on the door looking for her . . .

She brought her thoughts up sharply and chided herself silently, "Stop daydreaming like a silly school girl."

It was time for her to act like a grown woman now. A grown woman who was about to be married. She was certain that no one else indulged in such silly flights of fancy. Except for Lisette. Lisette was as bad as she was when it came to romantic foolishness, maybe worse.

She forced herself back to reality. She had to go down there and face Raoul and his guests sometime. She might as well stop putting it off, put a smile on her face and brazen out the rest of the evening like an adult instead of hiding up here like a timid child. She gathered her skirts and took a step forward. But what she heard next made her draw back and shrink even further into the shadows.

"How else can a man be expected to behave of in a sea of naked bosoms?" she heard a man say.

Another male voice answered, "You've been like a wolf on the scent of prey all evening, Anton. A very hungry wolf, I might add."

To her mortification, the speakers - she did not know how many there were - took up a position on the other side of the column, just beyond the curtain. They did not seem to be aware of her presence, and for a long, agonizing moment, Christine wavered, uncertain what she should do. Should she make her presence known? Should she stay hidden and wait until the men had gone away? She scarcely dared draw a breath as she heard a deep voice say, "Subtlety was never your strong suit. I suppose you really are safer up here. And so are they."

There was a low laugh and someone said, "It shouldn't surprise you in the least that he came up here. He's got a bird's eye view down the bodice of every female here. He knows he can't leer quite so openly down there as he can up here."

"You only wish that you had thought of it first," the first voice said, not bothering to deny the accusation.

There were more quiet laughs and then the first man admitted, "I'm damned if I can help myself. What am I supposed to do when there are so many of them putting on such a- shall we say, a *titillating* display? While looking from afar certainly is not as thrilling as an outright seduction, it has its moments, especially when they are so blissfully unaware that I can fondle them to my heart's content, even if it is only from a distance."

"I see that London hasn't changed you a bit, Anton," she heard someone say next.

"Why would I give up one of my most pleasurable pursuits? Speaking of pleasurable pursuits, your brother seems to have kept himself busy during the time I was away. When I returned to Paris and heard that he had gotten himself affianced, I didn't know whether to believe the tale or not. Is it true? Is he actually thinking of letting himself get shackled to- an *actress*?"

"My brother is quite serious about his upcoming wedding, I assure you."

Christine realized with a sudden stab of panic that one of the speakers was Philippe de Chagny, Raoul's older brother. If he should find her here in such a humiliating position, perhaps think that she was intentionally eavesdropping, she would never live it down. She pressed her hand against her own half-bare chest as if to quiet the pounding of her heart.

"I must confess, I have a hard time understanding why Raoul would take to wife a performer at the Opera House when there are a hundred other ladies that would gladly give their eye teeth to hold that position. Just how exactly did she manage it? The rivalry of the other females must be as fierce as the guns at Waterloo."

"She isn't just any performer," Philippe informed the man. "She has recently begun singing on the stage *and* she has been creating quite a sensation."

"Do tell."

"Raoul is completely smitten with her and when you see her, you'll understand why," Philippe went on. "He's not the first man and he won't be the last to let himself be snared by a beautiful face and, dare I say, an even more enticing body."

"Snared is the opportune word," the first man drawled. "I shudder at the very thought of how many ladies I would disappoint should I let myself become *snared* by one of them."

Someone scoffed under their breath.

"If it was a matter of his appetite needing to be appeased," the first man went on to say. "Couldn't he have just discreetly seen to it without getting himself entangled in the dreaded state of matrimony? Everyone knows that Raoul's popularity with the ladies is almost legendary. Why, by just crooking his finger, there are any number of ladies waiting in line for the taking."

"There is something about this one," was Philippe's reply.

"Ah, now you have intrigued me."

"You are certain to meet the little minx tonight," Philippe said. "You'll be able to see for yourself why she has such a hold over him."

There was a long moment of silence.

"Where has she been all night? I would think she would be glued to Raoul's side in an attempt to insure her claim on her territory."

"I haven't the faintest idea," Philippe replied. "Maybe she is perched like a frightened little bird in some obscure corner of the Opera House. I imagine being thrust in to the lion's den for the first time can't be easy for her. She can seem a little timid at times."

"Well, she will have to get over that soon enough if she is to become a de Chagny."

"Raoul will make sure of that. As we all know, he is very keen on keeping up appearances."

"Well, she must be something quite out of the ordinary. I can't wait to be introduced to her."

"Just make sure to keep that ravenous look out of your eyes when you do, Anton. Raoul is unusually possessive where she is concerned. He might take offense at you lusting after his future wife. Or, if you can't control yourself, at least be subtle about it."

"Does that include you as well, Philippe? Your usual rivalry has not flared up over the woman, I hope."

"I have restrained myself," Philippe assured the other man. "Although I will admit that it does get challenging at times."

"I knew it!"

"Just the other day she was trying to hold a conversation with me in the library, something about French history of all things. It was entirely my fault since I made the mistake of letting her get started in the first place. I gallantly pretended interest while she went on giving me her opinions about feudalism. Little did she know that I had stopped listening to her entirely and that the whole time she was talking I was thinking instead of what she would look like sprawled out naked under me on the davenport behind her."

"And she never guessed?"

"No, she was completely in the dark."

Christine felt her cheeks flush hotly when she recalled that conversation with Philippe. She'd had no idea, had actually congratulated herself that they were finally bonding and that she had impressed him with her knowledge of French history.

"You had better have a care when you are around your brother," Philippe was warned. "He knows you better than she does. I imagine he would catch on more quickly."

"If the opportunity presented itself and I had made up my mind," Philippe went on smoothly. "I assure you, there isn't a thing he could do about it. In fact, neither one of them suspected I'd had her completely and thoroughly by the time she had finished with her tedious discourse on the Reign of Terror. In fact, she had me so aroused that I had to stay planted behind the desk until Raoul fetched her out of the room."

"And you're going to be living in the same house with her after the wedding?" one of the other men asked and then laughed quietly, wickedly. "That should prove extremely interesting."

"I never said it would be easy resisting her," Philippe went on. "If indeed that's how it all plays out. As I said, there is something about this woman, and I am a healthy, red-blooded male after all. And I will wager that under that prim and proper, very gorgeous exterior, there is a flame that could be coaxed into a raging fire by an experienced hand. At least behind closed doors. After all, what woman parades herself across a stage for all the world to see? You should see some of her costumes."

"You realize, of course, that the mounting of your brother's fiancé, *or* wife, would be a shocking overstep," one of the men said brazenly. "But I can't say that it would surprise me. Your past history of running with the hare and hunting with the hounds is only too well known, Philippe. Unfortunately, it was also the reason behind your falling out with Raoul after Capucine. You might be brothers, but you two could barely be in each other's presence for almost an entire year. I 'm surprised you didn't come to blows over the woman."

Behind her consternation at the turn that the conversation had taken, Christine couldn't help but wonder who Capucine was. Raoul had never mentioned her.

"I, for one, shudder at even the thought of that unpleasantness," Christine heard one of the men say. "Thank goodness the entire family left France shortly after." There was a slight pause, and the same man asked with sudden dread in his voice, "Capucine isn't here, is she?"

"She wouldn't dare."

"That's a relief. I had no way of knowing if she had returned while I was away. I always said you must get your recklessness from the Beauvoir side of the family, Philippe," the man went on. "As I recall, you were twice Capucine's age."

"A fact that did not stop her in the least from participating in some very memorable hours of pleasure with me whenever we could find them. For such a young woman, Capucine could be a- shall we say, a very creative partner."

"Well, I haven't forgotten my part in that disastrous affair. Nor Capucine's outrage and threats when she finally realized you were also enjoying some memorable hours with Emilse. I can still see the look in her eyes when she took her riding crop to you."

"And I haven't forgotten what it took to keep the matter quiet," Philippe said. "I had to pay the family a fortune to hush it all up. To this day, I'm not at all certain that blackmail wasn't her intent from the beginning. There always was the matter of her questionable past. Nothing that could be proven, of course, but one has to wonder."

"True, where there is smoke, there generally is fire," one of the men commented. "In the end, it all worked out."

"Yes, as they say, blood is thicker than water."

"And no harm done. Apparently, Philippe has no complaints. Not if she was as good in bed as he said she was."

"Capucine was quite accomplished," Philippe assured them.

"You're certain this singer has no idea of your lust for her?"

"Not as long as there is a desk between us," Philippe answered.

There was a spattering of laughter and one of the men said, "I've seen her, Anton. All you have to do is to look at the woman and it's bound to happen."

To which Anton remarked, "Unfortunately, if Raoul should find Philippe literally with his trousers down again, he might not be so forgiving this time."

"No matter how tempting the woman is," Philippe assured him. "I shall make every effort to keep my baser instincts under control."

"An admirable goal. I should hate to have to play Raoul's second sometime in the future," came the drawling reply.

"I did not say it would be easy by any means," Philippe informed the other man. "*De vous a mois*, should she show any inclination at all that she is willing . . . " His voice trailed off suggestively.

"I wouldn't expect anything less. I would do the same thing myself."

"As for my calf-eyed brother," Philippe went on. "I hope that he is able to keep his wits about him and not allow this woman to lead him around by the- nose."

"Has *he* had her yet?" someone asked.

"No. Else I'm certain he wouldn't be able to keep from bragging about it. She is either unbelievably innocent or she is shrewd enough to realize that putting a man off only whets his appetite."

"Well, she is shrewd enough to have gotten him halfway to the altar. As for myself, I wouldn't think of limiting myself to picking a single rose when there is a whole bouquet ready for the plucking. Too many women would have their hearts broken. But it would seem we are in for an interesting few months."

"What do you say we make a wager on it?" someone asked. "We'll see if Raoul can get her to the altar before Philippe can get her into his bed."

"A wager. What a splendid idea."

"And the Dragon Queen? How do they get along?"

"They have their moments, as you would expect," Philippe replied. "Ligeia may be a vicious, bloodthirsty she-cat under the surface, but she is clever enough to be subtly devious. I'll give her that. There are times when I think Christine is about to stand up for herself. So far, however, she has proven to be quite docile and cowed before her majesty."

"Who wouldn't be? Ligeia makes even me quake in my boots."

"Amusing as this conversation has been, I'm in need of a brandy badly. And I am looking forward to offering my congratulations to Raoul on his engagement. Speaking of Raoul, he was certainly making himself scarce earlier this evening. There seemed to be some kind of intrigue that he and Eitan had been devising among themselves. Something very hush hush. Even I was not included in their scheming."

"Maybe there's to be a surprise during the musical programme," someone suggested.

"Yes, Raoul does tend to have a flair for the dramatic when it comes to entertaining his guests . . . "

The voices faded as the men moved off, thankfully without discovering her.

Raoul's jaw looked like it was carved in stone as he moved through the room, but he managed to keep a smile on his face as he forged a path through the crowd that was growing louder and more animated as endless trays of champagne made the rounds. He was halted several times by acquaintances before he could make his way up to the top of the stairs where he had just spied Christine standing by herself.

"Where have you been? I've been looking all over for you."

"I- " Christine was still struggling to compose herself after the shocking conversation she had just overheard.

Raoul frowned and peered more closely at her, perhaps becoming aware of her pallor and a decidedly hunted, lost look in her eyes. "What's wrong?"

What could she say to him? She certainly wasn't about to relate all that she had just overheard. Not here at least.

"What have you been doing all this time? I had begun to think you were avoiding me." Raoul's gaze narrowed and his mouth straightened into a thin line as he began to realize that something really was wrong. "Something is bothering you."

She opened her mouth to speak, but barely got two words out when he interrupted her. "Whatever it is, this isn't the time or the place to discuss it. Come. Take my arm. I'm sure people have been wondering where you are."

Christine reached for his arm with the hand of an automaton while Raoul said stiffly behind his smile, "This is a party, not a funeral, Christine. You're supposed to look happy on my arm."

He inclined his head and refreshed his smile for anyone watching as he focused his gaze on a point across the room. "Ah, there is my brother. He seems to have been avoiding me as well."

Chapter 3

In the faint red glare of the gaslights, the tall figure standing beside Madame Giry appeared almost sinister. Garbed entirely in black, except for a blue silk cravat knotted at his throat, he was an imposing six feet two inches tall, a man hard of muscle and broad of shoulder. His hair was black as a raven's wing, framing a face that remained a mystery, for he was standing well back from the balcony's curved railing, far away from the illumination of the chandeliers so that half his face was veiled in shadows. The other half was hidden behind a mask.

He was far enough away from the railing that his mask would not be evident to a casual observer, but close enough that he could see everything that was going on down below. Boldly staring eyes narrowed slightly. There was a cool cynicism in the unmasked portion of his face as the shadow of a smile briefly tightened one corner of his mouth. A muscle tensed in the hard, chiseled line of his jaw as he glanced casually over the balcony railing and said, "I see, Madame, that you are keeping yourself at a safe distance from the brood of vipers below us."

Madame Giry laid her hand on the railing and looked down as well. "I'm only here to make sure the vipers can slither around in comfort."

The man lifted one dark eyebrow as he turned his face to look at her. It was an uncharacteristic remark for the woman. Madame Giry was the epitome of poise and graciousness. No matter how demanding her job, seldom did she raise her voice and rarely did sarcasm fall from her lips. She had an abundance of patience which was essential to her job of overseeing the smooth running of the Opera House. She had been invited tonight for one reason only, to stay behind the scenes and make sure that everything went as it was supposed to during the Viscount's soiree. Of course, since she did not move in the same circles, one would not have expected her to have been invited as a guest.

"Venomous as they may be," she went on to the man's continuing surprise. "The Opera House could not run without them."

Beyond the tall arched window at the end of the long gallery where they stood, a flash of lightning briefly, but brightly, illuminated the black sky, drawing their attention at the same time.

The man's voice when he spoke reminded her of the low rumble of thunder that followed the lightning. It was a deep, low sound that lingered in the mind of the listener. "Snow *and* a thunderstorm tonight. A rare combination."

"Rare, indeed," Madame Giry agreed. She glanced up at the man's face for a second before she went back to watching the scene down below her. "I did not expect to see you here tonight."

"I had not planned to come. But at the last minute- " He paused and shrugged one wide shoulder. "My curiosity got the better of me."

Curiosity. She hoped curiosity was all that had brought him up here and that he would conduct himself with restraint tonight. But one never knew. Not where this man was concerned.

Although he never caused anyone any real harm, he had a dark and wicked sense of humor and if pushed too far, he could be quite diabolical with his pranks. Only she and the Persian knew of his existence. Only they knew how much the Opera House, which had always prided itself on its avant-guard innovation, was due to his talent and his genius. He stayed behind the scenes, but the truth was that his whims were indulged more than anyone realized. And if the new owners had any notions of changing the way things were run, he had infinite ways of making them bend to his will. Unfortunately, she also knew that there could be a certain ruthlessness in his methods.

"Someone said they saw a shadowy figure in a cape and a mask disappear down one of the hallways earlier this evening," she informed him. "In a mist no less."

"In a mist, you say?"

"Yes."

"Who saw the ghost?"

"Gaspar Belisard, I believe," Madame Giry replied.

"Perhaps Monsieur Belisard was in a fog himself. He has been known to sample his own kind of spirits one too many times."

Gaspar Belisard's fondness for alcohol was well known among everyone who worked in the Opera House. Still, drunk or sober, he was not generally given to false reports or wild exaggerations. The man must have seen *something*.

"I had wondered if, perhaps, *you* were careless for a moment," she went on. "But the mist had me baffled."

"I admit that I find the thought of the mist intriguing myself, but I assure you it wasn't me."

"Yes, I thought it was far too dramatic and obvious, even for you." The woman lifted a questioning eyebrow all the same as her gaze settled back on the man.

"Maybe some romantic rendezvous has someone lurking around in the dark," he suggested.

"But that does not explain the mist," Madame Giry pointed out.

"No, it doesn't."

"I had even considered the possibility that someone was masquerading as the ghost."

"An intriguing possibility," the man murmured thoughtfully. He was looking more intently over the railing now. "I'll wager that bored society is no doubt fascinated by the notion of a ghost making an appearance at their soiree. The rumors are probably making the rounds as much as the champagne by now. But it shouldn't be long before they move on to more- shall we say, venomous gossip."

Madame Giry agreed. "As long as there are no more disturbances to add fuel to the fire. If someone *is* running around masquerading as the Phantom of the Opera, however, we shall certainly hear of it before the night is over."

"No doubt. I see Carlotta has arrived."

"Yes, who could miss such an entrance?" Madame Giry said. "I have not seen Christine for a while."

"She is on one of the third floor balconies across the theater," the man informed her. "She has been there for some time now." He indicated the right balcony with a glance of his eyes.

"Whatever is she doing there?"

"Hiding, I imagine. Apparently, slithering among the serpents does not appeal to her, either. All that posing must be a strain on her."

"Yes, I suppose so," Madame Giry murmured her agreement.

"Likely she grew weary of being a decoration on the Viscount's arm and needed a moment to herself."

Madame Giry glanced up sharply.

"It's true, Madame, and well you know it," the man went on. "Raoul de Chagny has been displaying her like a shiny new bauble." He stared downward with a fair measure of contempt gleaming in his cobalt eyes. "At the same time he insults her by inviting Carlotta here to sing. We both know that Carlotta sounds like a croaking frog next to Christine."

"I imagine singing before such a- demanding crowd might be a little overwhelming for Christine."

"Demanding," he scoffed cynically. "That is not exactly the word I would use. But you may be right," he said half under his breath. "She might feel somewhat lost facing such an audience." After a silence, he added, "The pompous fool will not even acknowledge her singing. He doesn't know that she comes alive when she sings, that all the fire and passion she has for music is a part of who she is. He is asking her to give up a great deal. More than he realizes."

"She has said this to you?"

"Not in so many words, but- " his voice trailed off and Madame Giry was forgotten for a moment as Christine made an appearance on the Grand Staircase. She did look a little lost.

Madame Giry looked from the woman to the man, and back again. There was a troubled look in her eyes for a moment but she wisely kept her thoughts to herself.

"And while her success on stage has caused some embarrassment for him, ironically, it also makes her more desirable. This soiree is merely part of his efforts to groom her to play her role at his side." A hard smirk quirked his handsome lips. "He may not find that so easily accomplished."

"What do you mean by that?"

"Only that Christine has a mind of her own. She will not play the simpering, submissive wife as easily as he thinks she will. He is making a mistake by thinking she will mindlessly bury herself under spousal obedience and the weight of his immense ego and happily give up what she loves so much."

Madame Giry sighed, but then she admitted, "I had hoped that with his interest in the theater, he would be more understanding about that."

"We both know the reasons why the man insinuates himself in the affairs of the Opera House. He is like a vulture watching her every move to make certain she does not go beyond the length of her tether. He postures and pretends that he is motivated by some noble, undying devotion to the arts, and to her. But we both know it is something quite different. He is pretending right now. Under that pretty face, the Viscount looks quite annoyed, and I imagine that even now he is vexed that Christine is not proving to be as well-trained as he would like her to be."

Madame Giry stiffened at the underlying current of emotion she heard in his voice but she said nothing.

"I imagine she is feeling a little dazed, especially tonight, at the prospect of joining the ranks of the noblesse oblige," he went on. "Would it not seem, at some point, a little- daunting, even to you, Madame?"

Madame Giry looked back down below. She could not deny the truth of what he said. She also knew that the man beside her had a keen perception of human nature. During the long years she had known him, his shrewd perceptions had always proven to be startlingly, if not cynically, accurate.

"As for this little soiree, the night is still young and while they put on their finery and display their pretty manners for all the world to see, the truth is that with the libations flowing so freely, they are just as likely as anyone to bare their true souls. Eventually."

Madame Giry did, unfortunately, agree. She nodded slightly but said nothing as a worried frown lingered on her face.

"Christine is an exceptionally brave young woman," the man went on. "She will face the crowd tonight no matter how intimidating it may seem." He shifted his gaze. "Speaking of vipers, Carlotta has been growing bolder of late. And more defiant. She is looking daggers at Christine right now. I suppose she is annoyed at the mere thought that Christine may be getting more attention than she is."

"Carlotta looks daggers at everyone she considers a rival."

"She *should* consider Christine a rival. But the she-cat looks like she is out for blood tonight. Her eyes are boring into Christine as if she were savoring a slow, drawn-out torture before her final pounce. Give her time and she will sink her claws in to do some real damage."

They both looked over the railing to see Carlotta looking Christine up and down with barely disguised dislike.

"Do you think she would dare go against you?" Madame Giry asked.

"My instincts tell me that Carlotta's nature will make her eventually *have* to defy me."

Madame Giry knew from years of experience that his instincts were seldom wrong. And she knew Carlotta.

"Then again, my reputation alone may hold her back." His slow smile was wolf-like as his eyes gleamed with a dark humor. "There are times when being thought the devil incarnate has its compensations. But we shall see, Madame. We shall see."

Philippe de Chagny was an older version, by a full decade, of his brother, Raoul. He was just as handsome, but his waving chestnut hair was a shade darker. His eyes were a deeper blue. Anyone making a comparison might have said the older de Chagny's eyes were a little bolder, but perhaps that was because he was more experienced in the ways of the world. Philippe was also a little taller than his brother, a little broader of shoulder. But there was one way the brothers were undeniably, exactly alike. They were both every inch the blue-blooded aristocrat.

As he waited for his brother to make his way through the crowded room, Raoul hastened to make one more very brief, very low-voiced comment on propriety. "You cannot . . . " he began.

But he never finished. He stopped suddenly and stared down at Christine with a horrified look when, instead of a delicate sip, she drained the remainder of her champagne with a very unladylike gulp.

Rather than meet Raoul's shocked look, Christine continued to stare down into her empty glass. If she was going to have to face Philippe, she was going to need all the courage she could get, she thought as her bare shoulders lifted and then fell in a small hiccup. Just thinking about his comments about that day in the library made her face grow hot all over again. How was she going to smile and pretend that nothing was wrong? Because she had no choice. That was how.

Raoul waved the three men over. As they came to a halt, they immediately fixed their gazes on her, reminding her very much of a pack of wolves who had suddenly come upon a helpless, orphaned fawn with nowhere to hide. Under their combined, silent scrutiny, Christine not only felt trapped. She felt stripped down to nakedness.

As if from a distance, she heard Raoul making polite introductions. " . . . and this is Lord Anton Charlebois."

Her only hope was to get it over with as quickly and as painlessly as possible. She drew a deep breath, but the very moment that Anton Charlebois spoke his first word, she was immediately reminded of every wicked thing he had said. In excruciating and embarrassing detail. Had there been a trap door in the floor, she would have gladly disappeared through it.

Lord Charlebois caught her gloved hand in his. "I have been looking forward to meeting you ever since I heard about your engagement to Raoul," he said as he leaned forward and touched her hand with his lips. It came as no surprise to her that he held her hand far too long. It was all she could do not to jerk it out of his grasp.

Straightening, he smiled suavely and arrogantly down at her and said, "Allow me to offer you my congratulations on your engagement."

Somehow she managed to force a smile. "Thank you," she returned a trifle stiffly, but politely nonetheless.

"I see now why Raoul couldn't help himself," Anton Charlebois went on. "You are as breathtaking as a garden full of roses in bloom."

That had not exactly been his earlier words.

"I had heard about your talented singing voice," the man continued. "But I confess I was not prepared for such a rare beauty. Raoul is a very lucky man. I shall be in lasting envy," he said softly while his gaze lowered and lingered on the soft curve of her décolletage. "I have always said that France has the most beautiful women."

Christine's gaze shifted nervously and quite by accident she saw Philippe de Chagny's eyes on her. There was a sly subtleness in his gaze that she had seen before, a faint smile on his lips, but now she

52

interpreted it all completely differently. The blush on her cheeks deepened.

Even more distressing, she saw both men, Philippe and Anton Charlebois, share a secret glance, a glance in which they were no doubt comparing their earlier comments about her.

Luckily, the champagne had begun to flow warmly through her and it went a long way in reviving her dwindling courage. She refused to be *cowed and docile* before them. Suddenly from somewhere deep inside she was able to find her voice. "You are an exceptionally accomplished flatterer, Lord Charlebois," she said to the man. "Perhaps now that you have returned to France, you, too, will decide to choose a wife. Unless, of course, you fear that by doing so, you will be breaking the hearts of so many of the *unchosen*."

Anton Charlebois' expression changed. He looked confused as if he did not know if she was making a joke at his expense or not.

But as Christine continued to smile sweetly and innocently into his face, he quickly recovered and said, "I fear Raoul has already plucked the only rose that I would have had my eye on."

"Just be mindful of the thorns, Lord Charlebois," Christine reminded him. "One who wishes a rose must also respect the thorns."

Raoul's eyes shifted back and forth between the two of them. Philippe narrowed his own gaze, paying even closer attention to her as he hid a smile behind a crooked forefinger.

After the men had left, Raoul frowned down at her and asked, "What was *that* all about? Now I know with a certainty that *something* is bothering you tonight."

There was a great deal that was bothering her. The fact that she had been described as docile and cowed. The fact that Philippe was lusting after her in secret. The fact that she was being discussed in the most disrespectful terms behind her back. But perhaps the worst of it all was that Raoul thought *she* was the one behaving improperly.

Raoul, however, was not looking not at her now. "Whatever it is," he said as he looked out over the crowd. "We shall have to discuss the matter later in a more private place. We don't want anyone to see us quarrelling. Ah, there is Carlotta. Just the woman I want to see."

He immediately tucked her arm under his and began to lead her back up the Grand Staircase, while she was feeling very much as Philippe had described it earlier. Like she was a lamb being led into a den of lions, who, if they sensed even the tiniest bit of fear, or scented the tiniest drop of blood, would not hesitate to rip her to miniscule shreds.

La Carlotta had just emerged from the Grand Foyer. She paused at the top of the steps like an empress about to make an entrance before her subjects. Surrounded by a bevy of adoring admirers, she slowly descended the wide staircase with the train of her long gown trailing dramatically behind her.

Monsieur Peverell, one of the new owners of the Opera House, practically fell over himself as he rushed up the steps to meet her. The man made an absolute fool of himself over the woman whenever he saw her. As they met on the second floor landing, Monsieur Peverell gushed, "I can't tell you how thrilled I am that you have agreed to entertain us with your talented voice tonight."

Carlotta looked at him for a moment with her chin elevated and murmured an imperious, "Of course."

Her gaze shifted and her expression immediately changed as she caught sight of Raoul approaching with Christine. After smiling at Raoul, she sent Christine a look that would have scorched most people to a smoldering ash. Christine was aware of the hostility in that look, but she did what she always did with Carlotta. She decided to ignore the woman as best she could.

Monsieur Peverell was a good four inches shorter than Carlotta which made him have to constantly tilt his head back to look up at her face. But he had shrewdly positioned himself on the step above her so that they were eye to eye. His close proximity to Carlotta, however, also brought him closer to Androcles. The tiny dog yipped a few times and showed his tiny teeth, giving only the briefest warning growl before he tried to take a bite out of Monsieur Peverell's hand. The man jumped back, stumbling on the step above him so that he had to momentarily brace himself with one hand on the next step, only narrowly missing the furiously snapping teeth that were still trying to take a piece out of his hand. Although it was well known throughout the theater that Androcles was high strung, he was not usually vicious enough to bite. Except when it came to Monsieur Peverell. As long as the man kept his distance, there was no problem. But Androcles would not tolerate him getting too close to his mistress. Right now he looked ferocious with his little head tilted warningly to one side, his teeth showing and his small body trembling as he continued to growl menacingly at the man.

Carlotta, on the other hand, seemed amused by Androcles' hostile behavior. Either that, or she was perfectly content to let the dog keep Monsieur Peverell in his place. She continued to ignore the standoff between the man and the dog, and turned her attention instead to Raoul whom she tapped teasingly on the arm with her folded fan. As she leaned toward him, the material restraining her generous bosom was stretched to capacity, a fact that Carlotta was most likely well aware of. That the dress continued to hold everything in place was a small miracle.

"We have all been anxiously awaiting your performance," Monsieur Peverell said as he kept a watchful eye on Androcles.

"I am only too happy to oblige you een such a small favour," Carlotta purred without looking at him. She was looking instead at the Viscount. "And your wedding ees when, Veescount?"

Raoul told her the date.

"Ah, a Chreestmas wedding." Carlotta then came right out and said that she would be available to sing at the happy event. She had apparently already given some thought to the music.

"*Voi Che Sapete* by Mozart?" Carlotta suggested. "Or perhaps *Care Compagne* from La Sonnambula?"

"*Voi Che Sapete*, I think," Raoul said in a perfect accent, without even asking Christine's opinion.

"An excellent choice, Viscount," Monsieur Peverell chimed in. "Carlotta singing at your wedding will certainly make it a memorable event."

As for Christine, it was all she could do to hold her tongue. She had no intention of allowing Carlotta to sing at her wedding.

"Eet ees a good theeng the wedding weell not be held here at the Opera House," Carlotta went on in her heavy accent. She glanced briefly at Monsieur Peverell. "You have no idea what we have to put up weeth here."

"Put up with?" One of the listeners, Baron Edgard Robillard, asked as he raised a questioning eyebrow. "Whatever do you mean?"

"I mean," Carlotta replied. "The ghost. The Phantom of the Opera."

"But it won't be a problem much longer," Monsieur Peverell hastened to reassure her. "We shall take care of that soon enough."

"Ah, indeed we shall," Raoul said, and then he added, "But there is no ghost."

"You are a nonbeliever then?" the Baron's wife asked.

A small, tolerant smile touched Raoul's lips. "Of course I am. I don't believe in ghosts. I am a believer in the truth."

"The Viscount is right," Monsieur Peverell piped up again, insinuating himself in the conversation with all the air of authority that was due to him as an owner of the Opera House. "There are no such things as ghosts. Of course, convincing the performers of that fact is another matter entirely. They can be very superstitious." Realizing what he had just said, he looked sharply at Carlotta who was glaring down her nose at him.

"And ees a note signed by the Opera Ghost supersteetion?"

"Why, no, not at all," Monsieur Peverell quickly assured her, hoping she did not think that he had meant to insult her.

"He ees a very eensolent ghost," Carlotta said with a toss of her dark head. "He ees probably busy plotting what he weell say to me in hees next note."

As usual Carlotta was trying to manipulate the conversation so that it was centered on her.

"Notes, you say?" the Baron asked.

"Yes, notes," Carlotta affirmed.

"And just what does this Phantom have to say to you?" the Baron wanted to know.

Carlotta waved her hand airily. "He talks about my seenging, of course."

But Carlotta didn't go into detail and Christine knew why. The last note Carlotta had received had not been very complementary.

"Well, if there are notes . . . " the Baron's voice trailed off thoughtfully. "The Viscount must be right. It is no ghost. Surely a ghost would not be able to write notes."

"You would theenk not." Carlotta shrugged plump bare shoulders and said that ghost or man, the author of the notes was a nuisance and something needed to be done about him.

"Messieurs Telfour and Aleron gave een to hees demands," Carlotta went on half petulantly. "I suppose that ees why he theenks he can do whatever he weeshes."

"But you will find that things are different now," Monsieur Peverell was quick to assure her. And then he said to the Baron, "It seems that the previous owners were even more superstitious than their employees." He laughed and tried to make a joke of it. "We didn't know we had purchased a ghost along with the Opera House. It seems they took the idea of a ghost very seriously. Ha! They even reserved a private box for him. Is that not one of the most preposterous things you have ever heard? We were warned not to rent out the box or to change how things are done around here. But we are certainly not going to be frightened by the childish notion of a ghost roaming the halls of the Opera House, especially a ghost who needs his own private box." He lowered his voice and said confidentially, "Most likely the rumors about a ghost were started by the previous owners as a publicity stunt."

Carlotta arched a dark, skeptical eyebrow as she looked at the man. "Oh? And ees that why he was seen earlier tonight?"

There was a surprised murmur among the listeners.

"Where was he seen?"

"When?"

"What did he look like?"

"Who saw him?"

"Where and when? What does eet matter?" Carlotta questioned her wide-eyed audience. "The whole Opera House ees hees stage, eet would seem."

Monsieur Peverell obviously had not heard about the appearance of the ghost before this. "Someone has seen him tonight? The ghost?"

"Yes, of course the ghost. Gaspar told me. He said the ghost deessolved like meest right before hees eyes."

Carlotta looked down. Androcles had put his tiny black nose into her glass of champagne. After lapping up some of the bubbling liquid, the dog drew back, shook his head and sneezed. It was a very loud series of sneezes for such a small dog.

"You see? Even Androcles has been nervous tonight. Maybe he can sense the ghost's presence." Carlotta's eyes briefly swept the many balconies that surround them. "Who knows, maybe he ees watching us right now."

"This Phantom of the Opera may very well be watching us," Raoul spoke up.

"I thought you said you didn't believe in ghosts," the Baron said as he narrowed his eyes at the other man.

"I didn't say he was a ghost," Raoul told the man.

"Then what do you think he is?" the Baron asked.

"Something far more dangerous and sinister," Raoul replied. "Some low-life miscreant who hides out in the cellars of the Opera House. Surely, in a building that has seventeen stories, seven of which are below the stage level, there is the very real possibility of someone who knows his way around those cellars without anyone being aware of his presence. He could even be a criminal hiding from the law."

"That is hardly a comforting thought," someone said. "To think that some criminal is wandering around freely even as we speak."

"Perhaps that is the very reason people prefer to think it is a ghost," Raoul said as he lifted his glass of champagne and sampled it with the air of a connoisseur.

"I have heard people talk of this ghost," someone said. "And most describe the same thing. He's tall. He wears a black cape and a mask. No one has ever seen his face."

"And don't you think there may be a reason for that?" Raoul asked his listeners.

"I suppose someone could have secretly taken up residence here," the Baron said. "The Opera House is like a castle, complete with dungeons and torture chambers which were built during the time of the Commun. They say there are even hidden passageways in the walls. Not to mention that the place is built right over a lake."

"Isn't it possible that the ghost was a *victim* of the violence of the Commun?" the Baron's wife suggested. "It wasn't that long ago that the Commun occupied the building during their insurrection. With all the bloodshed and violence of that period, is it so hard to think that there might be a ghost or two trapped here?"

"Hmph," the Baron grunted. "With seven stories of darkness below us, I wouldn't be surprised at all to learn that there is still a body or two down there that no one knows about. They could be floating around at the bottom of the lake right now- "

"Edgard!" the Baroness sharply reproved her husband. "How you talk in the presence of ladies! But that is precisely my point. If there are- remains down there, would it be so hard to think that a restless spirit could be roaming the halls of the Opera House? It could very well be one of those poor souls massacred during the insurrection or someone who was tortured in one of those very dungeons my husband speaks about, someone who was left to die a horrible, agonizing death."

"Well, whoever, or *what*ever, is behind it all, we shall have the matter looked into right away," Monsieur Peverell told them all.

Carlotta all but rolled her eyes. "The last owners already deed that. They even tried renting out box five."

"Even if we decided to rent out box five, I'm not certain anyone would *want* to occupy it," Monsieur Peverell said, sounding a little uncertain for the first time. "Not after what happened the last time."

"And what exactly happened the last time?" the Baron wanted to know.

"Just what you would expect from a ghost," Carlotta answered him. "Cold weend, the curtains moving when no one was there. And eveel laughter coming from nowhere. Eet caused quite a deesturbance."

"Which is precisely why the practice of reserving the box for a ghost should be stopped," Raoul interjected. "So we can put the rumors to rest and show that there is nothing to be afraid of."

"But what of the violin music people say they hear in the dead of night?" someone asked.

"Violin music? What, no mournful wails or ghostly shrieks, no rattling of chains?" the Baron mocked.

"No, just the violin music."

"Our ghost is a musical one then?" the Baron asked with a laugh. Obviously he took the whole idea of a ghost as a joke.

"Our ghost is a fraud," Raoul answered him flatly.

"You think a criminal could play music so beautifully?" the Baroness asked.

"Yes, what of that?" another woman spoke up. "It sounds more romantic than frightening."

"Oh, posh," the Baron scoffed. "Listen how you women talk. How can a ghost be romantic? I am tall and I wore a cape here. Do you find me romantic as well?"

No one had a reply to that. The truth was that few women would find the gruff, portly Baron Robillard romantic in the least.

"Well, I for one would like to put an end to the rumors," Monsieur Peverell interjected. "It has gotten to the point where the girls working here are afraid to go anywhere by themselves."

Carlotta looked down at him. "The men are just as teemid."

"Yes, you're right, of course," he quickly agreed. "Some of the men can be timid, too."

"You are entitled to your opinion, of course, Viscount," the Baroness said to Raoul. "But as they say, seeing is believing."

"And you have seen something?" Raoul wanted to know.

"I have seen a great deal," the woman told him, but she hesitated a moment before she said, "But you said yourself you do not believe in ghosts."

"Do go on," Raoul encouraged the woman. "In spite of my skepticism, I always enjoy a good ghost story."

She ignored his scarcely-veiled skepticism and said, "I know something of the history of the Opera House and there have been too many sightings to discount entirely the idea of a ghost. *Tout au contraire.* I have talked personally to several of the theater performers and they swear that they have seen or heard things that could not be explained by the presence of some homeless person hiding in the cellars. What would you say if I told you that I myself have some experience with these kinds of things?"

Raoul arched one tawny brow. "Indeed?"

"Have you considered a séance?" the Baroness asked, shifting her attention to Monsieur Peverell.

"A séance? Whatever for?"

"To find out why a ghost would be trapped here," she answered him. "And then to free him."

"*Free* him? But are we even certain there *is* something here?" Monsieur Peverell hedged.

It may have been the champagne that made Christine say out loud, "I think I saw him once."

All eyes turned to her. Her statement also caused Raoul to look sharply down at her. She knew what he was thinking. He was wondering why this was the first he was hearing about this.

"I once saw someone in the rigging above me right before I went onto stage. He looked exactly as you have described him. He was dressed entirely in black, with a cape and a mask."

"Were you afraid?" the Baroness asked.

Carlotta scoffed out loud. "Oh? And why deedn't you say anytheeng before thees?" she wanted to know.

Raoul, too, was about to say something to her, but he apparently thought better of it.

"No, I wasn't afraid," Christine answered the Baroness. "Perhaps I was a little startled at first, but not afraid."

"Even more reason to believe that some poor, tortured soul is trapped here," the Baroness went on. "Would it hurt to hold a séance here to find out what we can?"

"I myself do not like unsolved puzzles," Raoul said thoughtfully.

"Which is precisely why a séance should be considered," the Baroness told him.

"Why? So that he can be drawn out of his secret lair in the cellars?" the Baron mocked.

The Baroness ignored his sarcasm. "I think perhaps it would be advantageous to hold a séance in the very box that is reserved for him."

Even Raoul looked intrigued by the idea, but behind his wife's back, the Baron was gesturing and waving his arms wildly while frantically mouthing the word "no".

While his eyes remained fixed on the Baron, Monsieur Peverell stammered, "Uh, er . . . We will have to give that some thought."

By the time the Baroness glanced over her shoulder at her husband, he was standing still, calmly picking a piece of nonexistent lint off his sleeve.

Raoul hid a smile and, after clearing his throat, said, "It's about time for you to get ready for your performance, isn't it, Carlotta?"

Pleased that the subject was back on her, Carlotta smiled broadly. "Why, yes, Veescount. Eet ees." She waved to one of the serving girls. "Mandarine."

The woman that Carlotta was waving to seemed confused. She looked around, first at the people around her and then at the ones standing directly behind her. Then she pointed to her chest. "Are you talking to me?"

"Of course I am talking to you," Carlotta said as if she was talking to a simpleton. "Come, take Androcles and put heem een my dressing room during my performance."

When they were informed that the musical programme was about to begin shortly, the guests began to migrate en masse toward the darkened auditorium. Christine sat down next to Raoul in the center of the front row seats. To her chagrin, Philippe took the seat to her left.

No one was occupying the private boxes tonight. To keep herself from thinking about Philippe sitting so close to her, Christine glanced up at box five. There was nothing there but darkness. So this is what it will be like, she thought to herself, to be sitting in the audience watching the performance rather than being a part of it. With a de Chagny on either side of her.

Raoul leaned over and whispered, "Why didn't you tell me you thought you saw the ghost?" He didn't wait for an answer, but, after giving her a prolonged, questioning look, he settled in his seat and stared expectedly at the stage. She knew very well that she wasn't going to get off so easily. They would surely talk about it later.

She was still wondering what she would say to Raoul about the man she had seen and about the conversation she had overheard earlier. As she tried to ignore Philippe, a flash of resentment shot through her. If Raoul had anything to say about her conduct, wasn't his brother's behavior even more questionable? After what she had heard tonight, she would never look at the man the same. And if Raoul thought that-

Philippe's long leg brushed her skirt and she drew the pink brocade closer, more sharply than she had intended. Philippe turned his face to look down at her curiously.

The rustling, murmuring sounds of the audience faded as everyone made themselves comfortable for Carlotta's performance. The stage was still empty as the conductor raised his arm. As his baton descended, the first strains of music filled the darkened theater.

Christine looked up at box five again. Was that thunder she had just heard?

She stiffened when Philippe suddenly leaned toward her. With his mouth close to her ear, she felt the warmth of his breath as he whispered, "Just how much of that conversation did you overhear?"

Magdeline Hugette was climbing one of the back staircases to the second story when she heard the low, ominous sound reverberating through the thick walls of the Opera House.

"Thunder?" she muttered as she paused to listen to the lingering rumble. How could there be thunder when it had just been snowing outside?

A little out of breath, she asked the woman who was climbing the staircase behind her. "Did you hear her? It's bad enough to have to deal with her colossal ego when we are rehearsing. But even tonight she thinks we were hired to personally wait on her hand and foot.

"*Mandarine*," she huffed. "She couldn't even get my name right even though I have been singing on stage with her for three years."

Magdeline paused at the bottom of the staircase which led to the third story. "Do you know that I could hate that woman quite thoroughly with hardly any effort at all?" she said as she stared upward, giving herself a moment to catch her breath. "I have been up and down these stairs running and fetching for her all day, and now she thinks I'm going to do it all night, too? If it wasn't for the extra money, I'd tell her- Well, I wouldn't hesitate one second to give her a piece of my mind."

She was supposed to be taking Androcles to Carlotta's dressing room, but the tiny dog had wiggled out of her arms and then run up the steps and disappeared in the dark. Carlotta's dressing room wasn't even on the third floor. So just what had possessed Androcles to go up there in the first place, Magdeline couldn't even begin to imagine.

"The little hellion is almost as much trouble as she is," she murmured breathlessly. After a fortifying sigh, she said, "Just a few more hours and we can both go home, Faustine. I'll tell you what would be good about now. A nice, hot cup of tea." Lifting her stiffly-starched apron in both hands, she muttered one last grievance, her voice fading as she started up the steps. "If she thinks I'm going to fetch that dog back again after she's done singing, she had better think again."

Suddenly she stopped and turned around. "What's wrong?"

It wasn't necessary for her to ask. One look at the younger woman's face and Magdeline knew, without asking, that she was too afraid to go up to the third floor in the dark.

"He's already been seen once tonight," Faustine whispered and looked around as if she was afraid she might be overheard by ghostly ears.

Too tired at the moment to even think about a ghost, or to argue with the other woman, Magdeline said, "If you're that afraid, Faustine, then stay down here. I'll go look for the little terrorist myself. Give me the candle and wait here. I won't be gone more than a minute or two."

But after she took the candle in her own hand, Magdeline herself hesitated and cast an apprehensive glance up the dark staircase. Surely Androcles would know if someone was up there and he would be barking, she reasoned. Even if it was a ghost. Dogs were supposed to be sensitive to such things.

Magdeline shook herself mentally. There was nothing up there, she assured herself. "I'm just tired," she muttered to herself. "The sooner we get this over with, the sooner we can go home."

Clutching her skirt in one hand and the candle in the other, Magdeline started up the wooden steps. They creaked and groaned beneath her weight as she asked herself, "Why would anyone bring a dog to a fancy soiree? I shall have dog hairs all over my clothes . . . "

When she reached the top of the stairs, Magdeline paused a moment to look over at the narrow window to her right to see what the weather was like. The last time she had looked, it had been snowing. Now the glass was streaked with rain. A vivid flash of lightning lit up the hallway where she was standing. A long, angry roll of thunder had the window panes rattling in their frames.

There was a cold draft blowing from somewhere, the window probably. The tiny flame on the candle sputtered and threw wildly-wavering shadows on the ceiling and the walls around her. There was a sudden, blinding flash of lightning beyond the window. Once again, it momentarily illuminated the long length of hallway and was followed by another long, lingering crash of thunder.

Magdeline wasn't looking forward to a walk home in the pouring rain, but she was looking forward to that hot cup of tea and getting off her aching feet. The third floor was a dark and isolated part of the Opera House. It was much colder up here and she couldn't suppress a shiver at the sudden change of temperature.

She had taken only one step down the darkened hallway when she froze. Try as she might, she could not make herself go any further. She moistened suddenly dry lips and swallowed heavily as a sense of uneasiness coiled in the pit of her stomach. She strained her eyes to try and pierce the blackness ahead of her but she couldn't see very far beyond the light of the candle.

She heard a sound. It was so slight that she wasn't sure she hadn't imagined it. It might have been Androcles. Then again, it might have been the rustle of her own clothing. Except she hadn't moved. A more likely explanation was that a draft was moving the curtains against the window frame or the wooden floor. But the next sound she heard was no curtain. It was a creak. A very definite creak. And it had come not from the curtains, but from the blackness of the hallway ahead of her.

Magdeline felt a stronger rush of cold air against her. The candle wavered and guttered and then went out completely.

If not for the brief, intermittent flashes of lightning, Magdeline wouldn't be able to see anything at all. As she tried to pierce the blackness before her, she felt an ice-cold, prickling sensation run down the length her spine. She swallowed hard and tried to tell herself that nobody was there and that it was foolish of her to imagine that there was.

Suddenly Androcles came running out of the darkness. Burning her hand on the hot candle wax, Magdeline actually cried out and jumped to the side as the little dog ran right past her. She had no chance of catching him as he disappeared down the steps with a rapid clicking of his toenails. Magdeline could hear Faustine's audible gasp at the bottom of the stairs.

It had only been Androcles. Magdeline pressed a wax-burned hand to her chest in relief and waited for her heart to slow its pounding. Now that Androcles was back downstairs, there was no reason to stay up here. She was about to go back downstairs when she froze at another sound. It was the creak of hinges and a door closing very softly.

There was a sizzling, vivid flash of lightning and another crash of thunder. Some sixth sense was already warning Magdeline that she wasn't alone. And then she found herself staring at a dark shape that had materialized in the darkness at the end of the hallway.

After a single loud, startled gasp, she called out, "Wh- Who's there?"

The lightning flickered again. Enough for her to see that the man, if it was a man, was wearing a long black cape with a hood pulled so far forward that his face was lost in its shadow. If indeed there was even a face there.

The shrouded figure did not move, nor was her question answered. The man, or whatever he was, just stood there looking huge. Menacing. Sinister.

Another flash of lightning threw the entire length of the hallway into to stark white for the space of one of Magdeline's erratic heartbeats. It was enough light for her to see that the face under the cowl was hidden behind a mask!

She knew then, without a doubt, that it must be the Phantom of the Opera standing before her.

Pale as a ghost herself, she began to back up, never taking her eyes off the terrifying vision before her. When one of his arms reached out towards her, her terror grew into a full blown panic. Without warning, the apparition rushed toward her like a bat out of the darkness.

But terror had already lent wings to Magdeline's feet. She turned blindly and all but fell down the stairs in her hurry to get away. She could almost feel the ghost's cold breath on the back of her neck. She could almost feel his hand dragging her back.

As soon as she reached Faustine, both women heard a sound that made their blood run cold. It was laughter, evil laughter that echoed through the darkness like a death knell. But by that time, both women were shrieking down the last flight of stairs, Magdeline leading the way with a squealing Faustine not far behind.

Carlotta had scarcely opened her mouth when she was interrupted. In fact she had only gotten two words out when an ear-piercing scream brought an abrupt end to her performance. The conductor's hand froze midair. The music stopped as musicians and audience alike turned to see what the commotion was all about.

In the darkened theater Carlotta's voice was replaced with terrified screams of, "The Phantom!" "The Phantom!"

The crowd reacted immediately. With a collective, startled gasp they swiveled around in their seats and craned their necks to see two breathless young women running down the center aisle as if the hounds of hell were fast on their heels. Both of the women were waving their arms and frantically gesturing behind them as their babbling cries of terror continued to echo in the darkness.

"What- " Christine began as Raoul stood up from his seat beside her. But her voice was drowned out by the alarmed murmur of the crowd who had surged forward to surround the near-hysterical women.

Up on the third floor, Madame Giry and the man beside her looked at each other with open surprise. Then they looked back out over the balcony and watched to see what was causing all the excitement down below.

"It was *him*! The dead come back to life!"

The masked man on the balcony continued to watch the two terrified young women with interest, thinking that their screams alone were enough to wake the dead. To add to the confusion, Androcles had followed the women down the aisle. His high-pitched, furious barking only added to the mayhem as the circle of agitated people pressed closer.

"Up on the . . . the third floor," one of the women gasped, almost sobbing as she flung her arm out dramatically and pointed in the direction she had come from. "I saw him with my own eyes," she told her horrified audience breathlessly. "It was the devil. It was the devil in human form."

By then, the bolder, more gallant men in the audience were assuring the two women that they would keep them safe, the bravest of them vowing to confront the threat with threats of their own.

"It was like staring into the face of death!" one of the women almost sobbed.

"He was dressed all in black, with a cape and a mask . . . just like you would expect. He just stood there with his demon eyes blazing like fire, staring at me like he had just risen from the pits of he- !" She remembered where she was and cut off the profanity just in time. But she brought her hands up to cover her quivering lips as she relived it all. "He reached for me. And then he- he flew at me like a bat with huge, terrible wings. He was after my soul," she moaned. "I know he was. And he was going to drag me back into the pit with him."

The man beside Madame Giry looked down at her and arched one dark brow. Turning his palms upward, he shrugged his broad shoulders. Neither one of them had an explanation for what had just happened. But they both knew that by tomorrow everyone would be talking about how the Phantom of the Opera had been seen during the soiree. Not once, but twice. The stories would get embellished until no one would dare go up to the third floor by themselves anymore. At least not in the dark. There was always an uproar when someone saw the ghost. Or thought they saw the ghost. This time would prove to be no different.

Chapter 4

Drawing aside the curtain at one of the tall, arched windows, Christine stared down at the Rue Scribe four stories below. It had rained off and on all night. It was well into the morning and the sky was still a dark, leaden grey with darker wisps of clouds floating by beneath the gloomy mantle. Rain was still spattering intermittently on the cobblestones far below while a light fog suffused the air, softening the sharp outline of the buildings of Paris in the distance. It was not the kind of weather that would make for a pleasant carriage ride and she sincerely hoped that Raoul would not insist on braving the elements and try to take her on one anyway.

She lifted her hand and laid her palm flat against the glass to test for the coldness there. Although the room was comfortably warm behind her, the streaming glass was as cold as she had expected it to be. Her slender fingers curved on the glass as she told herself that she hoped it would keep raining all day. Not only did she not want to have to answer the questions that Raoul would surely have for her. She would hardly be fit company today, for her mood seemed to match the churning chaos of the dark clouds drifting beyond the window.

Of course there was another reason why she hoped Raoul would stay away today. He didn't know about her singing lessons. She had wanted to be honest with him from the beginning, but meeting with a man in private without a chaperone definitely was not something that Raoul would consider to be appropriate conduct for his future wife. Her eyes flashed with a sudden dark fire as she recalled the conversation she had overheard last night. It was hardly fair that she should be the one that had to feel compelled to hide her behavior. She had done nothing wrong. What about Philippe and *his* behavior? And how was she supposed to live in the same house with the man and always wonder where his sordid imagination was taking him?

She let the curtain fall back into place, setting her jaw for a moment in an effort to compose her thoughts before she turned back to the room. As a deep rumble of thunder lingered like the protest of a caged beast, she straightened her shoulders and said in a half-hopeful voice, "I don't think there will be a letup in the rain today. The sky shows no signs of clearing."

"A most dreary day," a male voice agreed with her. The voice was deep and richly masculine with just a hint of an accent.

"We should expect a lot of rain this time of year," she said absently even though the weather was the last thing on her mind.

The man behind the curtain narrowed his gaze as he continued to watch Christine's distracted frown. She had seemed preoccupied all morning. Something was obviously weighing on her mind although she had tried hard these past hours to keep him from knowing it. She was far away from him this morning. Her distance reminded him that she would soon be even farther away and there would be no calling her back.

"You did well today."

"Did I?" she asked as she glanced over at the curtain.

"Yes, your voice grows stronger with each lesson."

"I have been aware of that myself," she said. "But I wasn't certain how this morning's lesson would go since I was up half the night."

"Ah, the soiree."

She continued to stare at the curtain with a new intensity in the depths of her eyes, as if she could will herself to see through it. "Where you there, perhaps?" she asked.

He smiled faintly at her efforts. She never stopped trying to probe the mystery of his identity.

"I hardly move in the same circles," he replied.

"Of course I know you only by your voice," she said. "But it seems to me that you would mingle quite easily with the nobility."

"I'm not sure if that is a complement or not, but I am afraid I would stand out in such a crowd," he said with a hint of irony in his voice.

He watched as Christine sighed deeply and crossed her arms at her waist as she stepped closer to the fire. Little did she know that there were moments when he had pretended that it had been him at her side last night, and not the Viscount.

"You are restless today," she heard.

"You read me so well," she murmured absently as she stared down into the flames.

Because of the light pouring through the windows and the glow from the fire, he could see her very well through the curtain although she could not see him. She was wearing a very becoming dress of soft lavender with insets of lace on the bodice and the sleeves. The firelight was blazing her hair into amber fire.

You have a faraway look in your eyes, Christine, was the man's thought. He watched as she tucked a rebellious strand of hair behind her ear.

"Something is preying on your mind this morning?" he ventured.

She answered with a slight nod, but she stayed silent. Even if she were to speak to him about all that was troubling her, where would she begin? She was very much aware of the passing moments. It felt as if sand was slipping helplessly through her fingers. Her gaze swept the room. She would remember this place always, she told herself. Every lesson and every conversation they had ever shared. She could not help but sense that things were already changing between them. He was quieter than usual this morning. His subtle humor had not been in evidence. She stared at the curtain with a fair amount of frustration. He had come into her life a complete mystery, like a closed door that had no key. He would leave it the same way.

She lightly touched the pages of the music he had brought her that morning. They lay on a small table before her, the pages etched with his bold, familiar scrawl. They had worked on a new song, one that he had written himself and she knew that the sad, haunting melody would stay with her long after their lessons had ended. It was his music. It was a part of him.

"It's a beautiful song," she said softly.

"One very suited to you. As I thought it would be."

She lifted her chin and tried mentally to shake off her dark mood. "It's very satisfying to be able to touch people with something as simple as my voice."

"Yes. Never has a voice touched *me* so deeply. Even I scarce imagined your talent in the beginning."

"If my voice is at all pleasing, it is only because you taught me. But I fear that I have wasted your time today?" It was a question.

"If you weren't up to singing, you could have cancelled the lesson this morning."

"No," she replied. "I had no wish to cancel. I wanted to come."

The truth was that the lessons had become something she eagerly looked forward to. At first it had been strange being spoken to by an unseen teacher, one that could see her while she could not see him. But over the past months she had found herself growing quite fond of him although she never did see his face. The rehearsal room was sparsely furnished but he never failed to have a cheerful fire in the grate and the door was always locked against unexpected intrusions so that the room always felt safe and comfortable. These past few months, she realized, it had become nothing less than a haven from the outside world for her.

They did not always stick to a strict music schedule. They would spend part of their time conversing about a wide variety of subjects. He was well read and proved to be an interesting and intelligent conversationalist. More than that, he had a very clever wit and a keen sense of humor. He had told her stories of his life in Persia and other parts of the world so that she almost felt like she, too, had visited those places.

He also had an uncanny ability to read her moods and her emotions, no matter how she tried to hide them from him. Over time, she had learned to feel comfortable confiding in him about her deepest feelings. She had, in fact, told him many things she had never told anyone else, even Lisette.

But could she tell him what she was thinking right now? It seemed that anything she was liable to say would come out all wrong. And would it be proper for her to discuss her innermost thoughts, her misgivings about her upcoming wedding to another man? She certainly couldn't talk about the things that Philippe had said.

"I'm only frustrated," she admitted with another long sigh. "Our time is running out."

"You are troubled at the thought of giving up your lessons?"

"Yes," she confessed. "That's a part of it."

The words she might have said, the ones that wanted to spill out, trembled upon her lips, but before she could voice those deeper thoughts, she bit her lip, hesitating. Finally, she found something safe to say. "Lately, when I sing, I feel that it comes from here." She lifted her hand and placed it over her heart.

"Music can have that effect on you. It can touch you deeply."

"Ah, like a lover?" she asked softly, though she wasn't sure if it was proper for her to put it quite like that.

There was a long pause before she heard, "Yes, perhaps."

The man behind the curtain drew a slow, deep breath. It was this pensive, wistful Christine that he knew he needed to guard his own heart against.

After a silence, he said, "I have been aware of the difference in you lately."

She was staring down at her clasped hands. "I think I am starting to understand now what you were trying to say to me from the very beginning when you told me I had to learn to let go of my insecurities and connect with my emotions. But you understand that, too," she said as she lifted her face to look at the curtain. "When you play for me, I *feel* the emotion in your music. You must be in touch with your own inner- passion to be able to write such beautiful songs."

She stared at the curtain with the intensity of a warrior contemplating the best strategy on how to get past the walls of a fortress under siege. "The truth is that when you first sent for me, I wasn't at all sure what to expect. I was afraid that you might expect something from me that I wasn't able to give."

"If you were afraid, you hid it well."

She laughed huskily under her breath. "Are you telling me you didn't know how frightened I was when I first sang for you? I pictured- Well, I didn't know what to expect. You were a stranger to me, and the circumstances were so unusual. I confess, my imagination was conjuring all kinds of things."

"I wasn't completely unaware of your- trepidation," he said. "Knowing your- shall we say, your very active imagination, you were probably envisioning some slavering beast waiting to leap out at you from behind the curtain. Much like the wolf in Red Riding Hood."

She laughed again. "I wouldn't go that far, but I admit I was a bit apprehensive." She eyed the curtain thoughtfully before confessing, "Did you know that the first time I heard you play the violin, I couldn't even speak? Your music was so sublime, so soul-stirring that it took me someplace I didn't even know existed. Your music is something you should share with the world."

"I have shared it with you."

"I'm not the world."

She was wrong. She was his world.

"It is satisfying enough to hear my music expressed through the emotion in your voice."

"Is that why you teach me?" she asked. "So that I can be a voice for you?"

"It's one of the reasons. Another reason is your ability. I didn't want to see it wasted."

She felt, at that moment, a deeper connection with him, and at the same time, a deeper sense of loss. Something rare was about to go out of her life forever and if she was to be honest with herself, she wasn't sure how she would bear it.

"You missed a great deal of excitement last night," she said, changing the subject, doing her best to hang on to an illusion of normalcy.

"Hearing Carlotta sing? I don't think I missed much."

"I'm not talking about Carlotta's performance. She barely got two words out when she was interrupted. By an appearance of the Phantom of the Opera, no less."

"The Phantom appeared on stage?"

"No, two women saw him on the third floor. It was the second time the ghost was seen last night."

"He sounds like a very busy ghost. But Carlotta being silenced would have been worth seeing. So what were *you* thinking while all this excitement was going on?"

"I found myself wishing that I had been the one to see the ghost."

"Indeed. Why would you want to see such a terrifying thing?"

"Maybe because the ghost does not seem very terrifying to me. I did see a man once, up above me before I went on stage, and he looked exactly the way the Phantom has been described."

"And you think that may have been the ghost?"

"I thought so then, but now I'm not so sure. It could have been anyone."

"Did it make you afraid to come up here by yourself?"

"No. In the daylight I'm not afraid, but if it was dark and I was alone," she admitted. "I might be a little frightened."

"A fear that would be completely understandable."

"The truth is," she went on. "I have always wanted to hear the ghostly music that other people say they have heard. A ghost that plays so beautifully does not sound very frightening to me. Only very sad. I have lived here at the Opera House for several years now and I have heard my share of mysterious creaks, and doors opening or closing when no one is there. And once or twice I have felt a cold wind blowing against me from out of nowhere. But I have never heard any music."

"Remi Botair heard violin music from box five when no one was there. Remi said it was the most beautiful music he had ever heard and that no human hands could have produced such music. Remi said the ghost must have been a man of soaring genius and incredible sorrow to play like that."

"Suppose you did hear such ghostly music. Would that make you too afraid to stay here?"

"I think I could only answer that if I actually heard him play. Then I should make up my mind on the way he made me feel. Here." She placed her hand on her heart again.

Little did Christine realize that the very man they called the Phantom of the Opera, the *ghost* who was responsible for both the frightening appearances and the music, was listening to her from the other side of the curtain. He was sprawled comfortably in a chair, one long, booted leg stretched out leisurely before him as he relaxed, content to watch her and to listen to her even if it was from behind a curtain.

Hers was the image that haunted *him* night and day. And now as he looked at the beautiful, wistful eyes, so full of innocence and womanly mystery, and the delicate, tempting curve of her lips, his heart, as it often did in her presence, ached with need and with love.

Her hair this morning was caught up in a slightly disheveled mass of unruly curls that seemed to be perilously on the verge of tumbling loose. A few stray tendrils that refused to be confined were drifting softly about her face and down her back. In the firelight, each shimmering, silky strand was touched with a copper fire and he would have liked nothing better than to go to her, pull the combs and pins loose and run his hand over the freed silken tresses.

The pale lavender gown she was wearing only enhanced her beauty, emphasizing the narrowness of her waist and the tantalizing curve of her hips that tempted and enticed him as she moved about the room.

With a will of iron, he clamped down upon his wayward thoughts and held his silence as he reminded himself that she could never be his. Not even remotely. Yet, as he sat looking at her, he marveled at how comfortable they had become with each other. Who would have believed that they could have gotten so close in such a short period of time? Even more amazing, who would have thought that he could have reached the point where he could share his own thoughts so freely?

Of course, he realized that the curtain was responsible for that. Not only did it keep her from seeing what he really looked like, it kept up an illusion on her part. Perhaps the worst part of his struggle lately was that he knew she had spun an almost romantic vision of him in her mind. She had built a fantasy surrounding his mysterious identity. Perhaps it was vanity on his part, but he did not want to destroy that image. There were times, he knew full well, when she was almost consumed by curiosity to see him face to face, but better for her to always wonder what he looked like, rather than destroy that fragile image with the brutal truth. She was about to take a different path in life and he would soon become nothing more than a fading memory to her. But perhaps when she was older, she might look back in some nostalgic moment and think of him with the fantasy still intact. Yes, better that she should always wonder. That was all he could hope for. That was *his* fantasy.

What they had shared these past few months would come to an end, as he had always known it must. What would be the point in destroying the girlish illusion she had built in her mind? He certainly was not inclined to see it destroyed, because it was all he would ever have.

"Aside from ghostly interruptions, you enjoyed yourself last night?" he asked.

She was staring at the rain-streaked windows again and she didn't give him a direct answer. Instead she shrugged noncommittally and said, "Here I have been wasting your time by talking about phantoms and ghostly music. Is it?" she asked, suddenly turning and staring hard at the curtain. "A waste of your time to go on meeting me here when these lessons will be ending soon?"

"I will meet you here as long as you wish me to."

"If my wishes mattered, then- "

"Then what, Christine?"

"Then the lessons would never end and we would finish what we have started. I can't thank you enough for offering them in the first place. I can't even begin to tell you how much these lessons have meant to me. I think part of it is because deep down I have shared something in common with you that I could not have shared with anyone else."

After a silence, he said, "Yes, I suppose there is a bond between us, one brought about by our mutual love of music. And since we have spent so many hours together here- " He did not finish. He did not know how to finish that thought.

"I will always be grateful," she said softly, almost impatiently. "But for some reason, I am at odds today. With- with everything."

"How so?"

"Something pulls me far from myself. I feel old things today. I feel unsettled inside."

He waited for her to go on, sensing that she needed to talk.

"In so many ways, these lessons have become my anchor of sanity amidst the madness of the outside world. Only when I am here, in this safe and secret place, can I let go and be who I truly am inside. You don't know that there were times during these past months when I felt that I had lost my way. But when I was here with you, I felt that I could stay lost if I chose. How strange that sounds when I say it out loud." She sighed deeply, frustrated at her woefully inadequate attempts to try and express it all. "You are patient. Infinitely so. You never gave up on me. You had faith in me even when I didn't have faith in myself." Her gaze became more intent as she stared at the curtain. "Somewhere along the line, music has become a necessary thing for my soul. I fear the days ahead will be empty. I fear that if I cannot solace myself with music, I shall feel lost again. Deep inside. As I felt when I first came here to the Opera House. I don't know how I will give it all up. And if Raoul really saw who I was inside, he would- " She stopped and closed her eyes for a long moment. "But he does not seem to understand what music has come to mean to me." There was a haunted look in her eyes when she opened them again. "When I am with you, I feel like I can be myself. But out there . . . "

At the mention of the Viscount, the man behind the curtain struggled with his own dark, unsettled feelings. The truth was that seeing her at Raoul de Chagny's side last night had been difficult for him. It brought home the fact that she would be marrying soon and he wondered how he could even begin to let her go. He, too, could not help but think about how empty the coming days would be without her. She did not know that her confession was only making things so much worse for him for it seemed that she, too, was regretful that the lessons would be ending.

"Sometimes I think I will never fit into his world," she went on. "We are so very different. I had a very humble background compared to the life he has led since birth."

Her gaze narrowed as she stared hard at the sky beyond the windows. "Last night I found myself thinking that if I had to put on a smile for one more pretentious, conceited, aristocratic buffoon, I would scream. And the truth of it is that I don't worry so much that I *won't* fit in, but that I *should* fit in. What would you think if you saw me somewhere a year from now, sitting in the de Chagny's private box watching someone else sing, with my viscountess nose in the air looking down on all the lesser mortals beneath me?"

She laughed humorlessly. "I suppose you are surprised to learn that there are so many doubts and misgivings inside me?"

She didn't wait for an answer. "It is a little overwhelming for me to think that my life will be an endless stream of soirees and formal dinners and carriage rides for show. Not because those are things I *want* to do, but because they are something I *must* do. That I will be expected to fill every moment of my existence with fashion and socializing and needlework and pleasing a husband rather than doing the things that I enjoy doing, that I will be perpetually surrounded by a group of emotional vampires that only masquerade as a loving family. I can't help but wonder if, in time, I will become just like them. The very thought distresses me.

"And if Raoul has trouble tolerating me now," she went on. "I can't imagine what it would be like to live with each other on a daily basis. Especially since I won't have you to talk to about it all. Who will I have in my life to unburden myself to? Who will I confess all my deepest, darkest secrets to?"

"What secrets could you have that you have not already confessed to me?" he asked a little huskily.

"I have my share of faults," she assured him. "Pride and vanity are among them. I also lie by omission. And I am cowardly as well. I have not told Raoul about these lessons for one reason only. Because I know he would disapprove and try to put a stop to them immediately. And did you know that I would secretly like to have a more important role before I leave the Opera House? Yes, that is, perhaps, my darkest secret. I actually envy Carlotta her freedom to have a singing career."

"So you're not only vain, prideful and cowardly. You are envious as well."

She ignored his teasing. "You may add vengeance to that list. After I heard that Carlotta had told the new owners of the Opera House that I would never be good enough to sing on stage with her, and that they were seriously questioning whether I should be let go, I felt very vengeful."

She tilted her head slightly to one side as if she was again contemplating her best strategy for a direct military assault. "Now that I have told you some of my deepest, darkest secrets, isn't it only fair that you tell me some of yours?"

She was feeling very reckless today, he thought. He had never seen her quite so bold.

"I fear there are too many to name," he answered her.

"Evasion then would be one of your faults?" she asked coyly.

She turned away from the curtain, certain he would tell her nothing. But with her back to him she heard, "I can covet, sometimes, what I desire but cannot have."

She turned back around.

"In what way?" she asked as she stared fixedly at the curtain.

"I cannot see you through to the end of your lessons, and that was something I desired very much."

There was a long pause before she said, "That isn't your fault."

"But it does not stop the coveting."

His voice was so soft and he sounded so sober suddenly as he admitted that truth to her, that she wasn't sure what to say. Only the sound of the crackling fire filled the prolonged silence.

"You have probably been wondering what you will do with all your talent," she began very quietly. "Maybe you will find a replacement for me?"

"A replacement?"

"Someone else to teach. You may stumble upon someone as you stumbled upon me."

"That won't happen." There was a new huskiness in his voice that had not been there before and it caused a strange breathless sensation in her own chest.

"When our lessons have ended, I will no longer be teaching," he informed her.

"But you will continue to write songs, won't you?"

"I suppose I will continue to do that."

"Will you perhaps leave France again? Go back to Persia?"

"I have no plans to do so."

She almost sighed out loud with relief and realized only at that moment how distressed she had been at that thought. As it was, if she needed to contact him, she could do so by way of Madame Giry or the Persian, although there had never been an occasion to do so. But if he should leave the country entirely, there was not even the remotest possibility of any future contact. But then she remembered that she would be living in the de Chagny mansion and she would be effectively cut off from communicating with him in any case.

She sighed again, regretfully. "I shall always remember you as a voice behind a curtain. Perhaps during our last lesson you should reveal yourself dramatically and then I would have something more substantial to remember."

He had to smile at her unrelenting efforts to learn his identity. "And if you were disappointed?"

"I don't think that would be the case."

"Ah, the optimism of youth. Since you have already envisioned what you believe to be the truth, I would hate to have reality destroy that vision. There is always that possibility."

"You move through my life like the Phantom moves through the Opera House, you know," she said seriously. "There, but always in the shadows. Do you think it's fair that I have not seen even a glimpse of you while you have been able to look at me all you like?"

"Perhaps it isn't fair, but life often plays itself out unfairly."

"Ah, you are harsh to me today," she said half petulantly.

"I don't mean to be."

"There is always a chance that someday we will see each other quite accidentally in passing," she went on thoughtfully. "You will know me, of course, but I won't have any idea that it's you. Unless you speak. Then I should know it was you by your voice. So remember that if you wish to remain anonymous. On the other hand, if you remain silent so that you do not give yourself away, I shall also know it's you, because your very silence would give you away."

He laughed outright at that. It was a deep, masculine sound. "So any man that does not speak to you will have you guessing? In that case, you may spend a great deal of your life wondering about strange men."

"I suppose that will be my fate," she sighed as dramatically as any actress on the stage. "Or maybe I will look into your eyes one day and know immediately that it is you, without either one of us having to say a word."

"Christine. Have I told you that your imagination is astounding? And that it is surpassed only by your boundless curiosity?"

"Yes, you have told me that. More than once," she said as she reached up again to try and coax a few rebellious curls into place. "I woke up late this morning. Since I was in such a hurry to get here, I fear I made a complete mess of my hair."

Using her fingers, she did what she could to try and tame the unruly mass of curls, but they refused to be confined. She fussed with the combs and the pins a while longer, but only succeeded in making things worse.

"Why don't you just let it down and be done with it?" she heard.

"Because I can't go back down through the Opera House in such a state of dishabille. People will wonder what I was doing up here. And if word were to get back to Raoul- "

They both knew what would happen. If word were to get back to the Viscount, he would start asking too many questions. And he would probably not stop until he had answers.

But she did let her hair down. The suddenly-freed curls tumbled over her shoulders and cascaded down her back like a shimmering, copper-hued veil. She tried to gather it up again, attempting, without success, to arrange it into a loose knot on top of her head.

"I'll braid it for you if you like."

Christine's hands froze. "How will you do that? Are you going to let me see you?"

"No, but you can sit in a chair with your back to me."

She lowered her hands and her hair fell loose around her.

"You mean with no curtain between us?"

"If I tell you not to look, I'm certain that you will honor my request, Christine. Turn around and I'll pull up a chair."

She did as he directed, turning her back to the curtain as a chair scraped across the wooden floor. With his voice as a guide, she backed up until she was sitting in the chair.

After a silence, he gave a soft, throaty laugh. "So here we are with no curtain between us and you have unfurled your colors before me."

His voice was so close that Christine experienced a heady excitement at the thought that there was finally no curtain between them.

"And again you can see me, but I can't see you," she reminded him. "You truly *are* a man determined to keep his deepest, darkest secrets hidden."

He smiled. "Isn't there a darker side to all of us?" he asked roguishly.

His hands lifted, then hesitated. Before he even touched her, he wondered what had possessed him to start this in the first place. He looked at the unbound glory of her hair and knew this was not going to be easy for him. At the first stroke of his hand he hesitated again.

"Should I sit up straighter?" she asked. "Am I high enough? Low enough?"

"You're perfect."

"You're about my height then?"

"No."

One corner of his mouth drew back when he realized it was another one of her efforts to discern how tall he was.

"You are shorter than me?" she asked.

"Taller."

"Much taller?"

There was no harm in her knowing one small detail so he said, "If we were both standing and facing each other, the top of your head would come about to my chin."

So much for Lisette's theory, Christine thought.

He could feel her thinking that over while he remained torn between his unexpected reaction to her and his vow to keep her at an emotional *and* physical distance, knowing he had already crossed lines he should never have crossed. She was beyond him for so many reasons. He must remember that. He decided it was best to get this over with as quickly as possible.

When Christine felt the first brush of his hands on her hair, she could have melted at the pure sensation that the light touch evoked. The gentleness of his fingers started a tingling sensation throughout her entire body, from her toes all the way to the ends of her hair, every single strand of it. In one way it was incredibly, intoxicatingly relaxing. In another way it started waves of awareness pulsing through every nerve and fiber of her being.

She closed her eyes as his hands continued to work with her tumbled tresses, lifting, untangling, separating. Should she be doing this? she wondered. But if she stopped him now, wouldn't that only make things suddenly very awkward between them?

"You make me think of when I was a child and I would have my hair braided," she sighed. "How far away those days seem now."

"You miss them?"

"Very much. I can't imagine a better place to live than the cottage where I grew up."

"A home should be one of our fondest memories," he murmured behind her as he worked with her hair.

"It always will be for me. I wish I could take you there. If it was possible, would you go with me?"

"If it was possible, yes."

"Just one day," she whispered as if she were envisioning such a trip. "I would show you everything. The flowers and the woods across the road and then we would walk on the beach."

"If I could make that happen for you, I would."

"When I was a child," she went on. "Everything seemed simpler, yet happier. The house we lived in was the type of house that the de Chagnys would look down on. It was not very big or very grand, but it was comfortable and, most importantly, it was filled with love. Across the road there was a forest. It was a magical place and I spent a great deal of my childhood exploring it. In front of the cottage, there was a white picket fence with rows of flowers of every color growing along it. There were roses everywhere. My mother had planted them and my father- Well, I think he wanted to keep them growing because they reminded him of her after she was gone.

"I think of those flowers sometimes. I think about them blooming and then dying and blooming again, year after year. And I wonder if there is someone living at the cottage now who is tending them and enjoying them as much as I used to. I can picture it all very clearly in my mind, but I still wish that I could see it all once more before me. Sometimes the music and the fantasy of the Opera House takes me back there."

"Yes, here illusions can become very real," he said behind her.

"Once I marry Raoul, I fear I will never see my old home again."

"And that makes you sad?"

"Terribly," she admitted. "Someday I will look back on *this* as a memory, as well."

After a long silence, she said, "I didn't tell you that had my own horse when I was a child."

"Did you."

"Yes, he was my best friend for many years. When he wasn't pitching me into mud puddles, that is."

She heard the smile in his voice when he said, "I've had my share of tumbles from horses."

"Into mud puddles?" she asked.

"Yes, mud puddles, and sand *and* tents."

"Tents?"

He had already told her that he had studied horsemanship and the military arts in Persia.

"Was that when you were training to become a fierce desert warrior?" she asked.

"Nothing so romantic as that. I was being instructed in the bow on horseback. It was a particularly grueling lesson. The horse was in a full gallop when he stopped short, as he was supposed to do. Unfortunately I was not aware of how well trained he was or for how quickly he would respond to the commands of my body. He stopped so abruptly that he pitched me headlong into a tent, much to the surprise of the people having a meal inside."

She thought about the bold life he must have led, envisioned him on horseback again as she had done many times before. She thought, too, about obeying the commands of his body, and another strange, breathless sensation went coursing through her.

"Hold still," he said under his breath.

She went very still, especially when she felt his fingers accidentally brush her back, so lightly that it was barely a touch at all.

She became aware of a faint male scent, a strangely intoxicating essence that surrounded her and drew her into another level of awareness of him. His nearness affected her deeply, so deeply that her voice caught in her suddenly dry throat before she swallowed heavily and asked, "If- If I fell into a mud puddle, would you pull me out?"

"Of course I would pull you out."

"Even if I was covered from head to toe with mud?"

"Yes, mud and all."

"I dreamed of him last night," she went on in a very soft voice.

"Who?"

"The Phantom."

"Ah, we are back to the subject of the ghost again," he murmured. "It was a nightmare, I presume?"

"No, no nightmare," she answered him.

"How can you dream of a ghost and it not be a nightmare?"

"It was actually a strangely beguiling dream. He was standing in the darkness and I had turned when I realized he was there. I felt his presence. But he stayed in the shadows so I never did see his face. Much like you."

"Maybe if you had seen his face, you would have been afraid of him."

She shook her head. "No. I don't think so. The idea of a lonely soul trapped in some place of darkness, wandering and searching for something for an eternity seems terribly sad. In my dream, at least, I was aware of his deep sadness. I was aware of *him*. He only wanted to be a man."

"So you pitied him?"

"No, not pity exactly. I wanted to know what had kept him from resting in peace."

"This supposed ghost must be in your thoughts a great deal lately if you are even dreaming about him."

"Yes, I suppose so," she said very quietly.

She was so close that he felt a sudden, overwhelming urge to take her into his arms. He could feel the very warmth of her body seep right through her clothes. Her fragrance, like the sweetest of wild flowers, beckoned him and he had to clench his hands into tight fists for a moment so he would not give in to the irrational urge to touch her.

"A dream can sometimes seem stronger than reality," he said, frowning as he tried to distract himself from what she was saying.

"Do you think that someone could fall in love in a dream?"

"I never thought about it. How would one fall in love with something that isn't real?"

"Don't you think a woman could fall in love with a ghost if his story was compelling enough?"

"I imagine loving a ghost would be difficult," he said with a trace of grim mockery in his voice.

"You're right. I'm sure that loving a ghost would be no easy thing."

After a pause, she heard, "I suppose if there really was a ghost in the Opera House and he was to hear your voice, he might be drawn to you. Like a siren."

"I had not thought of that," she said. "Do you think he hears me sing?"

"That's supposing he does exist."

"So many people have seen him. Or heard him. What if *you* were to run into the Phantom of the Opera down a darkened hallway some day?"

"I'm sure I would find that a most astonishing encounter."

He stretched one leg out to the side. Without turning her head, Christine glanced toward the leg and saw that it was long and muscular under the black material of his pants. Black boots came to his knees. The boots looked like they were made of the finest leather.

"Some people have talked of having a séance here," she informed him, still looking at that tantalizing view of his leg, absolutely fascinated at her first vision of him, even if it was only a partial vision. "But some people are afraid of what may be stirred up in the darkness. Maybe *we* should have a lesson in the darkness," she said as that thought suddenly occurred to her. "You wouldn't have to stay behind a curtain then. You could stand before me just like any other man and we would just hear each other's voices. I have heard that the senses are most acute in darkness. If there were no distractions of light, I wonder," she mused thoughtfully. "What it would be like to sing in complete darkness."

So innocent, he thought. She had no idea the images her words conjured up in his mind. Her hair was like strands of silk in his hands and he took his time braiding it, wanting to prolong and savor the moment now, knowing he would never have another.

Christine began to understand how a contented cat must feel, because if she was a cat, she felt she would be purring right now. His very nearness roused a strange, languid pleasure from deep inside her, a sensual awareness. He leaned a little forward and she felt the very warmth of his body. She continued to be enthralled by that black-clad, booted leg.

He could not help wondering, if his arms went around Christine, how she would react. Would she melt naturally back against him? Or would she run screaming from the room? If he leaned just a little closer . . .

Christine was a very proper young woman. But there was a sensuousness about her that ran deep. He had always been aware of it just below the surface. He was a man with a man's desires and he could not help but react physically to her.

"Do you think I might have gone very far?" he heard her ask.

"Far?"

"With my singing?"

When he spoke, his voice became even more throaty. "Very far. You have a rare talent, Christine.

"It's done."

The abruptness change in his tone startled her. In a moment the leg and the boot had disappeared.

"In spite of never having been a ladies maid, I think I did a rather decent job."

She groped at the end of her hair, pulling the long, thick braid forward. "What did you use to tie it with?"

"My own hair tie."

"You wear your hair long then?" she asked.

"Sometimes I do. I have seen many styles in the different parts of the world I have lived in. One style may suit me for a while, and then another. I suppose it depends on the mood I am in."

Her fingers ran lightly over the bit of black silk. "I suppose it's as black as your hair?" she asked, probing for details again.

"Very nearly."

He knew very well that she was adding another detail to her image of him.

"Stand up, Christine, and I'll draw the curtain. The morning is nearly gone."

She stood up regretfully, knowing it would probably be the closest she ever came to him.

Chapter 5

There was darkness all around him. The darkness was a void, a vast emptiness that seemed to throb with the heavy weight of a primordial silence.

"Where am I," he heard himself groan but the darkness gave back nothing save the faint echo of his own voice.

Gradually it came to him that the silence was not absolute but rather was pulsating with a deep, undulating sound. He realized it was the sound of waves lapping both near and far. And then he saw that he had been shipwrecked alone and that he was in the middle of a dark ocean, an endless sea of terrifying depths. All that kept him from drowning and being lost beneath the waves was a half-submerged, wooden raft, an unstable structure that had barely enough substance to hold up his own weight. Yet the raft was all he had, so he clung to the soft, water-sodden wood with his deteriorating strength as the water continued to press against him in unrelenting waves.

There were rare dreams where his face was perfect, unmarred by his curse. But this was not one of them. In this dream he was like some hideous, marked beast that had crawled up out of the depths of a watery hell. He was horrified to see that his deformity had gotten worse. His face was now pitted with rotted flesh and putrefying holes so deep that the whiteness of his skull showed through. The decaying flesh was crawling with maggots and the curse had spread to other places on his body. Even the good side of his face was decomposing. He felt exposed, even in the darkness. Where was his mask?

And then he saw Christine at a distance. She was a siren who had been condemned to the desolate rock upon which she sat. Her upper body was draped with her unbound hair as if she was some ancient, mythical mermaid. He could hear her voice which was very faint and faraway, but it was as soft and as sweet as honey as she commanded him to come to her.

A black shape took form in the dark, churning sky above her. It shifted and writhed in a jerky manner as it morphed into a hideous, winged creature, a dragon that began to fly in slow circles above her. Its scales were a dark, iridescent green. Its underbelly was like a toad's dull flesh. Its outspread wings were bat-like and membrane-thin and crisscrossed by a network of thick dark veins. With gnashing teeth and curved, razor-sharp talons that clasped and unclasped spasmodically, the beast looked down upon Christine.

Because she had called out with her siren's voice, she had attracted the attention of the dragon so that now the ravenous creature was slavering over her virginal flesh. It watched her with an unholy glare, tilting its head from side to side as its round snake eyes blinked with wicked fixation.

The wind had risen because of the beating of the dragon's immense wings and the water now roiled and seethed around him as he clung to the raft. Christine's voice grew ever fainter, drowned out now by the raging wind, but her faraway cries echoed her fear and her helplessness. He knew that he must save her.

She reached one arm out toward him. It was a hopeful, but pitiful gesture. He worried that she would see that he was an undead being, a half corpse, and wondered if she would prefer to be devoured by the dragon piece by piece rather than to look upon his loathsomeness. Yet he knew he would do what he could to save her. He would shield her body with his and offer himself up as a sacrifice instead.

He let go of the raft and felt himself immediately sink beneath the water. He continued to sink farther and farther from the surface. Everything was dark and murky and silent as death. But somewhere nearby, there was a light, a soft, golden light that shifted and wavered with the movement of the waves. If he could only reach it. But the light half blinded him so that he could not open his eyes fully and find his way.

The current carried him farther down into the darkness. As he sank deeper, he drifted helplessly through a rippling mirage of light and shadow, where long ribbons of entangling seaweed twined around his limbs. He tried to turn his face from the blinding light. At the same time, he realized that he was getting farther away from Christine. The water kept pulling him down. A hoarse sob broke from his throat as he realized that he would not be able to save her. He gasped for air as he fought the water . . .

Eric jerked awake, gulping in a deep, ragged breath of air as his eyes snapped open. He was still half caught in the dream and terror was pulsing through him with every beat of his pounding heart. There was still the sensation of seaweed wrapped around his limbs and for a moment he struggled, but eventually he realized that all he fought were his tangled blankets. As he waited for his heart to slow its pace, he realized that the light he had seen was nothing more than a candle flickering on the table beside his bed.

He rolled over onto his back as his mind continued to struggle to full awareness. In the depths of what some called his lair, he finally rose from his bed and went to the wash stand where he dipped his hands into the porcelain basin to splash some cool water onto his face. When he finally looked up, he almost winced at what he saw reflected in the mirror before him. The one they called the Phantom of the Opera stared back at him. The one some called a demon. The one that struck terror into the hearts of men and women alike. There were other words from far back in his past when he had been called an abomination. A freak of nature. A monster.

As the elusive Phantom of the Opera, he was more of a mystery now. Not because people had seen his face, but because no one had seen his face. He was more of a myth now, a figure from beyond the grave. A ghost. An enigma.

His dark brows drew together into a frown as he forced himself to survey the wreck that was his face. From his forehead to the corner of his eye, down over one cheekbone and all the way to the jaw the ugly mutilation that ran the length of his face was not the fleeting vision of a nightmare, but his own unending hell. No maggots, but the flesh was like one massive, uneven scar. No one had ever looked upon him without horror and revulsion. They saw little after that first glimpse, thinking him less than human, incapable of emotion.

He put his hand over the imperfection as if envisioning, if only for a moment, what it would be like to be normal. Then he ran his hand slowly across his unshaven jaw. Pulled back to the image of Christine in the dream, his deformity was brought painfully and sharply to mind. At best she could only think of him as a freak of nature. At worst, she would pity him.

Bracing his hands on either side of the small table that held the basin, he lowered his head and stayed that way for several long, silent moments. Then he let out a deep sigh and straightened, using both hands to shove the black hair back from his face.

Knowing the futility of trying to banish from his mind the woman who had become both his passion and his pain, he turned back to the room. The walls of his refuge were thick and solid. Secure. He could pace from one end to the other as many times as he wished, but there was only so far he could go. Walls, he already knew, could have a way of closing in on a man, especially when what he sought to escape from was inside himself.

There were times when he woke from his nightmares and he would feel the weight of his loneliness echoing like a death knell in his gloomy chamber, so deeply that he would go forth and prowl the darkness and the outside world like some nocturnal beast who had escaped, if only temporarily, from captivity. This would be one of those nights.

He thrust his arms into his shirt, prey still to his dark thoughts as he fastened the buttons. It had been his folly to let himself fall in love with a woman he could never possess. If that had not been foolish enough, he had done what he had vowed would never happen. He had drawn her close with no curtain between them at their last lesson. He had let down certain barriers that should have stayed in place. He had weakened for a moment. He had given in to all the soul-felt yearnings and the feeling of being alive that she had stirred to life inside him.

It was a cruel trick for fate to play on him, bringing her into his life and letting him imagine her at his side, knowing that could never happen. He should have known better than to touch her. He should have realized that if a smile from her could do so much damage from the other side of a curtain, how much more devastating a touch would be.

He had known all along that she was a temporary diversion in his life. He had sworn to himself that he would not forget that. Yet Christine had a way of making him forget a lot of things, it seemed. When she had first come to the Opera House, she had been mourning the loss of her father. He had watched her from afar and her depth of sadness had touched his heart. She had come into his life and caught him unaware. In the end, she had made him only too aware of the darkness of the solitary life he must lead.

He sighed deeply. He could make all the promises in the world to himself, but the fact remained that he had touched her. And he could not get it out of his mind. For her sake he must not let it happen again.

As he pulled his boots on, he whispered to the empty room: "I yielded to a moment of madness, knowing better. But I won't let it happen again."

He refused to let himself founder in thoughts of what the loss of her would mean to him, however, because then he would sink into a dark and wretched place and he could not bear that at the moment. He already knew he would soon lose her and the darkness would be so much worse for the knowing.

He searched for a distraction, then seated himself at his desk and spread out several sheets of foolscap. In the flickering shadows of the candlelight, his frowning expression remained intent as he took his quill in hand and dipped it into the ink well.

He could recall her every word, her every description. A cottage and a white picket fence. The flowers. The woods and the sea. He could envision it all in his mind as if he was really there. With his pen poised above the paper he imagined himself standing there on the seashore with her. Turning the darker things that resided deep inside him into something more bearable, he began to sketch a concept into a reality.

The scratching of the quill continued as the candles slowly burned down. After the better part of an hour had passed, he replaced the quill in the inkstand and sat back in his chair. He looked down at the images he had drawn, some of which were still drying. He had banished the images of his own dark nightmare from his mind and instead he had drawn a cottage bordered by a white picket fence and surrounded by flowers. The sea was a shadow in the distance.

Next he worked on the calculations and precise mathematical equations that would help make it come to life for her. And then, almost as an afterthought, he scratched a few bold lines onto a separate piece of paper and pressed a signet ring into a pool of blood-red liquid wax to seal it. When that was done, he allowed a faint, almost diabolical smile to curve one corner of his mouth.

"There is no ghost. There is only a man masquerading as a ghost. He is no more a ghost than I am."

Raoul de Chagny's lips straightened into a thin line as he fought for patience. His audience seemed to him more like a group of frightened children rather than logical, rationally-thinking adults. Who would think that their belief in a ghost could be so deeply-rooted? So irrational. So unshakable. Since he had taken it upon himself to gain control of the situation, he faced them now with all the air of authority that he could muster.

"He has dared to threaten Carlotta again with his childish notes," Raoul went on. "Do you not see that even if ghosts did exist, they would not write notes? Not only that, but he has repeatedly threatened the owners, the previous ones as well as the current ones, with vague and dire consequences if they do not do as he says. The villain has interfered with the running of this Opera House for far too long. And now that there has been an outright assault, is there anyone here who does not agree that he is a madman who must be stopped and that his reign of terror must come to an end?"

Reign of Terror? Those were provocative words to the French.

There was a growing crowd of agitated theater workers gathered around the Viscount. The incident had occurred only half an hour before he had arrived and so the particulars of the attack could only be guessed at until there was a thorough investigation. Even the reason for the attack was unknown. The only thing anyone knew for certain was that it had taken place in one of the backstage hallways and that Remi Botair had been the victim.

A few more people joined the crowd, and as the known details of the attack were repeated, the murmur of concern was raised to a new level. Raoul de Chagny raised both hands to quiet the nervous onlookers.

"What has changed?" someone asked. "The ghost has not been violent before now."

"Well, he is violent now," the Viscount replied grimly, his voice becoming louder at approximately the same rate as the crowd was growing. "*Someone* hit Monsieur Botair in the back of the head and left him lying unconscious in a pool of his own blood. The man was nearly bludgeoned to death. I tell you, there is something dangerous and sinister at work here. Is there anyone who will deny it?"

There was a general, though somewhat uncertain, shaking of heads as people looked around to see who agreed with whom.

The physician had just arrived. The crowd cleared a pathway that reminded more than one onlooker of the parting of the Red Sea. Especially with all that blood on the floor.

"Stand back and let him have some air," the doctor called out.

A hush fell over the crowd as everyone craned their necks to watch the physician lean over the wounded man whose face was the color of the chalk that the dancers used. Poor Remi, who was sitting in a chair, still looked weak and visibly shaken. His shirt was blood spattered and there was a white cloth bandage wrapped around his forehead that was also stained with blood. One of the dancers was holding another bandage to the back of his head.

Only one man had the courage to speak up, although he did so in a very subdued voice. "Is it possible that someone else is responsible for the assault? Maybe things got out of hand."

A bleary-eyed, obviously-hungover Gaspar Belisard was standing in the front of the restless throng, as concerned as anyone, when he realized that the crowd's attention had suddenly shifted to him. Horrified at the very suggestion that he might be guilty of the assault, he immediately held out his hands to silently, but vehemently protest against such an accusation.

"It wasn't me," he rasped hoarsely.

Everyone in the theater knew that there had been a verbal fight between Remi and Gaspar just two days ago. Over a costume of all things. Remi had made the costume of bright yellow satin with highlights of chartreuse. Gaspar said he was not going to wear such a hideous costume, that he was a man, not a canary. He went on to demand a costume in a more subdued, more *manly* color before he would step one foot on the stage.

95

Remi had told him that making another costume that would fit Gaspar would take time. He also hinted that because Gaspar was, as he put it, rather thick-girthed, making a new costume would take longer than usual. Gaspar, who was as concerned with every detail of his appearance on stage as he was with his singing, continued to push the issue of a new costume. To which Remi declared that he was a tailor not a magician. Then Gaspar accused Remi of purposely trying to downplay his manliness. What had brought that on no one really knew.

The argument had gone back and forth. In no time at all, it had gotten very heated. Insults started flying, ugly insults, and then outright threats. After enduring Gaspar's finger stabbing him repeatedly in the chest, Remi - who would have thought he had it in him? - had punched Gaspar in the nose, so hard that the blood had streamed down his face all the way to his shirt front.

Of course, the Viscount did not know about all of this, and so far no one had told him. It was well known that Gaspar did have a temper, especially when he was drinking, but no one actually thought he would go so far as to physically harm Remi who was normally quite docile as well as being very well liked by everyone in the theater.

"Only a stranger could have done this." The Viscount's gaze slowly swept the crowd. "It could be even more disastrous the next time the maniac strikes. Someone could be killed. It could be anyone of you."

"But how do you stop a ghost?" someone asked.

The Viscount looked up at the ceiling above him for a moment. Then he began speaking slowly and deliberately, as he might speak to a small child. "I have told you repeatedly. We are not dealing with a ghost. Only an ignorant mind would believe that to be the case."

The not-so-subtle insult was hardly lost on the listeners.

"The guilty party is most likely some homeless n'er-do-well that has been hiding in the cellars of the Opera House," the Viscount went on. "Obviously he is dangerous. He could very well be deranged. He might even be a fugitive hiding from the law. Therefore, he must be found and, even more than that, he must be brought to justice."

"What of the ghostly music we hear?" one of the dancers asked.

"What?" The Viscount was frowning now.

"Do you think a deranged fugitive could play such beautiful music?"

There were obviously some among the crowd who did not want to let go of the idea of a mysterious phantom residing in the Opera House. The rather romantic legend of a phantom had been around so long that, apparently, there were many who were not willing to give the idea up.

"Yes, what of that?" someone else asked.

The Viscount waved that detail aside as if it was inconsequential, like an annoying fly. "Someone is playing a trick on you. One of the musicians, I'll wager. Besides, there is nothing particularly magical about that. Anyone can pick up an instrument and play music. Or sing."

There were some in the group of listeners, perhaps most, who might not have agreed with that depreciating opinion, but the Viscount did not see, or he pretended not to see, the scarcely-veiled, hostile stares from a few of them.

"But how does he manage to do the other things he does? Like vanish into walls? Or disappear right before someone's eyes? He disappeared right in front of Henri Millard. And Gaspar saw him vanish into a mist the night of the soiree."

"Bah! Merely tricks. Illusions," the Viscount assured them. "You can see those things any night on the stage. As actors, you all know that the power of a suggestive mind can make anything seem real. It is really fear that has helped him keep up his illusions this long. And I will tell you one more thing," Raoul went on. "This ridiculous notion of a ghost having his own private box must stop. No wonder he thinks he can do anything he wants here. His ludicrous whims have been indulged up until now, but I am going to change all that."

"How?"

"For one thing," the Viscount said with a imperious lift of his clefted chin. "This building must be searched from top to bottom."

"The entire Opera House?" someone asked incredulously. "But there are over a thousand rooms. And no one *ever* goes down to the lowermost cellars."

No one *wanted* to go down to the lowermost cellars. There was only darkness and a lake down there. And quite possibly a ghost.

"Yes," the Viscount replied. "I know all that. But the Opera House *must* be searched thoroughly. Including the cellars. I will see to it myself."

"Just what will you be looking for?" Madame Giry asked as she stepped forward, separating herself from the crowd.

"If someone has been hiding there - and I'm sure that has been the case - we will find evidence of it," the Viscount answered her confidently. "We will rid the Opera House of this scoundrel once and for all. But first we must stop thinking of him as a ghost."

"What do you mean?"

"I mean, Christine, that it's time that you told Madame Giry that you have given your last performance."

"But I haven't given it. I will be singing here tomorrow night. And the night after that."

The Viscount, who was trying to be more authoritative, more *husbandly*, because he would have that right soon, lowered his voice to a more reasoning tone. "I cannot allow that, Christine. In light of everything that has happened, it is much too dangerous for you to even consider performing here again."

"I am not a child that I must be told what to do and what not to do." Her dark lashes swept up as her challenging gaze held his. "Just when did you decide that I cannot make my own decisions?"

"You know that I am only thinking about what is best for you."

"I have only a short time before I say good bye to this place - and my career - for good. Why are you trying to take what little time I have left away from me?"

He correctly read the rebellious look in her eyes as she stared up at him, but she needed to know that he was not going to get in the habit of backing down before her. That would be a disastrous way to begin a marriage.

"I am not trying to take anything away from you. I am only asking you to be reasonable. It's not safe here. And as your future husband, your safety is important to me. Would you expect anything less of me?"

Her chin lifted slightly. "Have you made the same request of the other performers?"

"I don't have to. They already know what they are up against and they can make their own decisions, which are no concern of mine. But as for you- "

She cut him off by turning her face to the side. It seemed that he was trying to make her decisions for her more and more frequently of late. She made an effort to suppress her growing anger, but resentment still smoldered in her eyes as she looked back at him. "But I will be on stage in front of an entire audience of people. What do you think could happen?"

Faced with that stubborn look in her eyes, the one he was beginning to know only too well, and the willful set of her chin he decided to change tactics. It had been necessary to feel his way through what he saw as her frustratingly mercurial moods of late, which seemed to be growing more and more unpredictable the closer they got to the wedding. He decided that his best strategy would be to ignore her challenging tone, so he summoned up a hurt expression on his face. "How can you be angry with me when you know that I am only concerned about your safety? As your future husband, do I not have that right?"

She drew a deep breath and forced calmness into her voice. She hated when he was like this. "Do you think you should be getting everyone stirred up when you don't really know what happened?"

"I know that a man was nearly bludgeoned to death by some deranged lunatic who is obviously becoming bolder with each dark deed. Have you forgotten about the serving girl the night of the soiree?"

"She wasn't attacked."

"She very nearly was. The man was reaching for her."

"We don't know what happened."

"Why do you feel the need to defend the man, Christine?" He blew out a forceful breath. And then he said in a sarcastic undertone, "Oh, that's right. You believe you saw the Phantom of the Opera one night yourself. Which you did not even bother to tell me about. Why would you keep that to yourself?"

"I don't know what - or who - I saw."

He saw her defensive walls go up even higher. His jaw tensed as he fought to control his own tongue. It was a battle he had been waging ever since he had walked into Christine's dressing room early that morning to see her calmly sitting at her dressing table with a rose held to her lips and a dreamy expression on her face. Recalling it now, his teeth clenched so tightly together that Christine looked around as she heard his jaw crack.

She frowned questioningly at the sound and said, "I'm not defending anyone. No one knows what really happened to Remi, or who was responsible."

"Not yet," Raoul said grimly. "But I have every intention of finding out. And until I do know more, I will not agree to let you become easy prey for some dangerous criminal who is lurking about in the shadows of the Opera House."

"Aren't you being a little- dramatic?"

"Not in the least." He pointed. "There is a bleeding man over there that proves it. With all that has happened around here in the past few days, you should be afraid, Christine. Yet you do not seem concerned in the least. And I must say that I find your attitude more than curious, especially since all I am doing is to try and save you from harm."

"I do not need saving."

"Really. And what about the roses?"

"Roses?"

"Yes, the roses. Clearly, someone has noticed you. And surely you are aware that people are whispering that the ghost is leaving them for you."

"You mean *you* think the ghost is leaving them?"

"No, I don't think the ghost- " He stopped and corrected himself. "Of course not. There is no ghost. The point is that you accept the roses, whoever is sending them. Aren't you sending a message that you accept *him* as well?"

"Carlotta receives flowers all the time."

"Carlotta is the star of the theater. What I am wondering is why someone would consistently choose to send flowers to you."

"My voice?"

There was a frown on her face as she glanced up at box five and its shadowed interior, but Raoul saw something else in her eyes, or thought he did.

He scoffed under his breath. "Don't tell me you have romanticized the notion of a ghost, too."

100

"In what way do you think I have done that?"

Because he had seen the way she looked up at box five. Because they were affianced, yet not once had she ever looked at him that way.

"I will continue to make the decisions that I feel I must make," he told her. "And you, as my wife, will trust that they are the right decisions. I must insist you leave this place."

"And go where?"

"You know my offer still stands. Move into the mansion and you will have servants to wait on you hand and foot."

"I can't live with you, Raoul. That would hardly be proper. We're not married yet."

"It would be perfectly proper. There would be chaperones around us at all times. Unlike this place, where you are completely on your own. You might at least have a care for *me*. How can I rest easily at night knowing you are here alone where some dangerous lunatic is lurking about?"

"I have lived here for three years and I haven't seen anyone-lurking."

The truth was that if she moved to the de Chagny mansion, she would have to give up her voice lessons, along with her freedom. She wasn't ready to do that.

"You're hardly suited for this life," he said testily.

"You forget, this life is what made you notice me in the first place."

"That certainly is not true. I noticed you from the very first moment I saw you."

"You scarcely took notice of me back then," she calmly reminded him.

"Of course I took notice of you. I remember very clearly how you tumbled down the hill and landed at my feet."

"You may have noticed me, but I didn't make a very good first impression on you. Admit it."

"That first meeting was quite memorable, I assure you. You were dripping with mud from head to toe after that hideous brute of a beast threw you from its back."

"Bonaparte was not hideous."

"That beast wasn't even qualified to be included in the equine family."

"As I recall, you didn't even offer to help me up. I would have helped you up, mud or no mud."

"I wouldn't have been on that beastly animal in the first place. So there would have been no need for your help."

"No, you would have been mounted on a splendid animal that was pure-blooded and pedigreed, and you would have had servants to attend to all your needs."

He looked at her like he didn't understand her at all. "And what is wrong with that? When you marry me, you will have those things, too. At least, that will be a reality, rather than you trying to live out the fantasy of some mythical heroine on stage."

He had gone too far. He realized it in an instant as her face suddenly looked like it had been carved out of stone.

"I do not wish to argue anymore," he said, wishing belatedly that he could take it back.

"Neither do I. But since you seem to be finding more and more fault with my behavior lately, perhaps we should re-consider this whole idea of a wedding- "

He interrupted her abruptly, worried that he had pushed her even farther than he had thought. "How can you say that?"

"I am only speaking the truth, Raoul. Lately everything I do seems to displease you."

"You are speaking nonsense. The wedding will go on as planned. Which is another matter that I had come here to discuss." He thought it wise, perhaps, to change the subject when she was like this. "Ligeia needs to go over wedding details with you."

"Tell Ligeia to make them herself. That is what she will do anyway, regardless of what I may want."

"You're acting like a petulant child, Christine. She has already gone through a great deal of trouble on your behalf. And she wanted me to tell you that she has already arranged for the dance lessons."

Christine suppressed a groan. "I know how to dance."

"What you do on stage is something entirely different from what a young woman of quality- "

She sighed impatiently. "And just what is your definition of a woman of quality? A woman who speaks her mind only to have her husband-to-be get annoyed or change the subject when she does so? Is this how things will be once we are married? You will continue to try and make my decisions for me and disregard *my* opinions and *my* wishes as if they are of no consequence? Will yours be the only ones that matter?"

"Christine, don't be like this," he said as he consulted his timepiece. "I have business to see to, which gives us little enough time to spend together today. We should not be wasting our time fighting with each other."

Whatever Christine had been about to say was interrupted by one of the dancers who was coming down the hallway waving a piece of paper before her. She handed the paper to Christine.

"Look, Christine. Gaspar has done a sketch of the Phantom of the Opera to show what he saw the night of the soiree. Who knew Gaspar was such a talented artist? Remi has seen the picture, too, and he said it is not the same man who attacked him."

Gaspar's bold strokes had rendered a very dramatic sketch of a cloaked figure with a mask covering half his face. There was a mist swirling about him. The mist looked very realistic.

Raoul snatched the paper out of her hand. "How can he know it is not the same man? The man in this picture is masked."

The dancer shrugged and said, "It is only a half mask." Then she looked at Christine. "There is something very intriguing about a man in a mask, *n'est-ce pas?*"

Christine glanced up at Raoul who was staring at the dancer. For once, it looked like he didn't know what to say.

Chapter 6

"Have you seen him today?" Madame Giry asked the Persian.

"No. He told me several days ago that he did not want to be disturbed. I am not certain what he is working on, but, as you know, I do not pry, and it is not unusual for him to disappear for long periods of time."

No, it was not unusual for him to seclude himself for days, or even weeks at a time.

As Madame Giry thought the man's answer over, the Persian shrugged his shoulders. "I know that this assault has been on his mind. Perhaps that is what has him so occupied. More than anyone, he would like to see it resolved. The inconvenience of all these gendarmes coming and going at all hours of the day and night can't be improving his mood any."

Madame Giry nodded thoughtfully. The entire Opera House was on edge. People refused to go anywhere alone. "It is difficult for the performers to concentrate on their roles without the added strain of having to be looking over their shoulders all the time. But," she added. "It has been quiet these past few days. I suppose we should be grateful for that."

Everyone at the Opera House had been questioned about the assault, yet they were still no closer to knowing who had attacked Remi Botair than they had been the day it had happened. And everyone was asking themselves the same question. If it hadn't been the Phantom of the Opera that had attacked Remi, then who had it been? Remi had had a brief glimpse of his attacker, but he said that he had not recognized the man. Which meant that his attacker was not one of the workers at the Opera House. And if that was the case, what was a stranger doing wandering around the backstage hallways? Apparently a very dangerous stranger. Some of them, at least, began to wonder if the Viscount wasn't right about a criminal lurking in the cellars below the Opera House.

"Thank goodness Remi has not suffered any long term effects from the attack," Madame Giry said. "When I saw all the blood, I - Well, I feared the worst."

"It must have all been very unsettling for you."

The Persian was well known throughout the Opera House. He was a tall, handsome man, dark skinned and dark haired. He was dressed elegantly, as always, but his style of clothing suggested a Middle Eastern influence. There were rumors that he had been a prince in Persia, but that he had fled to France because the state of political unrest in his native country was so unstable and so dangerous that an assassination attempt had been made on his life.

"He has been rather well behaved lately," Madame Giry said next. "Considering all that has been going on. But if the Viscount keeps insinuating himself in the affairs of the Opera House . . . "

"Then we may anticipate that he will eventually take some kind of action," the Persian finished for her. "I find it astonishing that he has tolerated it this long."

Madame Giry pressed her hand against her bodice and plucked abstractedly at a button there. "I have a bad feeling about this meeting."

"As have I," the Persian agreed. "They said they were going to be discussing security measures for the Opera House and finding this attacker. But- "

"But you don't believe that to be the case?"

"I'm not so certain the Viscount actually *wants* to find the person responsible. In spite of his loud talk, it may serve his purposes to have a ghost on the loose. We already know to what lengths he will go to have his way. Yet in the end, things may play out according to fate, with or without our interference. Indeed, it seems as if the pieces of a game of nardshir are being moved into place by some outside force and we have no control over anything."

"Do you think he knows about the meeting?"

"If he doesn't, I am certain he will know soon enough. Walls have mice and mice have ears."

"How long have they been in there?" Madame Giry asked.

"Not long. The Viscount just arrived."

The fact that Raoul de Chagny was meeting with the owners of the Opera House was nothing new. The fact that he was meeting with them behind closed doors was out of the ordinary.

"Whatever it is they are discussing, it cannot be good."

"Yes," the Persian agreed. "When the cat and the mouse agree, the grocer can be sure to expect trouble."

"The Viscount's threats to search the Opera House also have me worried," Madame Giry said.

"Even if he does search it from top to bottom, he won't find anything," the Persian told her.

"You're very certain about that?"

"If he does not want to be found, no one will find him," the Persian assured her.

"The Viscount seems very determined."

The Persian smiled. "I did not say he would not make things interesting for him."

They were standing on a second floor balcony, staring down at the closed office door and Madame Giry said, "I cannot help but wonder if this meeting concerns Christine in some way. This business with the flowers still has me worried. I haven't told her what I know which makes me feel like I have been dishonest with her, and I really don't know how long I can go on deceiving her."

"My advice would be to wait a while and see how things go. Sometimes a thing must play itself out in its own time. As for the Viscount, what percolates out of the jug is what is inside it.
He will give himself away eventually. As for Christine- " His voice trailed off and he left the rest unsaid.

A movement caught Madame Giry's eye and she lifted her face to look up at one of the third floor balconies on the other side of the theater. A black-shrouded figure stood there like some vampiric lord of ancient lore. Madame Giry could almost feel the intensity of the man's dark gaze as he looked down at the world below him. She had the distinct impression of the calm before a storm as he stood poised there for the space of several heartbeats. Then he turned abruptly and with a sharp flourish of his long cape, he disappeared, leaving Madame Giry and the Persian both staring after him.

Such a bold appearance in broad daylight could mean only one thing. He knew about the meeting between Raoul de Chagny and the owners.

"Somehow I think he is going to be displeased at what is going on behind those closed doors," Madame Giry murmured as she continued to stare up at the empty balcony.

"Displeased?" the Persian echoed. "Madame, I think that is going to prove to be one of the greatest understatements ever uttered in this Opera House."

The Viscount Raoul de Chagny had a glass of brandy in one hand. In the other hand he held a cigar that had come from the wooden box on Monsieur Vaussard's desk. Although the cigar was hardly the same quality he was used to, the Viscount lifted the cigar to his mouth and puffed deeply a few times before he let the smoke slowly unfurl into a thick cloud above his head. Settling back in his chair, he frowned down at the glowing tip of the cigar for a moment before he looked up and said to the other two men in the room, "I do not see the problem with my request, gentlemen. I do not make many of them."

No one had an immediate reply to that, at least not a suitable one. The truth was that lately the Viscount's requests had been coming with more and more frequency. First there was the business of the roses. Then he had asked to search the Opera House, which they had already agreed to. There had been no problem there. But this third request was something else entirely. Why, if they kept on giving into his demands, there was no telling how far he might go or how much he might affect the smooth running of the Opera House.

The Viscount took a long, deep swallow of his brandy, then waited for his original question to be answered.

Messieurs Vaussard and Peverell didn't dare share even the briefest of glances. They managed to avoid looking directly into the Viscount's eyes, as well, as they floundered about, trying to figure out the best way to handle the situation. But they could only stall for so long. The Viscount was waiting.

Monsieur Vaussard cleared his throat and asked, "What reason would we give her?"

"What do you usually say in these cases?" the Viscount asked.

"Well, we, uh, we haven't had to deal with such a case yet. But I suppose that if someone was giving a less-than-satisfactory performance, we should deal with them by promptly dismissing them."

"Then simply tell her you're not happy with her performance."

"But, wouldn't that be a bit- harsh?" Monsieur Vaussard asked.

Even Messeiurs Vaussard and Peverell, who could not be accused of being the most diplomatic or subtle of men, were nonplussed at the idea of crushing a young woman's dreams. Especially when she was making them a great deal of money.

"But we have been most pleased with her performance," Monsieur Peverell began. "Most pleased. And we have already told her this. Besides, the critics have nothing but the highest praise for her."

"And there is the fact that she was recommended for the part," Monsieur Vaussard reminded him.

One of the Viscount's tawny eyebrows lifted in surprise. He had not heard this before. "By whom was she recommended?" he wanted to know, his eyes narrowing suspiciously when both men suddenly looked even more uncomfortable.

Monsieur Vaussard had no choice but to tell him the truth. "By the ghost. The Phantom of the Opera."

Raoul's glass stopped halfway to his mouth. "You jest. Surely."

"No, from what we hear, it was a very specific request," Monsieur Peverell informed him.

The Viscount thought this over for a few moments. Then he speared both men with a more intent look in his eyes. "And when did this happen?"

"Some time ago. When the previous owners were in charge."

"You mean she is singing here at the request of a *ghost?*"

Messieurs Vaussard and Peverell could only nod in the face of the Viscount's outraged disbelief.

"Why would that come as any surprise to me?" the Viscount muttered under his breath. Looking up suddenly, he asked, "Does Christine know this?"

"No, actually we were told to keep it quiet."

"By the ghost?"

"Yes."

Several moments passed in silence. The Viscount's voice was quite low when he asked, "And did he have any other requests to make concerning Christine?"

"No," Monsieur Vaussard replied. But both men were looking at each other and Monsieur Peverell unfortunately spoke without thinking. "Only about the furnishings in her room."

Both men turned to look at the Viscount, having realized their mistake the moment the words left Monsieur Peverell's mouth.

"But, ahem, again that was already underway when Messeiurs Telfour and Aleron owned the Opera House," Monsieur Vaussard hastened to explain. "Of course we should point out that Christine's room was in need of new furnishings anyway."

"Have there been similar requests made for any of the other performers?" the Viscount asked.

"Not that we are aware of," Monsieur Vaussard replied. "Of course, Carlotta's dressing room is always being redecorated. But she makes the request herself."

"How considerate this ghost is," the Viscount said to himself. He looked up. "So, gentlemen, where do we stand?"

"The truth is that we have no one to replace Christine," Monsieur Vaussard told him.

"There is no understudy?"

"*Non*. There is no one who knows the songs as she does. And we believe she is one of the reasons the theater has been packed every night. People want to hear more of her."

"And you don't think it's possible that Carlotta has something to do with that?" Raoul asked. "Or that the current opera itself is popular?"

"The audiences have only increased dramatically since Christine began singing. And there are the reviews," Monsieur Vaussard reminded him.

"I see. In spite of such- obstacles, you do understand that I only have her best interests in mind?"

"Of course," Monsieur Peverell quickly replied.

The frown remained on Raoul's face as he got up out of his chair and walked over to the tall windows. "How long will it take to find an understudy?" he asked without turning.

"It takes time," Monsieur Vaussard answered. "One cannot simply sing on stage without first learning the songs and then rehearsing them for a while, both alone and with the rest of the cast.."

"To be perfectly honest, we're not certain how much time it will take," Monsieur Peverell said to the Viscount's back. "I mean, we haven't been in the opera business that long and on top of everything else, we have been distracted by this assault. What with trying to keep the Opera House running, which has proven to be a far more complicated undertaking than we had anticipated- "

The Viscount turned back to face both men.

Seeing the look on the Viscount's face, Monsieur Peverell finished meekly, "We'll see what we can do."

The Viscount remained standing before the large windows. To the two other men in the room, he was a dark, imposing shape against the daylight that was pouring through the windows behind him. He pushed his coat back and rested one hand low on his hip while he puffed contemplatively on his cigar. For a long time he didn't speak. And since he was obviously deep in thought, no one dared interrupt him. The truth was that Messeiurs Vaussard and Peverell weren't sure how to deal with him. They wanted to keep the Viscount happy, of course. In fact it was necessary for them to do so. But the Viscount's priorities were not the same as their own, which was running the Opera House as a business and making money. The Viscount's priority was more of a personal one.

"Are the police any closer to solving this incident with the tailor?" the Viscount asked.

"Unfortunately, no," Monsieur Vaussard answered him.

The Viscount nodded. He had nothing more to say about the assault, but there was something else on his mind.

"This business with the roses is troubling. I thought that we had put that matter to rest. How are they still getting through?"

"We had every intention of abiding by your request," Monsieur Peverell quickly explained. "But we have no control over the roses since they don't arrive through the usual channels."

"Yes, they can turn up anywhere," Monsieur Vaussard added. "It is never the same. *Jamais.*"

"We could say that you had requested that any roses are first delivered to you- " Monsieur Peverell began.

The Viscount looked at him as if he were a complete dotard. "I've already told you, I don't want my name mentioned."

"Well, er, you're right, of course. That wouldn't work. Then we would have to inform most of the staff to bring the roses to us first and the way that gossip makes the rounds of the theater- "

The Viscount was fast losing patience. They had given him a lot to think about. He cut the man off by saying, "And that brings me to the next matter I came here to discuss. I think you will agree with me that it is time to rent out box five. There is no justification whatsoever for letting it sit empty just to lose money night after night. This is a business after all, one which I have an interest in, and a business should be run without caving in to an extortionist, not to mention running a business based on unfounded fears and superstitions. Someone is making a fool of you, perhaps using fear so that he may watch performances for free whenever he wishes."

Monsiuer Vaussard would have disagreed, especially about the fool part, but the Viscount looked like he had said all he had come to say. Clearly the meeting was over.

The Viscount walked over to the desk, picked up his glass and downed the last of his brandy in one swallow.

"Think about what I said, gentlemen," he said as he stubbed out his cigar.

He then bowed his head briefly, turned on his heels and left the room.

Dazed by the difficult decisions they were being forced to confront, Messeiurs Vaussard and Peverell felt like they were caught between a hawk and a buzzard. It was not only the Viscount that wanted Christine off the stage. Carlotta had already made it very clear that she did not want to share the stage with an amateur. Carlotta was a little easier to handle. But just barely.

In the end, it came down to whether they were going to let the Viscount or the Phantom decide how the theater was going to be run. They understood that there would be consequences no matter which way they decided. They did not want to offend either one. Raoul de Chagny requested that Christine not sing. The Phantom requested that she did. What were they going to do?

In the end, afraid of angering both of them, they would make no decision at all. That is, until the Viscount forced their hand.

It turned out that Remi Botair had indeed seen the face of the man that had attacked him. It had only been a brief glance, but Remi was able to describe the violent encounter in chilling detail. In his own words the man had come lumbering at him out of the shadows like an enraged grizzly bear. Hearing the heavy rush of footsteps, Remi had had only a moment to look over his shoulder at his assailant.

Remi was very adamant about the fact that the man in Gaspar's sketch was not the same man that had attacked him. Magdeline Huguette had also seen the sketch and she said it was an accurate rendering of what she herself had seen the night of the soiree. So it was all becoming very confusing.

Remi was resting with his feet up in Madame Vernay's office when Christine walked into the room to see how he was feeling. He still had bandages wrapped around his head, but he was looking much better.

"Are you certain the man in the sketch could not have been the same man that attacked you, Remi?" she asked.

"I'm very certain about it. The man that attacked me was a coarse-faced brute, a giant of a man with a jagged scar down one side of his face."

According to Remi, it looked like the scar could have been from a knife wound, although he admitted he had never actually seen a knife scar before. But the important part was that the scar had been on the *unmasked* side of the man's face, according to Gaspar's drawing. Magdeline Hugette had confirmed that there had been no scar. Of course, she admitted that it had been dark and she had had only a very brief glimpse of her attacker as well. But the flashes of lightning had been very bright.

Remi continued to assert that his attacker could not have been the Phantom of the Opera.

"And how can you be certain it wasn't the Phantom?" Christine asked him.

"Because I saw his eyes, Christine. They were the eyes of a man fully capable of doing harm, even murder. Not playing the beautiful music that I heard."

Unfortunately, it was beginning to look like Raoul was right, that some criminal might be lurking around in the cellars of the Opera House. It was not a comforting thought for any of them. The rumor that Remi thought his attacker was definitely not the same as the ghost only made the Phantom of the Opera even more of a mystery. By now every curtain, every column and every shadow was suspected of hiding the Phantom. Or someone even more frightening.

Christine didn't say it to Raoul, but the man in the sketch looked strikingly similar to the man she had seen above her that night, except that the mask had not been right. The image had stayed with her throughout the day. So much so that in her sleep she dreamed about the Phantom again.

In her dream she was wandering the cellars of the Opera House. She found herself in a dark room where a square of moonlight filtered eerily through a single window. She saw a man's silhouette as he stared out the window. The long black cloak that was wrapped around him blended with the ebony darkness. From behind, it looked like the same dark figure that Gaspar had drawn. Somehow she knew that the Phantom of the Opera stood before her.

"Christine, have you finally come?" he queried without turning. "I have been waiting for you."

"Why is our lesson here?" she asked.

"Because no one will disturb us here."

He finally turned but his face remained in the shadows. He was a dark entity. Very intense. Very mysterious.

She was surprised when he told her that it was to be a dancing lesson, not a singing lesson. He walked a slow circle around her and stopped.

"Take a step toward me, Christine," he said in a low voice. "*Un pas*. Now spin."

She did as he told her, but when she turned she found herself in his arms with her back against him. There was a mirror in front of them and she stared at their reflection in the glass, but he was still faceless.

"Why haven't you disappeared?" she asked him.

"I'll stay with you as long as you wish me to," he said and she felt the warmth of his breath fan against the side of her neck. She was swept away on a tide of pure sensual sensation.

But then it was her teacher's voice that said softly, "Trust me, Christine, and I will take us both someplace far, far away where we will lose ourselves in the music."

113

She closed her eyes at the seductive whisper of that voice. Strong phantom arms tightened around her as she was drawn against his hard body, the place she had secretly longed to be.

As she watched him in the mirror, he pushed her nightgown down, exposing her shoulders and half freeing her breasts. Then slowly, lightly as a feather, he trailed a rose across her bare flesh, sending a sharp feeling of pleasure sweeping through her body. And then it was his hand trailing across her flesh instead. .

In the mirror his eyes held hers. "Shall I begin our lesson now?" he breathed close to her ear, watching her intently, the hunger in his gaze making her body come alive with a desire so intense that it that shut out all thought of anything save the two of them in that place of moonlit darkness.

He didn't wait for her answer. His mouth began to work its way down the side of her neck, caressing her, savoring her, drawing her into the unbridled rapture of the dream, drawing her to *him*.

She turned her face, seeking, hungering for a kiss, for the touch of his lips on hers-

But the kiss she sought never came. Her eyes opened and she was disappointed to find herself alone in the darkness.

For a long time she lay there as the sensual heat lingered. She had never had such a dream. Maybe it was wicked of her to think of another man this way, but she couldn't stop the feelings still coursing through her body. She couldn't help longing for more . . .

She closed her eyes and wound her fingers around the narrow piece of black silk that still faintly held his scent. She brought it close to her face, wondering in the darkness why she had kept it at all.

Chapter 7

"It was entirely my fault, Christine."

Raoul's apology had been completely unexpected. "I have given some thought to your feelings on the matter and I can now see your side of things. You have my word that things will be much better between us from now on."

He smiled magnanimously. He could afford to be generous with his apologies and his promises since she would be leaving the Opera House soon. And if he had his way, her departure would be even sooner than she realized.

"Of course I am jealous of anyone who would send you flowers," he went on, making light of their previous disagreement. "But you will have to get used to my protective nature. I like to hold on to what is mine. It is a de Chagny trait. But hereafter I will try to keep my jealous inclinations under control so they do not distress you. Let us forget about all that for now. The sun is finally shining and it's a splendid day for a drive through the Bois. I thought that afterward we might enjoy a brunch together at Les Deux Anges. But first, don't you want to open the gift I brought for you?"

Raoul was especially pleased at the way she looked today. Dressed in a very fashionable pink and white striped gown that he had never seen her wear before, he found her quite breathtaking. He watched with an expectant smile as she opened the dainty, rose-covered bandbox. Nestled under several layers of pink tissue was a bonnet. A very exquisite bonnet that was adorned with delicate lace, velvet roses and wide silk ribbons.

115

"Shall I help you put it on?" Raoul asked.

"You want me to wear it now?"

"Of course I want you to wear it now. Ligeia says it's the very latest style of bonnet. Don't you want to show it off when you are sitting next to me in the carriage?"

"It is a very beautiful bonnet," she said, wondering perversely if it was Raoul or Ligeia who had picked it out. She was already wearing her favorite hat, a straw chapeau that was adorned simply with black velvet ribbons and pink roses.

Raoul was waiting, however, and she knew he wanted her to wear his gift and that he would be very put out if she didn't.

"Thank you, Raoul," she said as she turned to her mirror. She took off her straw hat and then replaced it with the new bonnet.

As Raoul stepped behind her, she felt the weight of his hands come down on her shoulders. He massaged them warmly for several moments. "The way you look in it is thanks enough," he murmured close to her ear. She caught a glimpse of his eyes in the mirror and the unexpected heat smoldering in them took her by surprise.

"So much better than that old straw thing you have been wearing," she heard him say as he straightened.

That 'straw thing' had been a gift from her father, one that she cherished.

"Come, Christine. The carriage is waiting."

The moment they stepped outside her dressing room, she was caught unaware as Raoul's arm went around her waist and he drew her suddenly and possessively to his side.

"You might kiss me, Christine, if you want to thank me properly for the gift," he said huskily as he looked down at her.

Seeing no way out of it, she stood on her toes and was about to give him a quick kiss on the cheek. But he turned her in his arms, grasped her chin adroitly and held her face still while he kissed her full on the mouth. When he drew back, he merely laughed at the protest darkening her eyes.

"We're engaged, Christine. It's perfectly acceptable to be more affectionate towards each other. It's what's expected."

Perhaps it was expected, but neither of them was aware of the eyes that were watching from the shadows. Raoul opened his mouth to say something else, but instead he turned with a frown when Lisette approached Christine.

"Christine, there is something you should see."

An impatient scowl now replaced the frown on Raoul's face. "Whatever it is can wait," he told Christine as he drew on his gloves. "Let's be on our way."

"It won't take long," Christine said, curious now as Lisette led them along the hallway leading to the auditorium.

"What the devil is this?" Raoul demanded, stopping short when he saw the stage.

Christine was also looking at the stage, and the scenery she had never seen before. A beautiful cottage had been vibrantly and realistically painted. There was a white picket fence with rows of flowers bordering it. She stared in turn at the woods, the winding country lane and the sea painted in the distance. It was artistically brilliant. It was nothing short of breathtaking.

"*C'est magnifique, non?*" Lisette asked her.

Raoul turned to Christine and demanded to know, "What is this?"

"I don't know," Christine replied, but there was a softness in her tone and a wonder in her gaze as she turned to look back at the stage. "It looks like- my old home. Where I used to live with Papa."

"Yes, I can see that," Raoul said tightly. "You have never seen this scenery before?" he wanted to know.

Christine shook her head.

Raoul set off to make enquiries right away. He came back a few minutes later. "How is it possible that someone could have arranged something so elaborate and no one knows who is responsible? Doesn't anyone know what goes on in this Opera House?"

"It must have been done at night," one of the stage hands told him.

By now, a small crowd had gathered around the stage and they were all talking about the breathtakingly beautiful scene.

"Who would have access to the place at night?" Raoul wanted to know. "It must have taken an entire crew hours to create this and put it all in place."

But no one could tell him anything.

"Christine, this has been left for you," one of the dancers said excitedly as she handed Christine a note.

All eyes turned expectantly to Christine.

"For me?"

"Yes. With this."

The dancer also handed Christine a perfect red rose tied with a scarlet ribbon. Christine's name was boldly scrawled in black letters on the envelope. Before she could even open the note, Raoul snatched it out of her hand and tore it open.

"It says here that it is a wedding present," he said grimly. His lips thinned as he looked at the rose in Christine's hand. "The note is unsigned. Someone has gone to a lot of trouble to play games with us," he went on as he crushed the note in his gloved fist.

"Why do you say that?" someone asked.

"Because the same person- " He stopped himself just in time and silently answered his own question. Because the same person who was leaving the roses was obviously responsible for the scenery.

Raoul was fuming and he wanted answers. Of course, Christine couldn't give him any answers. And neither could anyone else.

"What do you want me to say?" Christine asked in the face of his anger. "I knew nothing about this."

"One thing we *can* do is to compare *this* handwriting to the notes that the Phantom left."

"The Phantom?" someone gasped.

That started everyone talking and conjecturing.

"You mean the Phantom is behind this?" someone asked.

"Of course it had to be the ghost."

"Who else could have done something like this?"

"What is he trying to tell us?" someone else asked.

"But you said there was no ghost," one of the stagehands reminded Raoul.

Raoul saw right away that referring to the Phantom had been a mistake. There was no taking it back, however. He must be more careful about what he said in the future. As it was now, the rumors would be even more difficult to control.

"Who would know what your home looked like?" he asked as he turned towards Christine. "Who have you spoken to about this?"

Of course Christine already knew the answer to that. But she could hardly tell Raoul about her teacher. She had already realized that he was the only one it could have been, the only one to whom she had described her home in detail.

She shook her head and shrugged. A silent lie was a little easier than an outright one.

"Make no mistake, I shall get to the bottom of this," Raoul vowed darkly. "There is no doubt now, Christine, that some madman has singled you out."

"So it *was* him then?" Christine asked later that evening. "My teacher?"

Madame Giry was wearing a dove grey dress with black jet buttons and a black crocheted collar that was offset by a cameo at her throat. Her skirts rustled as she went to close her office door. Christine had waited all day to be alone with the woman, who turned, but hesitated before giving her answer, "Yes, Christine, it was him."

"He must have worked a long time to finish it," Christine said with a frown as she thought it through. "Yet no one saw him. How is that possible?"

"He prefers to work at night when no one is around to disturb him," Madame Giry told her.

"He is here at night?"

"*Oui*, sometimes."

"I had told him that I missed my old home," Christine went on, half to herself. "He must have gotten the idea then." She paused for a moment. "It was a very thoughtful thing for him to do."

"Yes," Madame Giry agreed. "It was very thoughtful. As the note said, it was a wedding gift."

Christine was silent as she paced across the room. She stopped and whirled around, facing Madame Giry again. "I have so many questions and you're the only one I can go to for answers."

"I shall tell you what I can."

"How is it that he has so much access to the Opera House that he can come and go even at night?"

"He works as- a consultant to me on occasion," Madame Giry said. "He has a genius for turning fantasy into reality on the stage. The lavish productions, the breathtaking scenery, the special effects- he is behind them all. Nothing would be possible without him. You already know that he lived in Persia for a time. While he was there, he learned a great deal about magic and theatrics, among other things. He brought his knowledge back here to the Opera House."

"I have never met him except from behind a curtain. But you have seen him face to face?"

Madame Giry nodded.

"You say he works here at night. How is it then that I have never seen him?" Christine did not wait for an answer. "Is he here often?"

Madame Giry chose her words carefully. "He is here when he is in the mood for such things. He is also a brilliant composer, as you already know, and a musician with rare talent. I allow him his-whims because the truth is that the theater could not run as it does without him."

"Then the owners know of him?"

"Yes, they know he's here."

"And he works as a creative adviser to you?" Christine asked.

"He advises me on many things concerning the Opera House."

"Do you think he will ever trust *me* enough to let me see his face?"

"I cannot answer for him."

"Since I have spent a great deal of time with him myself, I can understand your loyalty to him, Madame Giry. That's why I didn't tell Raoul that I knew who was behind it."

Christine's long lashes swept up and then she regarded Madame Giry with a narrowed gaze. "And he has been sending me the roses as well?"

"He sends them."

"He must send them to encourage me since they're the only ones I receive. In the beginning, I had wondered if Raoul was secretly sending them."

Madame Giry made a scoffing sound. It was something very unusual for her, and she seemed on the verge of saying something else, but she kept her silence.

"Then he *does* watch my performances."

"Every one of them," Madame Giry replied.

"Did I get the part because of him?" was Christine's next question.

"He did suggest that you would be perfect for the role. But it is not such an unusual request for a patron."

"He is like Raoul, then? A sponsor of the Opera House?" Christine asked one more question. "Have I, perhaps, already met him?"

She was thinking about everyone she knew who worked at the theater. Was it possible he could be working at the Opera House right under her nose and she didn't realize it?

"You have never seen his face, Christine," Madame Giry answered her thoughts. "Please don't burden yourself with trying to guess who he might be. I only ask that you continue to respect his privacy. He has his reasons."

"Of course I will do that. You know him well then?"

"I have known him for a very long time, *oui*."

"Can you tell me where is he from? Originally. His accent is one that I cannot place."

"He was born in France, but he left a long time ago and travelled extensively for many years. The accent is a result of all the places he has lived in."

"What does he look like? Surely, after I have revealed myself to him from the beginning, you can tell me *something*."

Madame Giry's gray-clad shoulders lifted and then fell again as she sighed deeply. After a prolonged silence, she said, "Were you to look upon his profile, you would see an exceedingly handsome man."

Christine had not expected her to be so candid, and now she said, soft-voiced, "I knew it must be so." But now that she had learned that much, there was so much more she wanted to know. "And his eyes? What color are they?"

"They are the deep blue of summer storm clouds, dark but always changing."

"And what color is his hair?"

"As black as midnight."

"Yes," Christine murmured to herself. "I had already known that."

It was like putting the pieces of a puzzle into place. How much easier it was becoming to put a picture together and fit a face to the voice.

"And how does he really feel about me quitting the lessons?" Christine asked.

"Has he not spoken to you about this already?"

"We talk about many things. But I sense that sometimes he holds back, that he does not always tell me his true feelings."

"He is disappointed naturally. He saw great promise in you. But he respects your decision to end the lessons. He wants what is best for you. That is all he has ever wanted for you."

Madame Giry looked more closely at her. "You seem quite troubled about this, Christine."

"Of course I am troubled. We had come so far- " Christine's voice trailed off and she looked more intently at the other woman. "And you cannot tell me what his deep, dark secret is? The one that makes him feel he must hide himself from the world? And from me?"

"He would have to be the one to tell you more if he chose to do so. When you came to me, I thought that the lessons would benefit you both. I hope this hasn't caused trouble between you and the Viscount."

"Everything causes trouble with Raoul," Christine said under her breath. "I do not regret the lessons. I will never regret them. And I am glad that you gave your permission for they have meant a great deal to me and I will always be profoundly grateful for them. But I wish . . . I wish . . . "

She bit back whatever she had been about to say. Madame Giry had given her a lot to think about and she knew a great deal more than she had known before. Why then, did it seem like her curiosity burned brighter than ever?

Chapter 8

"The performers are expressing their apprehension about performing in a production that features so many ghosts in it. They are questioning how they will know a real ghost from a fake one."

"Tell them- " the man in black began. His dark mood was almost tangible tonight. Although he had stopped his restless pacing before the window, he was still staring out into the moonless darkness. He clamped his jaw shut and a muscle tensed in his cheek as he turned his profile towards her. Without looking at her, he said, "Tell them that no one has been hurt on stage yet. Tell them to remember that."

"I'll tell them," Madame Giry said to his back. "But it doesn't help that the Viscount seems intent on keeping things stirred up."

"The Viscount may well stir up more than he bargained for," she heard.

"Your- The wedding gift has vexed him further. He is very possessive where Christine is concerned."

The man at the window clasped his hands behind his back. He did not say that his black mood was due in a large part to seeing the Viscount's increasingly possessive attitude toward Christine.

"Possessive," he repeated curtly. "That is, perhaps, too mild a word, Madame. If he cared about her, he would not be going behind her back to stop her from doing what she loves doing. I overlooked it when they agreed to let him search the Opera House. But they go too far if they think they will indulge him in his latest demands.

"Indeed, the ignorance of those two fools is astonishing," he went on in increasing bad temper. "That they would even consider going along with the Viscount's scheming proves their own dishonesty. They have not even the most rudimentary grasp of what the opera is all about if they would contemplate getting rid of Christine. And they delude themselves if they think that Carlotta's bleating on the stage is necessary to the success of this theater. That is all the proof we need that they will run this opera house into the ground. They will make a shambles of this theater if I let them.

"And I shall assume from the Viscount's not-so-veiled extortion that he will go to great lengths to get Christine out of this theater as soon as he can," he continued. "As for those two witless buffoons who fancy themselves purveyors of the arts, their ignorance is only surpassed by their greed. And greed, Madame, is the surest path to a man's downfall."

His cobalt eyes narrowed thoughtfully and there was a certain recklessness in his gaze when he looked up and said quietly, ominously, "But something must be done."

"What are you thinking?"

"Only that a man should cross a bridge when he reaches it," he said vaguely, but there was a dark gleam in his eyes that did not put her mind at ease. "As for the pretty Viscount, I believe it is time to see just how much wolf is hiding under all that fashionable fleece."

He smiled at her tensed expression. "I assure you, it is not my intention to cause you even the slightest anxiety. But we both know that he plays a deeper game than anyone realizes. Just how deep remains to be seen. I have my suspicions. Just as you have your own. And if those suspicions should prove to be true, it will change things."

She was afraid to ask. "In what way?"

He did not answer her question directly. Instead, he said, "As for his personal campaign against the Phantom of the Opera, remember that I was not the one who fired the first volley. But he has done so blindly," he murmured with a calculating smile, looking as ruthless as any pirate who was sizing up a ship for plunder. His eyes, when he looked at Madame Giry, glowed with the boldness of a brigand's shrewd appraisal, and that was never a good sign.

"He may well have started a war that will prove to be more than he can handle. If the Viscount wants a memorable evening to be had in box five, then memorable it shall be. And we will see, Madame, who those two fools will listen to."

124

He stood for a moment longer looking out into the darkness. Then he turned and picked up a glass of brandy that was setting on the desk. Saying no word, he held the glass out to Madame Giry in a toast and downed the remainder of the brandy in one swallow.

"However did you manage the mist?" Anton Charlebois asked in a tone of half-bored amusement.

The man seated across from him answered with a question of his own. "Whatever are you talking about?"

"The ghost was said to have disappeared in a mist," Anton reminded him.

"Oh, that." Eitan Beauvoir, cousin to the de Chagnys, first finished chewing the bite of delicate raspberry pastry he had just put into his mouth, then he dabbed at his lips with a monogrammed napkin. "There was no mist. I can only assume that if you frighten someone enough, they will believe anything. I merely stepped behind a curtain to do my vanishing act. And I think that singer was already well sodden with champagne when he saw me. I dare say he would have believed anything at that point."

"But was it really necessary to reach for the serving woman?" Anton asked as he sprawled indolently in his chair and carefully surveyed the selection of delectable pastries in front of him before choosing one.

"I thought she was going to fall down the stairs," Eitan defended himself. "I wanted to scare the woman, not murder her."

There were three men seated around the table on the east balcony of the de Chagny mansion. The weather was mild and they were enjoying an early brunch as they talked amongst themselves in the strictest confidence. Even the servants had been sent away.

"Unfortunate that your man nearly bludgeoned the tailor to death," Anton said as he lifted his glass of bourbon to his mouth.

"That wasn't supposed to happen," Eitan told the other man. "He got lost, saw that someone was coming and panicked. I gave him orders to frighten a few people, not bash someone's head in. But what can you expect except incompetence from that type? Which only proves what I always say, that if you want something done right, you have to do it yourself. Well, it doesn't do any good to cry over spilt milk, does it? There was no lasting harm done. And as for that, it was hardly *my* fault. Raoul told me to get the biggest, ugliest brute of a man I could find for the job, which I did. Unfortunately the man turned out to be more of a brute than I had realized."

"I hope you at least paid him well enough to ensure his silence," Anton said as he swirled the amber liquid in his glass.

"Naturellement," Eitan answered him.

Actually, it was Raoul who had paid a pretty penny to keep the man quiet.

"I hope that we haven't gone through a lot of trouble for a bootless errand," Eitan said.

Anton Charlebois scoffed. "That's not likely. Have you ever seen him admit defeat?" They both looked at Raoul, who was sitting silently across the table from them. "I'm sure he already has something else in mind."

"Of course he does," Eitan said. "He is a de Chagny. He will move heaven and hell to get what he wants."

A silent, brooding Raoul acknowledged that thought with a dark, sidelong glance. His auburn hair was gleaming with red highlights in the early sunlight. The white linen at his throat was impeccable. He leaned back in his chair and blew a slow stream of tobacco smoke into the air, then took another deep drink of his own bourbon, something he was indulging in more and more of late.

His cousin Eitan was right. He would stop at nothing to get what he wanted, and it did not matter to him in the least what methods he took to achieve his goals. Indeed, to the other men who had known him all of their lives, Raoul de Chagny had always had a ruthlessly cold way of thinking when it came to business, and as things were turning out, that seemed to apply to matters of the heart as well.

"She's ravishing, Raoul," Anton remarked, closely watching the expression on the other man's face. "Well worth whatever lengths you have to go to. As I always say, however, to be shackled to a woman for life is bad enough, but to be shackled to a beautiful woman is even worse. Many a man has been blinded by a woman's beauty until he is stumbling around like a blithering, mindless idiot."

Raoul was reluctantly beginning to agree with that sentiment. His foul mood was nothing out of the ordinary lately. Not only his peace of mind, but his confidence was being slowly ripped to ragged shreds, one infinitesimal piece at a time. Given time, Christine *would* turn him into a driveling fool. *If* he wasn't careful. But he was not going to let that happen.

"She'll be singing until the day of their wedding at this rate," he heard Eitan say.

"Yes, it does seem she has taken the bit by the teeth," Anton said.

"Quite," Eitan agreed thoughtfully as he slowly nodded his head in agreement. "A slur on her reputation will be a slur on him. A woman who is going to bear the de Chagny name needs to be above reproach."

Above reproach. That was a sore spot with Raoul. First, there had been the business of the roses, and then finding out that she had been being recommended for a part by a ghost. There was also the matter of the new furnishings for her room. And now this damnable wedding gift was the final straw. A wedding gift, he scoffed silently. Who would go to such trouble? It was altogether too much. It made him even more determined than ever to put a stop to her singing.

His gaze hardened as he stared out over the gardens. Perhaps it was an open taunt. A challenge. And though he had never come out and said it out loud, there was something else preying on his mind. He couldn't help but wonder if Christine was really as innocent as she pretended to be.

Eitan was right. If there was even a hint of scandal, it could very well bring a stain to the de Chagny name. He didn't understand why Christine should be so stubbornly insistent about performing on the stage and about continuing to live in the Opera House. Why couldn't she just quietly take her place at his side and leave all that unnecessary business about a career behind her? Any other woman would jump at the chance to do so.

He had done what he had done to teach her a lesson, to frighten her, to show how vulnerable she was and he still felt perfectly justified in his actions. But maybe it was time he changed his tactics. Maybe it was time to try a more direct approach. Maybe a heavier hand was needed.

"Raoul will rein her in, surely," he heard Eitan say.

"He does hold some very formidable reins after all," Anton smirked. "He has his title in one hand and his fortune in the other. She surely won't turn her back on either one of those."

Raoul poured himself another healthy dose of bourbon. With a dark glance at the other two men, he said ominously, "I can assure you, I have no intention of letting her run wild. This so-called Phantom of the Opera has been thwarting my every effort to get her out of the Opera House. The damned rogue has become a thorn in my side. But that's not going to last."

"If he is not a ghost, then what is he?" a frowning Eitan asked.

"A damned nuisance," Raoul growled. "Which is why we must take steps to flush him out."

"Hmm," Anton remarked as he thought it over. "Just like any fox."

"What do you have in mind?" Eitan asked. "Do you want me to play the ghost again?"

Raoul blew a thick stream of cigar smoke into the morning air. "What I want is for you to rent out box five."

Raoul had already made his request of the owners, but so far the box remained empty. It seemed no one wanted to openly challenge the ghost.

"I say, Raoul. Are you serious?"

"Deadly serious. If this damned whoreson wants to test me, he shall find that he is up against a more formidable enemy than he had bargained for."

"What if this ghost decides to put in an appearance of his own?"

Raoul shrugged under his fine linen shirt. "That is exactly what I am counting on. Just don't indulge overly much that night and keep your wits about you. We will be waiting for him. And then I shall best him at his own game."

"Of course you will. *You* are de Chagny!" Eitan said heartily.

Rallying to the occasion, the three poured another round of drinks and toasted each other. "Gentlemen, here's to a most entertaining evening."

"In box five."

"Yes, in box five."

Marguerite Giry opened her bedroom window and breathed deeply of the heavy, rain-scented air. The storm that had raged earlier was still grumbling softly in the distance, well beyond Paris, but a stillness as deep and as unfathomable as the starless sky had settled, a stillness one could almost feel.

She sat down at her dressing table and unfastened the pins from her hair. Then she began to undo the heavy braid that she kept wound in a knot at the back of her head. The loosened hair fell about her shoulders and she shook it out. She stared into her mirror at the streaks of grey that stood out among the darker strands. Then she leaned forward and looked more closely at her reflection, critically assessing the small lines that had begun to appear over the years. She turned her face to one side and then the other. With the back of her hand held to the underside of her jaw, she critically tested the firmness there. Had so much time passed?

Her eyes grew distant as the memories came. She was pulled back to that night when she had seen Erik for the first time. Even after all these years, she had kept his secret. Even her husband, when he had been alive, had not known about him.

The images were still as strong now as when she had found him beaten and near death, huddled in the darkness with the cold rain beating down on him. She, too, had looked with horror upon his ravaged face, not knowing that the disfigurement had been with him since birth. Lost inside himself, his will for survival had been almost extinguished until there was only a tiny flame flickering. She had coaxed that fragile flame into life and gradually learned his whole story. Their friendship had grown and he had stayed with her, having nowhere else to go. Until the day came when he was strong enough to leave her, like a fledgling from a nest. Whether he had been running away or trying to find something that was missing from his life, she didn't know. Perhaps it had been a little of both.

She only knew that somehow he had found the strength to rise out of the misery that had been his dark existence. Wounded by the very world that should have protected him, his scarred soul almost destroyed, somehow he had found the courage to go out and seek something better. And then, after years had passed, when she thought she would never see him again, he had come back. With a hard veneer of cynicism around him. But she could hardly blame him for that. Maybe it had been necessary for his survival.

Music had been part of his healing all along. Maybe that's why he had been drawn back to the Opera House. He applied his talents and his intellect to the theater. He was, among other things, a mathematical genius. The mechanisms and automations he devised were truly a marvel and did much to heighten the audience's experiences. He had made the theater a place of wonder where anything was possible.

And now that he had found love, could she take that away from him? Did he not deserve, for once, something good in his life? Even if he loved from afar?

She sighed deeply. She saw trouble ahead of them and she, herself, had set things in motion the moment she had given her consent to Christine. But how could she have denied him his request? Being alone was no way for a man to exist. He had merely asked for what others took for granted their whole lives.

And while she wanted to believe that he had gotten beyond his past, the truth remained that the past overshadowed the present. He still carried emotional scars and what he referred to as his curse with him wherever he went. And there was no way to change any of it.

Above all, she did not want his heart to be broken, knowing full well it was not in her power to stop that from happening. Perhaps it was inevitable. She only knew that his passions ran deep and that his love for Christine was something rare. She also knew he had never intended to act upon those passions, but should something fan the flames . . .

. . . would he suffer more than he had ever suffered before?

Clasping her hands together, she did all that she could do. She prayed for him. And for Christine. She prayed for all of them.

Chapter 9

"What else can go wrong?"

Pressing a hand to her eyes as if she could not bear to look, Lisette eventually did take her hand away, only to gasp, "She's- How could she have forgotten the lyrics again? She's making them up as she goes along."

Lisette's eyes grew even wider as she stared at the stage. "What is she doing now? She was supposed to *die*! How is Gaspar supposed to mourn the loss of a wife who is still standing on her feet?"

"He's not going to have to kill her again, is he?" one of the stage hands asked as he peered over Lisette's shoulder.

All of the onlookers backstage wondered if, perhaps, Gaspar would have to strangle Carlotta all over again. And it did look like he might just do that, but there was another more pressing problem that rendered them all momentarily speechless and froze Gaspar's hands in midair.

The bodice of Carlotta's dress had begun to gape open. To a very noticeable, very perilous degree. In fact, the crimson material was separating like a slow parting of the Red Sea even as they watched. Carlotta was close to giving the audience a show they would never forget.

Gaspar, who was closest to her, had obviously noticed. After a moment of frozen indecision, he began to distract the audience as best he could by singing robustly. What was emotional performance and what was outright panic on his part, it was hard to say.

"What do we do?" the stage hand asked without taking his eyes off of what was happening on the stage.

"I don't know," Lisette murmured, unable to take her eyes off of the impending disaster, either. "She doesn't dare sing. If she takes another deep breath- "

It was very clear what would happen if Carlotta drew another breath.

"What is Gaspar doing now?"

"He's trying to maneuver himself in front of Carlotta."

"That won't work. He can't block her from all directions. And he can't keep singing with his back to the audience."

"Mon Dieu," the wide-eyed stage hand whispered. "I think Carlotta *is* getting ready to sing."

There were several horrified gasps as another hook came loose from Carlotta's dress. Everyone stood frozen in place as the large black hook slid down her crimson gown, all the way to the floor, and eventually skittered across the stage.

Carlotta didn't sing. She couldn't. Without moving her head even the slightest bit, Carlotta's eyes glanced downward. It was a monumental display of restraint on her part. She had no way of knowing just how exposed she was.

Ping!

Yet another hook had come loose. Carlotta's gown gaped even wider until her generous bosoms were barely restrained. She had no separate corset on. But it was her own fault. She had insisted that her corset be part of the costume.

The conductor's eyes mirrored his own horror as he glanced over his shoulder. Apparently not knowing what else to do, he, waved his baton and the music played on. Carlotta stood there like a statue, her arms half raised at her sides. Obviously she was afraid to move a muscle. The rest of the cast standing with her on stage watched with a dread fascination, not knowing what was going to happen next.

Henri Millard, who was partially hidden from the audience by the scenery, was the only one who had the presence of mind to actually take some action. He dropped down to his hands and knees. Still hidden from the audience, he crawled over to a table and snatched one of the fringed coverings off the prop and made his way over to Carlotta. He handed her the cloth which she promptly snatched out of his hand and flung around her shoulders with a flourish as if it had been rehearsed that way and went on singing.

The misadventure might have ended there, but a second cloth that was covering the table, and Henri, had fallen to the floor. There was Henri on his hands and knees crawling slowly across the stage. When he realized that the cloth had dropped, he stopped and turned his face to see the audience looking back at him.

What else could he do? He looked straight ahead and continued to crawl back the way he had come.

There was a spattering of laughter from the audience, but the show went on. Christine, in the next scene, was at her best and everything went smoothly after that. At least on stage. In box five it was something else entirely.

Raoul, too, had found the mishaps on stage amusing, if not provocative. As he settled back in his upholstered seat in the de Chagny's private box, he smirked in satisfaction at the thought that box five, which was directly across the theater from him, was not going to be empty tonight. When the owners had declared that they could find no one who was willing to occupy it, he had promptly put his own plans in place. Let this supposed ghost realize that he was dealing with a de Chagny now, not the bumbling, incompetent owners of the theater, he said to himself in the darkness.

While he had been temporarily distracted by the drama with Carlotta's costume, it was not until near the end of the third act that he rose up out of his seat and moved close to the balcony to stare intently across the theater. Without waiting to see exactly what was happening, he quickly left his private box and began to make his way to the other side of the theater.

In the hallway outside of box five he encountered a very agitated group of people. Anton Charlebois and his cousin, Eitan Beauvoir, were among them.

"I don't care . . . " a near-hysterical woman with terrified eyes blubbered. "I'm not going back in there."

"Just take us out of here, Anton," a second woman pleaded.

Raoul demanded to know, "What in the blazes happened in there?"

"Damned if I know," Eitan answered him.

"It was the ghost!" the first woman, who was still visibly shaken by whatever had happened inside box five, answered the Viscount's question.

The other woman was so upset she looked like she was about to burst into tears. Anton put his arm around her shoulders and tried to calm her down.

A few theater workers had come to see what all the commotion was about. One of them promptly crossed himself and stared fearfully at the door to box five when he heard that the ghost had been behind the disturbance. He clearly did not want to go inside.

Eitan drew Raoul aside. "What a disaster this night has proven to be," Eitan said in a lowered voice. "I thought you said there was no ghost."

"There *is* no ghost," Raoul asserted. "What exactly did you see?"

"I can't be sure. It was dark as Hades in there. Simone said she felt someone breathing on her. Drusilla said she felt cold air at first and then something lifting her hair."

Eitan hesitated a moment before he went on. "I thought I saw a death's head for a moment in the folds of the curtains. But to tell you the truth, I'm not sure my eyes weren't playing tricks on me. It was so dark that I could have imagined the whole thing."

Anton joined them and he began to tell Raoul his version of the story. "Simone said she heard the ghost say 'leave'. Drusilla thought he had said 'grieve', which made her think death was imminent for someone in the box. But the laughter that came out of nowhere was the worst of it. After that, none of us could get out of there fast enough. In fact, I tripped over something and hit my head." He gingerly rubbed his head and winced when he felt a large, tender bump already forming there. "I think it was Drusilla's skirt that I got tangled up in, but I can't be sure."

"Maybe you're right, Raoul, and it is only a man," Eitan said. "But that laughter made even my blood run cold. I'm not afraid to tell you that I'm glad I'm out of there. I've had enough of this ghost business for one evening."

"Not yet, you haven't," Raoul said grimly. "Not until that box is searched from top to bottom."

"In the dark?" Eitan questioned his cousin.

"Of course in the dark. We can't disrupt the entire theater with search lights. Not until the last act is over."

Eitan glanced over at the two frightened women. "What do we do about them? We shall have to spend half the night comforting them." He brightened suddenly as it occurred to him that the night might not be so disastrous after all.

Carlotta had been leisurely enjoying her breakfast when the note was delivered to her. The seal was all-too-familiar, so like a seething Charybdis, she slowly pried the parchment loose from the seal of thick, blood-red wax. She unfolded the letter, her eyes narrowing dangerously as they skimmed back and forth rapidly across the words. She was so incensed when she finished that she had to read the words all over again. And then she gritted a very unladylike oath from behind clenched teeth as she crumbled the paper into a ball and flung it away from her.

The Opera House would be preparing for a new opera, the note informed her, one written by the Phantom of the Opera himself. Christine would be playing the lead. The letter warned Carlotta that she would not be a part of the new production unless she accepted a lesser role. She was also warned against making any trouble for the other performers. The note was signed OG. The Opera Ghost.

Carlotta got up from her chair, leaving the rest of her breakfast uneaten as she stalked angrily across her dressing room. She placed both hands on her hips as she muttered, "Thees ees an outrage. He dares to threaten *me*? *Again*?" she fumed as her eyes narrowed to angry slits. "*I* am the star of thees Opera House." And then her thoughts shifted. "That conniving leetle weetch. She won't get away weeth thees. Thees must be her doing."

She wasn't sure who she was angrier with. Christine or that insolent ghost.

Warning or no warning, she needed to vent her fury on someone. Christine was the first one that came to mind and Carlotta had no intention of being stopped in pursuit of the matter.

When she jerked her dressing room door open, however, it was Monsieur Peverell who had the misfortune to be passing by. Her husky voice stopped the man dead in his tracks. He turned stiffly around to face Carlotta, then shrank back a little as he saw the fury blazing in her eyes. He continued to watch her with a kind of dread fascination, much like a tiny mouse who is frozen with fear before a cat who is ready to pounce.

"I thought you said you would take care of thees Phantom." She jerked her head towards the open doorway. "Eenside." With her hands still propped on her hips, she led the way into her dressing room and wasted no time in releasing all her venom on him.

"Wh- What has happened?" Monsieur Peverell stammered when she paused to take a breath. Anyone paying close attention, however, might have noticed that he looked a little sheepish as if he already knew exactly what was wrong.

Carlotta pointed. "There."

Androcles had the ball of crumpled paper between his front paws. He was shaking it furiously and tearing it to pieces with his tiny teeth.

"The dog?" Monsieur Peverell asked, completely at a loss.

"No, not the dog," Carlotta said impatiently. "The paper. Read eet."

Androcles wasn't going to let the man anywhere near the paper so Carlotta picked the shredded pieces up and handed them to him. Androcles who wanted the paper back, growled and nipped at the man's ankles a few times until Carlotta picked the dog up as well.

The paper was wet with dog saliva and punctured with teeth marks, but Monsieur Peverell gingerly unfolded it and held the separate pieces together. As he read the blurred words, the color receded from his face, leaving him more than a little pale. He looked up, nonplussed in the face of Carlotta's wrath. So she did know.

Her dark, flashing eyes roved over the man contemptuously.

"What are you going to do about thees?" Carlotta demanded. She didn't give him any time to reply. "And don't tell me you weell have the matter looked eento. That ees what you told me before."

Androcles, who had a piece of red wax hanging from one side of his mustache, gave a low growl and yipped once as if he, too, wanted answers.

Monsieur Peverell tried diplomacy, but Carlotta would have none of it. "You fools. You have let thees lunateec run thees theater and deceive you for far too long weeth hees treecks."

Carlotta had only begun to vent her fury and she launched into a more heated tirade, one that made everyone else wisely avoid any proximity to her dressing room for the next hour or so. Unfortunately for Monsieur Peverell, he had not been able to escape quite so easily.

Carlotta wasn't the only one who had received a note. The Viscount, who was sprawled on the davenport in the library of the de Chagny mansion, cast a baleful glance toward the letter that had arrived just that morning. He felt like he had been outfoxed. Cuckolded. Like the bastard had had the last laugh. Literally.

After a thorough search, nothing had been found in box five. No one had been hiding there. No one had come out. No one had been seen going over the balcony. At first he had thought that it was possible that Eitan and the others occupying the box had imbibed too much despite his explicit instructions that they keep their wits about them and refrain from doing so. He had thought that maybe in the darkness their imaginations had run away with them. But all of them? At the same time? Of course by the next morning, the details of the incident in box five had made the rounds of the theater even more than the mishaps on stage. And they had been embellished. Outrageously. Under Raoul's close supervision, the box was again searched by daylight. Absolutely nothing was found that would reasonably explain the presence of a ghost, or what people had thought was a ghost.

So he sat there rigid and motionless in the dark, and slightly disheveled, as his ire seethed through him like a slow poison. Unfortunately, people believed more firmly in a ghost now than ever. He had set out to outwit the bastard once and for all. Instead, he had played right into his hands. Again, the tables had been turned on him and the man had very thoroughly, very neatly trumped him.

He was not used to losing, so the more he brooded over the matter, the more determined he became to destroy the man who had become his nemesis. As his gaze shifted, his eyes narrowed dangerously with the flow of his thoughts. How dare the bastard make threats against him. How dare he have a letter delivered directly to his home. The letter had advised him to restrain himself in the future when it came to matters concerning the Opera House, and that he would be making a mistake by assuming that his, the ghost's that is, patience was without end.

The Viscount stared hard at the glass in his hand. The unmitigated gall of the man rankled deeply. The arrogant bastard had stated in the letter that he was aware of everything that went on in the Opera House and then enigmatically added that what began in darkness must eventually be exposed in the light. Had that been some kind of deeper, more insidious threat? Had this so-called ghost been hinting that he knew something he shouldn't know?

"He must have an immense ego if he thinks the Opera House is his own private theater where he can do as he pleases and everyone will cater to his demands," he muttered darkly to himself.

More disturbing was the thought that if the bastard could come and go at his will without being seen by an entire theater of people, he could be anywhere, at any time. Christine was living under the very same roof, which made her vulnerable. He needed to put an end to that. And it couldn't be soon enough. The damned roses would stop as well.

His sullen gaze was fixed upon the rising moon outside the library window as he nursed his glass of bourbon. His lips were set in bitter, vengeful lines as he was forced to acknowledge that he was dealing with a far more clever and cunning adversary than he had first believed.

As the clock on the mantle ticked loudly in the silence, he thought about Christine's behavior lately. She still didn't seem frightened in the least at the prospect of some lunatic prowling around in the shadows of the Opera House. She only seemed to have a kind of wondering curiosity that she took no pains to hide. And that both perplexed and annoyed him. He found her lack of fear strange. He kept seeing her after her performance when she heard about what had happened in box five. What she had been thinking he was not certain, but it seemed to him that her curiosity far outweighed any fear she might have felt, if, in fact, she felt any fear at all, and that made no sense to him. Or it made a kind of sense that he did not want to face.

His scowl deepened as he ran a hand across his unshaven face. To say that Christine was as different from the other women in his life as night was from day was an understatement. For one thing, in

138

all the time he had known her, she had shown no inclination to share his bed. He had waited longer for her than he had waited for any other woman. In some perverse way, this phantom business seemed to be making her even more desirable to him. It was also making his patience wear thin. He wanted to possess her now more than he had ever wanted to possess any woman. In fact it was becoming almost an obsession with him. He wanted to claim her as his and he knew that sleeping with her would go a long way towards accomplishing that goal. And yet he knew he must proceed cautiously with Christine. She had already shown that she would not be coerced into sharing his bed by the usual methods. Lord knew, he had tried.

So it rankled that someone, another man, was sending her flowers, and doing things for her that no man would do for a woman unless he had a romantic interest in her, unless somewhere down the road he expected something in return. Whoever this Phantom really was, he had a great deal of influence in the Opera House. He had recommended her for her singing role. He had personally arranged for her rooms to be newly furnished. And he had gone to great lengths to give her a lavish wedding gift, which, of course, was nothing more than an outright mockery. Obviously, the man was infatuated with her. And quite honestly, Raoul couldn't help but wonder if she was as oblivious to the fact as she pretended to be. True, she didn't know about everything, but if she was playing him for a fool, he intended to find out.

He cursed profanely under his breath, then looked up as Philippe appeared in the open doorway

"It's nearly morning," Philippe said as he stepped into the library.

"Yes, it is," Raoul acknowledged gruffly.

"Have you been drinking all night?"

Raoul's lip curled in a sneer as he gave a short, humorless laugh under his breath. "Very nearly."

"I take it Christine is responsible for your dark mood. Is she still being unreasonable?" Philippe asked.

"Damnably."

"You're right to be concerned. She is much more susceptible to gossip while she is performing at the Opera House. Which makes the de Chagny name more susceptible," Philippe reminded him quietly.

It was an unnecessary reminder, Raoul thought irritably. Did he think he didn't already know that?

"I heard about what happened at the theater last night," Philippe said as he dropped down into one of the velvet-cushioned, wing-backed chairs.

"You don't know the half of it."

"Perhaps it is time to get her out of there."

Raoul's sigh had a fair amount of impatience in it. He had been trying to do that all along. So far nothing had worked. He hated that his brother felt that he had to advise him on the matter.

"That is what I intend," he vowed under his breath before he drained the last of the bourbon in his glass.

"What will you do?" Philippe asked.

"Whatever it takes," Raoul said ominously.

Philippe waited for him to go on.

"The sly bastard might amuse himself with his jests, but I will do whatever it takes to unmask him once and for all and expose him for the fraud that he is. Whatever it takes."

Chapter 10

The reason for the near disaster with Carlotta's costume was immediately obvious. Because of his injury, Remi had fallen behind with the costumes, so at the last minute, Madame Vernay had hired two of the dancers to help him catch up. The two girls had tried their best and they had worked long hours, but they were not seamstresses by any means and their sewing skills had proven to be severely lacking, hence the loose hooks, hooks that, on Carlotta, had been strained to their utmost capacity.

This morning, there was a more pressing issue on Raoul de Chagny's mind than costumes, however. Word had gotten out that the Opera House would be doing a production composed by the Phantom of the Opera himself, as ludicrous as that sounded. He had gone to speak to Messieurs Vaussard and Peverell in person about the matter and found, to his astonishment and his chagrin, that the rumor was based on fact.

He turned in frowning amazement at the confession, but only after he'd had to practically threaten it out of the two men.

"Surely you realize that going along with him will only embolden him to make more demands," he said as he confronted both men.

Monsieur Vaussard was the first to speak up. "You have no idea the amount of free publicity this has been generating."

"Don't you see that you are playing right into his hands?"

"Perhaps he is the one who is playing into *our* hands," Monsieur Peverell had the temerity to suggest. "After all, our goal is to sell tickets and make money. That is exactly what is happening."

Raoul was livid and he took no pains to hide it. "Then your goal must also be to continue to let this man deceive you with his trickery. Does it not occur to you that by agreeing to the production of a second rate opera written by some unknown- extortionist only encourages him?"

"But the composer isn't unknown. The Phantom of the Opera wrote it," Monsieur Peverell reminded him inanely. "And *everyone* has heard of the Phantom of the Op- "

He stopped because Raoul looked like he was going to explode.

Monsieur Vaussard quickly tried to smooth the matter over. "Actually we have gone over the opera and find it- ahem, quite compelling."

"Compelling? Bah!" Raoul snorted. "This whole fiasco will turn out to be an embarrassment to the Opera House. Mark my words."

"Actually, Monsieur Guerin, the conductor, said the music was brilliantly written. He has been given a list of the songs and he is quite impressed by them. From the story itself to the music, it seems to be a- well, Monsieur Guerin called it a masterpiece of rare talent. He says the songs were not written by an amateur but that they show amazing talent and- "

He stopped when he saw the expression on the Viscount's face and finished quietly, "People are already showing an interest in it, especially since Christine has been offered the lead. That in itself, apparently, is a fascinating story. Not to mention that she has an astounding voice and a face to match it. A ghost choosing a relatively unknown singer for the lead- "

"This is insanity," The Viscount cut him off. He ground his teeth together and glared at the two men a moment longer before he stormed out of their office.

Christine was startled when she heard someone pounding loudly on her dressing room door. A very tense-looking Raoul stood waiting for her when she opened the door. She had not been expecting him. In fact, she hadn't even known that he was in the Opera House. She was a little shocked when he said no word to her, but boldly stalked across her dressing room and entered her bedroom.

"Raoul, what are you doing?"

He didn't answer her. Instead he looked around her bedroom as if he was searching for something, or for someone. He surveyed all the furnishings thoroughly, from the upholstered chairs to the chaise to the canopy bed and the mirrored armoire. He stood there for quite a while, taking it all in, as if everything he looked at made him more and more furious.

"What are you looking for?"

He finally answered her question with a question of his own. "Is *all* this furniture new?"

"Not new exactly," she answered him cautiously. She didn't know what was going on, but whatever it was, couldn't be good. "It's been here since last winter."

He flung his arm out to indicate everything in the room. "You don't think this is a bit grand for a dancer's room?"

He seemed to have forgotten that she wasn't just a dancer anymore. "Madame Giry said it is in keeping with the rest of the Opera House."

He gave her a dark, sidelong glance. "Madame Giry, eh? And did she also tell you *who* arranged for such elaborate furnishings?"

"I didn't ask. I assumed it was Madame Giry herself."

By the way Raoul was acting, Christine thought it wise not to mention that the very dresses she wore came from Madame Giry, as well. That she had, in fact, received several new dresses just yesterday that had been a result of cleaning out the vast storage rooms.

"What else is new?" Raoul wanted to know.

"Most of the furniture in here, and in my dressing room . . . " Her voice faltered as she watched Raoul come to a halt at the foot of her bed. He had slowly clenched his hands into tight fists at his sides as if he wanted to strangle someone.

"Even the very bed you sleep on?"

"Yes."

He spun around and abruptly changed the subject. "You're not seriously considering accepting this new role, I hope. This ghost-this charlatan will have you exactly where he wants you."

"Where he wants me?" she echoed. "You mean on stage?"

Her flippancy only infuriated him further. His face flushed with anger. "Christine, I forbid it."

"Forbid it?"

"When will it end, Christine?"

"When will *what* end?"

"This- this *Phantom* is the same man who viciously attacked the seamstress," he reminded her.

"The tailor."

"What?"

"Remi is a tailor, not a seamstress," she informed him. "And the Phantom has made it clear that he was not responsible for the attack."

"And just how did he do that?"

"He sent a note."

"Another note," Raoul sneered. "And just what did this note have to say?"

"That he had no part in what happened to Remi, but that the person responsible would be revealed at some time in the future."

Raoul was dangerously silent for a long moment. "And of course we should believe him. Must I explain to you that every guilty man claims he's innocent of any wrongdoing?"

"Raoul, what is going on? What does my room have to do with any of that? And why are you so angry?"

"I'm angry because this damnable ghost is making a mockery out of both of us. Because you would even consider accepting this role. And because, Christine, I am wondering just how far I will have to go to get you to come to your senses."

Christine knew she was dreaming because the music was so beautiful that it could only be part of a dream. She had awakened in the darkness and now she lay very still, listening as the soft strains of a violin drifted eerily through the darkness. She didn't recognize the melody, but she didn't need to recognize it. As she rose from her bed and hastily donned a robe over her dressing gown, she *knew*.

When she opened her door, she paused for only a moment on the threshold. She could hear the music more clearly now. Remi was right. It was enough to bring one to tears.

Of course in the Opera House she heard music all the time, but this- this was no ordinary music. This was ghostly music. It surrounded her. It got inside her. And she knew. She *knew*.

She remembered Madame Giry's words: *"He is a musician with rare talent."*

"He prefers to work at night when no one is around to disturb him."

"I allow him his whims . . ."

In her heart she knew it had to be him. Her teacher. No other man could play like that.

She followed the music until she found herself standing in the hallway outside of box five. The Phantom of the Opera's private box. Of course it would be coming from there. The door stood slightly ajar and she pushed it open.

She hesitated on the threshold and stared for a few moments into the pitch blackness, waiting for her eyes to adjust. There were no gaslights lit here, and the outside light barely penetrated the confines of the box, so it was too dark to see anything inside the small room. Except the dark silhouette of a man. The music had stopped but she could see his outline clearly. He was dressed in a loose linen shirt and he was holding a violin.

A familiar voice said, "Don't be afraid, Christine."

She wasn't afraid.

"It *is* you," she whispered. "Of course it's you. I would know your music anywhere. So this *is* where you watch."

There were a thousand different questions forming in her mind, far too many for her to immediately sort out. In the darkness she couldn't see his face, but for the first time there was no curtain between them. She had come this far. She could hardly turn back now, so she boldly stepped forward.

She stopped abruptly when she heard, "Don't come closer."

She didn't have to. He closed the distance between them himself.

He had stepped so close to her, in fact, that he was able to brace one hand on the wall behind her. Perhaps she should have been afraid, but what she was feeling wasn't fear and she made no move to draw away from him.

His voice was low, entreating as he whispered a single word. Her name.

She moistened suddenly-dry lips as she tilted her head back to look up at him even though he remained shrouded in darkness. As if to instinctively hold him at a distance, she lifted her hand and laid it against his shirt front. It seemed the very force of him flowed like a current through her hand. She could feel the hard-muscled warmth of him. She could feel the throbbing of his heart through the thin linen. She drew in a steadying breath.

"Why did you come?" she heard.

"You called me with your music."

"Why aren't you frightened?"

"Because I *knew*."

His hand lifted and he slowly brushed her hair. Lightly. So lightly that it was barely a touch. He laid his fingers softly against her cheek as he leaned closer.

Beneath her hand, she continued to feel the heavy thudding of his heart. Her own heart quickened its pace while his lips drew closer to hers. Somehow she knew that he wanted to kiss her. She raised her face to his, helplessly awaiting that kiss.

He lowered his mouth even more. Time seemed to come to a standstill as breath mingled with breath. Yet he held back.

"What do we do now?" he whispered.

His warm breath started shivers racing along her flesh. Sensual anticipation tingled through every fiber of her being.

He bent his head lower until he touched his lips to the corner of her mouth. It was the briefest of touches. As brief as the moment when he brushed his mouth across her parted lips.

It wasn't a kiss. Not quite. But the light grazing of his mouth was hungry all the same and it roused a hunger deep inside her, a tide of awakening desire. A low moan escaped her.

That sound, the evidence of her passion, took him by surprise. The very closeness of their bodies had already fanned every one of his senses fully to life like a brushfire in a tempest. He wanted to kiss her deeply, thoroughly. And he knew instinctively that she would allow the kiss. The knowledge that she wanted him, too, sent a molten fire coursing through his veins. It made him forget every single vow, every promise he had made to himself. In the space of a single heartbeat, he was like one lost at sea.

He fitted his hand very carefully to her waist. He leaned his hungering body closer to her. He was on the verge of kissing her the way he needed to, he was about to let his mouth have one deep, intoxicating draught of the sweetness that she was offering . . .

He drew back suddenly. There was a loud bang somewhere and the muffled sound of men's voices. Aggressive, shouting voices that penetrated the very walls of the theater.

"It seems we're about to have company," he muttered under his breath, fighting his frustration, clamping down on his runaway desire as he shut the door beside her.

"Search up on the third floor," he heard a voice call out.

"Search everywhere. Especially box five."

This time it was the Viscount's voice.

"Come," Christine heard. "I'll take you to your room."

He gave her no chance to refuse him. His hand closed over her wrist and he drew her along with him to the back wall of the box. She followed blindly through the darkness, still half under the spell of what had been about to happen between them. She could see nothing before her or around her. She only knew that they stepped through an opening and were immediately enveloped in an even blacker space.

Christine realized that they were in the walls of the Opera House. The very air felt different. It moved against her as if the walls themselves were breathing. The voices were more muffled here even though they sounded closer.

As she was led through the darkness, it all seemed like a dream to her, their passage through the darkness, the coolness of the air against her, the man ...

"This way," he whispered. He was still holding her hand.

She marveled at the ease with which he was able to move through the darkness. He was like some nocturnal animal that could see perfectly in the absence of light. There was no hesitation, no fumbling around even where it was pitch black all around them.

He said nothing more to her until they had halted before what appeared to be a solid wall. There were no more voices. They were alone. Utterly alone. His nearness in the darkness started that warm, languid feeling of desire flowing through her veins again.

"Your room is on the other side of this wall," he said, the low huskiness of his voice drawing out more heat.

He pressed on the wall. She heard a click and a panel opened up. "Hurry," he said as he turned to her. "You don't want him questioning your whereabouts at night."

He turned to go, but she stopped him with her hand on his arm. "Wait."

He turned and stared silently at her, but Raoul was already pounding at her dressing room door.

"Go, Christine."

And then he was gone, disappearing like a ghost into the darkness as the wall closed up after him. Raoul was still pounding on her door and she knew she must act as if nothing was wrong. She went to the door and opened it.

"Raoul, what are you doing here?"

Behind him she saw the silhouettes of men moving around in the darkness. Shadows flitted against the walls of the Opera House, elongating and shifting almost violently as lanterns waved.

"We're searching the Opera House," Raoul told her.

"*Now?*"

"What better time than the dead of night to catch this fiend?" His gaze raked her. "This is men's work, nothing you need to concern yourself with. Go back to bed and lock your door. I'll talk with you tomorrow."

When he had gone, Christine leaned her back against the door and released the breath she had been holding as relief flooded through her. Raoul had not suspected anything. She went back to her bed air like a sleep walker. She knew now that Raoul had been right in one regard. The Phantom of the Opera wasn't a ghost. He was a flesh and blood man.

Chapter 11

Remi stood in the hallway outside Christine's dressing room with a dress draped over one arm. "She's supposed to be having a fitting."

An unshaven Raoul grunted as he looked down at the smaller man. "You'll have to come back later. She doesn't have time for that right now." The corners of his lips tightened with irritation when Remi didn't immediately leave. "Do you really think she's going to spend time on a dress fitting when I am waiting for her?" he asked in a voice that was rough with impatience.

Christine's door suddenly swung open and she stood poised on the threshold looking from one man to the other. It wasn't until Remi was gone that she said to Raoul, "I heard what you said to him. Did you have to hurt his feelings like that?"

"Whose feelings?"

"Remi's."

Raoul, exhausted from his second sleepless night in a row, only frowned and shook his head as if he could not understand her mood. He was holding a steaming cup of coffee in one hand and he was wearing the same clothes she had last seen him in last night. It had been a long night of searching. Everything was quiet in the Opera House at the moment, however. Only Raoul's disheveled appearance and the muddy boot prints on the floors behind him were testimony to the invasion last night.

"Have you been here all night?" she asked him.

"All night," he confirmed as he took a sip of hot coffee.

"And did you find what you were looking for?"

"Not yet, but we aren't done searching yet. I'm going to go home and get some rest. We won't be able to move about so freely during the day when there are people here, so we'll resume the search tonight."

"You're going to be here another night?"

"We'll be here until we finish what we started."

"But if you haven't found anything by now- "

"That doesn't mean there isn't something to be found," he interrupted her with almost the same impatience he had shown Remi. "We'll keep looking."

"For how long?"

"As long as he is a threat to you."

He gave Christine a hard, possessive kiss, then abruptly turned on his boot heels and walked away.

The man they called the Phantom of the Opera was indeed a threat to her but not like Raoul thought. That night in box five was branded in Christine's memory in minute detail. In the days since it had happened, she had gone over it a thousand times in her mind. She had replayed every single touch, every single sensation, every single word he had said to her.

As she paced across her room now, she wondered how she was going to be able to wait until their next lesson when she could go to him with her questions. And yet, a part of her wondered how she could even face him after what had happened. Even more unsettling to her peace of mind, she wondered what would have happened had they not been interrupted. The terrible truth of the matter was that if she was to be honest with herself, she had wished many times, *many* times, that he had finished what it he had started in box five. That he *had* kissed her. For all the vivid imagination he had accused her of having, she had not truly understood, until that moment when his lips had brushed lightly across her own, how mindlessly enthralling being kissed by a man could be, or how devastating to her peace of mind. Raoul's hard, possessive kisses had not come close to affecting her like that. Not in all the time she had known him.

"It should not be this way," she whispered to the empty room.

But once again, helplessly, a flood of awareness seeped through her as she recalled the raw male power of the man who was called the Phantom of the Opera and that almost-embrace, that almost-kiss. Had it been a kiss? Amazingly, she still was not certain.

Kiss or not, she found herself reliving it again and again, at all hours of the day and night. The memory spilled over into every area of her life, at the most unexpected moments, even when she was singing on stage.

She had gone over everything they had ever talked about during their lessons, especially those things she had said to him about the Phantom. She recalled every enigmatic statement he had ever made to her in reply. To realize that *he* was really the man she had been talking about, that he was the man she was dreaming about was something she still could not fully reconcile herself to. She needed to talk to him.

But what would he say to her at their next lesson? And what would she say to *him*?

"Madame Giry, why?"

Christine placed both hands on the desk and leaned forward. "I know his secret now. There is no reason for this."

By way of the Persian, her teacher, the man they called the Phantom, had sent word cancelling their next lesson. Without an explanation, without saying if he would resume the lessons at some later date in the future.

"Have you spoken to him?" Christine asked as she slowly straightened.

"Yes, I have spoken to him."

"I don't see why things shouldn't go on as they did before," Christine went on. "He need not fear that I will tell what I know. I admit that at first I was somewhat shaken by the discovery, but I have had time to think it through."

"The circumstances have changed."

"But they haven't changed," Christine argued. "Not really. He is the same man he always was. I never even saw his face. I only saw the faintest glimpse of a mask in the darkness. Why *does* he hide? Can't you at least tell me that?"

"He hides because his face is- not perfect."

Christine thought that over for a few moments before she asked, "And so, because of that, he has decided to stop our lessons entirely?"

"He feels that, yes, that would be best."

"It is his intention then to shut me out of his life completely because his face is less than perfect?"

"He knew from the beginning that you would be in his life for only a short time- "

"And he has decided that I shall have no say whatsoever in the matter?"

Madame Giry folded her hands slowly before her as she chose her words carefully. "The truth is that your lessons have become a complication. Erik only wishes to keep himself hidden from the world- "

"Erik? That is his name?"

Madame Giry nodded.

Christine narrowed her gaze. "You said you have known him for a very long time."

"I have."

The woman's answers were maddeningly brief and Christine knew she had to proceed with some caution. "He trusts you," she said.

"We have known each other long enough to have developed a mutual trust in each other. I know that because of what he calls his curse, his imperfection, he sometimes makes decisions that we might not understand, but we must accept them nevertheless. He is not a man who can be driven."

"I assume he has had a difficult life because of this- curse."

"I have known him from his darkest days, and I watched him find a way out of that darkness. But his past has made him what he is today and we have to respect his decisions."

Christine sighed in frustration.

"We will never completely understand the depths of his struggle, Christine. What he calls his curse made him an outcast from birth and he did live a very hard life, more than you could imagine. He was beaten down for simply existing, but he found a voice through his music and transformed his pain into something else. He has applied his genius to many other areas as well. Math, astronomy, architecture, engineering. He is a man of rare talent and intellect."

"Why Persia?"

"Because covering the face is not uncommon in that part of the world and he could move about freely for the first time without fear. He even worked for a time on the design and construction of the Opera House as an architect. That is why he knows the Opera House as well as he does. He helped to build it. From the very beginning, there were complications with the underground spring. He was able to find a solution to the problem."

"And this is where he lives?" Christine asked. "Deep underground in the cellars where no one can find him?"

Madame Giry nodded once more.

"He really *is* the Phantom of the Opera," Christine whispered as that truth finally sank in with all its implications.

"And how does that make you feel?" Madame Giry asked.

"I should fear him, I know. But I don't."

"He had come back to France seeking a refuge. He wanted only solitude. Until you came. And though I do not wish to say this to you quite so plainly, while the lessons have brought him a great deal of satisfaction, it has also put him at risk and caused a great disruption in his life."

"Because of Raoul?"

"*Oui*, that is a part of it."

"His mind is set?" Christine asked quietly.

"He can be very stubborn when he has decided upon a matter."

"He doesn't realize that I have already seen the man *behind* the mask. That this- this *curse* doesn't matter to me in the slightest. Will you do me a favor, Madame Giry? Will you tell him what I said, and ask him for me if he will resume the lessons?"

"I can ask him, but I can't guarantee that he will change his mind."

"But you will ask him for me?"

"I will ask, Christine."

Lisette had been taking a shortcut through the Grand Salon when a voice startled her. Taken by surprise, she whirled around. "Viscount. I didn't see you sitting there in the darkness."

He rose up from the shadows, a shadow himself.

"I'm surprised to see you working here so late," he said as he came toward her.

Actually she had not been working. She had been visiting with Christine before going home. The Viscount had been at the Opera House a great deal lately. The search for the Phantom, however, had still turned up nothing.

Lisette could feel the steady intensity of the man's gaze even in the darkened room. "I didn't know you were still here," she said warily. The man often showed up out of nowhere when one was least expecting it. It could be quite disconcerting.

"Don't feel like you have to run away on my account."

"I- wasn't running away," she replied, suddenly feeling even more uncomfortable without knowing why.

"You're not afraid to be here alone with me, are you?" she heard.

"Afraid? *Non*," Lisette replied. But that wasn't exactly true.

"Good. Then perhaps we can visit for a little while."

"I was about to go home."

"Surely a few minutes of your time won't make a difference. The truth is that I have been waiting for you."

"For me?"

"Does that surprise you?"

"Yes," she answered honestly. "What is it you want to talk to me about?"

"This Phantom business for one thing. What do you think about it?"

"I think we should let well enough alone," she said guardedly. "If there is a ghost, he has his reasons for being here."

"I see. That is a very tolerant way of looking at things. Has Christine confided *her* thoughts on the subject of the ghost?"

"Christine? Everyone here talks about the ghost."

"I'm sure it's a very popular subject. But what does Christine have to say about it?"

The Viscount was close enough now for Lisette to smell the strong fumes of alcohol on his breath. She was startled to see the blatant heat that was simmering in his eyes, a heat that was discernable even in the darkness.

His gaze lowered and rested on her mouth for a moment. "Surely she has talked to you about it."

"Perhaps you should ask her yourself," Lisette hedged and then stiffened when he ran the back of his hand lightly down her arm.

"I'm only concerned about her," he said. "Just as you must be. Which makes us have a mutual interest. If we work together- "

She barely managed a nod for his hand suddenly fell heavily upon her shoulder and he leaned closer to her. His thumb slowly stroked her arm as his voice became lower, more intimate. "I'm sure we can come to an agreement that would be beneficial to both of us."

Chapter 12

Christine rose stiffly from the upholstered wing chair, and impatiently paced across the empty de Chagny parlor. She stopped before the open French doors and frowned as she looked out over the well-manicured, formal gardens. She was not looking forward to the rest of the afternoon, which meant only one thing to her, an exhausting mental battle with the woman they called the Dragon Queen, Ligeia de Chagny, Raoul's stepmother.

She had never been alone with the woman before. She had endured long, drawn-out meals across from her and that had been enough to make her feel tongue tied and awkward. In spite of Raoul's assurances to the contrary, the Countess' efforts to make her feel at home always felt instead like shrewd, calculated moves in a game of chess, or, rather, a battle of wills. Yes, Christine was certain this was going to prove to be a most wretched afternoon.

Where *was* Raoul? she thought impatiently. Why had he left her here alone so long?

She looked around the room. There were few houses in Paris that could equal the grandeur of the de Chagny mansion. The spacious parlor where she stood was richly and extravagantly decorated. As had been pointed out to her on her very first visit to the mansion, the massive mahogany furniture had been in the family for generations. Every piece gleamed with polish and not a fingerprint or a speck of dust was to be seen anywhere.

From the sparkling chandeliers that hung from the high ceilings, to the elegant furnishings and the ornate fireplaces, to the portraits and the gilt-edged mirrors that adorned the walls, all spoke of an abundance of wealth and a way of life that most people could only dream about. Even the entry hall behind her was lavishly decorated with marble floors and fine paintings, showcasing the huge, twin curved stairways that led to the second floor and the various wings.

It was the same in the dining room where they had just finished a late brunch. In fact, there was not a single place in the parts of the mansion that she had seen that were not magnificently and luxuriously appointed. Right now, Christine was watching the late sunlight slanting through the rose garden just outside the French doors. From here there was a commanding view of the grounds with its wrought iron gates, statues and fountains, as well as the well-tended woodland beyond it.

She heard voices and stepped closer to the open doors. She saw with some surprise that Raoul was in the garden with Ligeia. She could not fathom why Raoul should still be out there when she was waiting for him inside.

The woman was seated on a bench that was carved like a swan. Her hand was resting on Raoul's arm as she gazed up at him. A few words drifted through the open doors.

"I trust you will take care of it."

It was Raoul's voice.

As Christine watched, he bent his head and surprised her when he brushed Ligeia's hair with his lips. She would never have guessed that such displays of affection were common between the two of them, especially given the aloofness with which the members of the de Chagny family generally treated each other. Meals en famille were especially pretentious in the de Chagny household, for they were always formal affairs where strict rules of etiquette prevailed. Christine found herself having to weigh each and every word carefully before she dared utter it. And yet, in spite of her reserve, she almost always managed to say the wrong thing regardless.

It was not like her time spent with Erik where she never felt any need for pretense. She could say anything she wanted to him without having to first censor herself. He never appeared to be shocked by anything she had to say, no matter what it might be.

Suddenly she was drawn back as she remembered the stirring warmth of his breath against her mouth and his whispered, "What do we do now?"

Heat suddenly suffused her cheeks. Why did she have to think about that now? Especially since she heard footsteps approaching on the marble floor behind her. She turned. Standing in the doorway to the parlor, with one hand still resting on Raoul's sleeve, was Ligeia, looking every inch the Dragon Queen.

Her black hair was caught up in an elaborate chignon with a fashionable headdress of lace. Her elegant gown of sapphire blue silk was trimmed with glass buttons and wide bands of black velvet. Obviously made by the best seamstresses in Paris, it fitted her slender form snugly. A heavy piece of jewelry, probably another de Chagny heirloom, was nestled in the exquisite black lace at her throat.

She was the epitome of poise and fashion. Her black eyes flashed with a cool, yet almost disdainful smile, as she said to Christine, "So sorry to keep you waiting, my dear, but there is always business to discuss. You will have to get used to that."

Ligeia would have been an exceedingly beautiful woman had there been even the faintest hint of warmth in her eyes, or any sincerity in her smile. But she was decidedly lacking in both of these. When Christine had first become engaged to Raoul, Ligeia had been absent from Paris. She had been in the habit of spending a great deal of her time at the de Chagny's summer home. Lately, however, it seemed she was at the Paris mansion all the time. Ligeia's regal bearing never let one forget that the bluest of blood ran through her veins. Christine had also quickly learned that like others of her class, Ligeia could be astonishingly insensitive to the feelings of people she considered to be beneath her.

With an elegant sweep of her hand, Ligeia indicated the rose-colored settee beside her. "Please sit down, won't you? We can have tea together, just you and I. And Petrine, of course. Ah, there you are, Petrine," she said to the young woman who had just entered the parlor. "Raoul can take himself off somewhere for a while so we can have time to chat and get to know each other better."

A servant appeared with a delicate, gold-rimmed porcelain cup for Christine, which Ligeia promptly explained was another heirloom that had been in the de Chagny family for generations.

"This is the first time, that we have been alone together, isn't it?" Ligeia asked from beneath her dark lashes. And then she said with a measured laugh, "Raoul has been very *egoiste* keeping you to himself all this time, but since you are going to be part of the family, the besotted boy will have to find a way to get over that soon enough.

"You're very quiet at dinner time," Ligeia went on.

How could she not be quiet? Christine thought to herself. She often felt left out of the conversation since gossip about de Chagny acquaintances made the rounds of the table even more than the food did. Christine had no idea who they were talking about, nor did she care to know. The de Chagnys, however, seemed to thrive on it.

Ligeia took a dainty sip of her tea before she set her cup aside. "Are you interested in needlepoint, Christine?"

"I confess I've never had very much time for it."

"Well, we shall have to set you up with a hoop or two of your own." She glanced over at the young woman who was seated across the room. "Petrine is quite accomplished when it comes to plying the needle."

She ought to be, Christine thought. Petrine was a cousin of the de Chagnys and Christine had never seen her when she was not bent over one hoop or another. Apparently she had several projects going at all times.

Petrine had a mass of rather dull chestnut hair which she kept confined in a tight, braided chignon at the back of her neck. Not a single stray tendril was allowed to escape. She had a sweet enough face, but she was so pallid and reserved that it was usually hard to detect any signs of life in her downcast eyes. Because Petrine was an orphan, Christine had felt sorry for her in the beginning. She knew what it was like to lose both parents. But she had caught enough of the young woman's sly smirks when she thought no one was looking that she had revised her opinion considerably.

"What do you think, Petrine? Would you be willing to teach Christine some of the intricacies of needlework?"

Because she had been forced into the conversation, Petrine finally raised her head and swept her habitually guarded, somewhat cold appraisal over Christine.

Before Petrine could say a word, Ligeia spoke for her. "Of course she would. Petrine has been working on that particular piece of embroidery for nearly a year now. Tell her what it is, Petrine."

"It's the de Chagny mansion and the grounds surrounding it," Petrine replied dutifully.

"Don't be shy, Petrine. Show it to Christine," Ligeia said as if she were coaxing a small child. "It's quite lovely."

And so it was. The de Chagny mansion and the gardens surrounding it, though still unfinished, were stitched in minute, painstaking detail.

"I find needlework somewhat tedious myself," Ligeia said as she lifted her tea cup indolently to her lips. "But since it is one of the acceptable pursuits for a lady of breeding . . . " She shrugged one blue-clad shoulder as she let her words trail off. She directed her next question at Christine. "And how are the dancing lessons coming along?"

Christine had no doubt that the woman knew very well how the lessons were coming along. From Raoul himself, she knew that Ligeia kept a very close watch over every detail of the activities of anyone in the de Chagny household. Ligeia had set the lessons up herself, so she must know how they were going.

Christine didn't say what she really thought of the lessons. That they were tedious, pretentious and boring. And the very last thing she wanted to spend her time on. But she said politely, "Monsieur Pascal says I am a quick learner and that I should get through them in no time."

"Splendid. That reminds me, we will have to have you fitted for your new wardrobe soon."

"New wardrobe?" Christine echoed blankly.

"Hasn't Raoul talked to you about this?"

Christine shook her head. "No."

"The distracted boy. Naturellement, as a Viscount's wife, you will be expected to dress your best at all times. Which means you will need to be fitted for a new wardrobe as soon as possible. Since having an entire wardrobe made up takes a considerable amount of time and effort, we should get started as soon as possible. You must have proper garments for every occasion, which means we shall have to decide on morning and afternoon gowns, not to mention evening gowns and dinner gowns, and they must be of the finest quality, of course. You will also need all the accessories that go with them. As a de Chagny, you will have to give care to your wardrobe *toujours*. There will be no such thing as throwing something on at the last minute without first giving it careful consideration as to its appropriateness for the occasion."

"I hadn't really thought about it," Christine confessed.

"Well, you must think about those things now," Ligeia informed her. "And since we will be presenting you to a wider circle of people as we introduce you more and more into society, you must look your very best."

Petrine seemed to come spontaneously to life when the subject of fashion came up. She joined in the conversation with more spirit than Christine would have thought her capable of.

"Yes, you will need gloves, bonnets, collars *and* shoes to go with each outfit," Petrine said with a vigorous little nod. "And don't forget nightgowns and undergarments." She dipped her head suddenly as a deep scarlet color suffused her cheeks.

"Of course I will help you pick out styles and colors," Ligeia said with an amused smile as she watched Petrine's downcast face. "You would probably be a little overwhelmed all by yourself. But you needn't worry. I will be there every step of the way to help you with your choices. I don't mean to sound boastful, but I do have excellent taste in fashion. But then my family was always well-off, so I have had a good fashion sense all my life."

"That sounds like it will be taking up a lot of time," Christine said with a slight frown.

"Yes, of course it will, but it will be time well spent."

Christine's lashes lowered. Was this yet another of Raoul's ploys to get her to leave the Opera House? Was this what they had been discussing in the garden? She felt a surge of resentment, if, indeed, she was being manipulated behind her back.

"After all," Ligeia was saying with a calculating gleam in the depths of her black eyes as she stared at Christine. "We wouldn't want people whispering behind Raoul's back and saying that he isn't generous with something as basic as his wife's attire. How would it look to be under the wings of the Chagny family and yet to present oneself as plain and dowdy? You would quickly become the *on dit* of Paris."

Dowdy and plain. Was that how Ligeia saw her? Or was she trying to make her feel that way?

As she silently contemplated the woman's motives, Christine's gaze shifted to the oil painting hanging above the fireplace. Ligeia, with the steady fixation of a vulture, followed her gaze. "Both de Chagny brothers resemble their mama, don't you think? Melisande was a lovely woman, but I fear the poor dear had too much of la Bohemienne in her to feel completely comfortable here. In spite of that," she sighed. "I felt it was important for the boys to remember their mother, so I didn't have the portrait replaced."

Christine continued to stare up at the portrait and the heart-shaped face whose eyes seemed to hold secrets, and perhaps a hint of sadness, too. Somehow, in spite of her words, Christine felt that Ligeia would have liked nothing better than to replace it, especially with her own portrait so that her eyes could be everywhere at all times.

"Given her background, of course she would feel out of place," Ligeia murmured as she raised her tea cup to her lips, which made it impossible for Christine to accurately read her expression. Not that she would reveal a true one, of course. Christine had seen the woman slice a victim of her gossip to minute shreds with her merciless tongue on more than one occasion and maintain a perfectly innocent mien.

"Raoul has told me that you started working at the Opera House as a dancer," Ligeia commented behind a fixed, polite smile.

"Yes."

"How odd that I don't remember seeing you." Somehow, at that moment, Ligeia reminded her of a cat unsheathing its claws. She was very patient and she was very deliberate. "And you have worked your way up to singing on stage. How very diligent of you. And how do you really feel about giving all that up? You can confide in me, dear. After all, this is a very different world, and I can see how difficult it might be to go from mingling with the kind of people who frequent the theater to moving among people of a higher social standing."

Christine wasn't sure what to say in reply. She took immediate offense at the implied slur.

Ligeia took full advantage of her silence. "I must be frank with you. I thought you would have stopped singing the very moment

162

you became engaged. Yet you seem to need to hang onto that life, even now. I can see how being offered such an important new role would be a temptation. But to join the ranks of the nobility- Why, the choice should be easy enough."

Christine finally found her voice. "I cannot simply walk away with no one to replace me. That would hardly be fair to the other people on stage."

"So you feel you owe a certain loyalty to the Opera House. I can understand that. But do you not think you owe even more loyalty to Raoul? He is after all going to be your husband. And since Raoul has made the request of you- "

"It is not the request of a husband. *Yet*," Christine couldn't help saying. "Raoul knew that I worked at the Opera House when he met me."

From the corner of her eye, Christine saw Petrine's hand stop with her needle held aloft. She could almost feel the daggers of shocked disapproval in the other woman's eyes.

Ligeia gave a somewhat brittle laugh. "You're very young, Christine, and you have a great deal to learn about men. And about husbands. While it's true that they might like a bit of challenge in their daily affairs with the outside world, when it comes to their wives, well, they don't expect to have to shield them from the outside world needlessly. Especially when it comes to gossip. It is hardly fair to give them more to worry about at home, *n'est-ce pas?* Being the wife of a Viscount carries obligations," she went on. "I don't expect you to understand all those obligations and what they entail just yet. And I suppose it is a little daunting to be thrust suddenly into the middle of such an affluent family and be forced to interact with people who are practically strangers to you. But I do understand how much of an adjustment that will be for you, and I only want to make the transition easier for you. I am here to help you become one of us."

Was that what she truly wanted to be? Christine wondered. To be just like Ligeia? Or Petrine? Was this what her future life was going to look like? Was she going to be at the center of a constant barrage of mental skirmishes on a daily basis by people who outwardly professed to care for her when in reality they would be ready to pounce on her for the slightest infraction? Would Raoul even be on her side?

She felt like she had been silent long enough. "May I speak frankly?" she asked.

"Yes, of course. Please do."

She noted that Petrine had stopped stitching altogether, and that her head was no longer bent over her needlework.

"The truth is that singing at the Opera House it is the career that I have chosen. I have worked very hard to get where I am now. When I do marry Raoul, we are both in agreement that I will not become merely a slave to his wishes with no say of my own."

Petrine now lifted her hand and placed it just below her collar as if to protect herself from the shock of what she had just heard. With her mouth agape, she continued to look from one woman to the other.

Ligeia laughed under her breath as if she suddenly found something amusing, but it was the kind of laugh that could chill the blood of any listener. "I had underestimated what a modern, strong-minded young woman you are, Christine. And pray forgive me for not realizing that sooner. But then, I have forgotten what it is like to be young and newly fledged and to be testing one's wings for the first time." Those black eyes were piercing and shrewd as ever as they swept over Christine. "And since I am a few years older, it occurs to me that I am not the kind of company that is stimulating enough for you, or for Petrine. You two would have so much more in common. I'm sure that if we put some time into cultivating the relationship, you will be good friends in no time. *Non?*" she asked Petrine with a thin, sly smile.

"Of course," Petrine said obediently, although Christine was aware of a certain trepidation behind her eyes, as if she were a bird who had suddenly found itself caught in a snare. There was a new robustness in her movements as she stabbed her needle in and out of the fabric.

"In fact, I see no reason whatsoever to wait to begin this new friendship," Ligeia went on. "You two should begin spending time together now. Carriage rides. Social events."

Christine looked over at the drab, preoccupied woman across the room. Her heart sank at the very thought of spending hours in her company.

"You might begin with a visit to church with us next Sunday," Ligeia suggested as if the thought had just occurred to her.

Christine listened as the two women went on discussing plans for her as if she wasn't even present.

"Unfortunately, it is always a struggle getting Raoul to attend church on a regular basis. Isn't it, Petrine? But if people were to see him there with Christine," she said with a narrowed gaze. "They would come to believe that she was having a good influence on him, which could prove to be an asset both in his social and his business affairs. Yes," she said as if deciding the matter once and for all. "A display of religious respectability certainly wouldn't do Raoul one bit of harm."

Christine opened her mouth to protest. She did not mind going to church, but going to worship for such a self-seeking reason as to be *seen* going, seemed almost blasphemous to her.

"And perhaps Philippe will join us as well. Though I confess I had given up hope long ago for that miracle to happen."

The matter of Philippe was brought painfully and suddenly to mind. So far Christine had mostly been able to avoid him. Meals were bad enough, the rare ones that he did make an appearance at, but if they had to attend church together-

"Speak of the devil," Ligeia said. "So you finally decided to grace us with your presence. I missed you at brunch."

Christine drew a slow, calming breath as Ligeia presented her cheek and Philippe leaned over and dutifully kissed it.

"Ah, look at you, so docile and well-behaved. Just what are you about?" Ligeia asked as he straightened. "Are you actually joining us in the parlor for conversation? If so, I have to wonder just what would induce you to put in an appearance at a ladies tea. Something extraordinary, I am sure."

Ligeia glanced slyly across the room and arched one dark eyebrow. It seemed like she was purposely baiting the man when she said, "Perhaps it is because of Christine?" A subtle hint of venom crept into her voice when she said, "I'm sure Philippe does not want you to be aware of some of his darker sides just yet. *Qui sait?* It may be that he has taken a fancy to you and wishes to make a good impression. After all, you are a very attractive young woman and we all know how attentive Philippe can be when it comes to attractive women. He has always been quite entertaining when he wishes to be. He was only seventeen when I came to live here and he was a very wild boy indeed. I will let you in on a little family secret. It would be wise to keep in mind that one can never know what Philippe is really thinking. He is very good at concealing his true motives and feelings on any matter. Never assume that you know what is really going on in that clever mind of his." She laughed as if to take some of the sting out of her words. "Just when you think you have figured him out, he will surprise you." She settled back in her chair with a faint, predatory smile lingering on her face.

Christine didn't dare look at the man. She had already found out about Philippe's hidden thoughts.

"But I suppose that is what makes him so successful in business matters," Ligeia went on. "He can be absolutely ruthless in his dealings, but that is exactly what it takes to handle the de Chagny fortune."

If Philippe took offense at her words, he didn't show it. But anyone could see that there was an underlying, scarcely-veiled hostility between the two of them. Christine sincerely hoped she was hiding her own feelings. But when she saw Philippe's eyes on her, she could feel heat immediately flooding her cheeks. She looked away as Philippe instructed a servant to bring him a brandy, but she could still feel his eyes on her he slowly savored the dark amber liquid in his glass.

"What has been keeping you so busy lately?" Ligeia asked him.

"I was inquiring into the Beauchene castle."

"And whyever would you want to do that?"

"The place has always fascinated me," Philippe replied calmly.

"You're not thinking of- why, you're not considering purchasing that old place, are you?" Ligeia queried. "People say it's haunted, you know."

"If it was for sale, I would definitely consider it," Philippe told her. "Ghosts and all."

"It's a cursed place," Ligia said half petulantly as she regarded him from beneath her long black lashes. Obviously, she had no influence over Philippe's business decisions.

Christine watched the other woman curiously. She didn't know anything about the Beauchene castle except for a few vague rumors she had heard long ago about it being haunted.

"That is a wretched story," Ligeia said when she saw the interest in Christine's eyes. "There has never been anything but scandal

166

associated with the entire Beauchene family. In fact, it is hardly a proper subject for refined drawing room conversation. Besides, there are at least a dozen versions of the story. The only thing I know for certain is that the place is in ruins." She looked at Philippe. "Is it even habitable?"

"Probably not. And that is precisely why I thought I might acquire it at a good price," Philippe told her.

"I have to admit," Ligeia said, speaking to Christine again. "That Philippe has proven to be as sly as a fox when it comes to acquiring properties and making a profit on them." She looked at Philippe. "It's been what? A ten years since the Count died?"

"Eleven."

"I have never been to the castle myself," Ligeia went on. "Although apparently Philippe has visited it recently. The Beauchenes were a very powerful, very wealthy family. The de Chagnys did business with them in the past even though Count Beauchene had a reputation of being utterly ruthless in business matters, even moreso than Philippe. A trait which came from his pirate ancestors, no doubt. Or so the story goes. It would explain, however, how the Beauchenes were able to acquire such a vast fortune.

"It seems the Count approached his married life in much the same way that he handled his business affairs. After his first wife died without providing him with a son, he must have decided that it was time he produce an heir for his fortune."

"Completely understandable," Philippe commented as he leisurely sipped his brandy.

"And completely scandalous as it turns out," Ligeia informed Christine. "For his second wife, the Count chose a woman half his age. And he wasn't content with a French wife. *Non*, she was *Irish*," Ligeia said as if that was a scandal in itself. "In spite of coming from such a barbaric country, they say she was quite a beauty. *And* she came from nobility herself. Why she would have left everything she knew behind to marry a man twice her age, is something we will probably never know. There were rumors, of course. Some whispered that she was part of a business deal. Whatever the reason, the Count made up his mind that he had to have her. And after the wedding, he apparently had his hands full. It was a volatile combination by all accounts. There was talk that she tried to run away and go back to Ireland, but that the Count wouldn't have it. It was even said that she was kept at the Beauchene castle against her will. Whatever the case, it wasn't long after he took her to wife that she begat him a son. But the child turned out to be a misbegotten monstrosity. In fact, the child was so deformed that he was kept hidden away from the time of his birth."

"I have heard that he was a hunchbacked monster," Petrine added without looking up from her embroidery.

Philippe, who was leaning against the mantle with his arms folded over his chest, said, "No one knows for sure what he really looked like."

"That sounds terribly sad," Christine commented quietly.

"It *was* tragic," Ligeia agreed. "Especially since it was whispered that the child wasn't- Well, hadn't even been sired by the Count."

"Who was the father?" Christine asked.

Ligeia shrugged. "Who knows? The devil himself for all we know. Some said there was a curse on the castle itself. From its long, dark history, one can only wonder. As I have already said, in my opinion the place is best avoided." She gave Philippe a brief, sidelong glance.

To which Philippe only laughed under his breath. "Since I have no plans to sire a child there, I don't think we have anything to worry about. Actually, the castle itself was quite something at one time. And the view of the surrounding countryside is spectacular. The lands around it are well suited for hunting."

"Hunting," Ligeia repeated with a slow shake of his her head. "A pastime that Philippe is quite passionate about, as you will find out. But back to the Countess Beauchene. There was another child born, but that one only lived a few years and the Countess died shortly after. Of a broken heart, they said."

"What happened to the other child?" Christine asked.

"No one knows. After all these years, people have assumed that he is dead, else he would have claimed his inheritance by now. I can't imagine anyone turning their back on such a fortune. Others say he is still hiding in the castle somewhere or the woods surrounding it. If he is not dead, that is. Unless it is his ghost that haunts the castle. In any case, his mind was probably as deficient as his body. What would an imbecile do with such a vast fortune?"

Ligeia looked at Raoul. "He would be a man now, no child. If you purchased the castle, you do realize that you might be acquiring a beast along with it? How would you like to encounter something like that on one of your hunting outings?"

"I think that would prove to be quite an intriguing hunting expedition. Don't you agree, Christine?"

Without being obvious about it, his gaze moved slowly down her body. Jerking her own gaze away from him, Christine took a deep breath and forced herself to settle her thoughts.

"Erik."

Christine shot a glance in Ligeia's direction.

"That was the child's name. Erik Beauchene. Ah, there is Raoul now."

Christine had been balancing her tea cup on her lap. When she looked up to see Raoul in the doorway to the parlor, the scalding tea spilled over the rim and burned her fingers. Before she could stop it, the cup fell to the floor and shattered to pieces.

While she tried to gather her equally scattered thoughts, Christine stared down at the broken pieces of delicate heirloom china and the pool of dark liquid that was spreading perilously close to the Aubusson carpet.

Without thought, she grabbed up an embroidered linen napkin and got down on her knees to wipe the tea up before it could reach the carpet.

By now, Raoul had crossed the room in several long strides. "Let the servants do that," he said above her.

"But it was my fault- "

"Christine," he said sharply. "I said leave it."

She felt her arm firmly gripped and she was hauled her to her feet as Raoul gave orders to the servant who had just entered the room.

The early morning was fog-shrouded. There was no sun. Only the palest ghost of light could be seen behind the grey mantle of scudding clouds.

The man was a solitary dark figure against the grayness as he stood on a rocky ledge high above the surrounding terrain. While the wind whipped the cloak about his body, his dark brows were drawn together in a frown. His black hair was wind-blown. He lifted his face as dark cobalt eyes searched the turbulent clouds above him. Then he bowed his head, yielding for a moment to the turmoil that seethed like a churning sea inside him.

He had set out well before dawn and now that he found himself standing among the familiar, time-ravaged stones that rose bleak and desolate against the agitated sky, he wondered again why he had come at all. Because, he reminded himself, this was his legacy. This was his past. His beginning. It was here that he had learned he was an abhorrent beast, a monster that was not quite human. It was here that he had learned to hide himself.

The place had always seemed to be haunted by ghosts, even from his earliest memory and he himself had moved among them like a shadow. The ghosts might remain, but the living human figures from his past were gone now. Only he was left, and the ravens and the sparrows that had taken up residence here in this gloomy abode that seemed to give back only echoes of desolation and loneliness even now.

He had needed the strenuous activity that the long journey required, but he was still asking himself why he had returned. He still had no answers. There were few good memories here. Nearly all of his childhood recollections were of an isolated, wretched existence. Not once since he had returned to France had he been motivated to return. Until now. Perhaps he had been drawn back because he himself fitted the gloomy ruins of the castle. Was he not as much a ruin?

He had known all along that returning could give him no resolution. It was like trying to find solace where no solace could be found. It was like seeking an escape from that which followed him wherever he went. The past, like his curse, was like the ghosts. It was a thing that could not be confronted. And he had no desire to retrace it all. Yet he understood that the pain of the past was a tangled thing inside him whose roots went deep.

But there was nothing more here than there had been before. Only the lonely wind whispering through the trees and mourning through the cracks and crevices of the lichen-mottled stones. There had been one bright spot of light that had briefly overshadowed the darkness of those years and that had been his mother. That she had loved him, he had no doubt. Not that she had been allowed to love him freely. Then, some years after he had been born, she had given birth to her second child, a perfect boy. But when the child had died at the age of three years, she had retreated into a darkness from which she had never emerged. Weakened by her grief, she had followed him in death less than a year later, leaving her first child to grieve alone. Leaving him at the mercy of a man who had only one thing in his heart for him and that was hatred. Pure, deeply-rooted hatred.

Years of brutality had etched themselves across his life. He had learned one lasting lesson from those years. That one could not change true evil. But one could build walls against it. He had learned, too, that he had too much hunger inside himself to settle for starvation. He had learned too much to lay down and die before that wall of hatred. While his mother had been alive, she had stood as a shield between him and the man who had reluctantly called himself his father. But with her passing, all the restraints had vanished. Fueled by alcohol, the hatred had grown to murderous proportions, until he did the only thing he could to get away from it. He ran away.

Unfettered finally by the darker things that had bound him for far too long, he had left France in search of something that even he did not understand. In Persia, he had embraced life to its fullest. He had become almost a legend there since some believed that he bore the mark of Cain. Others gave him a wide berth because they believed it was some other kind of curse. But in the end, he was to learn that evil and brutality could be found anywhere, and so he had become disillusioned with the life there.

The Persian had warned him that his life was in danger because he knew too much. Because of the political intrigue there, an assassination attempt had also been made on the Persian's life. The man had been grievously wounded and left for dead. But he had survived and eventually the two men made their way back to France together.

He had found a measure of peace in the underground cellars of the Opera House. And then Christine had come along and shattered his world of solitude. He had found, finally, that piece that was missing, that filled the aching, lonely void. She became the fulfillment of all the things he could never hope to find in another human being. And he knew full well that when she left him, when she was finally gone from his life forever, her memory would haunt him mercilessly in his lonely existence.

"Even if I'm the only one who remembers us," he whispered to the restless, churning sky. "I shall hold the memory of you forever, Christine. No matter how much time passes, in my heart I will not forget you. I will keep you by my side."

Braving the raw winds blowing in off the water, he walked up to a small, desolate cliff where the dreary morning light filtered through the branches of a stand of ancient cedars. He frowned down at the tombstones half buried in the weeds, reading the words chiseled there.

He got down on his heels and with a gloved hand brushed the weeds away from two of the stones and stared down at the name of the woman, Ailia Beauchene, and that of the little boy who was buried beside her, Enan Beauchene.

He shifted his gaze to the gray, turbulent waters far below him. Almost as an afterthought, he brushed the weeds away from a third stone that had not been there before he had left France and his lips twisted with bitter irony. There was a single name etched there. Erik.

He got to his feet and stared down at the final mockery, one that he knew should come as no surprise.

His decision and been a difficult one for him and he had wrestled with it for a long time. But now that he had decided on his course, a small measure of peace flooded through him. He would resume the lessons.

Chapter 13

Christine hardly knew what to expect. She could still hear the Persian's words: "He would like to speak with you."

She was now following the man through an underground passage somewhere beneath the Opera House. The lantern in his hand cast leaping shadows on the stone walls all around them. When they stopped, she was looking up at a wide flight of stone steps that disappeared into the darkness above them.

"Where are we?" she asked the Persian, her voice sounding small in the cavernous space.

"In the third cellar below the Opera House."

"And this leads to?" she asked as she stared up at the staircase.

"Another level of the Opera House."

"Is he- " she began, but when she turned back around, the Persian had already disappeared, leaving the lantern on the floor behind her.

A heavy stillness hung over the deserted corridor. But that was soon broken by a soft creak, a door perhaps. She heard footsteps and looked up to see a dark figure materialize from out of the shadows at the top of the steps. Catching sight of her, the man they called the Phantom of the Opera paused for a moment. Then, without saying a word, he began to descend the staircase. When he reached the bottom of the steps, he halted again.

Christine had her first real look at the man that had sent for her and she took in every detail from head to toe. He was wearing a pale linen shirt with a dark vest over it. A silk cravat was knotted at his throat. He wore no cape so she could see that the broad shoulders under the shirt were wide and powerful looking. His booted feet were placed slightly apart as he silently regarded her.

His hair was indeed as black as Madame Giry had said. He wore a mask, or a half mask that covered one side of his face. His cleanly-shaven jaw was lean with strong masculine lines. Madame Giry was right about something else. The part of his face that she could see was exceedingly handsome.

She opened her mouth to speak, but no words came. Now that the face her mind had wondered about for so long was before her with no curtain between them, and no darkness, she could only stare mutely. Every question she ever had flew away like startled bats into the shadows.

"So you are the one they call the Phantom of the Opera," she finally said very softly. "My teacher."

He nodded once, very slowly, and then he paced silently for a few moments before her as if he was considering his own words. His every movement held her gaze for he moved with the feline grace of a caged panther. It was a decidedly unnerving thing to watch him, she found, when she remembered that her hand had rested very intimately against his hard, muscled chest. And that his mouth had brushed intimately against her own-

She cut those thoughts short because they were the cause of a strange disruption inside her. She did not want him to read that disruption in her eyes.

"You came," he said in a low voice as he finally came to an abrupt halt and faced her.

It was the same voice she remembered from their lessons. But as she stood there trying to adjust the face to the voice, as she had wanted to do for a very long time, his physical presence before her now seemed as dark and as wild as a storm crashing against the walls of the Opera House. It made her unaccountably apprehensive.

"Did you doubt that I would?"

"I had no way of knowing," he replied.

"Why did you call me here?"

"I have decided to resume our lessons. If you are still willing."

Her brows arched in surprise. "I am willing."

"When I thought things over," he went on. "I realized I was being unfair to you. Your role in the new opera will be much more

174

demanding, and you still have much to learn. To leave you unprepared would hardly be fair."

"There will be no curtain between us?" she asked.

"I think we are beyond that now."

"Madame Giry has spoken to me about- why you wish to keep yourself hidden."

"Yes, I know."

"And has she told you that I intend to keep your secret?"

"I know that as well."

"You have decided to trust me then?"

He did not answer her immediately. He bowed his head as if he was deep in thought for a moment. "Do I have any choice?" he finally asked as he looked up.

Without waiting for an answer, he said, "I have given much thought to the matter. We will have our lessons somewhere other than where we had them before. Somewhere where there will be more privacy and less chance of interruption. If it becomes necessary, we may have to work at night to avoid being disturbed. With people invading the Opera House at all hours, we must be more careful."

She closed her eyes for a moment as the familiar, deep voice moved over her and she tried to reconcile it with the voice from their past lessons. It was a voice she thought she might never hear again.

She opened her eyes again as he said, "I'll work out the final details and send word so that you may decide if they are acceptable to you."

"I'm sure they will be acceptable. When you cancelled the lessons, I wasn't sure if I would ever see you again," she said somewhat impulsively. "When I realized who you were, that you were a real person- "

"Now you know that I am no ghost," he said bluntly. "But neither should you think of me as a flesh-and-blood man."

"Then what should I think of you as? Did you want me to go on thinking of you as a ghost when you played that night in box five?"

One corner of his mouth tightened in an ironic half smile. "Perhaps. But that night- I didn't know you would be so bold as to actually try and confront a ghost.

"My mistake was in teaching you in the first place," he went on. "And making it all seem so mysterious. I should have realized that you couldn't help but be curious." His laugh was low, but self-deprecating. "I knew from the moment you stepped into box five that night that things had changed between us, and that was my fault."

"What made you change your mind about the lessons?"

"Because I began the lessons and then I left you. I merely wish to make things right. I knew from the moment I heard you sing that you would become a disruption in my life and that has proven to be the case. But I intend to finish what we started. Does that help you understand?"

His eyes, one of them half shadowed by the mask, seemed to have the power to pierce straight to her soul. She drew a slow, deep breath and forced herself to meet his penetrating gaze.

"In light of that, I don't see why we shouldn't go on just as we did before."

"Nor I," she said so quietly that he barely caught the words.

"We will spend time getting ready for the new opera," he went on. "Where you take it beyond that, Christine, is up to you. I only request that you keep the lessons as you have in the past, a secret."

A deep silence lengthened between them as he watched her face to see what effect his words might have on her.

"The only question remaining is, can you do it with this?" His hand came up and his fingers indicated the mask.

"If you feel more comfortable that way, I can."

"It is one of my conditions."

"Of course I can do it."

"Then I'll leave you now. Wait for the Persian. He'll come and take you back."

He turned to leave her then, but after he had climbed several of the stairs, she called out after him.

"Wait! What shall I call you?"

He half turned, but he kept his face averted from hers.

"Erik," she heard.

And then he was gone, vanishing like a wisp of smoke she could not hold onto.

"If this is a ploy to get out of your lesson, it's not going to work."

Christine's chin was resting in her palm as she listened to Erik play the guitar very softly. He had been teaching her a new melody, the last song of his opera.

"My past is of no consequence," he said in reply to her last question. "Are you ready to sing the song with me?"

He guided her through the song in his deep masculine timbre. This song was nothing like the others he had written. It was as beautiful as the other ones, but there was a dark, deep-lying undercurrent in the music. It was more intense, more passionate than any other song he had taught her. It was a lover's song. A song about unrequited love.

She closed her eyes and let herself be carried away by the music as she tried to remember the words and follow him.

When she opened her eyes again, he was staring at her very intently and very deeply, as if he had the power to see into her soul. She lowered her own eyes in confusion. What was he was thinking, she wondered, as he leaned back in his chair and regarded her so seriously?

Unknown to her, the truth was that while he chided her for not being focused, he himself had been distracted. She looked too beautiful this morning. She was dressed in a gown of soft blue with accents of lace, another one that she did not realize he had picked out for her. What would she say, he wondered, if she knew that he had personally picked out most of her clothing himself?

There were a dozen candles lit and the candlelight was only enhancing her beauty, which was no longer filtered by a curtain and therefore was making things more difficult for him. She was also sitting closer to him than she had ever been before. He still wore a mask. He had been apprehensive at first, worried that she might be frightened at his half-hidden appearance. So far, however, that had not proven to be the case.

But this was still as much a change for him as it was for her. It was strange sitting so close to her with no barrier between them. To look into her eyes and have her look back so openly at him, to be aware of the subtle changes in those fascinatingly beautiful eyes, to be surrounded by her faint, intoxicating perfume - all those things were proving to be a distraction. He remembered when he had had his hands in the silken depths of her unbound hair, when she had been so close that it had been an agony not to put his arms around her and draw her closer. Very much aware of where his thoughts were taking him, he tore his gaze away from her and tried to discipline himself against any more wayward thoughts.

"Try it one more time," he said.

"What was the first line again?"

He groaned and let his head drop heavily back against the chair he was sitting in. "Have I been playing all this time to the walls?"

"No," she said slowly as she watched him from behind her lashes. But by the way she had dragged out the word, he knew he had challenged her. And she always, *always* rose to his challenges.

She closed her eyes and drew a deep breath before she sang the line by herself. Perfectly. Her voice was much stronger this time. She surprised him by singing the song almost all the way through with very few hesitations.

"What were you thinking about when you wrote this song?" she asked after she had finished.

He tried to be stern as he raised a half-mocking eyebrow. "A very beautiful woman. One who talks when she should be singing."

Did he really think she was beautiful? she wondered silently. And why should that stir such an inexplicable pulse of pleasure deep inside her?

"I have been singing," she said. "You said I should not push myself beyond my limitations."

Since he had avoided a direct answer, she asked another question. "How did you learn to play so many instruments so well?"

"I had a lot of time to myself. When you work at something for so many years, you should become good at it."

"Like you worked hard at being a ghost?"

"*That* took hardly any effort at all."

Her gaze was intent and searching as she regarded him, as if she was trying to visualize what lay beneath the mask. "Should I tell you I worry that if I say the wrong thing, you might abandon me again?" she asked.

"I won't do that. I thought your curiosity would be satisfied once there was no curtain between us, but that doesn't seem to be the case." He set the guitar aside. "What are *you* thinking?"

"I was thinking how unique my situation is. How many women can say that they have been summoned by the Phantom of the Opera himself? Ghosts are usually the ones who are summoned."

He ignored her wit and reminded her again, "This is supposed to be a music lesson."

"We always talked during our lessons," she reminded him back.

"So we did."

"This is the same song you played in box five that night. I knew from the moment I heard it that it was you."

"You may have suspected it was me, but you couldn't be sure."

"But I was. I was very, very sure. Just as when I heard the story of your past, I knew it had to be you."

He sighed deeply. "We are back to that again. Do not make a romance out of this, Christine. There is nothing romantic about my past. In fact, it's best forgotten."

"I told you about *my* childhood."

"Yes, you did. But my childhood is very different from yours. It's not so pleasant."

"I have heard that it is in ruins."

"The Beauchene castle? It was a dark, forbidding place even when I lived there. It didn't have far to go to fall into its current state of disrepair." His gaze narrowed as he looked at her. "Just what did you hear that has made you so curious?"

"Not very much. Only that Count Beauchene was not a very pleasant or agreeable man. And yet, he did manage to marry. Twice."

"I suspect it was mostly because he wanted an heir. Unfortunately for him, he got me."

"And what of your mother?" Christine asked quietly.

He sighed again, knowing she wasn't going to let it go. "I suppose her life would have been called a tragedy had it been performed on the stage, what I knew of it. When she had first come to France, they said she was like a bright ray of sunshine in the bleak castle. By the time I was born, however, it seems the life had gone out of her. But a man can take that out of a woman quickly enough when he sets his mind to it. From what I heard, she did not want to marry the Count. She was forced into it." His voice trailed off as he shrugged one shoulder. "Given the circumstances, it should come as no surprise that she fell in love with another man."

Christine raised a questioning brow.

"We can't always choose who we will fall in love with. It's a cruel twist in life, but one that is common enough," he went on. "It seems she tried to run away with this man before I was born. I imagine it was a desperate time for her and it must have been a hard choice. But in the end, love won out. Some said that the man she was running away with was from Ireland and that he had followed her to France and was going to take her back home. Unfortunately, the man, whoever he was, disappeared and was never heard from again. The Count eventually found her and dragged her back to the castle. By then she had found out she was with child, which was me. The Count apparently did not want the scandal of a wife who had tried to run off with another man, so he kept my mother virtually as a prisoner to avoid such speculation. Not that it quieted the rumors. I suspect he would have kept her out of spite anyway to punish her for defying him. As for me, there was the inevitable question about my parentage since there was another man involved. Admitting that I wasn't his would have created another scandal for the Count, so he tolerated the situation. At least outwardly.

"Of course, what was true and what was not is hard to say. I only know all this from second hand gossip among the servants, and only when they did not know I was around to hear. I had learned to keep to the shadows at a very young age.

"In any case, when I was born, the Count told my mother that I was her punishment for her unfaithfulness. And then he finished what he had begun the day he married her. He set his mind to making her life a misery."

"So- "

"So, yes, there was some question as to whether I was a true Beauchene. But as I grew, it became plain to everyone that there was Beauchene blood in my veins. Aside from my curse, I greatly resembled the Count." His mouth twisted sardonically. "It was the greatest irony that I became the sole living heir of everything he owned. What he did not drunkenly gamble away, that is."

"That sounds very sad." She looked up at him. "But your mother loved you, surely. A mother's love isn't conditional."

"As much as she was able. But suffice to say that loving me did not make her life any easier. When I was born, she did not get a son that was a comfort to her in her loneliness. And she could not love me openly. If she did not pay the price for her displays of affection, then I did, so she learned to keep her distance. She suffered greatly because she was so torn. A grim sentence, but one she lived until her dying day.

"When my brother died, it was like the life went out of her, too. She never stopped mourning him. Or blaming herself. The last words she spoke to me were, 'Forgive me for bringing you into this hell that I have created.'"

"Have you been back to the castle in all this time?"

"Only once. Since I am the sole living heir, I was curious. I suppose *living* is the opportune word. There is a tombstone with my name on it. The Count must have had it put there sometime after I left, perhaps to say I was dead to him." He paused. "Now your face looks very distressed. It was a mistake to tell you."

"No," Christine hastened to assure him. "I only wish that you could have had the kind of childhood that I had, one that left you with fond memories."

"There's no sense wishing for things that are beyond our grasp, Christine. Don't feel sorry for me. The last thing I want is your pity."

"I have pity for the child who grew up in loneliness and darkness. As for the man- "

What did she feel for the man?

"I can only admire the strength that it took for you to survive and become who you are. You might have let anger and bitterness rule you. But you didn't."

"I have had my share of destructive emotions, I assure you."

"But you were able to find solace in music."

"Yes, my mother did instill that in me."

"The music was a fond memory." He smiled faintly. "And tourtiere."

"What?"

"Tourtiere. It's one of the few good memories from my childhood. I was expected to keep myself hidden away, but the cook at the castle would bake them and leave them where I could find them."

A smile lingered at one corner of his mouth as he remembered. And Christine watched in wonder as that smile transformed the uncovered half of his face.

"Have I finally satisfied your curiosity?" he asked.

"For now," she answered him back.

"Good. Then we can get back to our lesson."

As his gaze dropped to her mouth, he suddenly found himself remembering that near-kiss in box five. Again. He had thought about it many times since, while she seemed to have been completely unaffected by it.

She was about to become another man's wife, he reminded himself. Of course she didn't want to think about kisses with someone else. Of course she would want to pretend that it had never happened. No doubt she hoped that it would never come up in their conversations. *If* she even thought about it at all.

He reminded himself again why they were there. "Encore un fois, Christine. Doucement . . . "

Chapter 14

The elegant black carriage rolled slowly through the sun-dappled Bois. It was a handsome carriage, one well known in the park and in the fashionable districts of Paris. The sun gleamed on the sleek, polished exterior. On the doors, the de Chagny crest was painted in exquisite detail. Even the horses were a flashy pair of pure-blooded animals. Halfway through the Bois, the carriage slowed and drew up before the Grand Cascade.

There was no lack of comfort inside the carriage. Dark burgundy velvet covered the thickly-cushioned seats and every luxury that was possible was available to the occupants, but to Christine the long ride had seemed endless and tiresome.

Raoul, who was lounging comfortably back in the seat across from Christine, continued to stare thoughtfully at her face as if he was trying to read her through her expressions. "Why do *you* think I invited you for this ride?" he asked her as he continued their conversation.

"To be seen, of course," she replied as she glanced down at her gloved hands. She looked up. "That's what these rides are all about, aren't they? You haven't told me yet. Am I dressed fashionably enough to please you?"

A hard, humorless smile briefly tightened the corners of his mouth. He did not understand her mood today. She was far from pleasing him.

"I take it you didn't have a very good visit with Petrine."

Christine hesitated a moment before she said, "Actually, if I am to be perfectly honest, I find it to be a bit of a strain to be in her presence. And if *she* were to be honest, I think the sentiment is mutual."

To her surprise, he laughed outright. "I can't think of two women who are such complete opposites in temperament. You, Christine, are unlike any woman I have ever met. And Petrine, admittedly, does take some getting used to."

"I don't know if I want to get used to her," Christine confessed.

"She's only trying to get closer to you. Can you really fault her for that?" His gaze narrowed slightly. "Did she talk with you about your new wardrobe?"

"She brought it up again, yes," Christine replied. "It's about all we ever talk about."

"And?"

"And I don't know if I will have time for all those fittings and decisions right now. Don't you think it is a little early to be thinking about such things?"

"Not in the least. Do you have any idea how long it takes to have quality garments put together?"

"As opposed to what I am wearing?" she asked testily.

"I didn't mean that and you know it."

"And this matter of a tour of Europe," she said as she frowned out the window. "Why am I only hearing about this now?"

"I wanted to surprise you."

"I think what I'm feeling is overwhelmed instead."

"I want you to feel overwhelmed. I want to sweep you off your feet. Isn't that how a bride is supposed to feel?"

She was still frowning and she had a faraway look in her eyes as she said, "You have kept me away from the Opera House all day and I missed an important rehearsal, but you already know that since we discussed my schedule before we left this morning."

"If I were any other man, I might think you were choosing the Opera House over me."

"You agreed that we would be gone for the morning only. The day is almost gone and we haven't even started back yet."

"I have been enjoying your company. If I would rather not see it end, can you blame me for that?"

She didn't reply, so he couldn't tell what she was thinking.

"Any other woman, you know, would be thrilled at the idea of a new wardrobe," he said. "Not to mention a tour of Europe. Yet you seem- almost annoyed. Why?"

"Maybe because I am never included in the decisions you make."

"Yes, I know. You are a very modern and independent woman with a mind of your own."

"Would you rather I was like Petrine who buries herself in her needlepoint and is so timid she has admitted to me that she would probably faint dead away at the sight of a tiny mouse?"

He sat back against the velvet cushions and regarded her with a bland smile. "The truth is, I *have* seen Petrine almost swooning over a spider, if it is big enough."

"With men there to protect her, what reason would she have to be afraid?" Christine asked half flippantly.

"She enjoys the life she lives, Christine," he said, suddenly becoming very sober. "She herself admits she wouldn't change any of it. So she plays a helpless, damsel-in-distress role and lets men take care of her? It's small compensation for the luxuries that surround her."

"Well, I am not like that. I do not want to feel like I must play a role. Or that I should have to pretend or to feel obligated- "

"Obligated? What on earth would *you* feel obligated for?" he interrupted her in a tone that made her stare back at him.

"What do you mean by that?"

"I mean, Christine, that so far I have had very little compensation for the things I have done for you."

"What are you trying to say?"

"Only that you resent everything I try to do for you. Yet this so-called Phantom of the Opera can do no wrong."

"What are you talking about?"

"He sends you roses. He arranges elaborate wedding gifts. And he has also recommended you for your roles at the Opera House." There was sarcasm laced through his words, but behind the sarcasm she knew that he was seething with anger. "Surely it has occurred to you to wonder what *he* wants in return."

Her eyes grew wide. "What are you implying?"

"Only that a man would not do those things for a woman unless he expected something in return. There. I've said it. You may not like hearing it, but that's the plain, unvarnished truth."

"Is that how you think it must be between a man and a woman? That acts of kindness should be done only with the anticipation of receiving something in return?"

He took no pains to hide his anger now. He sneered openly as he leaned slightly forward. "You accept his gifts, every single one of them, yet you refuse a wardrobe from your own fiancé? What am I supposed to think? We are to be married, Christine, yet I am a beggar for the slightest display of affection from you. Even a kiss or an occasional embrace is something I must work like a bricklayer on a pyramid to coax out of you."

"A br- " she sputtered. "So you think I should do those things because I am obligated to do them? Maybe you are used to a different kind of woman- "

"I can assure you I am used to something *quite* different. From any number of women."

"Like Capucine?"

"Capucine? Where did you hear- So you know about Capucine." There was a subtle change in his tone. "Does that mean you are jealous?"

"Jealous? No."

"I will not make excuses or explanations for my past, Christine," he said and a coldness now crept into his voice.

"I am not asking you to."

But the truth was, it was a past she was beginning to question more and more. And it wasn't only his past that had her wondering. Earlier that morning she had seen another strangely-intimate scene between Raoul and Ligeia, something which seemed completely out of character for the cold, aloof Ligeia. She had observed Ligeia touching Raoul's face with her hand. It had been a slow, lingering touch and it had seemed to Christine more like a lover's caress than a sign of affection between a stepmother and her stepson. It had disturbed her enough that she could not get it out of her mind.

"Enough of this quarreling," he grumbled. "Let's not ruin the rest of our day."

An uncomfortable silence deepened between them. As the carriage started off again, leaving the Grand Cascade behind them, Christine chose to watch the scenery passing by rather than argue with him anymore. For the rest of the trip they barely spoke.

Raoul's hand clenched and unclenched on the silver head of the cane he was holding. There was a wolf in the family crest, so the head of the cane was in the shape of a feral wolf. He was feeling somewhat predatory himself at that moment himself. While Christine continued to stare out the window, his gaze raked her slowly from head to knees. He had a good reason for keeping her away from the Opera House as long as possible, but he was beginning to wonder if his surprise was going to please her or if it was going to turn out to be yet another reason for her to accuse him of making her decisions for her.

He was beyond frustrated with her. So far his efforts to impress her had been a dismal failure. He shook his head slightly as he continued to regard her. She looked quite beautiful as she sat there, quite desirable, but she had a faraway look in her eyes, as if she was miles away from him.

Perversely, that only made him want her more. In fact, bedding her was becoming almost an obsession with him lately. Once he made her his, this Phantom *and* this singing business would cease to be a problem for him. And once they were wed, he would have full authority over her. Every decision, every facet of her life, would be his to control. He looked forward to crushing, once and for all, her defiance and the damnable independence she prided herself on. She would belong to him in every sense of the word. In the meantime, he resolved then and there that he would get her into bed long before the wedding vows were spoken. And after he had staked his claim on her in that most primitive of ways, she would not dare to defy him. She would not dare.

As he put more thought into his plan, he felt himself grow hard and rigid with his lustful imaginings, so much so that he had to position his hand and his arm in such a way as to hide his arousal from her. By the time they were headed back through the gates of the Bois, he was throbbing and straining against his pantaloons as he envisioned everything he would do to her in full and rousing detail. But until then, he could not touch her and in his frustration he swore under his breath which drew a questioning look from her.

Christine saw a muscle tensing in Raoul's tightly clenched jaw as he scowled across the carriage at her. She completely mistook the desire glittering in his eyes as anger as he said, "Someday, Christine, you will come to appreciate the things that I do for you."

The long day had taken its toll on Christine. She wanted only one thing and that was to be back in the quiet comfort of her room. But as she pulled her gloves off, she still felt like a bow string that had been stretched too tightly.

"I take it you didn't have a very good visit today?" Lisette asked as she watched her.

"Hardly."

"Does that mean you are still having doubts about the wedding?"

Christine looked sharply at the young woman sitting in her dressing room, but she avoided a direct answer. "A great deal has changed," she said as she threw her gloves on the dressing room table and took off her hat.

"Do you want to talk about it?" Lisette asked.

Christine shook her head. "No."

"You were gone a very long time."

"I know. I had not anticipated that."

"It's not getting any easier with them, is it?" Lisette asked. "I mean your time with the de Chagnys."

"No," Christine sighed. She was tired. The last thing she wanted to talk about was Raoul, or Petrine, or Ligeia or Philippe for that matter. She turned towards the doorway of her bedroom, but hesitated when Lisette said behind her, "Before you go in there, I should tell you- "

But Christine was already standing in the doorway. After her first gasp of astonishment, she remained silent for several breathless moments. A change was slowly coming over her face. She whirled around to face Lisette and waited for an explanation.

"I tried to tell you before you went in there. It happened while you were gone."

Christine clamped her jaw shut. Her breast rose and fell as she fought against the tumult of emotions seething within her, but nothing she did was going to bring about a calming. Not for a very long time at least.

"Do you want to be on stage and forget the words as you just did?"

"I won't forget them. Have I not worked hard enough today?"

"No," he growled. "Not nearly hard enough."

He was being very severe with her today. He was exacting. He was demanding. And while he often pushed her to do her very best, this new brusque, impatient manner of his was not like him at all.

"Where is the young woman who threw everything she had into her lessons?" he asked as he stopped his pacing and regarded her sternly for a moment. "You used to be single-minded, Christine. You used to focus and give yourself to the music."

"I am still that way."

"Then let yourself *feel* it. You must make your audience believe your emotions."

But when she sang the song again, he stared out the window as if he wasn't even aware of her presence in the room with him. When she had finished, he had nothing to say to her.

"Wasn't that better?" she asked as she stared at his back.

"You're supposed to be a woman who is passionately in love," he said without turning.

"And I wasn't convincing?"

He turned around to face her.

She was wearing a mahogany-colored dress with accents of black velvet and a delicate fall of ivory lace on the collar. The richly-hued dress brought out the pale amethyst of her eyes and the effect was distracting. Damned distracting. But that was his fault, too. He should have picked out plain, serviceable clothes for her to wear. Not gowns that made her look like- like that.

"I let this go too far," he said before he could stop himself.

"Let what go too far?"

"We have worked long enough for one day. You obviously have other things on your mind."

"I have been distracted," she admitted. "But we don't have to quit. I'll try harder. It is not my intention to waste your time."

"Don't do this for *me*," he growled. "I told you I don't want your pity."

"I do pity you," she made the confession, her own ire rising in the face of his dark mood. "But not in the way you think. Maybe pity isn't the right word."

"And what, pray tell, would the right word be?"

She opened her mouth, but a few silent moments passed before she spoke. "However scarred your face might be, I think it is your soul that is far more damaged. That is the reason I pity you."

He scoffed in derision. "Save your pity for someone else. I don't want it."

She faced him boldly. "What has changed between us?"

"Do you really wish to know? You used to stare at a curtain. Now, you stare just as intently at my face. I half imagine it is because you are trying to figure out what kind of monster lies beneath this mask."

"I don't think of you as a monster. No monster could create the music that you write."

He turned away from her again and bowed his dark head as if he was wrestling with his thoughts.

"I don't understand you today," she said. "The moment you came here, you reminded me of a caged tiger, one that has been locked up for far too long."

"Does that mean I frighten you as a tiger would?" he asked in a very quiet voice.

"I'm not afraid. Whatever lies beneath that mask, you're a man and someone should have told you that a man is much more than just a handsome face. Or half a handsome face."

She stopped as he slowly turned back around. Had he realized that she had just admitted that she found him handsome? In truth she did find his features strong and manly, what she could see of them. And she was on the verge of telling him that very thing when he said in a very low voice, without looking at her, "Do not make the mistake of thinking that your flattery will blind me to the other half of my face."

"My flattery? Is that what you think it is?"

"I have said as much."

"You are hard-hearted today," she said outright. "And, dare I say, insulting."

She was probably right, he admitted to himself. They had taken away all her furniture, the very things he had picked out for her, yesterday. The Viscount had then taken it upon himself to replace every single piece with furnishings of his own choosing. Better to be hard-hearted than to let her know how that had affected him.

"I should be vexed with you for even suggesting that I am being insincere," she said.

"Impossible child," he growled under his breath.

"I'm not a child."

No, she wasn't.

And then he found himself wondering testily if she was as vexed and preoccupied when she was in the Viscount's presence. They had been spending more and more time together lately. She had been gone all day yesterday, in fact, which had been time enough to completely refurnish her rooms. They had taken all her old things, the very ones he had picked out for her, out of the Opera House completely.

He had not intended to bring it up, but he heard himself say, "I heard the Viscount had a surprise waiting for you yesterday."

"So you know about that."

"There is very little that goes on here that I do not eventually find out about."

"I was not expecting it," she said as she glanced up to see him staring at her with eyes that were dark and unfathomable.

"Did he please you?"

"Please me?" she echoed scoffingly. "To be honest, I really don't know what would motivate him to do such a thing."

"Maybe he wants you to be surrounded by a constant reminder of him."

"You may be right. If he wasn't so jealous- "

"Whatever does *he* have to be jealous about?" he interrupted her as he stared at her intently.

"You," she answered him.

"Me?"

"Yes, he knows about the roses. And he has found out, too, that you have recommended me for my roles in the Opera House. And there was the wedding gift."

There was an almost feral gleam in his eyes now. "Are you telling me he is worried that the Phantom of the Opera is your secret lover?"

She wouldn't have put it quite that way, but her silence was answer enough. She nodded slowly, unable to take her gaze from his, and said, "If he finds out about these lessons, he will have even more to worry about."

"So," he went on thoughtfully, half to himself. "He wonders if you are meeting some secret lover in the shadows of the Opera House. Not being sure, it must be eating away at him." He didn't say it to Christine, but for some reason that image gave him a great deal of satisfaction. He turned to her. "What he suspects is half right. We do meet in secret and we do go out of our way to keep him from knowing about it. I *am* the Phantom of the Opera and if he knew that I have kissed you- "

"Was it a kiss?" Christine asked without thinking.

He watched her with a questioning stare. "You're not sure?"

She shook her head almost imperceptibly.

"It must not have been a very memorable kiss," he said as his gaze boldly held hers. "Let's call it then a momentary lapse in judgement."

She stared back at him in silence.

"Whatever we choose to call it, it is something that won't happen again. And for the sake of your lessons, we'll try to forget that it ever happened."

Maybe he could forget, but she didn't know if that was possible.

"Can we?" she asked in a ghost of a voice.

"Not if- " He closed his eyes and didn't finish what he had been about to say.

Not if you keep looking at me that way, Christine.

"Not if *what*?" she pressed.

"Never mind. It's me," he said as he shook himself mentally and tried to gain some semblance of control, not only over the whole situation, but over his volatile emotions as well.

"It is something *I* have not forgotten," she confessed, low-voiced. "And Raoul . . . "

"Must never know since he already fears there is something happening between us," he finished for her.

It was a dangerous thing, Christine found, to talk so openly about that kiss. It started a strange, quivery sensation down low in her stomach. A kind of breathless anticipation. Unsettled by the subtle change in his dark eyes, her gaze dropped to his chest. Which didn't help in the least. She still felt the raw masculine force of him reaching out for her from across the room when she thought how she had touched him that night in box five, and how *he* had touched *her*.

"Does that change your mind about these lessons?"

She shook her head. "No. Not if you can forget- "

"I said I would *try* to forget."

Something had changed in his voice, and it kindled an answering heat deep inside her. As he stepped closer to her, she inhaled the subtle male scent of him. Overwhelmed by his sudden nearness, his focus, which seemed to be centered upon her, she drew a deep breath and let herself be drawn into the power of his dark gaze.

"And since you're so uncertain that it *was* a kiss, perhaps I should erase any doubts."

Without saying another word, he put his hand under chin and lifted her face to his. Before she knew what was happening, his mouth had swooped down upon hers. He silenced any protest with a deep, devouring kiss, one that seared her very soul. This time he made very, very sure that she knew it was a kiss.

Every rational thought Christine ever had seemed to fly out of her mind as his arms went around her and he dragged her unresisting body against his own. As if they had a will of their own, her arms crept up around his neck as he kissed her again. True to his pirate blood, he plundered, he ravaged, he showed her no quarter, yet it was hard to say who was the captive of the other.

They came apart breathlessly, overcome by the unexpected storm of their passion. Still reeling from the onslaught on her senses, Christine stepped back, but found that her legs were unsteady as her bosom rose and fell with her effort to breath.

"Forgive me, Christine," he breathed in a raspy voice as he took another step away from her. "I didn't mean to do that. "

But it was a lie, he knew. He had meant every breathless second of that kiss, and if he could, he would very willingly do it all over again. Yet he clamped down on his runaway lust and, after that succinct, woefully inadequate apology, he walked out on her. Because only he knew how close he had come to forgetting every vow he had ever made and he meant to keep it that way.

"What did you say?" Christine's tea cup stopped halfway between the saucer and her mouth.

She set the cup down and stared at Remi who had made the outrageous statement in the first place, and then at Lisette who seemed to be avoiding any eye contact whatsoever. Indeed, both of them seemed to be trying to pretend she wasn't even there in the room with them.

She looked around her dressing room as if seeing it for the first time, at each and every new piece of furniture. "Surely you can't mean- Where did you get an idea like that?"

"I heard it from Monsieur Peverell himself," Remi informed her after a quick glance at Lisette.

Christine got up from her chair and then walked slowly across her dressing room. For a moment it looked like she was going to go into her bedroom, too, but she stopped and suddenly whirled around.

"You mean Monsieur Peverell himself said that the Phantom of the Opera was responsible for changing the furnishings in my room last year?"

Remi nodded slowly. And then he shrugged as if he had decided it was time she knew the truth. He lifted his tea cup to his lips and sipped the dark liquid as he watched her over the rim.

"So Raoul also knew? And that's why he- "

"*Oui*, Christine," Lisette affirmed.

Christine stared at them both for a silent moment. Then she took a deep breath and said, "It seems I am the only one in the dark." And then something else occurred to her. "Raoul must have been furious when he found out."

"From what I hear, yes, that was the case," Lisette told her.

"So he really was motivated by jealousy," Christine said half to herself.

"It appears so," Lisette affirmed as she narrowed her gaze over her own cup. "Does that come as a surprise to you?"

No, Christine thought. Now that she knew the truth, it wasn't a surprise at all.

"You must beware of a jealous man, Christine," Lisette went on very soberly without looking at her. "When he lets his jealousy rule him. Such a man can become very irrational. Desperate even."

Lisette didn't say anything else. Why, then, did Christine have the distinct impression that Lisette *wanted* to tell her more?

Hours later, when she was lying alone in the darkness of her room, hating the new furnishings and wishing for her old things back, Christine was still going over everything that had happened. She thought back over every detail of her last lesson. Erik's frustration and his anger had been evident. And now she thought she understood what was behind it.

Raoul had known about the furniture all along and he had not said a word to her. He had gone behind her back and taken matters into his own hands, once again making her decisions for her. Decisions that had not been to her liking at all. She thought back over Raoul's visit that morning. He had obviously been expecting her to be grateful and pleased over his generous gift. In truth, she was feeling just the opposite.

There were so many conflicting emotions warring within her that her life lately seemed to be becoming more and more hopelessly entangled. Erik had been right. She *was* distracted. She *was* having a hard time concentrating on her lessons. Part of the reason was that she was constantly thinking about him. And about that kiss in box five that night, especially now that she knew it had actually been a kiss. He had admitted it himself. Of course, there was no doubt about the second kiss which had taken her completely by surprise. She thought she now understood what had motivated such an impulsive move on his part. He had been upset about the furniture being replaced. He had been angry. Anger had made him kiss her.

But perhaps the worst thing of all, the thing that really played upon her guilt, was that she had let him kiss her, and she couldn't help comparing kisses. Raoul's kisses had never affected her the way Erik's had. Raoul had never made her feel like she had been swept away in a storm of mindless passion. Ever. She couldn't imagine him kissing her until the whole world faded away, leaving just the two of them. She couldn't imagine Raoul leaving her breathless and waiting for more. So much more.

"I must stop this," she whispered to the darkness as she clasped her hands together and held them against her mouth.

She should be remorseful. She knew that. She should be guilt-ridden over the shamelessness of her behavior. But the truth was that she wasn't. Those kisses with Erik had felt so right. Was that why she kept reliving them? Was that why she was suddenly questioning everything about her life and her future with Raoul as she never had before?

Chapter 15

"We must go over your dance steps to get the choreography right and we can't do that with Gaspar here. Besides, there is no telling how long Gaspar will take getting over his cold. The man has already been confined to his bed for three days." Madame Giry made a slight scoffing sound. "You would think that no one in the world has ever suffered so much from a cold."

Madame Giry had arranged a private, late-night rehearsal for the final act of the new opera. She was on the stage alone with Christine.

"We'll begin when Erik gets here."

Christine looked up. "Erik?"

"Yes, I didn't have a chance to tell you earlier, and I didn't know if he would actually agree to it. I decided that this rehearsal would be far more productive if he was here. He can play the music for you. He can also sing Gaspar's part. It won't be any different than one of your lessons. Ah, there he is now."

Christine's heart picked up its pace as she tried to look anywhere but at Erik. She had not seen him since their last lesson and she couldn't even begin to imagine how things would be between them after that kiss.

"You move as silently as a cat," Madame Giry said to the man who had just stepped up onto the stage.

Christine finally looked at him, but it was difficult not to betray any outward sign of her inner turmoil. As for Erik, he flashed her a brief dark glance, the apology in his eyes telling her that this had not been his idea.

He held his violin casually in one hand as he listened to Madame Giry's instructions. Now and then, he interjected his own ideas. This was a different setting for them and Christine couldn't help thinking how strange it felt to be standing on the stage with Erik. All his attention was focused on Madame Giry at the moment so she was able to study him in detail. How tall he was, how broad-shouldered, how potent his maleness, and how the gaslights brought out highlights in his dark hair . . .

It took her a moment to realize that Madame Giry was talking to her. "Since this opera gives you the opportunity to sing *and* to dance," she was saying. "There is so much more for you to learn. I arranged for this rehearsal tonight so you can dance to the actual music without the constant disruptions and distractions of the other performers and so that I can see exactly how the choreography is going to work out. That way I will have plenty of time to make any necessary adjustments."

Madame Giry had asked Christine to wear the same costume she would be wearing on stage. The dress was the color of liquid emeralds and it shimmered in the gaslight as it clung to every curve, but bared her bosom and her shoulders.

"I have never seen anything so beautiful," Madame Giry told her as she looked over the dress critically. "Remi has been working on this all day so that you could wear it tonight. He will have to make a few more adjustments, of course."

Indeed he would. The bodice was quite low, perhaps a little too revealing.

"But the dress is exquisite, isn't it Erik? Is it what you had in mind for this scene?"

"It's, ah- yes, perfect," Erik answered and Madame Giry gave him a curious glance at the hesitation in his voice. For a moment, she wasn't quite sure if he was looking at the dress or at Christine. And when she asked if they were ready to get started, he merely nodded and by now was avoiding looking at Christine altogether.

"Give me a moment to get my papers so that I can take notes," Madame Giry said as she disappeared off stage.

Christine knew a moment of panic. What would she say when she was alone with Erik? What would *he* say?

"You seem surprised to see me here," he said as he walked over to her.

"I am," she admitted. "I wasn't sure if you had decided to end the lessons again."

"I would have sent you word if that had been the case. I thought I would give you a few days to consider if the lessons were worth it."

"Worth it?"

"If they were worth being set upon by a madman. I have no excuse for my behavior the last time we were together, save that the lack of a curtain, apparently, can bring out the worst in me." He smiled faintly. "It won't happen again."

She drew a deep breath as she pushed several loose curls back from her bare shoulder. "Of course I think the lessons are worth it," she said, and silently congratulated herself on the steadiness of her voice.

"I knew you might be uncomfortable doing a private rehearsal with me," he went on. "But Madame Giry asked me to come and I couldn't think of a valid reason for refusing her. Besides, we will properly chaperoned for once. You should be safe enough."

"I never felt *un*safe," she said, daring to look straight at him. "We have been together many times without a chaperone."

"But that was before- "

He didn't finish what he had been about to say and an uncomfortable moment of silence fell between them.

"I didn't know you had been responsible for furnishing my rooms," she said to break the silence. "I mean before Raoul changed everything. When I learned that, I realized that you must have picked everything out based on our conversations during our lessons. I understand now the thought that went into every piece. And I- you had every right to be angry."

"Perhaps it was time for a change," he said, his hand flexing on his violin as he looked down at the instrument.

"That was certainly not the case," she informed him with a slight lift of her chin. "I liked my bed. It made me feel like a princess. And everything else was perfect as well."

Did she imagine that his expression changed, softened? If so, the change was transient, subtle. He held her gaze. "Whatever I was feeling, I should not have taken it out on you. Does that mean you forgive me?"

"Of course I forgive you."

But what was there, really, to forgive him for? she found herself thinking.

199

He gave a very slight, very gallant nod of his head, and his cobalt eyes dipped momentarily as he conceded to her generous pardon.

"Christine, are you ready to begin?" Madame Giry asked as she walked back onto the stage.

"Yes."

Christine walked to the center of the stage. She was not looking at Erik now, yet she felt his dark gaze following her.

"In this last scene," Madame Giry was saying. "You have finally come to realize that you have fallen deeply in love with your mysterious, unseen lover. He has been in love with you all along, but from afar."

To Erik she said, "You have not dared to approach her. I think it would be best if you stood *there*." She pointed to the place she meant.

She was speaking to Christine again. "Christine, you feel him there in the darkness. You sense him with your heart. As he pours out his love to you, you can't hear him singing, but your heart is really answering him every time *you* sing. During this scene, it is morning. The sunlight will be falling through the trees and woods will be veiled with mist. Erik has something very special planned. The scenery will be quite elaborate, and, I dare say, breathtaking."

She went on to describe the scenery in more detail, where Christine would be standing and how the special effects would work. "How that is going to be accomplished I am not certain. But if Erik decides it will work, then we can be assured that it will.

"You will sit here first," she said, indicating the place where a bench would be. "Here in the garden while the first flush of dawn grows around you. The roses are in bloom and it is a very hushed, very haunted moment as you are pulled by things you cannot see. It is a moment of pure awareness."

She paused a moment and said to Erik, "This is where you will stand before you walk away from her for the final time. She will never know what you have given up, or that you have sacrificed yourself for her happiness."

And then Madame did something very strange. She half turned away from them and said with a catch in her voice, "I imagine there won't be a dry eye in the theater."

Was it possible that there were tears in *her* eyes?

While Christine wondered at Madame Giry's unaccustomed display of emotion, Erik lifted his violin and began to play. Christine sang her aria, the same one they had practiced several times already. When she had finished, she stood there completely absorbed in the music as he played on. Somehow on stage his songs came to life even more than during their lessons.

Following Madame Giry's instructions, she did several graceful spins across the floor. As Erik played on, in no time at all, she lost herself in the music. When she came to a breathless pause in the center of the stage, Madame Giry seemed more than pleased.

"Magnifique, Christine. The audience will be enthralled. It's a shame you will be singing with Gaspar instead of Erik. While Gaspar is quite capable, I have also heard Erik sing and I think that *you* two would sing beautifully together. Since the next song is a love duet, I will have you both sing it together this time."

Madame Giry could not help but be aware of their hesitation when she asked them to sing the song together. Her gaze shifted from one to the other. Erik acknowledged her request with an air of studied indifference, but she noted that there was a brief flicker of something dark in his eyes that he quickly concealed.

They finally did sing the song together. They were so finely attuned to each other that Madame Giry knew she was watching something rare. Something beautiful. Erik was hopelessly, deeply in love with Christine. She already knew that. But it was Christine who held her gaze now. Seeing them together-

Christine's softly lingering glances when she looked at Erik, the wistful look on her face and the emotion in her voice, Madame Giry realized, had less to do with the music and the dancing than they had to do with Erik himself. Christine was not merely acting. It came as a shock for her to realize that Christine was-

A woman in love.

He knew full well that he was guilty of an unreasoning jealousy. And he knew he had no right to that emotion where Christine was concerned. But try as he might, he couldn't seem to help himself. Seeing her with Raoul de Chagny that morning had left him in a dark and disagreeable mood.

He felt possessive of her. How could he not? He had held the woman in his arms. He had kissed her. And he wanted far more than that from her. He wanted her heart, as unreasonable as that was. But even if there was a chance for that, what could he offer her? A life of darkness and solitude? And while he suspected she was becoming infatuated with him, or rather, the mystery of who she *thought* he was, how long before that wore off in the harsh face of reality? She was Beauty. And he was the Beast. And, unlike the fairytale, a kiss would not change any of it. Her fantasy was like all fantasies. It was not based on reality. If she should have even one look at him, the fantasy would vanish as if it had never existed at all, and he would not be able to bear the look of horror on her face when she saw him for who he really was.

He knew that he had taken her by surprise with that kiss. He wrestled with his own culpability. Was he guilty of feeding her infatuation in spite of his vows to keep her at a distance? While she had not exactly responded to the kiss, neither had she pushed him away. Nor had she exhibited the outrage he would have expected from her. He knew the danger of continuing on with the lessons. He had weakened once. If, *if* he should kiss her again - and *if* she should kiss him back - then there would be no hope for him. His torment at losing her completely would come close to destroying him.

And yet he was brutally honest with himself. He wanted to kiss her again. He wanted it with everything in him. He also knew that the longer they went on, the deeper she drew him. He had opened the door to the darkness inside himself and let her light shine straight down into his soul. And now he did not know how to close that door again.

He undid the fastenings from his linen shirt and drew it over his head. He was pulling a new shirt on when he became aware of the Persian's approach.

"You promised Christine a copy of the finished song," the man reminded him.

"Ah, yes, the song. She may have to wait a while," he said as he worked at the buttons of the shirt. "It may take a little longer than I had anticipated to get it down on paper for her."

"She sent this to you."

He turned around.

"Sent what?"

He froze and stared at the neatly-wrapped package in the Persian's hand.

"She asked me to bring it to you."

He took the small package in his hands and opened it. He'd had very few presents in his life and he didn't know quite how to act.

"She put quite a great deal of effort into making it," the Persian informed him. "She spent half the morning in the Opera House kitchen. She said it wasn't easy finding all the ingredients at this time of the year."

He looked at the Persian but he didn't know what to say. It wasn't until after the man had left him that Erik said to the emptiness that surrounded him, "Christine, Christine, what are you doing to me?"

The early sunshine fell through the stained glass windows and fractured into beams of intensely-vibrant colors. Christine was seated in one of the front row pews, the one reserved for the de Chagny family.

It was a quiet Sunday morning and the church doors were open behind her. The weather outside was perfect. The sky was a deep, cloudless blue, exactly the color of a robin's egg. Maybe it was because of the peaceful weather outside that Christine was finding it difficult to pay attention to the sermon inside. Who would not want to be enjoying such a day? But she knew it was more than that. It was becoming harder and harder to think about anything other than Erik. No matter where she was.

The times she felt most alive were when she was with him. Probably because he had always allowed her be who she was. And she'd had her first taste of passion. The mere thought of his kisses left her in a dazed, distracted state of mind. Just thinking about the possibility of being in his arms again had the power to make her feel weak, to draw her once again into this spell he had woven around her. Even more confusing to her was that, in the end, she felt no guilt. Or very little, at least. It felt right to be in his arms, as if that's where she was meant to be.

She looked up from her hymn book, chiding herself for her wayward thoughts. They were hardly the kinds of thoughts she should be having in church. She said a swift, silent prayer for forgiveness, but even as her lips whispered the words, she felt herself melt all over again at the remembrance of his mouth moving over hers. Hungrily. Passionately. Blissfully.

Deep down, she knew that part of the reason she was so distracted was because now that she'd had time to think it through, not only did she realize how deeply *she* had been affected by those kisses. She realized that he had been affected, too. Every glance he gave her, every word he spoke took on a new, deeper meaning. She read more into those things now. Something powerful was happening between them, something that both awed and frightened her with its intensity, and denying it would be less than truthful.

As she found herself wondering what his reaction had been when he had received her gift, a small smile curved her lips. But when she felt Raoul's gaze upon her, the smile vanished and she was jerked abruptly back to the present. She didn't dare raise her eyes to his. Sometimes lately, Raoul stared at her with a steady fixation that she found disconcerting. She could not read his thoughts, however. Whatever they were, he kept them to himself.

Standing to join in another hymn, she kept her eyes lowered, sincerely hoping that Raoul could not read the guilt that she tried so desperately to hide.

Chapter 16

Dark clouds had been gathering all day and the threat of rain had hung ominously on the air. In the greyness of an early dusk, a few raindrops spattered against the glass. Christine turned from the window and quickly made her way back down the dark, deserted corridor.

Even as she half ran, she was fastening the velvet frogs at her throat and pulling the hood of her cape forward. Downstairs, to her relief, she found the vestibule empty, so she boldly went forward with her plan, completely unaware of the dark figure that was watching her silently from the shadows.

Her hand was just reaching for the brass door handle when she felt someone at her side. Startled, she whirled around and stared up at the man who was flinging a cape about his own wide shoulders. As he raised his hood, he said, "Come. We'd best make haste. The storm is about to open up on us." He paused a moment to ask, almost as an afterthought, "Where are you going?"

"Anywhere."

The moment he pulled the ponderous door open, heavy drops of wind-driven rain rushed through the opening. But there were voices behind them and so there was no time to delay. With his hand on her back, Erik guided Christine out into the stormy night.

A blast of cold wind and rain immediately blew under her hood and billowed the hem of her cape. With a breathless gasp she turned away, only to be caught against Erik's chest and shielded from the worst of the onslaught.

"This way," he said, half covering her with his cloak.

Heedless of the wind and rain, Christine hurried along with him to a waiting carriage. She wasted no time climbing in. Erik followed her inside and pulled the door shut behind them.

"Who are you running away from?" he asked as he sat down in the seat across from her.

"Everyone," she said as the carriage jerked into motion.

After her performance tonight, she had wanted only one thing. To be alone. If she had even tried going back to her dressing room, she would have been immediately surrounded by a crowd of people, Raoul first and foremost among them.

She drew her wet hood back and spent a few moments adjusting her skirts. As she leaned back on the velvet cushions, she heard, "Shall I light the lantern?"

"No. Leave it dark," she replied.

As the carriage rattled over the wet cobblestones, the rain began to beat down harder upon the roof.

"The poor driver," she murmured sympathetically. "It must be miserable to have to be outside on a night like this."

"Don't worry about him," Erik's deep voice assured her. "He is being more than compensated for his time and his discomfort."

There was just the sound of the rain for a while, and the clip-clop of horses' hooves on the cobbles. She could barely see the man across from her in the darkness, but she heard him comment, "You are still in your stage costume."

"I didn't dare go back to my dressing room to change. No doubt, I would have been waylaid for hours. Carlotta seems to be able to manage socializing after a performance, but I apparently, don't have it in me. Where are we going?" she asked, bracing herself as the carriage bumped along a heavily-rutted stretch of road.

"The Bois."

"I have taken many carriage rides through the Bois," she mused. "But none at night. And none in the rain with a ghost sitting across from me."

Very low, almost wicked laughter came from the darkness on the other side of the carriage. Because the space was so confining, she felt his long legs brush lightly against her skirts.

"The Viscount will be livid when he finds that you are gone," she heard him say.

"No doubt."

"I see you are not overly concerned at that image."

"Oh, I assure you, I will be repentant enough tomorrow. He will make certain of that."

"A lover's spat?"

"Nothing specific, but the night is not over yet. Were you following me?" she asked.

"Yes," he confessed without even a moment's hesitation. "You were being very mysterious."

"As mysterious as you?"

"Moreso."

"How was my performance tonight?"

"Perfection."

She pulled the curtain aside and looked out the window. "I don't think the rain will last. It is already letting up."

"Where were you going if I had not come along?" he asked.

"I don't know. Given the weather, I might have turned around and gone back inside."

After a silence, he said, "Thank you for the tourtiere."

"Did you enjoy it?"

"Very much."

"I wanted to repay you in some small way for all that you have done for me."

"There was no need, but I did enjoy it."

And then she heard, "It seems we are improperly unchaperoned again. I hope that doesn't cause you some concern."

"You're a man of many moods," she said honestly. "Some, I confess, I cannot even begin to anticipate. Truthfully, I never know what to expect from you."

"You can expect more gentlemanly conduct tonight than I have exhibited in the past."

That should have set her mind at ease. Why then, was she feeling a vague sense of disappointment instead?

Christine saw that they were just now passing the gate leading into the Bois. The rain had already ended but the sky was still a very black, starless void. A faint mist was beginning to rise from the damp ground as the deep, melodious croaking of frogs and the descant of nocturnal insects filled the night with a music all its own.

"There's not a soul out there," she murmured.

"You wanted to be alone."

"I'm not really alone. I'm here with a man who- " She hesitated, not sure what she had been about to say. They were far away from the rest of the world and somehow the usual rules didn't seem to apply. But then with this man, they rarely did.

"Who what?"

"Who leaves me confused."

"How so?"

"I suppose it's because you are so contradictory. First you keep me at a distance, then you are taking me on a carriage ride. One minute you are reprimanding me and telling me very harshly that I am not giving my all to my lessons. The next you are- kissing me. What am I to think?"

She should not have said that, Christine knew, but some perverse mood seemed to be driving her.

"Ah, you dig the spur in deeper. So merciless, Christine. I thought you said you had forgiven me."

"I have. But that does not necessarily mean I have forgotten. Do you never think about it?" she dared to ask.

"I think about it."

"You say that like you're recalling a loved one's death."

He scoffed softly in the darkness. "Truthfully? My behavior leaves me confused as well," he admitted.

For a while there was just the sound of the horses. And then again, Christine felt compelled to fill the silence between them. "One kiss was barely a kiss at all," she went on. "The other one was because you were angry. I suppose we can agree that makes both kisses meaningless."

"Meaningless? Did it ever occur to you that when you are referring to a man's kisses, such a word could be considered to be a serious blow to his pride?"

"I hardly think your pride would be wounded if you knew- " she said, cutting herself off just in time. She began again, choosing her words more carefully. "Since we work so closely together, I suppose we should expect to have a quarrel now and then."

"A quarrel?" he echoed, something that sounded very much like disbelief edging into his voice.

"I don't know what else to call it. You *were* angry."

"Whatever you choose to call it, be assured that I would do it over if I could."

In the darkness, he could not see the change in her face, and it was better that he did not.

"You would?" she asked in a voice scarcely above a whisper.

"It seems I have left you with a two opposing extremes, neither of which, apparently, have left you with a true sense of what a lover's kiss would be like."

A *lover's* kiss? Was that not a dangerous word to use between them? Christine wondered.

"And *that* would be different?" she asked softly.

"I assure you, Christine, if we were lovers, those kisses would have been very different."

There was a prolonged silence and before he could stop himself, he said, "I confess I have a question of my own."

"And what would that be?"

"Did you kiss me back?"

"You don't know?"

"No, apparently I am the one who is uncertain now. I have learned much about you in these past months, Christine. I have memorized your every feature and expression. I know that moment of fear before you go on the stage and the moment you overcome it. I know how you look when you give yourself over to the dance and to the music. But I do not know, apparently, when you- "

"I most definitely remember that I- had returned the kiss. Did you really not know?"

Part of her was very aware of the sway of the vehicle and the sound of the wheels as a deep silence lengthened between them. But through it all, she was waiting for one thing only, and that was his answer.

"I didn't. But definitely," he said in a lowered voice. "I would do it over, just so you would know what a proper lover's kiss should feel like."

She felt his weight shift to her side of the carriage and he was suddenly looming close to her in the darkness. And then, with hardly a moment's hesitation, he began to demonstrate very slowly, very thoroughly what a proper lover's kiss should be like.

It was a kiss of exquisite tenderness. And love. Unspeakable love. It went on and on and swept her away on a tide of inexpressible, breathless wonder.

This kiss did not end abruptly as the others had. It deepened as he took his time, letting his mouth move slowly over hers as his hand lifted to lightly touch the side of her face. His lips caressed. They courted. They savored. They seemed to possess the power to pervade her very heart and soul. And there was no mistake about it this time. She kissed him back.

Again, his kisses seemed to have the ability to make time stand still. The world faded away until there was nothing left but the indescribably-intoxicating feel of his mouth working sensuously over her own, loving her, worshipping her, adoring her. And Christine was lost, drowning in the sensations. She was so far from herself that she thought she might never be able to get back again.

When he finally drew back, she could find no words. Not a single one.

As for Erik, he knew there would be consequences for such a rash and impulsive move on his part, but for several breathless moments in time, the emptiness that normally yawned inside him had been filled. He closed his eyes, the better to linger in the madness that had just taken place, the easier to pretend that nothing was wrong, that reality could be undone and re-invented just as he wished it to be and not remain what it was.

The memory of the sweetness of her mouth was something he knew he would carry to his grave. For one blissful, rapturous moment in eternity, he had let himself be carried away by the illusion that they were lovers. Of course he wanted her. He had wanted her from the first moment he had laid eyes on her. But tonight, she had wanted him, too. That was his one consuming thought. She had wanted him, too.

He had not wanted the kiss to end. For several earth-shattering moments there was no curse between them. There was no Viscount. There was just the sharing of a tenuous dream in the darkness. But, of course, the sun would rise in the morning and banish away the dream and everything would look different in the harsh light of day. So he tamped down the desperate need that had taken root far too deeply and said the only truthful thing he could think of saying to her, the same words he had spoken to her before.

"I did not mean for things to go this far. It's time to go back. Before your viscount works himself into a state of frenzied panic at your absence."

As the carriage continued on through the weeping, night-shrouded Bois, he knew with no doubt whatsoever that he had made things worse. So much worse.

The sun was a flaming crimson ball settling over the distant buildings of Paris when Christine heard a knock at her door.

"Remi, what are you doing here with Androcles?"

Remi was holding the tiny dog in his arms, and he looked down at Androcles with a look of mock sternness. "It seems he has escaped again. But who could blame him? I would run away from Carlotta, too."

Remi rubbed noses with the little dog and received several exuberant dog kisses in return. Lately it seemed the two were inseparable.

"How is your head, Remi?" Christine asked as she led both of them into her dressing room.

"Honestly, I still have nightmares about that whole dreadful affair. But," he shrugged. "I refuse to let it stifle my creative efforts."

"That is very obvious. What do you have there," she asked, arching an inquisitive brow.

"Swatches."

"For me?"

"Heavens no. These are for Carlotta. Or I should say, they're for Androcles. Carlotta wants a little wardrobe made for him. As for you, Christine, I hope you trust that I know the right colors for you."

"I wouldn't trust anyone else."

"I'm nearly finished with the alterations to your costume. While I'm here, I should also warn you that Carlotta's wrath against you hasn't lessened in the least. In fact, it seems to be getting worse. Not that bitter rivalries and jealousy aren't a normal part of theater life, but I thought you should be aware of it.

"This morning's rehearsal was like nothing I have ever heard before," Remi went on. "The music of this new opera is sheer emotion."

"Yes," Christine murmured softly. "It is beautiful, isn't it?"

"From beginning to end," Remi agreed. "Someone has poured their soul onto the pages. Someone has wrung the very emotion from their heart."

There was a great deal of conjecture about who had really written the opera. Some thought it was an out and out publicity stunt. Others believed that a copy of the opera had been found hidden away in the cellars of the opera house and that the identity of the composer was a mystery. Still others believed the Phantom of the Opera had, in fact, written it. But they had all stood in awe at the sheer beauty of the music. No one had been unaffected. Even the stage hands stopped what they were doing to listen during rehearsals.

"The opera almost seems to have been written for you personally," Remi said. He was watching her face closely as he petted Androcles.

"Do you think so? I would not be singing at all if Raoul had his way."

"I hope you're not even considering that," Remi said with a shudder. "People don't like to see the lead singer in any opera changed at the last minute. Can you imagine how bad things would get around here if Carlotta was to fill your place? And altering *your* costumes to fit her? It makes me cringe just to think about it. I have been working day and night on your costumes as it is. To start over from scratch would be a nightmare. I was told to put everything into your costumes. To spare no effort."

"By Madame Giry?"

"By Madame Giry," Remi answered her with a shrug. "Or the Phantom himself. It is hard to say. It is after all his opera. Whoever he is, *what*ever he is, he has ensured a packed house for opening night. And from what I have heard and seen at rehearsals, no one is going to be disappointed. Yet something has been bothering you?" Remi went on. "Is it because your time is running out here?"

"I suppose that is a part of it."

"Are you still having doubts about your wedding?" he dared to ask.

"Would that sound foolish at this point?"

"You should always follow your heart, Christine, no matter where it leads you. True love is rare enough and if you really love someone, there should be no doubts, and no hesitation."

"Have you ever been in love, Remi?"

"I did love someone years ago. But only from afar. I was afraid to face my real feelings so eventually we went our separate ways."

"I'm sorry."

He shrugged again. "It was years ago."

"Have you forgotten?" she asked. "Really?"

"No," he answered her honestly. "I still look back after all these years and wonder what might have been if I'd had a little more courage."

"That sound very sad, Remi," she said sympathetically.

"Perhaps, but there's no time for sadness today," he said as he looked down at Androcles. "This one is ready for a fitting."

"Remi? Before you go, there's something I have wanted to ask you. What do you really think of Raoul?"

Remi looked like he was struggling to find something good to say. Finally he looked straight at Christine and said, "You should ask yourself if spending the rest of your life with the prince means submitting your very soul to him. And if that is the case, will you really have your happily-ever-after?"

As she thought that over, he added as an afterthought, "But the Viscount does wear nice clothes."

Chapter 17

"It's not time for our next lesson." Erik looked at Christine more closely. "You have sought me out. Why?"

"I thought you should know that they are planning to hold a séance here in the Opera House."

Without looking at her, he breathed out a low, scoffing laugh. "That shouldn't surprise me. Séances are all the rage right now."

They were in their old rehearsal room on the fourth floor, the very place where they used to hold their first lessons. Obviously, he was not happy to see her there. He had very specifically told her that he did not want her wandering around the Opera House by herself until the man who had attacked Remi had been caught.

"How did you find me?" he asked, glancing at her with a lingering frown.

"The Persian told me you were here. He said you were working on some musical arrangements."

He went back to his papers as if he was making a point of ignoring her. "I'll take you back to your room- "

"They are going to hold the séance in box five," she informed him.

His frown was still in place. "And who exactly is going to do that?"

"Raoul and some others. I thought you should know that Raoul will be trying to flush you out. Remi heard him say so."

"No doubt." His gaze narrowed. "And will *you* be there, too?"

"I have no wish to be a part of it, no. But given what has happened in the past when the box was occupied, I couldn't help but wonder if we should be expecting *something* to happen."

"*We* shall have to wait and see," he said ominously as he set the papers aside, then stood and faced her. "Let's go back downstairs now."

"I don't want to go back."

His face grew carefully blank. "You've told me what you came to say. There's no reason for you to stay."

"There is every reason. We have spent very little time together this past week, and I- I *want* to stay here with you."

"I don't think that would be a good idea. There is no end to the things I must see to with this opera," he said, trying to evade the real reason he was trying to avoid her.

"I thought I would be one of those things."

He suspected where this was going and he knew he had to put an end to it before he did something foolish. Yet again.

"You are one of the distractions I have been trying to avoid," he told her bluntly.

"Because of what happened the last time we were together?"

He shook his head slowly without taking his eyes off of her. "Because of what might happen *now*."

It was a bold answer. One that stirred the embers of her own desire.

"Can you not just decide what will or will not happen?" she asked.

"No, apparently that's something that seems beyond me where you are concerned. My best intentions seem to go so far away from me that I cannot even begin to call them back."

"Maybe your intentions need adjusting."

He blinked with open surprise, obviously not expecting such a daring statement from her. And then, as if suddenly remembering who she was, who he was, he straightened and half turned from her. "You don't know what you're saying."

"You're wrong. I'm very much aware of what I'm saying."

When she stepped closer to him, he went very still but kept his face averted from her.

"Christine, don't do this."

"Don't do what?" she asked as she stepped even closer. When he didn't answer her, she lifted her hand and laid her palm lightly against his chest. "This?"

His hand immediately closed around her wrist. "You have no idea what a dangerous game you're playing."

He was very wrong about that. She did know.

He released her hand and tried to look very stern as he warned her in a low voice, "I am weak enough in your presence. As I have already proven on more than one occasion. And that is with *no* encouragement from you. But if you- keep acting this way, I shall lose very quickly every last shred of my resolve."

Another bold admission.

"And what would you say if I told you that I have imagined you losing that resolve that you work so hard at maintaining?"

He stared at her helplessly for a moment. Then his jaw tightened as he dragged his gaze away from her.

"Have I misread what was behind those kisses?" she asked very softly. "Even the angry one?"

"You should not have come here. When I am with you- "

"You feel the same way that I do?" she finished for him.

Passion kindled in his eyes a moment before he was able to conceal it.

He let go of her and shook his head slowly. "You try my patience, Christine, in ways that test my very soul."

"I make you impatient then?"

He did not answer her.

And then he scoffed very softly, "Have I not proven that to you already? Do you want the truth? My passion for you would frighten you, so deep is it."

The dark look in his eyes made her draw a slow, steadying breath. "Have you perhaps considered that it only matches mine?"

He weakened for a moment in the face of her own confession, but was able to summon up a last vestige of resolve from some unknown corner of his soul. "I shall give you one last chance to leave me, Christine."

But she made no move to leave him. She couldn't.

"And was that passion there during our earliest lessons?" she questioned softly, not sparing him.

"Yes, then," he admitted.

"Even when you were behind the curtain?"

He nodded silently, not trusting himself to speak.

"Why do you find it so hard to tell me how you are really feeling?"

"Let me take you back now," he said in a husky whisper.

"If you did that, I should warn you that you would get no rest, because my heart would be calling out for you. You would hear me, would you not?" she asked as she placed her hand over his heart one more time. "Here."

She could feel the strong and steady throbbing of the heartbeat beneath her fingers. This time, he did not stop her hand. Emboldened, she lifted her hand to his face and ran her fingers lightly over the hard, chiseled line of his jaw, feeling the slight rasp of beard there. His eyes closed.

With slow deliberation, he took her hand away from his face, turned it over and held it to his lips. His expression remained intent, his gaze fixed on her face as he pressed a kiss into her upturned palm.

"If you stay, I should warn you that I can't guarantee even a pretense of gentlemanly conduct. You already know how quickly my best intentions crumble to utter ruin before you."

She took that as a surrender of sorts on his part.

"You're assuming that I want gentlemanly conduct. Maybe what I want is something entirely different. Maybe what I want is for you to make me forget everything else outside this room."

His chest rose and fell as he drew a deep breath.

"We could do that, Christine. Forget the rest of the world for a while." His gaze held hers. "But not all that stands between us."

In spite of his words, his arms went around her and he drew her close to him.

"The time may come when you regret what you have just asked me," he said as he rested his chin against her hair. "I had vowed that this would never be."

"Even if without you my heart would be empty?" she breathed softly against his shirt.

He tried one last protest. "Christine, we should not begin this . . . "

But even as he spoke, her lips were trailing slow kisses along his jaw and down the side of his throat.

"We have already begun," she said between kisses. Emboldened by the change in his breathing, she began to undo his shirt buttons, taking time to lavish kisses on the flesh that was gradually revealed beneath. When the shirt lay completely open, she drew it down his muscled shoulders, admiring the hard, masculine contours, stopping only when his hands caught her wrists again.

"Things would never be the same between us. You would be haunted by this. As would I- "

She kissed him again, silencing his protest. Her lips were sweet as honey against his mouth as she whispered, "I am already haunted by a ghost."

He slanted his mouth over hers and kissed her so deeply that she thought she might perish from the sheer ecstasy of it. She slid her hands up under his gaping shirt, reveling in the smooth male flesh, then drew her hands down lower to explore his flat, hard belly. It was as if she could not get enough of the feel of him.

Under her bold caresses, a shiver of unbridled lust raced through his veins and went straight to his groin. It was almost his undoing. It brought him nearly to his knees. Her touch was like liquid, molten lava, scorching him, consuming him.

"I have warned you, Christine," he said in a hoarse whisper before his mouth came down on hers once again in a kiss of smoldering, impatient need.

His unleased passion roused her own. His arms were like iron bands as he drew her tightly against him. She could feel every part of his body against her own. His bare chest. His hard thighs. Even through her skirts, she could feel his arousal thrusting boldly against her. It should have frightened her, but instead it stoked her own feverish heat. She knew what he wanted. She wanted it, too. Her arms slid up around his neck as she pressed her body even closer to him.

She was so overcome by the ardor of his kisses that her legs felt unsteady. But his arms were strong and tight around her as he laid her back and lowered her to the davenport where she would sit during their lessons.

As he leaned over her, his eyes burned darkly into hers. Her head was tilted back on the pillows. Her eyes were half closed, her mouth parted in anticipation of more of his kisses.

He didn't make her wait for long. The sheer ravishment of his kisses took her breath away. The heated sensation throbbing low in her body made her breath come quicker, intensifying the need in her.

The bold, slow thrust of him between her thighs heightened the exquisite tension that was building inside her. He must, she realized, be feeling the same thing she was feeling. That knowledge heightened her own passion.

Even as his mouth continued to devour hers in a long, rousing kiss, he drew the pins from her hair. The silken strands of amber tumbled free around her. He broke the kiss only to trail a sensuous path down the sensitive arch of her throat. Under the slow hungering of his mouth, she felt herself rising to a new level of desire.

He continued to stoke the fire with his mouth and with his body as he unfastened her dress, loosened it and pushed it down her arms. When the dress was out of the way, she reveled in the strong feel of his hands on her body and the hard heat of his flesh wherever it touched her own. When his thumbs brushed across the peaks of her breasts beneath the thin material of her chemise, she gasped as it forged a searing path downward to her most sensitive of places. He stroked the hardened, sensitive peaks until she was breathless from the sweet, erotic torture. Then his lips seared a path along the soft curve of her breasts that were so temptingly displayed beneath his heated gaze. He pulled the chemise aside and she groaned as he took one rose-hued tip into his mouth and then the other,   ing her until the sensation was almost more than she could bear.

But there were still the layers of her skirts between them and she watched him with a hungry gaze as, with quick, efficient movements, he pushed them up.

"Shall I tell you that I have dreamed of you like this?" he asked in a low, tantalizing voice.

There was only a single thin layer of cloth between them now, and as he spoke, he moved against her, making her breath catch in her throat.

A low growl sounded deep in his own throat as he ground himself against her, making Christine gasp at the feel of his desire pressing against her. He was so hard, so hot, and it roused an answering heat inside her.

She arched against him, panting, desperate for some kind of release she did not understand. She felt like she could not get close enough to him. And although it was the most exquisite kind of torture, the aching need inside her built to almost an agony.

Instinct made her seek him. Instinct made her press into his hardness. She was very close to the brink of *something*. She was teetering on the very edge ... Whatever it was, she only knew that she needed it with a desperation she had never known before. She knew, too, that Erik was the only one could appease the hunger.

The heat increased, intensified as her breaths came in low whimpers and soft moans.

"Yes, Christine," he whispered above her as his own breathing deepened. "Come undone for me."

And in a moment of mind-shattering bliss, she did just that. Suddenly she found herself lost among the stars, spiraling, soaring, consumed by unimaginable waves of pleasure that surged through her like some indescribable, unstoppable, rapturous tide.

Slowly, gradually, she floated back down to earth. Sated. Contented. Changed.

He had not meant for things to go so far. And now, even though he was still consumed with his own need, he gently kissed and caressed her. Even though he was adrift in a churning sea of raw sexual want. Even though his body was crying out for him to finish what he had started. He was poised on the very edge of control, and yet he held back by sheer will power alone. Summoning up some superhuman strength, he denied himself and simply held her against his bare, pounding chest while she buried her face against his shoulder.

Christine was not prepared for the rush of emotion that came over her. In the lingering afterglow of her passion, he continued to brush the tangles away from her face and smooth her tossled curls with a tenderness that touched her heart very deeply. In her innocence, she did not understand all that had happened. Not the emotional torrent that threatened, nor the tears that wanted to come from some place deep inside her. And especially not the outpouring of tenderness she felt for the man as he continued to hold her very lovingly, almost reverently.

"I was foolish to have let things go so far," he said, though the gentleness of his voice belied the regret that should have been in his words.

He wanted to be stern with her. He needed to be stern. His own need was still pulsing through his body like a raging inferno. But he was well aware of the change in her. He saw not only the new-found wonder and the almost-shy confusion in her eyes, but also a look of innocent trust that smote his heart very deeply and made *him* feel very vulnerable. His arms tightened about her as he wondered how he could bear to give her up when it became necessary to do so.

"I'll not have you hating me in the morning," he said quietly as he half rose and dared to look down at her.

His shirt was open and hanging loose, the buttons still undone. His arousal was still rigid and throbbing.

He knew she might be temporarily sated but she was not completely satisfied. He was drawn helplessly to her in a weak moment as she looked back at him and her lips parted invitingly. He kissed her again, gently at first, and then the kiss deepened as his passions flared anew. His tongue thrust into the welcoming heat of her mouth with a rhythm that roused them both. Mindlessly, helplessly responding to her, he settled himself back against her as his tongue continued its marauding.

"No," he ordered himself sternly, suddenly wrenching his mouth away from hers.

He drew back and promptly distracted himself with straightening her clothes. He would not take her innocence, not completely. Even if she was practically inviting him to do so.

Not that his body wasn't urging him to forget all his noble impulses, even as he drew her skirts down over her exposed skin and closed the bodice of her gown. He then fastened the buttons, before he could give in to the urge that also told him to tear the clothes from her body and make her his in the most primitive of ways.

She was all softness and seduction. A temptress that could steal his very soul. A siren that owned him body and soul. She was almost more than flesh and blood could bear. But somehow he found it in him to resist her, and when her clothes were finally straightened, fastened and secured, he began to work on his own buttons.

When she reached out to caress the bare flesh between his gaping shirt, he drew in a deep breath and growled, "Don't touch me, Christine. It is taking everything in me now to walk away from you."

And with that briefest of explanations, he promptly did just that. Because if he didn't, he knew the fire that was still smoldering inside him was going to burn completely out of control and there would be no stopping him this time.

Carlotta arched a dark, expressive eyebrow. "You might ask her about her secret lessons."

Raoul turned slowly from the window. "What secret lessons?"

"The ones weeth her meesterious teacher. Do you theenk she learned to seeng like that on her own?" There was a sly glitter in Carlotta's dark eyes. "I only tell you thees because you should know the truth. She ees not quite so eenocent as she pretends to be."

"And you know about these secret lessons how?" Raoul wanted to know.

"I have people who are loyal to me een the Opera House. Not much happens here that ees not eventually brought to my attention."

Carlotta had intentionally saved her sharpest arrow for last. "Some people theenk eet ees the Phantom of the Opera heemself that has been teaching her." She saw immediately that the arrow had hit its mark. "Eet makes sense," she went on. "He has eenseested on her playing the lead role een thees new opera of hees. What reason would she have for keeping the lessons a secret? Even from you. Her ambeetion, eet seems, ees only exceeded by her deception."

Carlotta carefully watched the Viscount's reaction. At first, after hearing the news, his face had grown quite pale. Now it was suffused with a deep red color.

"I'm sure you weell agree that eet ees outrageous that he should have any say een the running of thees Opera House."

The notorious Phantom of the Opera had been a bane in Carlotta's existence for a very long time. If anyone could get rid of the impudent ghost, then the Viscount could.

"How long?" she heard the Viscount ask hoarsely. "How long has she been taking the lessons?"

For a moment she was almost afraid of the look in the Viscount's eyes, but then she plunged ahead recklessly. "No one knows for sure. But eet must have been quite a while seence she has learned so many songs already. And she- " Carlotta did not want to admit that Christine had any talent. So she said instead, "A good teacher can make anyone sound passable. Not just anyone can be a star, however.

"Whoever thees Phantom ees, he does have some musical skeell," she went on. "Who knows why he chose Christine. Just a few months ago, she was a complete unknown, a dancer."

By the look on the Viscount's face, Carlotta was quite satisfied that she had accomplished what she had set out to accomplish. Every one of the seeds she had planted seemed to have taken root. Once Christine was out of the way, she would go back to occupying the position she had always occupied. She would be the star of the Opera House once again. Because surely, surely the Viscount would not tolerate such deception on the part of the woman he was supposed to wed.

The empty glass shattered into a million pieces against the papered wall. Shards of broken glass lay glistening in the bright sunlight that was pouring in through the tall, mullioned windows of the de Chagny library.

Raoul was staring hard at the mess he had just made, but he was blind to it, so enraged was he. He was too beside himself with fury to notice much of anything that was happening around him.

"Damn the faithless, deceiving bitch," he gritted out between his tightly-clenched teeth.

He had suspected something was wrong all along, but now he knew that she had been lying to him from the beginning. Carlotta had been right. Christine's ambition was exceeded only by her treachery. He could not believe that he had bought her innocent act, or that he had allowed her to play him for such a fool. It was like she had cast some kind of spell over him. Why else would he be lusting for her even now? Even while he hated her for the lying witch that she was.

Damn her.

She would pay. She would pay dearly. He would see to that.

If word got out that she had made a laughingstock out of him-Well, he didn't intend to let that happen.

He had wanted to confront her immediately, but he had decided against that. His revenge must be carefully planned out, the blade of his vengeance honed so finely that it would cause her the most amount of pain and regret. And to do that, he needed to get her out of the Opera House once and for all.

He brought both fists down on the desk as his dark passions flared once more. He bared his teeth and ground them in savage fury.

"*Damn her.*"

There was hate in his eyes now. For Christine *and* this Phantom.

Revenge would be had, he vowed. If he lost Christine to this low-life nothing, he would never be able to show his face in Paris again. The humiliation of it would be almost too much for him to bear.

Chapter 18

"You won't be coming with us?" Christine asked.

"I know we were supposed to go together and I was looking forward to spending the day with you," Raoul lied. "But I have unexpected business to attend to first. Petrine has agreed to go with you in my place."

Raoul pretended not to see the bleak look on Christine's face. Watching her, he couldn't help yielding to a momentary lapse in his control. His lip curled just the slightest bit as he told himself she deserved even this inconvenience. "Don't be so difficult, Christine. You will go to church with Petrine and I will join you afterward. I really don't have the time to stand around here arguing with you about it any longer."

"We'll talk?" she asked him.

"Yes, later."

Christine had decided that this would be the day she would tell Raoul she wasn't going through with the wedding. There was no putting it off any longer. She should have done so a long time ago.

With a fixed expression, Raoul handed her into the waiting carriage and said a brief farewell. Petrine climbed in, dropped down into the seat opposite Christine and fussed with her skirts as the carriage rolled away.

It was frustrating for Christine to think that she had been so easily manipulated into another change of plans. She could only hope that in church she would find the peace that had eluded her lately. And then- Then later she would tell Raoul. No matter what happened.

But not five minutes later, Christine was staring at Petrine as if she wasn't sure she had heard her correctly.

"Yes, let's skip church," Petrine said as if her mind was made up. "We'll go to the Bois instead. It will be much quieter there and we'll be able to think more clearly. Isn't that what we're supposed to do on the Sabbath? Take time for quiet reflection?"

"I'm not sure if- "

"I'm just not up to sitting quietly in church for the next hour," Petrine interrupted her petulantly. "Indulge me, Christine. Do I ask much of you?"

Petrine was not a sparkling conversationalist on the best of days, but this morning she was proving to be an even more unsociable companion. She barely spoke a word for the next half hour.

Christine was looking out the carriage window, lost in her own thoughts. Since they had entered the Bois, not a single carriage had passed them by. There was no one on foot or on horseback, either, not at this unfashionable hour of the morning. It was too early for the population of Paris to be taking to the park. In any case, most people were attending church, which is exactly where they should have been.

As the wheels of the carriage rattled over a bridge, Petrine suddenly seemed to take an interest in her surroundings. She began to stare intently out of the carriage window. So intently that Christine finally asked, "What are you looking at?"

"The Grand Cascade, of course," Petrine answered her. "The waterfall would make a splendid tapestry, don't you think?"

Christine frowned. Petrine wasn't acting like herself at all. And she wasn't really looking at the waterfall, in spite of what she had said. Her normally pale cheeks were flushed with spots of color and there was an intensity in her eyes that Christine had never seen before.

They had entered a thickly-wooded, isolated part of the Bois when the carriage suddenly jerked to a stop. Christine was alarmed when she heard angry male voices immediately barking out commands.

"What's going on?" Petrine whispered tensely as if she was a bad actress on a stage as she pressed one gloved hand against her mouth and sank back into her seat.

Christine tried to see what was happening. When she looked out the window, she was startled to see a masked man on a horse, and a riderless horse beside that one.

As Christine drew back from the window, Petrine suddenly didn't seem to be interested in what was going on outside. She was looking down at her gloved hands as intently as she had been looking at the scenery a few minutes ago.

The carriage began to shake almost violently. There were alarming sounds of a scuffle, grunts and someone crying out.

When everything was silent again, the carriage door was flung open and a voice behind a mask snarled, "You. Out."

When Christine did not immediately obey the man who was filling the doorway, he seized her wrist and dragged her brutally out of the carriage.

"I'll ask the questions," he growled. "You do what I say or this isn't going to end well. For you at least."

There were two masked men, Christine discovered. There was the one on the horse and the other one who had forced her out of the carriage. She could not see the driver. Petrine was allowed to stay in the carriage. In fact, it seemed she had been forgotten entirely. The man who had dragged Christine out of the carriage seemed completely focused on threatening and bullying only her. It was as if he was putting all his efforts into intentionally frightening her. In the crudest of terms, he began to paint a very disturbing, very detailed picture of what he was going to do to her. Apparently he didn't get the reaction he was expecting, so he suddenly shoved her to the ground, tearing her sleeve as she fell painfully to her knees in the grass.

The man was huge and he towered over her. His eyes behind the mask roamed over her lewdly from head to toe. That's when she noticed the scar. Or the part of it that showed beyond the cloth that covered the lower part of his face.

As the man continued to loom over her, he doubled his efforts to terrorize her while she was on the ground, much to the amusement of the second man who was still seated on the horse. But both men froze at the sound of another carriage approaching.

Like the coward that he was, the man who had dragged her out of the carriage mounted his horse and both men immediately rode away without further incident.

That's when Christine saw the driver sprawled in the grass. He groaned as he struggled to a sitting position, then pressed his hand gingerly to his forehead where a stream of blood was still trickling from a deep gash.

A near-hysterical Petrine was almost beside herself when she saw the driver. She wouldn't come out of the carriage. "This wasn't supposed to happen," she moaned as she leaned out the window.

Of course it wasn't supposed to happen, Christine thought to herself. People weren't waylaid by robbers in the Bois anymore. She ignored Petrine and made her way over to the fallen man.

"He's not dead, is he?" Petrine blubbered from the carriage window.

Christine pressed her lips together and shook her head with vexation. Would a dead man be sitting up? She held her handkerchief carefully against the man's wound to try and stem the flow of blood just as the other carriage pulled up alongside them.

"What's going on here?" she heard someone shout.

There was another voice. "It's Christine!"

How ironic, she thought, that Eitan Beauvoir and Anton Charlebois should be the ones to come to their rescue.

Nearly an hour had passed, but Christine's hands were still unsteady. Obviously, she had been more affected by the violence in the Bois than she wanted to admit, even to herself.

In one of the bedrooms of the de Chagny mansion, she explained to Raoul once again, "I already told you. I didn't see the man's face. He was wearing a mask. Both of them were. So I cannot tell you what they looked like."

Raoul's probing about the incident had been relentless. He turned now and frowningly listened to Anton Charlebois' recounting of the story.

"We were unarmed," the man explained. "Luckily by our persons alone we were able to scare them off."

"There's no telling what might have happened if we had not come along," Eitan added, looking from Raoul to Christine.

"Yes, it was lucky," Raoul agreed. "Christine needs to rest now. I'll see you downstairs."

The two men took their leave and Christine was left alone with a still-scowling Raoul. And Petrine.

"I should have been there with you," Raoul said. "You can see now how dangerous it is for a woman alone."

He had repeated the same sentiment several times.

"How is the driver?" Christine asked.

"Bloodied, but he'll recover," Raoul answered her.

With a crisp rustle of silk skirts, Ligeia swept into the room. She took one look at Christine's disheveled appearance and her lips thinned. She then glanced at Petrine silently. The younger woman offered no remark save that she had a headache and wished to retire immediately to her own room.

With Petrine gone, Christine dreaded the questions she knew were about to follow. Indeed, she expected nothing less than an inquisition from the woman that was rightly called the Dragon Queen.

Ligeia continued to silently take in every detail, from the grass stains on Christine's skirt to her torn sleeve and her tousled hair.

"How did this happen?" she asked Raoul.

When Raoul finished telling the story, Ligeia asked, "You mean they were out there alone? Why? I was expecting them in church."

Raoul looked at Christine and said, "Apparently, a drive through the Bois was Petrine's idea."

"And you went along with that?" Ligeia asked Christine. "Do you know the scandal this could cause? For everyone?" She dragged her dark gaze away from Christine. "For you, too, Raoul."

"Why should we feel that we have done something wrong?" Christine asked the woman. "Neither one of us invited that attack. And Raoul had nothing to do with it, either."

Ligeia turned on her and said in an icy tone, "Do you think that makes a difference? Once the gossips get their greedy claws into what happened, they won't let it go."

"But it was clearly a failed robbery- " Christine began.

"We will never know for sure what their motives were," Ligeia cut her off. "The speculation will be the same. You were two young women set upon by ruffians in the Bois when you shouldn't have even been there in the first place. People will assume the worst. Especially if anyone were to get wind of your torn clothes."

"That is unfair," Christine said, feeling the need to defend herself.

Raoul hadn't said a word, and she looked at him now.

"Ligeia is right," he said. "This should be a brutal awakening for you about what can happen to a woman alone without an escort."

She couldn't believe he was taking Ligeia's side. There shouldn't even be sides.

"We weren't alone. There was the driver," Christine reminded them both.

That apparently made no difference to Ligeia, who said, "There is only one way to put the rumors to rest. And even that may not be enough. Christine, you will stay here. Raoul has already sent for the family physician to come and make sure you have no serious injuries."

"There's no need for that," Christine started to protest. She had no intention of being ordered around like a child. Nor did she think there was any need to see a physician.

"The best thing for you to do is to spend the rest of the day in bed," Ligeia went on as if she hadn't even heard her.

"That won't be necessary- " Christine tried to argue with her.

"Nonsense. That is where Petrine has gone. And that is precisely what you will do, too. While you let *us* determine how best to handle this whole unfortunate incident."

Christine tried to protest again, but Ligeia interrupted her in a frigid voice. "It is already done, Christine. Are we going to waste more precious time by arguing?"

After Ligeia had left the room, Christine said, "Raoul, none of this is necessary."

He took her completely by surprise when he slammed his clenched fist down on the table, which effectively stopped her from speaking further.

"Do you *still* fight me? How will it look if I sent you off on your way after *this*? Do you think I will let you go back to the Opera House where you can continue to incite the passions of every man in the audience night after night as you flaunt yourself on the stage?"

Taken aback by the vehemence of his words, Christine felt the blood recede from her face. "I do not flaunt myself," she said coldly. "And just what does my performing on stage have to do with any of this?"

"You dress to seduce every time you sing. Do you deny it? Does it not occur to you that those men might have first seen you on stage and then stalked you? As it will occur to everyone else?"

"How could you think that is what this is all about?"

Saying no word, he reached out and cupped her chin in his hand, forcing her face upward until she had no choice but to stare into his flashing eyes. His teeth were clenched tightly together as he hissed, "How could I think it? Because I myself have had my passions roused by watching you. I had thought maybe you were doing it for me alone. But that isn't the case, is it?"

Christine held her breath as she experienced a sudden moment of panic. Did he know something? Was that why he was so angry?

"I- " she began as he suddenly let go of her. "We need to discuss the wedding."

His eyes narrowed to dangerous slits as he looked down at her. "We'll discuss it," he said grimly. "But not right now. I have things to attend to and you need to rest before we go any further."

His anger seemed to suddenly dissipate, or at least he was making an effort to hide it. "Everything will work out," he told her as he straightened. "You will see. You are overwrought because of your ordeal this morning and you are obviously not thinking clearly. Therefore, I will make the decisions that are best for you. The more I think about what happened, the more I realize what a close brush you had with disaster. Which is why I am going to take measures to ensure your safety. From now on I want to know where you are at all times. I don't want you leaving this house or going anywhere without me as an escort. Do I make myself clear?"

"Raoul, you go too far. You can't keep me here."

"You're wrong, Christine. I can and I will do exactly that."

"You know I was against this marriage from the beginning. I knew she could never be a proper wife to you and that she would bring you nothing but trouble. And that very thing has born itself out. But what would you expect from someone with her breeding?"

Despite Raoul's warning, Christine had left her room. It was Ligeia that she overheard talking and Raoul answered her, "Are you waiting for me to tell you that you were right?"

"I am waiting for you to come to your senses and call off this wedding."

231

"You needn't worry. There will be no wedding," he said in a low voice.

"Then why did you bring her here?"

"Because I'm not finished with her yet." This last was said so venomously that it took Christine aback. "Am I not entitled to have this end as I see fit?"

After a silence, Ligeia asked, "What will you do with her now?"

"Keep her here. For a while at least."

"You frighten me when you look like that." Ligeia's voice lowered. "Let's not quarrel. Come to my room tonight. I'll make you forget all this unpleasantness."

Christine could not hear the words Raoul spoke in reply, but what she had heard was enough. She had to get out of this house.

She backed up slowly, hoping she would not be seen. Then she turned and hurried as quickly as she could down the hallway from which she had come, wanting only to get back to her room where she could be alone to figure out what she must do next.

She made her way safely upstairs and was rounding the corner of the hallway that led to her room when she collided with something hard. Something immoveable. It was Philippe's chest.

"Are you supposed to be out of your room?" he asked as she took several steps away from him.

His buff-colored pantaloons were tucked into black Hessians. His white shirt was immaculate and offset by a silk vest and a deep umber cravat. His pale blue gaze seemed half amused as he looked down at her. "Now what could have put that look on your face?" he asked as his eyes narrowed shrewdly.

He glanced briefly in the direction she had just come from. "Ah, since Raoul and Ligeia are downstairs discussing what is to be done with you, I assume you must have overheard something. Something shocking," he went on as he searched her face. "There is only one thing that could have put that look on your face. Usually they are very discreet, but lately . . . " His words trailed off suggestively.

"Let me go to my room."

She tried to pass by him, but he took a step in those black Hessians and effectively blocked her.

"Of course I will let you do that. But first, take a moment to hear me out. I knew you would find out eventually. I have merely been biding my time. And now that you know, you should also know that a little knowledge can mean the difference between winning and losing. You need an ally, Christine. A powerful one. And I can be that for you. Once you realize just how powerful, you will be in a better position to figure out your best strategy."

She looked at him warily from beneath her lashes. "You make it sound like some kind of military campaign."

"It is very like a war, isn't it? At least in this household."

She couldn't completely disagree with him there.

"You may think that you have found Raoul out, but he is playing a deeper game than you realize. And once you come to terms with that, we can make this work to our mutual advantage."

"What do you mean?"

"I mean, you can have your revenge."

"What makes you think I want revenge?"

"What woman would not want revenge? You can have that, while I can have something just as satisfying."

Heat suffused her cheeks, then quickly receded. "I don't know what you're talking about," she lied.

"But I think you do."

Her eyes flared with indignation. He was right. She did know and she was not very good at hiding it.

He laughed lowly and heat kindled in his eyes as he dropped his gaze to her mouth like a vulture eyeing its next meal.

"Raoul is no innocent by any means. And someday, when we have gotten to know each other better and you are ready to hear the whole sordid truth, I will tell you just how ruthless he can be."

"And are you not just as ruthless?"

"I won't deny that, but I do not pretend to be something I am not. When I want something, I state it very plainly. I have wanted you from the moment I first laid eyes on you. But you already knew that from the conversation you overheard that night at the soiree. If you will only trust me, Christine, I shall help you through this."

Trust him? A man who would betray his own brother? A man who was so debauched he thought she would willingly accept a role as his mistress?

"And if you are honest with yourself, and with me," he went on. "You are drawn to me, are you not?"

"If you believe that, then you have misread me."

"Is that why you blush whenever you see me?" he asked with a slight smile curving his hard mouth. "I have already told you that I state my desires very plainly. I want you, Christine, to play the part of my mistress. Discreetly, of course. I would be more than generous. You would have everything you could possibly wish for."

Although he was talking as if he was negotiating a business deal, the lustful glow in his eyes showed that he was deadly serious.

"You don't have to answer me now. After all, it has been a difficult day for you. Take some time to think it over."

"I assure you, I will give your proposal all the consideration that it merits."

He laughed as if he found her delightful and said, "We shall get along very well together."

And then, before she knew what he was doing, he bent his head and brushed a presumptuous, possessive kiss against her parted lips.

Christine leaned back against the closed door and drew a fortifying breath. Her thoughts were scattered, chaotic. Her mind was still reeling from the shock of discovering Raoul's relationship with his stepmother. And Philippe's indecent proposal.

But she did not have long to collect herself and come up with a plan to leave the mansion. Ligeia came back upstairs promptly with the de Chagny's personal physician who poked and prodded her in various places and asked her endless irrelevant questions. She tried her best to look unconcerned, just as if she had not just overheard that conversation downstairs. She did not want Ligeia to suspect that anything was wrong. But she was aware of the woman's close scrutiny as those cold, black eyes narrowed on her during the examination.

She did manage to calmly reply to every one of the physicians questions. It was, she told herself, very much like playing a role on the stage. She could make it believable.

"You are a very lucky young woman," the physician said to her. "You are fortunate that you escaped with nothing more than a few minor bruises."

Shortly after the physician left, Christine asked Ligeia, "What happened to my hat?"

"That shabby old thing? I had it burned."

"You what? You had no right to do that. That hat was a gift from my father."

After a moment of insincere remorse, Ligeia shrugged in unconcern. "Was it? I didn't realize that it had such sentimental value to you. But I shall give you a new hat to make up for it. Right now you should be resting, not worrying about a hat."

She looked at Christine appraisingly and frowned at the tear in her sleeve. "We can't have you going around in a torn gown that has mud and grass stains all over it. Get undressed and I will have a new gown brought up."

But before she had finished undressing, Raoul entered the room without knocking.

Christine tried to cover her half bare bosom with her hands.

He looked her over in much the same assessing manner that Ligeia had just done, then said, "You parade yourself across the stage night after night with less than that on, yet you are worried about me seeing you with a few of your buttons undone?"

"Wait. We need to talk," she said to his back as he turned to leave the room.

He turned back around to see her still fumbling with the buttons as she tried to cover herself up.

"You've just had an upsetting experience. I think it's best if you stay in bed and rest first."

"I don't want to stay in bed."

"Maybe you do not understand me. I insist."

"You are treating me like a prisoner."

"Being with me makes you feel like a prisoner?" he queried with a narrowed look in his eyes.

"Being forced to stay in this room against my will makes me feel like a prisoner. Are you forcing Petrine to stay confined to her room?"

"I don't have to. Petrine knows what is best for her. And," he added. "She had sense enough to stay in the carriage."

"I was *forced* out of the carriage."

"Yes, so you said."

She stared back at him. Did he not believe her?

"You sound like you think that attack was my fault."

"What I believe is of little consequence. You *will* stay here tonight."

A knot of panic began to grow. It was not just the way he said it, it was the cold look in his eyes that she found so troubling.

"I have rehearsal first thing in the morning."

"That's out of the question," he said, making the decision for her. "I will send word that you won't be able to be there."

"You will do no such thing."

"But I will," he said and then waited as if he dared her to defy him.

Ligeia came back into the room with a servant who was carrying a tray that had on it a pitcher with a cup and saucer.

"Here," Ligeia said as the servant set the tray down. "Drink this."

Without thinking, Christine sipped the tea that the servant handed to her.

She frowned down into the half-empty cup. "It tastes strange. What kind of tea is it?"

"Something the doctor left for you."

She looked up, alarmed.

"Don't be so suspicious," Raoul grumbled. "It is only something to help you relax."

"I don't need something to help me relax."

"Don't you? You seem quite distraught right now."

She did not miss the look that he shared with Ligeia.

Panic began to course hotly through her body. It seemed very much like both of them were working together to force her to stay here.

"Finish your tea. It will help you relax," Raoul told her. When she did not immediately obey him, he sighed heavily. "Later when you are not feeling so emotionally distressed, we can talk. And I will convince you then that you are not a prisoner."

To make him think she was going to comply with his wishes, she sat down on the bed and pretended to drink the tea. But despite his assurances to the contrary, she was under no delusions. She was very much a prisoner.

When she was finally alone, Christine wasted no time. She had to get out of this house and go back to the Opera House. No matter how she had to do it.

She kept her own dress on and listened at the door until she was certain that no one was outside. Miraculously, she ran into no one as she cautiously descended the stairs. She was able to make her way outside and to the stable without being seen. Night was descending when she was finally able to find a groom and convince him that Raoul had decided that she was to go back to the Opera House tonight and that he should take her there immediately.

Luck was with her. In the darkness there was less chance of Raoul seeing the carriage leaving. He would follow her, of course, when he learned that she was gone. But at the moment, she had one thing in mind only, and that was to put as much distance between them as possible.

By the time the carriage arrived at the Opera House, a terrible weariness had come upon her. She realized that the tea had to be responsible. Or more precisely, what they had put in the tea.

"The fresh air will revive me," she said to herself as she stepped down from the carriage steps. In fact, she almost fell down the short flight of steps. The driver had to steady her and then walk her into the Opera House.

By the time he left her, she was feeling alarmingly lightheaded. She knew she must reach her room before she collapsed completely. The drug was now in her blood stream, coursing through her veins with every beat of her heart. But if she could clear her head enough to . . .

Only a few of the gaslights were lit, so the shadows were deep around her. She was climbing the grand staircase when everything began to swim around her.

She steadied herself on the foot of one of the brass torcheres for a moment. When she let go, she wavered and clutched blindly at the marble railing. Her cloak slipped off her shoulders and fell unheeded to the floor while she struggled against the waves of darkness that threatened to engulf her. She began to think she wasn't going to make it to her room when she heard a voice behind her.

"Christine, what has happened?"

She looked up and tried to focus on Erik's frowning features, was drawn instead to the glittering, rainbow-hued prisms of a candelabra beyond him.

Alarmed at how pale she was, he gripped her arm and asked her again what was wrong.

"There was an attack . . . in the Bois. Afterwards at . . . the de Chagny mansion, the doctor gave me something . . . "

Her voice trailed off as she shook her head, wanted nothing more than to lay down on her bed and give in to the darkness before she collapsed right here. "Raoul did not . . . want me to come back here. But I . . . managed to . . . "

She braced her hand against Erik's chest and leaned against him. "I fear that I- I . . . "

He put his arm around her because she did not seem able to stand on her own. In an instant, she half collapsed against him.

Her eyelids fluttered, trying, for a moment, to focus on his words right before she fainted dead away in his arms.

As Erik scooped Christine up in his arms, he heard the Persian's voice behind him. "What's wrong with her?"

"I'm not certain. Apparently, there was some kind of attack in the Bois. The Viscount has had his doctor sedate her," he said with his mouth set in grim lines.

She stirred only slightly in his arms. Her head was against his shoulder as he began to carry her up the wide staircase.

"Until I know what has happened to her and what kind of danger she may be in, I must take her someplace where she will be safe."

"Where will that be?"

He only had to look at the Persian to give him his answer.

Chapter 19

Heavy draperies were the first things Christine's eyes saw when they fluttered open. She tried to focus on the dark, unfamiliar velvet hangings that were tied back by tasseled cords to intricately-carved posts. Whatever bed she was lying on was an elegant one, a very comfortable one. She wanted to go back to sleep, but a flickering candle beside the bed drew her gaze and kept her from drifting back into the darkness.

A moment of panic rose up inside her. Was she back in the de Chagny mansion? Had Raoul found her and brought her back? Wherever she was, it seemed to her that she had not been completely alone in the darkness. Her mind held onto strange images of moving shadows, a black shape that passed back and forth before the candle flame, a voice that spoke in low, soothing tones. But as she lay there in the strange bed, she was unable to take a firm grasp on reality and sort the fleeting impressions out so that they made sense.

The candle became a focal point for her. Its slow flickering drew her and she found it almost mesmerizing. She tried to sit up, but found that movement made her vision blur alarmingly.

By gradual degrees she managed to sit at the edge of the bed. She knew with a certainty that she had not been alone. Someone else had been with her at the edge of the darkness. And hadn't there been a moment in that darkness when someone's lips had pressed lightly, briefly against her own? Or was that part of a dream?

She saw a chair next to the bed. There were other candles in the room that were glowing softly and holding back the darkness. She stood on trembly legs and had to immediately fight the wave of dizziness that threatened her. She took a step at the same time she became aware of a man's dark shape. He suddenly turned . . .

He was at her side in an instant. He picked her up and laid her down gently back down on the bed.

"Erik," she whispered as a deep sense of relief flooded her. She was not back at the de Chagny mansion then.

"Where am I?" she asked weakly.

"Underground."

"How long have I been here?"

"Several hours."

Actually it had been quite a few hours. So many that he had begun to worry.

"You should not be walking around yet."

She didn't argue with him. She didn't know if she was even able to walk. "My head feels so strange," she said, her voice not much more than a whisper.

"You had me worried," he admitted. "I wasn't sure what you had been given."

"They said it was something to help me sleep."

He pulled the chair closer to the bed and sat down.

"Is this where you live?" she asked as she gazed around at her surroundings.

"Yes. I thought it best to keep you here until I know it is safe up there for you. I sent word to Madame Giry where you are. You needn't worry about anything. You should just think about resting for a while longer."

She closed her eyes, silently agreeing with him. And then, as if the effort of speaking and getting out of bed had been too much for her, she fell into a deep sleep once again.

She woke later to the sound of music being played very softly. Erik's music. This time when she tried to get out of bed, she was able to stand on her own with only a little weakness in her legs. She walked to a door that stood ajar and pushed it wider.

In another room, several candelabrums were lit. The room that was luxuriously and elegantly furnished, from the Persian rugs to the oil paintings and the rich tapestries on the walls. In the midst of it all, Erik was sitting in a chair playing his violin.

The music stopped abruptly when he saw her.

"I thought music might be the easiest way to wake you," he said as he got to his feet. "How are you feeling now?"

"Much better."

"I'm glad to hear that." He set the violin aside and pulled up a chair for her. "Why don't you sit and tell me what happened."

She sank down into the chair and recounted most, but not all, of her story. She did not tell him how Raoul had insisted she stay at the mansion against her wishes. Nor did she tell him about Philippe, or the conversation she had overheard between Raoul and Ligeia.

"The Viscount has been to the Opera House making inquiries about you," he informed her.

"Has he gone away?"

He nodded, watching her face closely.

"He'll come back," she whispered half to herself.

"I brought you here so that you could have time to yourself. From what has happened, it sounds like it is something you need."

"Is it morning?" she asked as she looked around and realized that there would be no windows. "Or night?"

She didn't know how her innocent question affected him, how it reminded him that she was not made to live in the darkness.

"Morning," he answered, thinking to himself that she had never looked so beautiful or so desirable. So out of reach.

Her hair gleamed with strands of glistening gold in the candlelight. Her dress of deep indigo only heightened the pale amethyst of her eyes. He had, in fact, been so struck by her beauty while she had been asleep that he had stolen a kiss from her.

Her dress was muddied and stained with grass. One sleeve was torn. When he thought of the danger she must have been in, when he thought of what might have happened to her, it was all he could do to maintain a calm façade.

Christine felt Erik staring at her, but when she looked up, his eyes slid away so she could not read the emotion that simmered under the surface.

"We should talk," she said quietly.

"We are talking."

That's not what she meant. "About what happened- " she began.

He stopped her there. "What happened cannot happen again."

He heard himself say the words, even though he wanted nothing more than to take her in his arms and love her more thoroughly and more completely than she had ever imagined being loved.

"Things have changed," she began again.

"Nothing has changed."

She stared back at him. Of course things had changed.

"It was a moment of weakness for us both," she heard him say. "And we both know it would be a mistake to let it happen again."

She folded her hands carefully in her lap. Had she misread him so badly? Why did he sound so cold, so unemotional? It was as if he had put up some kind of wall between them. Yet that wall proved to be no hindrance to her heart, she found. It did not stop all that *she* was feeling.

"I am not going to marry Raoul," she informed him straight out, thinking that should make a difference.

While he had not been able to suppress a secret leap of joy when she had said that, he reminded himself that nothing had really changed. She was still who she was, and so was he. He would not take her from the life she was meant to live. Most of his life had been an agony in the shadows. He could not sentence her to the same kind of existence. In time she would feel like a prisoner in his dark world and in the end she would come to despise him for taking her away from the world she was used to.

"I brought you down here to rest. Nothing more than that."

He saw the hurt in her eyes and agonized inwardly over the fact that he had been the one to put it there.

"Then- are you saying that what happened meant nothing to you?"

He pushed his own pain deep inside and hesitated only a moment before he said to her, "You are a voice to me, Christine. As I once was to you. I let myself get distracted. I won't let that happen again."

"Then you regret what happened?"

"I regret my weakness, yes."

He reminded himself that it was better for her to experience a little pain now than to suffer an agony of regret later.

"I wanted someone to sing my music. You served that purpose."

"And our lessons?"

With his expression cast in stone, he asked her, "Why would you need them at this point?"

He had already decided that it would be best to end the lessons because he did not trust himself to be alone with her any more.

Before she weakened him again, before he got down on his knees before her, he must finish this. When he spoke, his voice sounded harsh, even to his own ears. "You have been too much of a disruption in my life, as I have been too much of a disruption in yours. What we shared was the music. Beyond that, I think we can both agree that it would be best not to complicate our lives any further."

She stared at him for a silent moment and barely managed a nod.

It took everything in him to not take her into his arms and wipe that wounded look from her eyes. The one he had put there. But she had her whole life ahead of her, while he- He was destined to live in the shadows. All he could offer her was solitude and darkness at his side. That was not the life Christine was meant to live. He wanted to remember her as she was now, not after she had grown to hate the only existence he could offer her, not after she had grown to hate him.

"So it really did mean nothing to you," she said in a ghost of a voice.

"You came to me, Christine."

"So I did," she said so softly he barely heard her.

She felt a sudden tightening in her throat. Because she did not want him to see the tears that were gathering beneath her eyelids, she did not look at him. "I see."

But she didn't. Not really. She didn't see how he was falling apart inside.

"Rest here a day or two," he said in a hollow voice. "I have much to do, so you need not fear that I will be hovering over you. When you are ready, I'll take you back."

She still would not look at him. The silence deepened between them, and then she said, "I have no wish to complicate your life further. I am ready now, so by all means, take me back."

He bit back the words he wanted to say. He dared not let his heart rule and do what he wanted to do, lower the wall that he knew must remain in place between them.

"Christine has been different lately," Madame Giry said. "She has seemed distant, preoccupied."

Erik was sprawled in a chair across from her, looking just as preoccupied. He shifted his weight slightly and stretched out one long, booted leg but he made no comment to her last statement.

"I couldn't help but wonder if she has realized how you feel . . . " she began carefully, not sure how she should put it or if she should even broach the subject.

His dark brows were drawn into a frown as he considered his answer. He didn't look at her as he answered, "Regrettably, I fear that is just what has happened."

After a moment of silence, she asked, "And has this- changed things between you?"

"Things have changed, yes."

"I know your feelings run deep- " she began. "And that this has been difficult for you from the very beginning."

He straightened in his chair. Raking his fingers back through his dark hair in a gesture of frustration, he sighed and said almost irritably, "Difficult? *That* is an understatement that you could scarcely understand. But I will deal with it."

"Can you?" she asked as he abruptly got up out of the chair. "Or have things gone so far that- "

He had paced once across the length of the room. She could feel the suppressed energy in him as he stopped and pivoted towards her. "Will it make things any better if I say the words out loud, the very ones we so carefully try to avoid? That I am so deeply in love with her that I cannot think straight, let alone concentrate on this opera or any other aspect of my wretched life? That she is the center of my thoughts? You already know that. But I also wish with everything that is in me that it wasn't so."

"You're no different than the rest of us, Erik. You're not immune to love."

"Love?" he scoffed. "It has proven to be an agony that almost consumes me with its intensity. I do not want this. If only by saying it out loud to you, I could find some peace at last . . . " He almost groaned out his final words. "But I cannot banish it. Not with words."

"What will you do?"

"I will do what I must. I will put my efforts into the opera. *And* find a way to deal with my weakness for Christine."

"And you think that will be enough?"

"I sincerely hope that it will be," he sighed.

After a silence, she asked him, "And Christine, do you know how she feels?"

Another deep-felt, frustrated sigh was his only answer.

Chapter 20

"The Viscount has just arrived," Madame Giry announced and then waited nervously for Erik's reaction.

"For Christine?"

"*Non.* At least not entirely. He is not alone."

At Erik's questioning glance, she said, "He has moved the séance to tonight. He did not inform me of the change beforehand so I am just as surprised as you are. He has a medium with him, and there are others who are still arriving. They are setting things up in box five."

"Is he doing this on his own?"

"No, Monsieur Peverell will be there."

Erik's lips thinned for a moment. "Even though he knows there will be consequences for such a blatant disregard of my request?"

"In the man's defense, I think he was taken by surprise, too. He tried talking the Viscount out of it."

"Has the Viscount approached Christine yet?" he asked.

"Not yet. Have *you* spoken to her since- "

Since he had brought her back from his lair.

"No."

He had promised himself that he would stay away from her, but he had not been completely successful in keeping that vow. Staying in the shadows, he had secretly watched her on more than one occasion during her rehearsals.

"What will you do?" Madame Giry asked.

"I assume this medium is priming the sitters right now for some dramatic occurrence tonight, in addition to calculating how much money she can bilk out of them. I will see for myself how good she is at slight of hand tricks and illusions."

This medium, Madame Giry thought, didn't know she was up against. Erik was a master of illusions, trap doors and elaborate special effects. With emotions running high between everyone, she feared what might happen tonight.

She was definitely not reassured by the look on Erik's face when he said, "It seems, Madame, we have a séance to prepare for."

Since Christine had not yet answered him, Raoul repeated his question. "Why did you run away from me?"

"It would not have been necessary if you hadn't insisted on treating me like a prisoner with no say in the matter."

Christine had decided to tell him once and for all that their wedding was off. She had avoided it for far too long.

Raoul thrust his clefted chin out belligerently. "You have been missing for two days. Where were you?"

"I was here."

"Here?" he scoffed. "If that is the case, you certainly kept yourself well hidden. Is that what you were doing? Hiding from me?"

He grabbed her chin in his hand and forced her to look up at him. "At least look at me so I can see the truth in your eyes." He let go of her abruptly as his lips twisted into an ugly sneer and he said coldly, "Well, I'm not here for you. I imagine that will come as a huge relief to you."

"I have been wanting to talk to you," she said. "We keep managing to put it off."

"You're right. But unfortunately that talk will have to wait a little longer. We are getting ready for the séance."

"The séance? You mean you are going through with it? Tonight?"

"Yes, tonight. And I expect you to be there."

She shook her head. "I won't be a part of that."

"You already are a part of it. Besides, aren't you the least bit curious about what will happen?"

"No, since I don't believe that anyone can conjure spirits out of the air."

"Well, tonight one may make a believer out of you," he said with a strange gleam in his eyes.

"What are you planning?"

"Just like the other guests, you will have to wait and see."

"I told you, I won't be there."

"But you will. In fact, you will be the guest of honor."

He gave her no chance to say no. Ignoring her protests, he grabbed her wrist and dragged her out of her room. He kept a hold on her arm as he forced her to go with him up the stairs and along the corridor which led to box five. Only then did he release her.

"An hour of your time, Christine. Don't you think you owe me that at least?"

She stood rubbing her wrist. "I told you, Raoul, I don't want to be here."

"Why? Because you're afraid of what might be revealed tonight?"

"You said yourself there is no ghost."

His eyes narrowed as he looked down at her. "Does that mean you have come to believe that the Opera House is haunted by a man after all, the very same man that has been sending you roses *and* giving you lessons?"

He laughed harshly at her chagrined expression. "It seems you neglected to tell me about that. Or is that what you have been trying to tell me about these past few weeks? Well, ghost or man, this should prove to be one hell of a séance." He looked beyond her. "The other guests are arriving."

He leaned closer to her. "I hope you're not going to be vulgar and make a scene."

Ligeia was coming down the hallway with Philippe. The very two people she never wanted to see again. Baron Robillard and his wife were there as well. And so was Monsieur Peverell. Anton Charlebois and Eitan Beauvoir had also just arrived.

Madame Villeneuve, the medium, stepped out of box five behind them.

"Quite a little crowd," Raoul said as he rubbed his hands together. "There will be thirteen of us here tonight. Of course the ghost will make fourteen," he said with a dark current of mockery in his voice.

Ligeia was elegantly coiffed and gowned in what Christine could only assume was proper séance attire. The woman gave Christine a brief, insincere smile.

After being introduced to the medium, Monsieur Peverell asked, "Are you certain we should be doing this here?" His eyes shifted to the open doorway leading to box five.

It was the Baron who answered him. "Since the ghost has been seen here on more than one occasion, what better place to try and communicate with him? Isn't that right?" He had posed the question first to his wife, and then to Madame Villeneuve.

The medium inclined her head in a silent, almost regal reply, then said, "Let us go inside. Everything is ready."

All the seats had been removed in box five. In their place a round table had been set up in the center of the small room.

"You seem uneasy, Christine," Raoul whispered as he leaned toward her. "Are you really worried that this will be a waste of time? Or are you afraid that he *will* be here and end up being exposed for the fraud he is?"

"You know very well that this is only a show," she said under her breath.

He gave a sarcastic snort. "Well, I am paying good money for this show, so sit down." He brought his hand heavily down on her shoulder, then pressed her into the seat, giving her no chance to refuse.

"This should be a memorable evening, indeed," Philippe commented as he approached the table.

Raoul smirked and said, "That is exactly what I am counting on." He took a seat beside Christine. "I feel that with Christine's presence we have a better chance of contacting the ghost. She is after all the star of his opera. And he does seem to have a fascination for her."

The other people around the table readily agreed with him.

"Shall we begin?" the medium asked.

"Yes, by all means," Raoul replied. "Summon him."

The medium was younger than Christine would have thought. Her long, waving dark hair was worn loose over her shoulders. Her dramatically bare bosom almost glowed in the darkness.

"Philippe is right," Eitan Beauvoir whispered. "I'm certain this will be a night we won't forget."

Anton Charlebois, whose eyes were fixed on the medium, or rather on her overflowing bosom, agreed. "Yes, I am sure it will be fascinating."

After Madame Villeneuve's assistant lit the candles on the table, she instructed everyone to join hands. Philippe, who had taken a seat next to Christine looked at her, took her hand and squeezed it as if to convey some secret message. Apparently he still thought there was a chance of her accepting his offer to become his mistress.

"I can sense a presence here already," Madame Villeneuve said with a mysterious air.

After the candles had been lit, the Baron expressed his surprise at seeing a bowl of soup and a loaf of bread in the middle of the table.

"It is for the spirits who still seek physical food," the medium explained. "We are all believers here," she went on, as if to assure the darkness that surrounded them.

That wasn't exactly true, Christine thought. She wasn't a believer. And she knew that Raoul didn't believe, either.

"Commune with us, Phantom of the Opera," the medium called out.

Nothing happened so she repeated the chant. "Come join us," she invited in a dramatic stage voice. "I can sense that you are already here. Let your presence be known."

Most of the people around the table had their eyes closed. Raoul, however, was one who did not. He was looking around intently, watching everything like a hawk.

Suddenly, there was a loud rap which startled everyone. Madame Villeneuve did not seem to be surprised in the least. She was as good as any actress on the stage when it came to drawing the attention of her audience. "Spirit of the Opera House, speak to us."

She began to moan and sway back and forth.

"Come, enter my body," she said breathlessly, earning her the attention of everyone present, especially the men. There was something disturbingly erotic about her movements and her moans.

The table thumped once again, making the people around the table gasp collectively.

"What are you trying to tell us?" the medium called out.

"Can you hear that?" Anton Charlebois asked tensely. "Something is in here with us."

"Yes. Yes, it sounds like- someone is breathing," Countess Robillard whispered.

Madame Villeneuve ignored them. "Were you a victim of the Commun?" she asked the darkness. "Were you tortured in the cellars below us?"

Raoul was squeezing Christine's hand tightly, almost painfully. Philippe was intently watching the medium as were the other people around the table. No one dared close their eyes now.

A tambourine suddenly appeared above the table. It shook jarringly a few times and then disappeared as if whisked away by an unseen hand.

An icy wind came out of nowhere and blew against the sitters. Several of the candles wavered and then blew out. As Madame Villeneuve gasped, Raoul half rose from his seat.

"Do not leave your seats for any reason," the medium's assistant whispered anxiously. "It could be dangerous to Madame Villeneuve."

The table thumped twice, very violently this time. In fact, it actually lifted off the ground. Both the medium and her assistant gave a little cry of consternation. That had not been faked, Christine realized.

Christine looked around at the darkness, suspecting that things were about to get very interesting.

The medium suddenly sat up straighter in her chair. "Is that you, Phantom? Are you here?" she asked breathlessly as her own gaze darted around the room.

She wasn't swaying any more. She seemed to be frozen in her chair as she continued to look wildly about the room. She even turned to look behind her.

Her voice was even more dramatically imploring as she lifted her arms and called out, "Come forth, oh Phantom of the Opera House. We wish to know who you are and why you are trapped here."

The rest of the candles went out and there was total darkness. An eerie blue light began to glow in one corner of the box.

"What's happening?" Monsieur Peverell whispered anxiously.

"Maybe this wasn't such a good idea," Eitan Beauvoir whispered. "He has made it clear that he doesn't want anyone here- "

"Shhh," Madame Villeneuve hissed, her face and her bosom looking very ghostly in the blue light. "Everyone, stay where you are. Do not let go of your hands."

A violin was suddenly floating in midair above their heads. No one knew where it had come from. A single, drawn-out note was played, but it was a discordant, jarring sound. The violin suddenly crashed violently to the ground.

Madame Villeneuve, who at first had seemed to be confused, now looked almost alarmed. She looked at her assistant and asked in a strained whisper, "Have I finally done it?"

Her assistant shook his head as if he, too, was confused. "This is going too far, Madame," he whispered back as he leaned close to her. "Stop this."

"I- I can't," Madame Villeneuve told him as her eyes searched the darkened, blue-tinged space. "Wh- What do you wish to tell us?"

Suddenly there was violin music, sans the violin. It came from everywhere and nowhere at all. The soft, sweet sounds were expertly and beautifully played. Christine knew instantly that it could only be Erik.

But the music stopped abruptly and the atmosphere suddenly changed in the small room. Cold air again wafted over them all.

"Where is that coming from?" Raoul wanted to know.

"There. Behind the curtain," Eitan Beauvoir cried out.

Everyone looked to see that the bottoms of the curtains were billowing forward.

Raoul bolted out of his seat. He began to slap at the curtains frantically in an attempt to see if someone was hiding there.

The blue light gradually faded and disappeared. Madame Villeneuve's assistant re-lit the candles, but they blew out all at once, leaving them in total darkness once again.

Then came the laughter.

Baron Robillard rose so abruptly that his chair overturned. Philippe, too, had risen. Raoul was already out of his seat.

"I say, Raoul," Eitan Beauvoir began. "Isn't that the Phantom standing in your private box?"

It was indeed the Phantom who was watching them from across the theater, from the de Chagny's private box.

Raoul immediately lunged for the railing. Unfortunately, he didn't know about the wire that had been strung up earlier by Madame Villeneuve's assistant. The woman saw the impending disaster, drew in a sharp breath and tried to warn him. "Watch out for the- "

But it was too late. Raoul tripped and sprawled headlong into the railing. The gun that had appeared in his hand went off, but it did no more damage than to put a hole straight through the eye of one of the brass statues on the third floor.

"Raoul, are you mad?" Philippe cried out in the darkness.

But his brother didn't answer him. Raoul's head had bounced off the railing at precisely the same moment that his gun had gone off. Moments after, the gun fell from his hand, leaving everyone who saw the gun sliding across the floor to wonder where the next shots had come from. There were three of them in rapid succession.

That was the last sound Christine heard before a hand closed roughly over the lower part of her face and an arm clamped around her body like a vise.

A small group of curious theater workers had been watching the séance in secret. They had kept themselves well-hidden and thought of the night's unusual activities as a novel kind of performance, one that they thought would provide them with an evening's worth of entertainment for a change. Things had taken a turn for the worse, however, when the gunshots rang out. Most of them dove for cover when they heard the shots. They were whispering nervously amongst themselves now that everything was quiet again.

"Who was that shooting?" one of them asked cautiously.

"I think it was the Viscount Raoul de Chagny," someone answered. "He was leaning over the railing in box five and I saw a gun in his hand."

"He must have been hurt. I saw blood on his face," someone else whispered.

"What was he shooting at?"

"I suppose it was the ghost. I saw the Phantom of the Opera in the de Chagny's private box."

Everyone in the group was silent as they thought that over. And then someone asked, "Why would anyone be shooting at a ghost when they are trying to summon it?"

No one had an answer to that, at least not one that they could agree on. But everyone did agree to make themselves scarce. It didn't take them long to scatter like mice into the shadows of the Opera House.

In box five, things were far more chaotic. When the candles were relit for the third time, Madame Villeneuve, who was still sitting in her chair, looked deathly white. She wasn't talking at all. Her assistant was equally silent. Baron Robillard was sputtering out his confusion as to what exactly was going on, and wondering out loud why a ghost was in the de Chagny's private box, because seeing was believing, and he declared most adamantly that he now believed.

His wife was trying to stem the flow of blood from the Viscount's face with her handkerchief. Blood had begun to stream down profusely below his nose after he had hit the railing. It was still dripping onto his white cravat and shirt. The Viscount put his hand gingerly to his nose and winced. It felt like both his nose *and* his upper lip were swollen to almost twice their normal size. Being a vain man, his first concern was that he looked nothing short of monstrous.

But he quickly reminded himself that a swollen nose was the least of his worries. He drew himself up and straightened as he jerked his coat into place. His teeth showed in a vicious snarl as he forgot himself and expressed his rage in searing, colorful oaths, in spite of the women present.

"Show yourself," he shouted across the theater as he shook his fist. "Or are you too cowardly to come out and fight like a man? Mark my words, I will hunt you down like the damned dog you are."

Behind him, Monsieur Peverell, who looked like he wasn't at all sure the danger was really over, said, "Should we not let well enough alone?"

The Viscount ignored him, but he spun around on his heels when Philippe asked, "Where on earth is Christine?"

But no one had an answer. Christine was gone.

Chapter 21

After the hand had clamped brutally over her mouth and powerful arms dragged her out of box five, Christine had immediately begun to fight for her life. Something more frightening than a ghost was half carrying, half dragging her along the deserted corridor and then down several flights of stairs into what she knew was a lower level of the Opera House. The man was huge so he was able to subdue her easily in spite of her struggles. She had heard the gun shots but she didn't know who was shooting.

The giant leaned over her and snarled, "You want to keep fighting me, that suits me just fine. But *he* doesn't want me to mark you up too badly, so you'll be doing both of us a favor if you keep still."

He dragged her to a door and grabbed a handful of her hair to keep her restrained while he shoved a key into a lock. As he pushed the heavy door open, rusted hinges groaned a loud protest in the darkness. And then there was only shuffling sounds and the man's heavy breathing mingling with hers as he forced her along with him through another narrow hallway and down even deeper into the depths of the Opera House. Finally he opened another door and shoved her roughly inside, letting go of her so abruptly that she fell painfully to her hands and knees on the ground.

As he stood over her, his evil chuckle echoed off the stone walls that surrounded them. "It won't be long. I promise you, he's very anxious to see you."

A lantern was radiating a garish yellow light in the center of the room, but the far corners still remained dark. As she stared up at the man, Christine knew he would show her no mercy. She could plainly see his scarred face. She knew it was the same man who had attacked her in the Bois. And quite possibly it was also the man who had attacked Remi.

She became aware of faint footsteps right before Ligeia appeared in the doorway. Another lantern made her shadow loom monstrously against the walls as she entered the room.

As Ligeia glared silently down at her, Christine could not detect a single shred of compassion or surprise in the woman's black eyes. Even as Christine struggled to her feet and the man who had dragged her here jerked her hands behind her and tied them with a length of rope.

"*You* are behind this kidnapping?" Christine gasped as the rope was tightened painfully.

Ligeia did not deny it. "And you have only yourself to blame," she said, completely unconcerned about any discomfort Christine might be experiencing. "Thank goodness Raoul finally came to his senses. But better now than after the wedding."

Christine stared back at her. "So you can have him all to yourself?"

"Silence," Ligeia hissed with sudden venom. She spoke sharply to the man. "Leave us."

When they were alone, Ligeia could not help gloating a little. With her face heavily etched in shadow, she laughed quietly under her breath. "So Raoul was right. You have figured it out. You should also know that you could never please him as I do."

When Christine did not react to that the way she had expected, she said coldly, "Raoul will be here shortly. He can tell you that for himself."

"I don't care what Raoul has to say."

Ligeia sneered. "Still so impudent for such a vulgar little nothing. I confess I do not know what Raoul saw in you. You would have undoubtedly made his life a living hell. Not to mention that you would have brought the de Chagny name down into the mud. Fortunately, you will never have a chance to do that, nor will you ever see a single franc of the de Chagny fortune."

"What are you planning to do?"

"We are planning- not to let you become an embarrassment to him." She heard footsteps and looked at the door. "Ah, that must be Raoul now."

Raoul appeared in the doorway a moment later. There was a long, dark gash beside the bridge of his swollen nose. His lip was split and his mouth was twice its normal size. Both his face and his shirt were smeared with dried blood.

Ligeia's chin jerked a little higher as she glanced at Christine. "This is where she belongs, Raoul. Like any common trollop."

Raoul didn't say anything, but he seemed to agree with that sentiment.

Ligeia was still looking at Christine. "I hope you are going to finally put her in her place."

Raoul didn't immediately answer her. When he did, his voice was low with suppressed emotion as he said, "Ligeia, wait outside."

Christine had never heard him speak like that to her and Ligeia clearly resented his tone. But she quickly gathered up her skirts and disappeared through the door.

Raoul waited until she was gone. And then he stepped closer to Christine until she was forced to face him.

This was all like a horrible nightmare, she thought. Maybe he would untie her. Maybe he would tell her it had all been a terrible mistake.

But through his swollen, misshapen lips, he only snarled, "She's right. This is where you belong."

Fearing that she might make his anger even worse, she asked cautiously, "Why have you brought me here?"

"Since you already felt like a prisoner, you may as well be one in reality, don't you think?"

"What happened during the séance? I heard shooting."

"Since *I* am standing here before you safe and sound," he said mockingly. "The only one you could be worried about is your phantom lover."

He watched her face closely to see her reaction to that and saw a brief flash of the guilt he had been expecting.

"I see you deny nothing. Not even a pretense of denial."

He turned away from her for a moment as if he could not bear to look at her. But he suddenly whirled back around. Even in the lantern light she could see the rage that suffused his face.

"Those must have been some lessons," he spat out in a hoarse voice. "You played the innocent with me so very convincingly. But then you are an actress. What else would I expect? So tell me, what

257

are you thinking now?" When she wouldn't look at him, his fingers closed brutally around her upper arms and he shook her. "Answer me."

An impulsive answer trembled on her lips, but she bit it back, knowing better than to rouse his anger any further. She looked straight at him as she said, "That I never knew you at all."

He shoved her away from him, so hard that she stumbled backward and almost fell.

With his misshapen features, he leered lewdly in the lantern light. "A situation that will soon be remedied," he told her. "You will get to know me very well before this is all over. Now that I know what a conniving little whore you are behind that innocent façade."

Her eyes grew wide at the implication of his words. And then she turned her face aside as she frantically wondered what she was going to do.

"Come now, Christine. You can't ignore me, you know. You must realize that." He ran a hand over her loosened hair but drew it aside when she jerked her head away from his touch.

"It seems you need some time to consider the seriousness of your predicament. Obviously, your mind has been poisoned against me."

"You did that yourself," she couldn't help retorting.

He shook his head. "You should have been happy with me, but apparently you have decided that you can do better." He laughed unpleasantly. "You promised to be my wife and you shall fill that role, even if it is without the formal vows."

"I never will!"

His face grew distorted as his anger rose again. "Who do you think you are to defy me? You were a nothing, a nobody when I first met you. A woman who displayed herself before an entire audience of men just to make herself a paltry living. I tried to lift you above all that, and look how you have repaid me. But know this." He brought his swollen features closer to her. "I will bring you down lower than you ever could have imagined. There will be no wedding, but we will still have our wedding night. I confess, even now I am looking forward to the opportunity of seeing you as a blushing bride. It will be the final act of the not-so-amusing comedy that was to be our marriage."

He was clearly enjoying the look of horror on her face.

"You can't mean- "

"I mean every word I say. I will make you regret every last moment you spent with him behind my back. I have already taken steps to ensure that he is never going to interfere with my plans again."

"What have you done?"

"As you well know, I am an excellent shot. You did hear the shooting, of course. By the trail of blood we found, your phantom lover is already dead. Or he soon will be. Whatever his condition, I shall find him, even if I have to drag him back from the very gates of hell. And when I do, I will have his body buried where no one can ever find it."

Her eyes reflected the fear that his words instilled in her. But there was no pity in him.

"You never were very good at keeping your thoughts hidden," he said unfeelingly. "If you were hoping that your masked lover will be coming to your rescue, get that idea out of your head. He has most likely crawled off like an animal to die in some dark hole somewhere. You won't be seeing him again. No, Christine, I am the only one who will decide what your fate shall be."

"They'll search for me."

"They won't find you. Do you think I have not already thought this all through very carefully? It won't be hard to convince them that the Phantom took you. And when neither one of you are heard from again, you'll both become just another legend of the Opera House, a mystery that was never solved. Until then, let's see how cooperative you become after you spend some time alone in the darkness thinking about how you have wronged me."

His distorted lips curled in another short, ugly laugh. "I'll leave you now with a single image to keep you company in this rat-infested darkness, that of a corpse rotting forever down in some obscure, unmarked grave below the Opera House."

He called the man back in. "Take her down below where no one can hear her screams. When things quiet down, I will have a carriage brought around. Have her ready then." He swept Christine with one last, unpleasant look. "She'll soon be leaving the Opera House for the last time."

They left, taking the lantern with them and Christine found herself bound and alone, surrounded by pitch blackness.

259

The three shadows emerged from a little used stairway that led down to the cellars beneath the Opera House. They stayed well back in the darkness and talked among themselves in hushed whispers even though they thought no one was listening.

But someone was listening as the Viscount asked, "You are sure you hit him?"

"At least once, yes. As I told you, there is a blood trail. But it ends before a wall."

"Then there must be something on the other side of that wall." It was the Viscount's voice again. "We'll tear it down if we have to. Obviously the rumors are true and there are secret passages that he hides in."

A woman's voice asked, "What are you going to do with her?"

Raoul turned to Ligeia and said, "She is the least of my concerns at the moment. No one will hear her even if she does manage to scream. Finding out if he is dead is my first priority right now. That is one loose end that cannot be ignored."

After a brief silence, the Viscount said, "I have to make an appearance. I'll have Philippe take you back to the mansion."

They were so concerned with their evil scheming that they did not see the eyes that were watching them from the darkness beneath another little-used staircase. Remi pressed his back tightly against the wall, praying that the shadows were deep enough to hide him. He waited until after they were gone and then he wasted no time in seeking out Madame Giry.

He sucked his breath in through clenched teeth as the hole in his side continued to burn like hell's fire. He was breathing heavily, for it had been an arduous climb up to the third floor, and then a long walk through the dark, narrow tunnel he was in now. He knew they had found the blood trail and then followed it. He also knew they would eventually find the hidden passageway because with his own blood he had led them straight to it. But it couldn't be helped and there was no undoing it now.

He leaned his back against the wall, then slid to the floor where he took a few moments to catch his breath and inspect the raw, gaping hole in his flesh. There was still a good amount of fresh blood welling from the hole. He pressed his hand against his side, ignoring the pain, but every time he moved, warm blood came out in a rush. He knew he needed to stop the bleeding, and soon, but he also had to make sure that Christine was all right. She was his first priority.

He got back to his feet, swayed a moment, but steadied himself. Then resolutely, painfully, he began to make his way through the darkness.

Chapter 22

She had been dragged down several more dark hallways to another flight of stairs and now she was alone in a cavernous room with thick stone walls. She had no idea where she was. She only knew she had been taken further down into the cellars below the Opera House. She was far underground and it was tomblike down here. And silent. Deathly silent.

When she had tried to resist, the man had lost both his patience and his temper. He had thrown her brutally down a final short flight of steps. Now she was lying at the bottom of them, still tied, still in complete darkness. But it was so much worse now because her mouth was also bound so that she could not scream for help, even though she knew that no one would be able to hear her screams anyway.

For several terrible, agonizing moments, she almost gave in to the fear that had been clawing at her relentlessly through it all. Erik couldn't be dead. He couldn't. She wouldn't let herself think that way because if she gave in to it-

She choked back her tears. She needed to get out of here before they came back. She needed to find him. She needed to know that he was alive.

In the eerie stillness she heard the scurrying and squeaking of rats all around her. She had no idea how many of them there were. She only knew that if they kept their distance, she might be able to bear this. But if they got too curious or aggressive-

She cut those thoughts short. She wasn't going to think about that, either.

She struggled to get back to her feet, but once she did, she was so disoriented in the darkness that she had no idea which way to go, except back up the stairs, wherever they were. She would have to be very careful, because she had been lucky the first time she had fallen down them. But if she fell again, with no hands to break her fall, she might be seriously injured and then she would be even more helpless.

Her arms were cramped from being pulled so tightly behind her and numerous places on her body screamed in pain from being pushed down the stairs, but she had to ignore those things. There was one consuming thought in her mind. She had to get out of here before they came back.

She took a step forward in the inky blackness. And then another. Where were the steps? She finally ran her foot up against the first one. Then she sat down and maneuvered her bound hands along the edge of the step until she felt the roughest section of stone. She began to work the sharp edge against the rope that bound her hands. It was hard work and she didn't know how much of an effect it was having, but she kept going. She needed her hands free to open the door once she did reach it.

At times the coarse stone would scrape against her bare flesh but she made herself ignore the burning pain. Her progress was painstakingly slow and through it all she kept listening intently for footsteps. But finally the rope loosened, then separated, freeing her hands. She jerked the cloth away from her face and drew a deep breath of air into her lungs.

Now that she was free, she needed to get out of here. She gathered her skirts in both hands and began to climb upwards.

"Madame Giry."

It was Remi's strained voice on the other side of the door.

Remi didn't wait for her to answer him. The door suddenly burst open.

"Madame Giry, you have to get word to the Ph- "

After the first gasp of astonishment, Remi froze in his tracks while his eyes fixed on the scene inside the room.

Madame Giry looked at him a moment before she said quietly, "Remi, close the door."

He immediately did what she said, and then he turned back around to stare in open-mouthed shock at the sight of the man standing with Madame Giry.

The man was bare chested. Madame Giry was tying the ends of a bandage that was wrapped around his body, but blood was already seeping through the white cloth. There was another pile of bloody rags on her desk. He saw something else. The man was wearing a half mask.

There was no doubt in Remi's mind. He knew that the Phantom of the Opera stood before him.

With an effort he tore his gaze away from the man and said to Madame Giry, "Christine is in trouble."

A change came over the man's face. His eyes grew cold and alert as he slanted a brief, dark look in Madame Giry's direction.

"The Viscount is holding her prisoner," Remi told them.

"Where?"

The man - the Phantom - was already pulling on his shirt.

"I'm not certain exactly," Remi answered him. "They came from a staircase off one of the backstage hallways, the one that leads to the cellars."

"I know the place," the man said in a deep voice that rumbled ominously like low thunder.

"They said that they had taken her down to the cellars where no one could hear her screams and that they would take her away when things settled down here."

The Phantom said no word, but his lips were set in grim lines.

"I'll take you there," Remi offered.

"No, you stay here. I know a quicker way to get there and I can find Christine faster on my own."

Not knowing what else to do, Madame Giry sent for the Persian. And then she and Remi did all they could do. They waited.

A slight scraping noise caught her attention. Christine scrambled away from the door where she waited with her back pressed against the stone wall. Her heart was pounding in her throat.

The heavy door creaked slowly open. Every instinct she possessed was screaming at her to hide, to run, to get away, but she didn't know where to go in the darkness. She had expected a lantern, but not even a sliver of light shone beyond the partially open doorway.

Could she take whoever it was by surprise, run outside the door and then close it before he knew what was happening? Could she find her way in the darkness after that? And if she was not successful in her escape attempt, what would they do to her then?

She couldn't think about that right now. She had to focus. She had to try and escape no matter what happened.

The door creaked opened a little wider. Although she couldn't see anything in the darkness, someone was definitely there. As she dug her back into the wall, fear crawled up her spine and lodged in her chest, making her heart pound even harder. She took a step away from the door, stumbled when she caught her foot in the hem of her dress and nearly fell down the steps again. She quickly righted herself, then panicked when she felt a presence close behind her. But before she could run, someone's hands were on her and she was being dragged backward.

All she could think about at the moment was that she had to get away and this might be her only chance to do so. She had been warned she would be punished if she tried to get away again. The man had hurt her before. What would he do to her this time? As he continued to drag her backward, she continued to fight him. She silently vowed she would not make this easy for him. She clawed. She kicked. She scratched. But as hard as she fought, she could not break free of his iron-like hold. Though she squirmed in his arms, he spun her around as easily as if she was a child.

"I've got you," she heard as strong arms went around her.

Her muffled sob against the man's chest was one of unutterable relief.

Erik's voice!

Erik was alive and, although she didn't know how it had come to be, he was here with her.

"You found me," she whispered.

"Yes, and I won't let you go again." He gathered her closer to his heart. "I love you, Christine."

"You what?"

"I love you," he repeated.

"I love you," he whispered once more, filling her heart, filling her soul.

And then he did what he told her he would never do again. He covered her mouth in a deep, healing kiss that spoke for itself.

Epilogue

A peaceful stillness held the morning in a spell. While the light grew, a soft mist suffused the air. The picturesque cottage was covered with vibrant, abundant blooms where roses climbed the trellises. Roses were also tumbling over the picket fence in a glorious profusion of color that filled the air with their sweetness. Across the road, the woods were alive with the trilling of birds. Through the trees, bright gleams of the dawn sky could be seen all along the winding road that led to the seaside.

The man leaning against the wooden picket fence smiled as he imagined her playing here as a child, surrounded by the hollyhocks and the balsam. He had built her a bench and placed it just so, that she might sit and enjoy the sunrises and the sunsets with him. She had been right. He could think of no better place to live than right here.

The cottage had sat empty for a long time, just as if it had been waiting all those years for her to come back. After they had shaken out all the shadows and the dust, after they had swept out all the cobwebs, they had spent the past three years adding new memories to the ones she already held in her heart.

He passed through the open gate and went inside where he stood in a shaft of warming sunlight, listening to Christine sing a lullaby. She didn't know he was there as he leaned a shoulder against the door frame and watched her. In a moment, he was called back through the years to the first time he had heard her sing. She had been unaware then, too. He continued to listen to the magic of her voice as it wove its spell around him. Her voice was so beautifully sweet and so full of love, even moreso now than when he had first heard her. The early sunlight sifting through the lace curtains made a gory of her unbound hair. It lit the curve of her chin and cheek, lending an almost ethereal softness to her features. Motherhood most definitely agreed with her.

She must have become aware of him standing there because she stopped singing and turned around. A tender smile formed on her lips as she saw him and, as always, it had its effect upon his heart. How he loved her, this woman who had banished the shadows from his life and filled his heart with more love than he had ever dared dream of.

She rose from the bed where she had been seated and watched him come into the room.

"You are up early today," she said.

"I've finished the bench."

Her eyes lit up. "Did you?"

"Yes, we'll have to try it out. There's room for the three of us."

She turned to look at the little boy who held his arms out to the man. She smiled again, her eyes softening as the child was picked up and held against the man's heart, the small arms tightening around his neck. She had learned much about the man in the three years they had been together. She knew that he gave to his child all the love that had been missing in his own life, and therein he had found his own healing. And he had grown to love the cottage as much as she did, especially since it was filled again with music and a child's laughter, which was the most magical music in the world.

As they walked hand in hand to the yard, the wind came gently up the winding road, fresh with the smell of the sea. The sun was warm and it bathed them in its nurturing warmth. They cherished the memories of the past, but the future held promise for them as well, for he had kept his vow not to lead her into the darkness, but instead had let her lead him into the light of her love.

"About the bench," she said as she looked down at his handiwork and ran her hand admiringly over his craftsmanship. "I'm glad there will be room for *four* of us."

And then her hand was on his heart as she turned to him and told him of the child who was still unborn. She saw the surprise, and then the happiness that glowed in his dark eyes, knew that he was grateful for the precious miracle of love that had been given to him. Saying no word, he bowed his head and kissed her.

Deeply.

Thoroughly.

Lovingly.

Till there was no doubt whatsoever that it was indeed a kiss.

Or that she had kissed him back.

And then she asked him, "Should we walk down to the water and watch the sun rise?"

"I'll go wherever you want me to go," he answered her as he pressed a kiss into the dark, sun-struck curls of the little boy in his arms. "As long as you're both by my side," he began, and then corrected himself. "As long as all three of you are by my side, I'll want for nothing more out of this life."

"Ah, does that mean you are planning to be with me for a very long time?" she asked teasingly as she looked up at him from beneath her dark fringe of lashes.

There was a smile lingering in the depths of his dark cobalt eyes as he answered her. "It means I am planning to be with you forever, my love. And forever again," he promised her as he handed her a single, perfect, blood-red rose.

47907575R00169

Made in the USA
Middletown, DE
05 September 2017